M J HOLLOWS was born in London in 1986, and moved to Liverpool in 2010 to lecture in Audio Engineering. With a keen interest in history, music, and science, he has told stories since he was little. *Goodbye for Now* is his first novel, which he started as part of his MA in Writing from Liverpool John Moores University, graduating in 2015. He is now researching towards a PhD in Creative Writing, and working on his next novel. Find out more about Michael at his website: www.michaelhollows.com.

Goodbye for Now

M J HOLLOWS

ONE PLACE. MANY STORIES

HQ
An imprint of HarperCollins*Publishers* Ltd
1 London Bridge Street
London SE1 9GF

This paperback edition 2018

First published in Great Britain by
HQ, an imprint of HarperCollins*Publishers* Ltd 2018

ISBN: 9780008323004

MIX
Paper from
responsible sources
FSC® C007454

This book is produced from independently certified FSC™ paper to ensure responsible forest management.

For more information visit: www.harpercollins.co.uk/green

Typeset by Palimpsest Book Production Ltd, Falkirk, Stirlingshire

Printed and bound in Great Britain by
CPI Group (UK) Ltd, Melksham, SN12 6TR

*For everyone who fought and died in war,
and everyone who fought and died for peace.*

1923

They all stood in silence, with hats and caps doffed under arms, focusing their vision on their shoes. Meanwhile the bishop droned on in his fashion, extolling the virtues of sacrifice.

He stared with them, trying not to dredge up the memories of the past. *I have lived through hell, but in that I am not alone*, he thought. Bile stuck in his throat and he desperately tried to swallow it away. No one noticed, or if they did they attributed it to his grief.

Everyone had suffered and sacrificed, not just the soldiers. He wondered how his brother might be now. How much he would have been changed by the war. They had both endured their own private hells, and as the dead would keep their solace, so would the living. No one would ever truly understand their plight and those that had experienced it didn't need the others to remind them. That was what the nightmares were for.

So he stood there, in silence, with their neighbours and people from the nearby streets, waiting for the bishop to finish his sermon, for the memorial to be revealed.

Somewhere in the distance a baby cried. No one reacted, empathising with the child, who was probably too young to know what was going on but was joining in nonetheless.

The bishop stopped and was replaced by a Major young enough to have been a junior Lieutenant at the outbreak of war. His voice broke as he began reading out the names of the lost, Morgan, Norris, Oliver, the endless torrent of the dead. They were just names now. Their legacy, the brass plaque that was being unveiled.

He patted his coat pocket, remembering the bundle of letters that he kept there. That's where they would stay, sealed, but not forgotten.

The Major continued reading out the names of the fallen, some of whom he knew, others he had never met.

When he could bear to think of him, he had spent most of the war angry with his brother. Not angry, that wasn't strictly the right emotion. They had never really understood each other. They were very different people, with different stories. He had had high hopes for his brother, they all had, yet he threw it all away. He chose his path. When he should have turned to his family he turned away. It was hard now to remember him as they were when they were children. Too much had happened. His name had not been spoken aloud since. They all missed him, but it was too painful a memory.

The Major had finished now and had disappeared. There was a cough from someone amongst the crowd. The only sound apart from that was the occasional sniffle of a nose or the sound of stifled weeping. Heads were still bowed and would remain that way for some time, some years perhaps.

At first he hadn't understood his brother's decision; they stood on opposite sides. But as the war dragged on and on, past its first Christmas and into a new year, year after year, he had started to understand his brother a lot more. He begun to understand the need to fight for something, to believe in something and to not give up. No matter what life would throw at you. That was a sentiment he could agree on, and he guessed it was something their father had managed to instil in them both, despite their differing opinions. It had been a clear dividing line at first, but things were less clear now. The world had changed for all of them. The horror of the war had left no family unaffected. They couldn't change their decisions, but they could make sure that they counted for something. That things hadn't just changed for the worse but would be allowed to change for the better too.

He just wished his brother was still around to say this to, but he would never have the chance now. Their paths drifted apart, on what was to be a fateful day for millions of people...

4

1914

Chapter 1

'It's war!'

George Abbott would never forget where he was that day, when those very words were spoken. He was sat at the family kitchen table, a roughly cut dark wooden frame, with an off-white cloth draped across it to hide its wear and tear. He leaned over a bowl of oats, playing them around with his tarnished spoon. Beside it was an enamel plate with some bread and milk.

His sisters, Catherine and Elisabeth, sat either side of him. Catherine was looking over at George to see if he would eat his bread, or if she could take it. Her hair was a deep black mess of curls, the same as their mother's, framing a pale, chubby face, whereas little Elisabeth's hair was a distinct copper colour, more like their father's. At the other end of the table, across the other side was George's brother Joe, gaunt and long like their father, although with a growth of unkempt curly black hair. He wore the deep brown suit that he always wore to work, even at the breakfast table. He was careful not to get any food on it.

The back door had burst open and their father limped in clutching the *Daily Post* to his chest and calling to the family. If George were to look him in the eye, it would be like looking in a mirror, except his father was older and thinner. Their faces were exactly alike and the resemblance was uncanny. It was only his father's eyes that looked different, like they had seen a thousand things, and crow's feet pulled at the edge of his face.

'It's war!' he said. 'We've declared war.' He carried on as if unheard. 'Britain has declared war on Germany.'

Everyone stared, not knowing quite what to say. War had been brewing for some time, so they weren't surprised.

'Pass your father the kedgeree,' their mother said to Catherine and she did as bid, passing the dish of flaked fish and rice that everyone but their father despised. He must have picked up his taste for it in India.

'I thought we were allies with Germany?' Their mother was ever the practical woman. She carried on eating while the rest of the family grew excited and agitated. George pushed his plate of bread towards Catherine to distract her, but she just stared at it, then at him.

Their father finally found his seat, hanging his cheap coat behind him as he wrestled his body onto the chair.

'No, no, love. Belgium. They're the ones. They invaded there, so ol' squiffy told 'em where to go.'

'Belgium invaded Germany?'

'No. The other way round!'

She didn't appear to be listening and smiled conspiratorially in her husband's direction, before collecting up more plates.

Joe stared across the room at the news their father had brought with him, wringing his hands in front of his face. Joe was older than George, but in this moment he looked even older, worry lining his face. His hair threatened to grow too long on his head and his feeble attempts to grow a beard in patches on his chin was a constant source of ridicule. The object of Joe's gaze was a faded photograph of their dad dressed in his uniform, beaming with pride at the South Africa medal pinned to his breast. He still often wore his medal, stroking the silver disc absent-mindedly. Father turned to Joe, putting the paper down.

'D'you know what this means, son?' Joe didn't respond and their father looked around the room, at the rest of them, testing everyone's reaction. 'The papers say they're going to issue a call. They're gonna need more men.'

George carried on playing with his oats, knowing that this was between Joe and their dad. Joe looked into the middle distance, the edges of his mouth moving as if about to form words but thinking better of it.

After a tense pause, Joe spoke. 'I won't do it,' he muttered under his breath, so quietly that George almost didn't hear.

Their father banged a fist on the table, and cutlery jingled as it was disturbed.

'What do you mean you won't do it?' he shouted at Joe. He kept his fist firmly on the table, flexing his fingers, but managing to keep it balled. His other hand gripped the arm of his chair and George could see the blood draining away as his flesh turned a pale pink. 'Every generation of this family has served. As far back as I know, the Abbotts have fought for our country. What makes you so different?'

'Dad...?' By simply calling out to him Catherine brought him out of his tirade. His hands relaxed and the blood flowed back into them. She had a way of calming him that none of the others could manage.

The legs of Joe's chair screeched on the tiled kitchen floor as he pushed it back and stood up. Without taking a step he turned to face their father. His voice was calm despite the speed with which he had risen.

'I'm not different. That's not the point. I won't, I don't have to, so I won't. You know exactly what I think about war, and I mean no disrespect to you or our ancestors, but I won't fight. Not ever.'

He rushed across the kitchen, opened the door and, without looking back, left. The door clicked shut behind him. The room was silent.

The action was completely out of character; Joe was never angry. He never had any reason to be angry, he was always quiet and kind when he needed to be.

His sisters appeared as shocked as George surely did, trying to cover it by intently focusing on their food, and stuffing their faces with whatever was left.

Their father looked over at their mother and shook his head. 'I told you that teacher had put funny ideas in his head,' he grumbled.

'Eat, love.' She pushed a plate of breakfast in front of him, stroking his shoulder before going back to the worktop.

He ate in silence, as the rest of the family finished their breakfast. He occasionally looked up at them, his eyes resting on George, before he carried on eating. When he had finished he left the room himself, hobbling in his usual manner towards the front room. George waited a few seconds for him to be gone, before getting his mother's attention.

'What was all that about, Ma?' Elisabeth said, before he could phrase the question himself, her six-year-old inquisitiveness winning out.

Their mother continued her meticulous dish washing. Her voice had to compete with the scrape of crockery and the splash of water as she poured more into the sink from the jug she had got in from outside, but she knew well enough how to project. A skill that he expected came from having four children.

'Don't worry, love,' she said quickly, but not without care.

'But why were they arguing?' he asked, interrupting his younger sister's reply. He had always felt close to his mother, she cared for them all well, but she had always been honest with him and spoken to him like an equal.

Another stack of plates clattered onto the draining board. 'They'll be looking for young men to volunteer, I don't doubt. Your father wants our Joe to go and give his name, join the regiment. It's the family tradition after all.' She paused as a blackbird flew past the window. 'But your brother has no interest in your father's traditions. He has other plans for his life, what with all the things that he's learnt.'

'I've never seen our dad so angry before,' Catherine said, finally eating George's unwanted bread and pushing the words out between mouthfuls.

Mother finished her washing up and returned to the table, taking a look at the sisters then at George where her gaze lingered for a moment.

'You're too young, George, or your father would be having the same conversation with you too, love,' she said as she took a dishcloth to his cheek to wipe away whatever leftover food was lodged there. That would explain why his father had kept looking at him.

'Now get on with you and get yourselves ready. I need to go speak to your father and try to calm him down. Up the stairs now.' She ushered the family out of the kitchen with a wet dishcloth, and a smile.

*

Upstairs, the house was a cramped affair, with the rooms close together, leading off from a shared landing. Four children was common for a family around Liverpool, and they all had to fit into what space their parents could afford. George and Joe brought what money they could into the house, but they still slept in a shared bedroom.

George walked into the room that had been his and Joe's for as long as he could remember, to find his clothes for work. There were three other rooms leading from the landing: their parents', their sisters', and a small room that they used for cleaning and getting changed. Having one changing room between six people was never easy, but they made do. There was a kind of unspoken agreement about the order of who got to go in first. Their mother was always first. Their father would shout at them and push them away if they tried to get in before her. The rest was a hierarchy of age within the family. Catherine would usually have to go downstairs and boil a tub of water then bring it up for cleaning. They would often share the same water and rub as much soap as they could afford on their bodies. They had a tin bath that they kept next to the outhouse, but that was only for special occasions.

He sat down on the thin mattress of his wire bed to wait, and the frame creaked as it took his weight. Across from him was Joe's side of the room. Both sides were marked out as separate, and neither of them ventured to the other's. He couldn't help but think just how different Joe's personal space was compared to his own. Though only a couple of feet apart, an outside observer could easily see the two different personalities in the room.

Above his bed, Joe had a couple of cluttered shelves, so full that often things fell off whenever someone opened or shut the door to their room. He had put them up himself, forever keen on being self-reliant, even when George had offered to help. The bottom shelf contained a number of books, a few were great dusty tomes. Every time George looked he suspected there were more books. Joe would smuggle them in from somewhere, George didn't know where.

Sometimes, in the evenings he often caught Joe pulling them off the shelf one at a time and running a finger along the words while softly mumbling to himself. He thought that George didn't notice, but he did. He often wondered what Joe was thinking, while he read the words under his breath. He seemed so separate, so distant, as if he were born to another family and had been given to the wrong parents at the hospital. There were times when George was about to ask him what he was reading, but then Joe would start another book or go to sleep.

To say he wasn't interested in things would be untrue. However, when it came to Joe's interests George just didn't understand.

There was a difference between them that was more than age. Unlike a lot of his peers George could read, but he found more fun in other things.

He looked back over his own bed and at his own possessions. In pride of place was his favourite landscape, and various other pictures. They were all prints that he had managed to find for very little expense or trade for with what little he had. Some were cutouts from newspapers or magazines, of particularly interesting scenes. Some were postcards. Some were larger copies of paintings of places that he had no hope of visiting. Underneath them, if you looked carefully, were some of his own sketches. They were poor in comparison, but he practised whenever he could snatch a moment. With work at the dock, time was scarce.

The changing room door opened and Catherine walked back out. She smiled at George. 'Your turn,' she said, shutting the door behind her. George didn't follow into the now empty room, there was no point in him washing when he was due to go to work, he would only end up dirty again in a matter of minutes. The dirt didn't bother him, he was used to it, but the sweat always wound him up, as it ran down his temples and pooled on his chin. Instead, he got ready for work, throwing on a pair of overalls and making sure that his boots were securely tied to his feet. A loose lace could cause a serious injury in a hurry.

*

Less than half an hour later, he was out of the front door and facing down the road. Egerton Street was a quiet street hidden just off the main road. Terraced, brick houses lined the road without break, built for the workers in the city. The Abbotts weren't completely poor, but they weren't wealthy either. The army gave their father a meagre pension and he had found work at the docks bookkeeping, thanks to a friend. The others brought in what they could.

Most of the houses that George could see were occupied by the families of other dockworkers. The red brick buildings trailed off down the hill, meeting at a point in the direction of the Mersey which was still covered in a grey sea-mist at this time of day.

As George stepped out of the yard, closing the wooden gate behind him and making sure the steel latch stuck, a group of young children pushed past him, their leather soles clattering on the pavement as they chattered in excitement, on their way to the local school. They played soldiers running around with their arms outstretched in mockery of a rifle. One mimed shooting at him and George pretended to be hit, falling to his knees and clutching his chest. The child laughed and ran off, and George shouted a friendly warning after them as they disappeared down the road.

Mrs Adams from next door waved as she saw George on his knees in the street.

'Mornin', George,' she said, smiling. 'Get up now, you'll get dirt all over you.' She carried on tending to the small trough of plants she kept in her front garden, with a pair of secateurs.

'Good morning, Mrs Adams.' He pretended to wipe himself down. 'D'you know where Tom is?'

'Oh, he's on his way to work, not long gone. You only just missed him. But knowing him, he's probably off scrumping for apples.' She smiled knowingly. Mrs Adams always smiled, no matter what happened. It made George feel happy to see it, knowing what she had been through. He smiled back despite the feeling of embarrassment that washed over him. The Adams' smile was infectious.

She referred to the time that George had first met her son. Before then, they had never had so much as a conversation. After school one day, George had been walking home, and came across Tom, Harry and Patrick loitering at the end of a road. They were trying to climb over the brick wall of the corner house, to get to its orchard, but couldn't make it over.

Being taller, George was asked to help, but there was a shout from over the other side of the road. The local copper had spotted them and was crossing towards them. They ran, the policeman giving chase. They turned a corner and hid in a hedgerow.

George's lasting memory of that time was of laughing uncontrollably. The boys had been friends ever since.

George chuckled to himself as he carried on walking. A lady walking up the road glanced at him out of the corner of her eye and took a step around him. 'Morning,' he said, still smiling.

He hoped to catch up with Tom, but he had no idea how far ahead he was. He could feel the excitement of all those around him, from the running children, to the busy adults.

He crossed the tramway that ran along Catharine Street, careful not to trip on the rail that was indented into the stones of the road. He always preferred to walk to work, but Tom would most likely be waiting at the stop, hoping to jump on if George was too late.

George turned the corner and there he was, leaning against a lamppost, smoking a cigarette in his usual, cocky manner. Tom didn't look up as George approached him. 'Morning, George,' he said, without looking. 'You're later than usual. I was just about to leave without you.' He dropped his finished cigarette on the floor and stamped on it. 'Lovely day for it.' He smiled wryly, and shifted his coat, knowing that the heat would only make him sweat more. 'Let's be getting on.'

George carried on walking past the tram stop. Tom sighed, before rushing to catch up with him. 'Walking it is then.' Tom smiled wryly whenever he spoke, it was what was so endearing about him. 'I always enjoy a good walk. Hey, perhaps there will even be some work left for us when we get there too?' They walked on together down the hill towards the Mersey and the docks.

'Walking is better, you know the tram takes just as long by the time it's stopped at every station,' George said. 'If we're lucky we might get there first.'

Both boys had found work down at the docks, like most young men from these parts. George had left school three years before, at the age of thirteen, and he was glad to see the back of it. The old bastard of a teacher still haunted his dreams, his idea of drill was the worst, and you would get a cane if you couldn't stand up straight afterwards.

It was hard work, unloading ships and carrying box crates of tea, or tobacco, and bales of cotton to another part of the dock. There were hydraulic cranes, but the boys were needed to move the goods into storage, or transport, and as George was large for his age, he easily found work.

'So, you've no doubt heard the news then?' Tom said as they crossed the dock road, dodging a horse and cart that clattered along without a warning. The coachman shouted back over his shoulder, telling them to watch out. You could easily get killed by a horse and cart if you weren't on your watch.

'Who hasn't?' George replied. 'Our dad brought the paper in this morning. It's why I was late.'

There had been talk of war for a while now, ever since that Austrian got shot. People had been talking excitedly about Britain going to war and he had felt excited with them, eager to join in. The talk was of going to show Fritz that they couldn't do what they liked. It was hard not to join in with the sentiment, but then there was also talk of not having enough troops to deal with Germany's warmongering. Talking about the war was fine, but George didn't really want to talk about why he was late, nor about his brother.

'My dad reckons they'll be after more troops before long,' he continued. Tom hadn't asked.

Tom paused for a moment, then grinned again in his usual, contagious manner. 'We should go and sign up,' he said. 'We'd be like our dads. Make them proud.'

Tom was always joking around.

'Aye, it will be like South Africa.'

16

'Perhaps, not as hot though. Sounds like they had a great time. It's what our dads would want. Well, I know my dad would have encouraged me to sign up if he was still here. I bet your brother has already gone to enlist.'

George hesitated. He hadn't really wanted to talk about it.

'No,' he said. 'He stormed off at the very mention of it. He has his own ideas.'

Tom shut up and stared ahead, not saying anything for the rest of their journey.

The walk took them past the Custom House, that magnificent building glittering in the morning sun, and into the dockyard, through the wrought-iron fences. The smells of salt water and the cargo were strong. Everyone here was too busy working hard to think about any prospect of war. George waved to a few dock hands and they nodded as they carried on their jobs. For now it was time to work, the war could wait.

Chapter 2

Joe let the door click shut behind him. He wanted so much to slam it, but in the end he backed down. What point would he make if he crashed about the place like some bull? He liked peace and the quiet protest of knowing wholeheartedly that he was right, no matter what anyone else said. It kept him going.

He had known what this morning's breakfast conversation was going to hold, he had expected it. They had been edging ever closer to war, and every day he felt nearer to the time his father would ask him what he was going to do. This morning had been the breaking point.

He took a deep breath before opening the front door and walking out of the house. It was earlier than usual to leave for work, but he could always find something to do at the newspaper. It may be early for him, but the bakers on the end of the road were just finishing their morning cycle. The smell of warm bread was somehow comforting.

A horse and flatbed cart went past carrying large steel milk churns. Its wheels rattled on the cobbled road. Workmen were on their way to the factories, wearing heavy, protective clothing.

He forced a smile to them as he passed. Some of them were people he knew well, people he had grown up with, friends and

18

relatives. They lived in such close confines that it was impossible not to know each other.

Already, people were running about and calling to each other, with a cheer that didn't reach Joe. He was trying to push his father's words out of his head, but he couldn't forget how badly the conversation had gone. He had always known that he would refuse to join the army, but that wasn't how he had wanted it to happen.

He turned the corner away from their little street and on to the main road. Upper Parliament Street glowed in the summer morning sunshine. The further he went the easier it might be to forget. Children in scruffy brown clothes with dirty white collars ran down the road, some waving Union flags and others pretending to attack their friends. The boys ran into a couple of regulars dressed in khaki coming out of a house. One of them smiled at a child and the other grabbed one and put him on his shoulders before joining in the chase of the other boys, laughing.

It was a fine morning and the walk would do him good. The air was light and clear, feeling good in his lungs as he walked. A motorcar went past, its engine chugging out fumes, easily overtaking the lumbering horse carts. The roads rose up as they moved away from the city, giving a view of the River Mersey, houses built onto the hills to the south of the city. The Mersey reflected sunlight as the tide came in, a faint mist beginning to grow.

In the distance he could just about make out the recently opened Liver Building, its two domes each housing a stylised Liver Bird. He remembered the opening that the newspaper staff had been invited to. At the time one of the workers had told him a story about the two birds on top of the building. 'The female bird, ya see, is looking out to sea for the returning ships, right? And the male bird is looking into the city to see, to see if the pubs are still open.' The man's laugh had been deep and booming, and the memory made Joe smile.

He ended up on Wood Street, one of the small roads that

intersected the city centre, housing the many offices and shops. The Liverpool *Daily Post* building was one of the largest on the street, rising above the horizon in an edifice of brick and glass. The other buildings along the road had grown up to it, but none matched. At this time of the morning the low sun was hidden behind the building, which cast a shadow on the road. The *Daily Post* sign looked down on all those in the street, ready to proclaim its news.

Joe walked in and nodded to the clerk at the front desk. Stephen nodded back and carried on with whatever he was reading. It was a ritual, but today Stephen paused, putting his magazine down, and looked on the verge of saying something. Joe climbed up the wrought iron stairs that turned back on themselves, avoiding the conversation, and into the main offices on the first floor.

He hooked his hat on the hat stand that always stood by the door. The large post room had rows of metal desks across the middle, machine-built in a large quantity by the same smith that had built the press. It always made him proud to see the amount of work they put into the newspaper, and proud to be involved.

The journalists and copywriters hadn't all arrived yet. Those that were already in the building were looking through the other morning papers, the *Manchester Guardian*, and *The Times* all the way up from London on the morning train. They were too busy pretending to work and talking amongst themselves. They didn't look up as he sat down at his desk.

Two other workers came into the room at that moment and called to the ones that had already arrived whilst putting their hats and coats on the stand at the doorway.

'Good morning!' they both shouted, almost in harmony.

'I guess you've heard the news then, Frank?' Charlie called back.

'Stop shouting, Ed will hear you, and you know what he's like about noise,' Frank said as he walked past the desk, giving Joe a quick wink.

He could still hear the conversation once they had passed; despite telling each other to be quiet they were talking in loud voices as they sat together, any pretence of work forgotten. The customary snap of a match signalled that they were smoking, before the smoke filled the room.

'…Not before time,' one said in the kind of voice that suggested he thought he knew everything there was to know about everything. 'Them Austro-Hungarians were just spoiling for a fight. Can't have 'em taking over Europe.'

Even though Joe couldn't see the speaker from where he was, he knew Charlie would be looking smug with himself, whilst trying to pretend he wasn't. He could hear it in his overconfident voice.

'Ahh whaddya know, Charlie Mason? You'd make an awful soldier. Look at you.'

'What rot, I'd be great. Just you wait and see.'

There was an almighty laugh as the other men had fun at Charlie's expense.

The boisterous camaraderie of the office and the type room was not for Joe. Idly, he pulled a sheaf of papers towards him and took out a fountain pen from its slot in the desk. He couldn't concentrate and instead sat, holding the pen, and looking out over the office, staring blankly at the opposite wall.

'Abbott.'

The hard, croaky voice of Edward Harlow made Joe look up at the slightly fat man, whose bald head shined in the electric lights of the office. The editor let a puff of smoke drift around Joe as he stood above him. He was always smoking; it was as if he had decided that it was something that an editor should do. As a result, it made his voice somewhat distinctive, along with the heavy breathing that accompanied his walking. It sounded like he was trying to talk through the reed of a woodwind instrument. It was a sound that the other men in the office had found especially useful when trying to avoid working. They

21

always knew when he was coming, even if they didn't smell his cigar first.

'Good morning, Mr Harlow. How do you do?' Joe made the pleasantry without wanting an answer. It was just what one did.

'I take it you've heard the news then? You can hardly avoid it round here, what with all the noise and excitement.' With that he looked over at the other men and then at the still empty desks of the office. They were once again pretending to read the newspapers. Research, they would call it, if pressed.

Joe nodded, not knowing what to say. The news had been coming, but he wasn't a war reporter, so it wasn't his responsibility.

'I'm sorry, Abbott,' Mr Harlow coughed. 'The news came through last night, almost immediately after you left. I had to give the article an edit myself when it came through. Priority you see, when it comes to declarations of war. We had to get it ready for this morning, see. The typesetters were about ready to go. "You know how much it costs to stop once we've started," they said, but I had to. If it didn't go out this morning, the owner would have my neck.' The apology was unnecessary, given Joe's position, but characteristic of the man. He wanted to be every one's best friend.

'But forget that. It's happened now, and no doubt we'll pay the price for it sooner or later.' Mr Harlow wagged a finger at Joe as if telling him off then paused, thinking about his own words and taking a puff of his cigar.

'I've got this here for you. Something to work on, and I need it pretty sharpish. Forget that other rubbish.'

He pushed the piece of paper under Joe's nose. 'Enlist to-day. The Germans pillage Belgium!' the headline read. If that was how the headline started, then he daren't read the rest.

Why was Mr Harlow giving him this piece to edit? Could it be because he felt bad about working without him last night? Joe doubted that. It made a change from his usual job of looking through the local pieces for any mistakes or spelling errors, but it wasn't what he wanted to be involved in. It wasn't like he had shouted it from the rooftops, but surely Mr Harlow must know of his opinions.

'When you're done with that and it goes out, the office will empty.' Mr Harlow sighed. 'Seems that some of the lads have already deserted us. That or they're just bloody well late!'

So that explained the empty desks. He only swore when he was angry and he was giving Joe this piece because there was no one else around to do it. So much for taking his mind off the pressure of the war, instead he had to edit this abhorrent article. Albert Barnes had written it to encourage other young men like him to sign up, whatever the cost.

'I'm not sure this is my thing, Mr Harlow,' he said with hesitation. When he looked up, the editor had already gone, the waft of cigar smoke following in his wake.

He looked back at the article, pushing aside his other work. The headline was no worse than the rest. Crammed into the tiny article were all the atrocities that the German army had already engaged in during their short time marching into Belgium. He had no idea where the information had come from; he knew for sure that Barnes had never left the city, he wasn't the kind of man to go off in search of a story. How could he possibly know that any of this was true?

Joe couldn't bring himself to endorse it.

Allegedly, men were already leaving their jobs to sign up for the war they had been anticipating for months. To see off the invading Germans and send them home with their tails between their legs. They didn't need the help of this propaganda and supposition to encourage them, many had already made that decision on their own.

'Wondering what it'd be like to be in uniform, Joe lad?'

Frank Gallagher liked the sound of his own voice and, seeing as he occupied the next desk, Joe was often on the receiving end of it. Joe hadn't noticed him come over, but now Frank was sat side-saddle on his chair and smirking. His face was pockmarked with the remnant signs of acne.

'I fancy me in a bit of khaki, like. Reckon the girls will lap it up.'

He smiled stupidly, enjoying himself, and Joe reluctantly smiled back. He had to admit that even though Gallagher could be annoying at times, he did have a certain charm. He made you want to laugh and join in with his japes.

Joe didn't say anything and just shook his head in a playful manner. For once he could imagine why people might sign up, with the honest camaraderie of people like Gallagher, but it was still war.

'Come on, lad. Ya never know, you might find yourself a sweet lass too.' With that he laughed and punched Joe lightly on the shoulder. 'But then we'd have to drag you away from your work.'

What would it be like once the war started proper, if everyone went off to fight? Would it be him and Mr Harlow left all on their own to run the paper? How on earth was the country going to cope? He didn't like the thought, and once again tried to push thoughts of the war out of his mind and press on with work.

'Is that where Barnes and Swanley are, Frank?' He nodded over at their empty desks.

'What? Them two? Lost if I know where they are. They live by their own rules them two. Even the territorials would give them a wide berth.' He scoffed and shook his head. 'They'd look rubbish in a uniform. And they already get all the girls anyway. Leave some for old Frank, that's what I say.'

Joe laughed despite himself.

'I just saw Mr Harlow, and he gave me one of Barnes's articles.' He held up the sheet of paper he was supposed to edit.

'Aye, I saw him on the way in too, muttering to himself. He didn't even notice me. Thought it were best to leave him to it.'

'I don't suppose you could take it off my hands, Frank? I'm a bit busy you see.' He pulled the pile of local articles and adverts closer and smiled at Gallagher. There was no point in telling Frank that he didn't want to work on it himself. He wouldn't understand.

'Oh no! You're not getting me in trouble that easily.' The big smile lit up his face. 'I've only got a few more days' work to get through before I can get out of here. Last thing I want is old Ed Harlow coming down on me for doing your work for you. He's given that to you. I've got other stuff to do.' He shuffled a pile of papers on his own desk. 'Gotta make this lot respectable. Half them journalists can't write for toffee. I'd swear on me old gran that they make up some of this stuff. Some of these words I ain't even heard before.'

Joe didn't doubt it; Frank was a nice guy, but he wasn't the most intelligent. Joe suspected the questioned words were in fact real words, but he was better off leaving Frank to it – he had his style, which was popular with the readers.

'You'll have to find someone else to pass the boring ones to.'

'This one isn't exactly boring, Frank.'

'I know, just glancing at it has already made me want to sign up.' He gave Joe a thump on the arm in jest, and Joe resisted to urge to say 'ow'. 'But, well, that's not the point. I've already decided I'm going. Perhaps reading what Fritz is up to might give you that kick you need to join in the fun too.'

'But, how do we know any of this is true, Frank?'

'What do you mean, true? Of course it's true. We're newspaper men, if we don't know what true is then who does? True...' He shook his head.

'But all these horrible things, I can't believe that they would do that. We have no proof, other than hearsay.'

'Of course they're up to no good. They started a war, Joe. That's not a particularly friendly thing to do now is it?'

'I suppose not.' He put the sheet down. 'Really though, we should be staying neutral, Frank. It's not our war.'

'Don't be stupid, Joe. That's not like you. Of course it's our

25

war.' For once Frank was serious, his usually bright eyes surveyed Joe in a way he hadn't seen before.

'Them Germans want Europe for themselves. All this stuff that's happened leading up to this was just rot, designed as an excuse. They've been spoiling for a war for ages now, and it's been left to us to stop them. We'll see that we do. Our Tommies are the only ones that'll stand up to 'em.'

It was no use. Frank was just like all the rest: well meaning, but misguided. Joe wouldn't get anywhere by trying to make him see reason, and to question what he was told. Everyone was determined that the only way to stop the – alleged – despicable acts of the Germans was to counter them with yet more despicable acts. He would have to try another tactic.

With that thought, he pulled out the copy of the *Labour Leader* from the top drawer of his desk and flicked through the pages for the article he sought. With a pen he began crossing out lines and rewriting them with added argument, inspired by the words of Fenner Brockway and the other socialist writers. It wasn't much, he didn't know how many people would read the article now that he had crossed out the headline, but he could dissuade some men from fighting. He hoped he could make a difference. He had to do something.

Chapter 3

'There's a ship mooring at the Duke's dock,' someone shouted. The men picked up kit, off to find some maintenance work, but George had none. He got a running head start on them, with Tom by his side. They pounded along the cobbled streets, the soles of their boots clicking on the surface with each footfall. At first his boots had rubbed his feet to tatters, but now they were so worn in that it felt like he was running barefoot. Sweat caused by the glaring sun dripped down from his temples and ran round the curve of his neck, under his clothes. It was almost unbearable, but he kept running, otherwise he wouldn't get there in time.

War had almost been forgotten in the last few days, as work had taken over. They crossed Gower Street and ducked around a carriage, the coachman swearing at them, before running into the Duke's dock underneath the brick arch of the dock house. The dock smelled strongly of salt water and that ever present stench of fish that got into the nostrils and never left. There was a ship mooring at the dock. George craned his neck to see around the men in front of him. It was a small ship. Its sails were furled and it was being guided in by a small motor. Rope was already being pulled over one of the mooring posts. A man assisting in the mooring saw them coming and blocked their way. 'Easy now,' he said, raising the palms of his hands. The men almost didn't stop. 'Easy,' he said again, louder.

This time the men stopped in front of the dock master. 'I need ten able-bodied men to unload this cargo,' he said. 'No more.' There was a collective groan from the group, about fifty, most of them in tatty clothes. 'She also needs some caulking, if you can do it.'

A man towards the back of the group with a heavy tin toolbox put a hand up and pushed forward past the dock master. The master started assigning men tasks. 'You, you, and you,' he said to three men a couple of rows in front of George. The rest of the men jostled to get noticed, but the master just scowled, picked the rest of the men from elsewhere.

Tom cursed. 'I thought we had got lucky there, George,' he said with a shake of his head.

'Back to the custom house?' George said. 'We can look in on the arrivals there.' Work was scarce on the dock, and down to luck.

The dock master came back over to the group. 'There's a big haul coming in, lads. If you're quick.' There were calls from the crowd, asking where.

'...King's dock' were the only words George heard, as he dragged Tom after him. The two of them spent most of their days running from one place to another. He didn't mind the running, but it was the sweat that he couldn't cope with. In winter it was fine, the running kept you warm, but in the summer it was unbearable. He tried to wear as few layers as possible, but the clothes were for protection. If a piece of cargo slipped it could cut a hole, he'd seen it happen. The boys crossed to the King's dock. It was a good distance to get to King's dock. Some part of George suspected that it wouldn't be worth the effort, but they had to try. Their families depended on the income. Even if it was only a few pence.

As they turned the corner the expanse opened up to a much

greater view. King's dock was much larger than Duke's. Here the buildings were spaced back, allowing the cargo to be offloaded and moved to better locations. There was indeed a ship entering the dock, larger than the last. It was crawling into the moorings, carefully using the rudder to make sure that it didn't hit the dockside. It let off its horn, blaring across the dock, almost deafening, and some of the men following George and Tom cheered, feeling their luck was in.

This time the dock master agitatedly waved them into a queue at the side of the dock without saying anything. If the men pushed their luck they would be dismissed without a chance to earn any pay. So they waited, eager, but cautious.

He started assigning them off into queues, and only a few minutes later George and Tom were busy rolling heavy wooden barrels of brandy away from the dockside to a horse-cart that would take them away to a holding area. It took two men to roll each barrel, one guiding while the other put all their weight behind it and gave it a great shove. George and Tom had plenty of experience and idly chatted amongst themselves while they worked. They stopped for a moment to catch their breath, having just loaded the last barrel that would fit onto the cart, rolling it up the wooden chocks that formed a slope to the hold. The coachman put up the tail board with help from Tom to seal the other side.

'You were right,' Tom said, holding up a paper he had taken off a bench. The headline indicated that the war was in the morning paper again. It had been all that people had talked about since the ultimatum had expired.

George wondered what Tom was talking about. Staring at him, he urged him to continue.

'About them wanting more troops,' he said. 'You were talking about it the other day, remember? It says right here that Lord Kitchener has asked for another hundred thousand men.'

There was a loud crack, accompanied by the snap of breaking

wood, which seemed to drag the sound out from its initial burst.

He turned to see a shape rushing towards them. He called out to Tom but it was too late. He just had time to reach for Tom and push him out of the way before an escaped barrel knocked into his back with force.

Tom fell to the ground with a cry as the metal-clad wood knocked into him. It carried on rolling past, and George was just about able to get out of its way, before it crashed against the brick wall of the dock house and burst open, spilling its contents all over the cobbles.

The coachman rushed to the back of his cart. The back plank had come undone, allowing the barrel to slip off the cart and run free. With the help of a few others, he managed to stop any more barrels falling off the cart and lashed them to the decking with some spare rope.

George ran over to Tom, sprawled on the cobble floor. Tom had been hit in the back and was lying face down. He feared the worst, but Tom just groaned and tried to roll over.

'Don't move, Tom. I'll get help.'

Tom just smiled back at George as he always did and he pushed George away as he tried to check him for wounds.

'Ah, don't worry, George.' He groaned as he sat up and put a hand to his back. 'I'm all right, I'm all right.'

He finally accepted help but shook his head. George helped him up with a hand under his armpit and then dusted him down. There was a bit of blood on his forehead, but nothing on the rest of his body except for a bruise that would blacken over the next few days. George wet his handkerchief and handed it to Tom as he motioned for him to wipe his forehead. Seeing that George was taking care of Tom, the coachman got back up on his cart and led the horse away – any delay would cost him money.

'Are you sure you're all right?' George asked.

'Yeah. It was lucky you shouted,' Tom said as he wiped the crusting blood from his forehead and winced at the pain. 'I would have been stood stock still if you hadn't. That shove helped too. I avoided most of the barrel.' He stretched his back. 'Still gave me a bloody great thump though. I'll feel that one in the morning, no doubt. Let's see what else they need us to do.'

He turned to walk away, but George grabbed him by the arm.

'We should call it a day. You've had a nasty bump. That could be a head injury too,' he said, gesturing towards Tom's forehead again.

Tom shook his head and tried to hide another wince. The smile was back again. 'There's nothing wrong with my head,' he said. 'If we're quitting work, do you think we should volunteer?'

George let go of his arm. 'Come on, let's go home. I've had enough for one day.'

'I'm serious.'

George wiped the smile from his face, knowing it was doing him no favours in this situation.

'I've been thinking about it a lot. No matter what else I do, I keep coming back to the same thought.'

George tried to show compassion and lighten the mood. 'I know, you haven't shut up about it since the other day.'

At that moment the dock master ran over to them and started shouting. He was an overweight man, his belly threatening to escape his waistcoat, and his hair was balding, leaving a sweaty pate of pink flesh.

'What the hell is going on here?' he shouted when he had got his breath back from the run. A frown crossed his face.

'You.' He pointed at Tom, who was still stretching his back, visibly uncomfortable at the pain. 'What did you do? Why are you slacking?'

Tom shrugged. 'I'm not,' he said. 'The cart's full, and we're going back for more.'

The dock master wasn't appeased.

'Don't lie to me. I heard a commotion, what's going on? If you've caused any damage...'

It was at that moment that he noticed the destroyed brandy barrel. It was a wonder he hadn't seen it sooner, the stench of brandy was strong in George's nostrils. The dock master's eyes widened as he took in the broken wood and the precious cargo draining away through the cobbles.

'You damaged the cargo,' he said through gritted teeth.

'What?'

The dock master grabbed Tom by the collar, even though Tom was a good foot taller than him.

'Do you have any idea how much that barrel was worth? More money than you'll ever have.'

'What?' Tom said again, unsure. 'I didn't do anything. You're mad.'

'Damn right I'm mad. How are you going to pay for that?'

George moved to help Tom, but couldn't see how without angering the dock master further. Instead he tried to calm him down.

'Tom didn't do anything, sir. The tail board on the cart broke and the barrel rolled off. If you ask the coachman he will vouch for us.' The coachman wouldn't be back for a while, but at least it might buy them some time.

The dock master turned to George, still holding Tom by the collar.

'Who asked you? As far as I know you're just as much to blame as this idiot is.'

Tom used that moment to break free of the dock master's grasp. With a lurch, he pushed the smaller man away with both hands. He moved backwards and tripped over a cobble, but thanks to his low centre of gravity, managed not to fall.

'I didn't break the barrel, sir. In fact, it almost broke me.' As a gesture of goodwill, Tom checked the man over to make sure he wasn't hurt. 'Now, if you don't mind, my friend and I would like to get back to work. There are plenty more barrels like that that need moving and if that doesn't get done, then I guess you'll lose even more money.'

The dock master trembled, in shock from Tom's shove, then nodded.

'Fine. I'll chase that coachman for this. But if either of you lads does anything like this again, if you put one finger where it shouldn't be, then I will make sure that you never work anywhere on these docks again.'

He walked away, his pace slightly quicker than a walk like someone trying to escape a confrontation with an enemy without drawing attention to himself.

'Now get back to work,' he called over his shoulder, as if it was his idea and not Tom's.

'That was close,' Tom said, grabbing George by the arm and leading him away. 'Come on, let's get this over and done with.'

They went back to work, but before long the conversation had returned to the war.

'Well now, I think they'll take me,' Tom said out of the blue, and George rolled his eyes at him, even though Tom wasn't paying attention. 'They need more men, they'll take anyone that can hold a rifle at the moment. Besides, what have I got to lose? I've not got much here except my old mum. It's gotta be better than this. Anything is better than this.' He stopped and gestured at the barrel he had been rolling towards the new cart. The previous coachman hadn't come back.

He stretched his back and groaned at the pain. Injuries were common around the dock, and Tom was lucky it hadn't been worse. Every week one or more of the lads working on the dock ended up in a ward, or sometimes worse: a mortuary.

George grunted. It wasn't so much that he agreed with Tom – he resented the fact that he had only thought about his mother and not his friends – but Tom had that way of getting you to see his point of view.

George thought about Tom leaving, and about working on the dock alone. It didn't appeal to him. They made a good team.

'If you go, Tom, I can't go with you,' he said.

'Sure you can, if that's what you want. Why not?'

'For a start, I'm not old enough. You have to be nineteen before they'll send you abroad, eighteen if you just want to stay at home doing something boring.'

He saw the dock master prowling along the path and gestured to Tom to resume their work. 'At least, that's what my dad always told us. He's been counting down the days.'

'Ah, come on now, George.' Tom shook his head as he always did when he thought George was being unreasonable. 'If you want to sign up, they'll take you. By the sounds of it they'll take anyone. That old dock master over there might even be in khaki soon. You'll see.'

They both laughed at the thought. It was a welcome relief to the melancholy that had settled on them during the day, and finally Tom was smiling again.

'You don't want to wait till eighteen or nineteen to go down the recruitment office. You'll be sat twiddling your thumbs, hearing about all the heroic deeds we've been up to out there. It'll all be over by the time your eighteenth birthday comes, then what'll you do? Start another war, just so you can fight in it?'

He was poking fun at George, but the smile was so warm it was difficult not to get dragged along in his wake.

'Perhaps I will. It'd show you.' George thought for a moment. 'They'll know I'm not old enough and I'll get turned away from the office. It'll be humiliating watching you and the rest of them get your khaki and being told to come back when I'm a man.'

'Ah, that won't happen, trust me. You're bigger than any eighteen-year-old I know. You even look older than me and don't forget, I'm two years older than you. Besides, you'll be with me. That'll be enough to help you out. They won't want to turn away any of the famous Tom Adams' army.'

George laughed as he pushed the final barrel onto the cart and fastened the rear hatch, eyeing it suspiciously. Tom gave it a big thump and was satisfied that it wasn't going to come loose. 'Ready,' he shouted to the coachman. He then stood with his hands on his hips, like George's mother often did when he was in trouble. 'If I didn't know you, I wouldn't believe you were any less than nineteen,' he said.

George pushed Tom away and they went to find some more work.

Tom was right. George was unlike his father and brother, who were both thin and gaunt. His broad shoulders and chest may have come from his mother's side. Uncle Stephen was a much larger man. George had more in common with him than his father. His uncle was like a giant when stood next to his father, even if his father didn't have a crooked leg. His father always stood as tall as he could when Stephen was around. His mother always argued that George looked just like his father had done in the army, and pushed old, brown photographs in his direction to prove it. Back then he was a stronger, prouder man.

The rest of the day continued largely without incident. They moved more barrels, and their backs became sore from the effort. George suspected that Tom was in a lot more pain than he let on, but he didn't complain, except for stopping occasionally to stretch with a wince. Once the cargo ship was emptied and the other dock hands were on board, fixing and caulking, the two boys left. There was little extra work to be found, but they had managed to earn some money.

'So then, George,' Tom said, as if unsure how to broach a difficult subject. Tom was seldom lost for words, but this time he seemed unable to speak. He kept biting his lip.

'What's wrong?' George asked, trying to force the conversation.

'Nothing's wrong.' Tom stopped speaking again and then shook his head. 'Well, except for all this,' he said, waving an arm behind him to indicate the dock. 'This... this isn't what I wanted from life, George. When we were back in school I thought so much more of life. All the things the teachers talked about. Every time I thought… "I could do that." I should have tried harder. Perhaps I wasn't intelligent enough. Who knows?'

George just nodded along.

'I didn't think I would end up down here in the docks. My ma was happy when I got a job. So was I for that matter, but now look at me.' He waved an arm up and down his body and at his back. 'Covered in muck and sweat. Just look at this bruise, George. That's really going to hurt in the morning. Ouch.' He had touched it with a finger. 'It hurts now!'

'Be careful, Tom.' He wasn't used to his friend being so glum.

'We can be much better than this, George. Both of us. We're not as daft as some of those idiots down that dock, so why not? Everything we've done, we've done well, right?' He didn't wait for an answer. 'Right, so it's settled then. When I get a chance, I'm putting on my Sunday suit, I'm going down the recruitment office and telling them I want to fight the Germans.' Red threatened to break out on Tom's cheeks, but then he held his head high, pushing his chest out at his decision.

George wasn't surprised. He had felt that it was coming since he had spoken to Tom that morning. Tom had mentioned the war at every opportunity. George preferred to keep his thoughts to himself, but Tom appeared excited. The mood of the city was of excitement, Tom wasn't the only one. The way George's father often talked about his time in the army, it sounded like an adventure, like a way of life to be proud of. His father had served in the King's Liverpool regiment and his uncle too. It was the only thing he ever remembered his father talking about with happiness in his voice. The troubles of recent times seemed forgotten, everyone was pulling together in the same direction, as his dad would have said. George reflected as they climbed the hill.

'I think you should do it,' he said to Tom, after a silence. Tom let out a deep breath as if he'd been holding it. 'If it's what you want to do, then why not? You'd make a good soldier, I don't doubt.'

'It's my ma I'm worried about. After my old man… Ah, I can't talk about it. She will understand, and your folks will look after her, won't they?'

'Sure.' Their mothers were close. 'Say, why don't we go to the pub tomorrow night? It's been an age. See what the other lads are up to. You can run your idea by them too. Let's go to the Grapes.'

Tom's grin returned. He always loved a drink.

'Great idea!' was the only reply George needed.

Chapter 4

Joe was walking through Chinatown the next day when he saw George and Tom Adams across the road. The signs on the shops and even the street signs were in Chinese. The Chinese seemed to be the largest of the sailor communities, huddling around the area of Nelson Street and integrating with the Liverpudlians in the area.

Joe couldn't imagine settling in another country, especially one so far away from his home. But perhaps it had been easier for them than returning home. Who knew what kind of prospects they had back in China? At least here they had families and work.

His brother and Tom were walking along the road in the opposite direction to him. Of course, he saw them first, and as of yet they hadn't noticed him. It was always the same way. He had a habit of disappearing into crowds, and he was so far outside their world they didn't have any reason for acknowledging his presence. They must have been on their way home from the dock, chatting together in their usual way. Unusually, they didn't look as happy as they normally did. Often when Joe saw the pair of them, they were too happily tied up in some inane conversation to notice him go by. Most of the time he didn't mind, happy to meld into the background and avoid an awkward conversation with them. Today, however, he walked closer to the side of the road to make himself more noticeable. He wanted them to see him, he wanted to speak to his brother, if only in passing.

With luck, Tom crossed the road, George shortly behind him. They weaved between a couple of carts, before making their way across the cobbles.

'Afternoon, Joe,' Tom said, upon seeing him. He was always the more friendly of the two, with a smile for anyone he passed – though Joe suspected he wasn't always the best influence on George. Recognition dawned on George's face as he came closer, but he simply nodded. 'On the way to work?' Tom asked, before Joe had a chance to say hello.

'Err, well, I have a few things to do first,' he said, put off by the unexpected conversation. George had his hands in his pockets and looked around the road, seeming disinterested in any conversation. 'George, could you tell Mum that I will be late this evening and not to worry about food?'

'Sure,' he said, nodding slightly. 'We're on our way home now. She probably won't be surprised.' This was the most they had said to each other in weeks. Sharing a bedroom was one thing, but working different hours meant they seldom saw each other.

'No, I suppose not.' The atmosphere was awkward, and Joe felt uncomfortable standing still on the pavement, but he so much wanted to talk to George, to reach out and feel something between them. He never could say the rights words, and it hurt him. He felt as if George believed that he had nothing to say to him, but it couldn't be further from the truth. 'The war's creating a lot of work for us at the paper.' He scratched at his collar, feeling more uncomfortable by the minute. 'A lot of the men at the paper have already left to sign up, and we're having to do extra work to make up. I shouldn't complain. You two possibly have it a lot worse.'

'Yeah, there's not much work on the dock at the moment. It could pick up with the war, but who knows?' Again, Tom was the one to speak. George nodded at his words, as if thinking of something else. How had they grown so far apart? Joe was only a few years older than his kid brother, but the divide was a gulf. 'We've been considering the war ourselves. Everybody is talking about it. We've been wondering what's going on out there, what our lads have been up to. We should read your paper.'

George gave Tom a dig in the ribs with his elbow, and Tom yelped with mock pain. 'We'd best leave you to it, Joe. Come on, Tom,' George said, finally finding his voice.

'Yes. There's some stuff I need to do before work,' he said, feeling the newspaper in his jacket's inside pocket. 'See you at home?'

George nodded with a slight hesitation as the pair of them walked away from Joe.

'Goodbye, Joe,' Tom called after him.

'Goodbye, George,' Joe muttered under his breath, ignoring Tom.

Chapter 5

George had been looking forward to a drink all afternoon and he didn't take any time in pushing open the door of the pub and rushing inside. Clinking glasses, laughs and the occasional cheer filtered through the doorway to the Grapes, their local drinking haunt.

From the entranceway two doors led off, one to the private patrons' bar and one to the public bar, the latter more brightly lit through the frosted glass of the door. Shadows moved inside. The patrons' bar, by comparison, appeared empty.

George knew which side they would be welcome in and walked straight through the public bar door, taking his hat off, to where the smell of stale ale mixed with sweat, and the heavy fog of smoking hit his nostrils. The noise was louder inside as men tried to talk over each other and make their orders heard at the bar.

'Let's find the lads,' Tom said, from behind him, raising his voice to be heard as they pushed their way into the pub.

The bar was a loose 'L' shape and as they moved around the corner George heard Tom's name being shouted.

'Tom! Get over here, lad. Pull up a stool and get your lips around a nice bevvy. Don't waste any time!' Patrick waved them over as he shouted.

George could just about see them through the cloud of smoke and the press of bodies. He and their other old school mate Harry had already got themselves a table in the corner and sat around it with pints of ale.

'Evening, lads,' Tom said as they got through the crowd. 'Cains again, is it?' He gestured to the glasses of thick, brown ale.

'Aye,' Patrick said. 'Harry won't drink anything else, will he?'

Harry tried to say something but had a mouthful of ale.

'Everyone has their family pride,' Patrick continued. 'The only time I ever got him to drink something else was when he lost at Crown and Anchor. And even then he spat most of it up.' He took a short drag on his cigarette. 'Say, lads. Why don't we play another game now?'

Harry lurched forward and ale spat down his front and across the table. The others laughed, and he joined in with them as the remnants of the ale frothed around his lips.

Patrick was always trying to be the life of any gathering and tonight was no exception. His blond hair was ruffled as if he had just dragged himself through a bush, and his thin, wiry frame would definitely aid in that.

Harry, on the other hand, was exactly the opposite; he cut his brown hair close to his head and his short thick frame would easier knock the bush over than slide through it. He was also slightly slower on the uptake than the others, and found himself lagging behind most conversations and, indeed, jokes.

'Stop being cruel to Harry, O'Brien. He drinks what he wants to drink and no one should tell him otherwise.'

Tom sat down on a stool next to Patrick and pulled one out for George. Harry handed him a cigarette, and he lit it, taking a long drag, letting the cool, blue smoke escape his mouth.

'So what news, Tom Adams?' Patrick asked, puffing smoke while waiting for an answer. Tom put the glass to his lips and waited for a long moment, refreshing the taste of his beer, before answering.

'Not much to say, Paddy. Work, work and more work for us.'

The others nodded in sympathy. Patrick shot him a look.

'Can't we talk about something else?' Harry asked. 'Like football or something? Is anyone going along to the match at the weekend?'

'No, Harry, I don't think so,' Tom said, humouring him. 'I think we have other plans.'

'Come on, Williams. It's only a friendly, why bother?' Patrick put his arm around Harry's shoulders, who deflated at the response.

'The season doesn't kick off for another month, Harry,' George added. 'Paddy is right. Besides it's not like you support a proper football team.' He tried to flick a cheeky smile to show Harry that he was jesting, but Patrick slammed his glass down.

'You know I don't like that name, Abbott. Don't ever call me that again.'

He leaned over the table and raised a fist at George, a little stylised cross on a silver chain dropping out of his shirt. He reached for it with his other hand.

Tom put his hand around Patrick's fist and slowly pushed him back towards his own seat.

'There's nothing wrong with the reds, George,' said Harry. 'Just because they're not as old as Everton, doesn't mean they're not a proper club. You take that back.'

As always, Harry seemed to have missed the undertones to the conversation and the others laughed, breaking the uneasy tension that had built up from nowhere.

'Sorry, Harry. I'm sure they'll do better this season, but not if we can help it!' George pushed another pint of ale in Harry's direction and gave him a wink.

'So how's the rice industry, O'Brien?' Tom broke his silence, then had another drink. He lit another cigarette from the butt of his last one.

'Work is much the same as always, I guess it's the same as down at the dock.'

George very much doubted that, but didn't say anything.

'Always back-breaking and sweating buckets without any thanks. I'm sure I constantly smell like rice,' he laughed wryly.

'Better than smelling like brandy,' Tom interjected. 'My old mum thinks I always come home drunk from work. She won't listen that it's thanks to those barrels.' He sniffed his armpit in mock theatricality. 'Brandy and sweat, a fine combination, fit for the middle classes.'

George chuckled. 'Well, at least she'll be right tonight, when you go home flat drunk,' he said as he passed his mate another pint from the dwindling row of full glasses on the table.

'That's right!' Harry shouted, and the others roared with laughter.

'I'm not going to lie to you, Adams.' Patrick leaned over conspiratorially and covered one side of his face with a hand, as if he was going to whisper into Tom's ear and he didn't want anyone else to overhear.

'Things have not been going well at the millers.'

'Oh, aye?' Tom feigned interest, but Patrick didn't seem to notice.

'Yeah. The supervisors are getting jumpy. Things have been going badly for a while. We've kept on working, doing our thing, but they've been getting worried nonetheless. The unions are urging us to strike, and winding up the owners, but we don't know what's best.' He leaned closer. 'I think Bailey's going to call a picket any day now, you wait.' He sighed. 'There's too much trouble at the moment.'

'You're right, O'Brien, there is. I don't know what you should do, but you should try listening to the union man. Surely they've got your best interest at heart?'

George took another sip of his beer, listening to the conversation between the other two. Patrick was hardly being quiet, despite what his body language suggested.

'And to add to that, my da is worried about his family. I thought we were his family? But no, he wants to go home, to help out with all the trouble there. He says he's gotta help 'em.'

'What's he going to do in Ulster? What can he possibly do to help them?'

'I don't know, but he's got to try, hasn't he?'

'I guess so. Your father's an honest man, O'Brien. And don't worry, he loves it here almost as much as he loves Ireland. This is home now.' Tom patted Patrick on the back in a friendly gesture and stood up. 'Time to get some more in.'

He pushed his way to the bar, and the conversation died out. Patrick studied the bottom of his empty pint and George averted his attention. The pub was busier now, and there was a group of men by the bar having a heated discussion.

Tom came back, precariously carrying four pints of ale. He plopped them down and beer spilt over the rims.

'Easy, Adams,' Patrick said.

'Well, give me a hand next time then, won't you?'

He made sure that the fullest pint was sat in front of Patrick.

'Listen, there's a group of lads over there getting quite rowdy. Keep an eye out for them. There might be some trouble.'

A glass shattered and Tom cringed. A tall, thin man, with yellow hair came flying through the crowd and almost fell over in front of their table. He was being pushed in the chest by a stockier, balding man.

'What do you mean you don't think we should fight, Smith?' The smaller man was shouting in the other's face, prodding his front with a finger. 'Or should I call you "Schmidt"? That was your family name before you came over here, wasn't it? Taking good, British jobs from good, British workers.' He punctuated each word with a jab.

The two men were nearly at their table now. A hush had descended across the bar.

'You ought to be ashamed of yourself. Saying that they

45

shouldn't be defending their right to work. What gives you the right, you Prussian bastard?'

'Actually I was… well, I was born here. And our King is cousins wi—'

'I don't care,' the other man said. A great shove propelled the other man into Tom's back, almost spilling the pint he was holding.

'Sorry,' the thinner man said from the floor, but Tom had had enough. He turned to the two men, standing taller.

'That's enough,' he shouted. 'There's no need for that in here. Good and honest British workers are trying to enjoy their downtime. You hear me?'

The stocky man looked up at him.

'Now go and have another pint or go home. Either way, leave us in peace.'

The other man glared at Tom, before he grumbled and pushed his way through the crowd. George didn't realise that he and the others had stood up to help Tom, and he sat down again, feeling embarrassed.

Tom helped the thin man to his feet, brushing him down.

'Be careful what you say in here, lad. This *is* a workers' pub.'

'Thank you, I'm sorry. All I said was that it seemed odd that our King had gone to war with his cousin, and that our soldiers should have to fight for it.'

Tom frowned.

'Well, even still, be careful.'

The other man nodded and walked away, eyeing the customers as he left the pub.

'See what I mean, lads? Too much trouble,' Patrick said as Tom sat down.

'Well, I think the Germans are a much bigger problem than anything else, O'Brien,' Harry replied, wiping the beer's head from his lips with the back of his hand, while Tom remained silent.

'I mean, how dare they try to start a war? Over what, some

pompous Duke's death? What's that gotta do with Belgium and France?'

'Archduke,' George said.

'I mean,' Harry continued, ignoring George, 'I thought their problem was with the other side? Not with the French.'

'I think they have a problem with everyone in Europe, Harry. Most of the Royal Houses are at war with each other now. What next?' Tom had calmed down enough to rejoin the conversation and he lit another cigarette.

'Well, our boys will show 'em where to get stuffed!' Harry took a large swig of beer.

'Dad says that their army is much bigger than ours.' George finally managed to get a word in now that Harry's mouth was full. However, he was met with scoffs of derision and chuckles.

'Don't worry, Georgie,' Patrick said, with a big grin from ear to ear. 'The Kaiser may have a bigger army but he doesn't know how to use it!'

George spat beer across the table, and they burst out laughing.

Tom put his hand on George's shoulder and smiled before saying, 'Lad, George's right. That Kitchener is building a new army, to counter the Germans.'

He paused for breath, weighing his next words, then plunged straight ahead. 'Listen, I'm going down the office tomorrow, lads. To sign up.'

'What? You?!' Patrick and Harry replied almost at the same time.

'Yes, me. I've had enough of trying to scrape something together. I think you lads should join me, but I'll understand if you don't.'

'But you're a cad.' Patrick was smiling despite the insult. 'They'll never take you.'

'Then they'll be losing out.' Tom grinned back, and slapped Patrick on the arm. 'I'm not worried, Paddy. Just wait and see, they'll be begging me to enlist. I bet they'll sign me up as an officer right away. They'll give me my own battalion. I'm sure that they'll let you join it. You can be my servants, lads.' He held up his arm with his palm outstretched. 'They'll even call it Tom Adams' Army.' He punctuated each word with his hand as if imagining a hoarding.

'What about your job, Tom, lad?' Harry sounded concerned. 'What'll you do when the war is over?'

Tom shook his head.

'I'll cross that bridge when I come to it, Harry. There's no use in worrying what might be. Plus, I hear the army pays better.' George caught the hesitation in Tom, but he carried on, apparently hoping the others wouldn't notice. 'It'll be an adventure.'

'Besides, he'll be back soon when it all blows over.' Patrick was clearly warming to the idea. 'He might not even get a chance to go over there before our boys have sent them Germans packing.'

'Aye,' Tom said. 'But I might stay on after the war. See where it takes me. I could go all over the world.'

'When he served in the King's, my dad was out in South Africa,' George added. 'Not to mention Afghanistan and India. Who knows where they might go after this war?'

'It's gotta be better than good old Toxteth,' Patrick laughed.

'My dad has always said he misses it, ever since he got injured. Though I was too young to remember much about it.'

'So, that's why your old man's so grumpy,' Harry said, trying to elicit a laugh, but bringing the conversation to a halt. The colour drained from George's face, his anger swelling. He wasn't quick to anger, but he couldn't let someone insult his dad.

'Come on, Harry, there's no need for that!' Tom came to George's rescue. 'George's dad served our country proudly for years. You should show him more respect.'

Patrick drank his beer as if he hadn't noticed the awkwardness.

'Sorry, uh, George… lad. I was, er, ah… out of line,' Harry apologised.

George could only nod, not wanting to open his mouth for fear of what he might say.

'You can't go alone, lad,' Patrick said, returning to what he thought was a more interesting topic, leaving George still fuming.

'I won't be alone, the rumours of war have been going for weeks. I've heard whispers all over the city about signing up.' Tom was grinning wider with every word, engaging his audience with enthusiasm in every breath.

George quickly forgot about the insult to his father, and envisioned a great British soldier rallying his troops and leading them into a glorious battle against the despicable enemy. He could see Tom doing that sort of thing, pulling every other soldier along with him in his wake and winning the day, with a big grin on his face. Men would follow Tom into anything. He would, too.

'Besides, that's why our George is coming with me.'

That one sentence ripped George out of his daydreaming and back into the present. He tried to hide his surprise by grabbing his ale and taking a swig. He hadn't told Tom that he would be signing up with him, but as usual Tom had assumed he would follow. They had talked about it, yes, but he hadn't said that he wanted to sign up. It had all been Tom.

Although, now it had been said, he liked the idea. He couldn't imagine working down at the dock without Tom to keep him company and get him through a hard day.

'Oh, you too eh, Georgie?' Patrick obviously wasn't willing to let the matter lie. 'Going to follow in the footsteps of your father? Keep it in the family? Make him proud?'

Without thinking George replied. 'Yes,' he said. He very much wanted that, to make his father proud. George's father was a hard, uncompromising man, but he had always done everything he could to do right by his family. George knew that his father loved both his sons, even if he never showed it, but he desperately wanted to see that sense of pride on his father's face. His mother always said that the reason he was so sullen and withdrawn was because he was forced out of the army by injury. George wanted to do anything possible to give him some of his pride back. His father couldn't fight, so he would.

He had tried to make a living, urged by his mother to do something honest and constructive, but it wasn't working. The dock was its own special kind of hell. Heavy, hard work, and if he was truthful, he hated it as much as Tom did.

'So, what about the football then?' Harry urged again.

The others continued talking without George. He didn't care what they thought. 'I'm going to enlist,' he said, more for himself than for any of the others, testing the words out on his lips, to say it out loud. Tom was the only one to take any notice and smiled at him, before turning back to the others, deep in conversation. They were too drunk now to talk about anything serious. George had another drink.

Chapter 6

'It's a dacks-hound, one of them German ones, lad,' said one of the group of small boys with dusty brown hair, as Joe walked nearer. They were surrounding a small, whimpering dog. Another boy taunted it with a stick.

'It's the enemy, get it,' shouted another, lost in the crowd.

The boy, a gaunt thing with scruffy clothes and thick curly black hair, whacked the dog with his stick. It fell on its side and elicited a great wail. Its pain didn't deter the boys, and as the boy raised his stick again Joe grabbed it from behind. 'That's enough,' he said, and yanked the stick out of the boy's hand.

'Hey, that's mine,' the boy complained. He must have been about eight or nine years old, his face covered in the muck and grime accumulated from playing in the street. The dog used this distraction to limp off and disappear from sight around a corner.

'Not anymore,' Joe said, calmly, making sure not to talk down to the boy. 'There's no need to abuse that poor dog. What has it done to you?'

'Hey,' someone shouted from behind Joe, and he turned. 'What are you doing to my son?' A slightly plump woman wearing a pinafore rushed across to road to confront Joe. He thought of the stick in his hand and dropped it.

51

'Nothing,' he said. 'They were having a go at a poor dog, saying it was German. Hitting it with a stick.'

'And you think it's right to tell them what to do, do you?' Her big cheeks were flush with anger. 'They're just showing their patriotism. Are you some kind of pacifist or something?'

'Well actually—'

'You're all the same, your lot. Go on, leave my boy alone, or I'll give you a good hiding like your mother should have done.'

'I was just helping the dog,' he said, the sound struggling to get past his throat.

Her anger didn't abate, but she focused on her son and Joe walked away as fast as his legs would allow. Behind, he could still make out her voice, yelling at the boy.

He crossed the road past the horse carts, as a lone motorcar trundled past. Outside the greengrocer's boxes of fruit and vege-tables shone in the late morning sun. He picked up a couple of apples. One was thick, ripe, and juicy, the other was thinning and clearly older, bruised in parts. He put the ageing apple back on top, feeling sorry for it. Perhaps a customer might see it first and buy it.

He entered the newsagent's next door, which opened with the jingle of a bell. Posters lined the walls, showing various headlines from different newspapers. Light filtered in through the window panes casting long shadows across the stands. It smelled of musty paper and ink, a smell Joe was well used to. At the far end of the shop the shopkeeper was having an argument with another man. Their voices were rising and falling. The shopkeeper, a bulky man wearing an apron, and with silver hair around his ears, was moving bundles of papers away from the counter. A smaller man followed him. They hadn't heard the entry bell. Joe couldn't make out what was being said.

He read the first newspaper on the stand, waiting for them to finish. The terrible 'Hun' was plastered in a headline across the first page. He shook his head and put the paper back, sliding it behind another, then picked up the copy of the *Labour Leader* that he had come in for, folded it under one arm and walked to the counter.

'Don't expect me to do your work for you,' said the shopkeeper to a smaller man as he moved another bundle of newspapers aside, dropping them with a bang.

Joe coughed into his fist.

Both men jumped in shock. 'Sorry, sir,' the shopkeeper said, letting go of another bundle and rushing around the counter to serve Joe. The small man's cold blue eyes stared.

'Joe?' he said. 'Joe Abbott?'

Joe didn't reply. He put the paper down in front of the frowning shopkeeper.

'Joe, it is you. It is.' The other man moved to shake Joe's hand. He was a head shorter than Joe, with, short brown, bushy hair. His cheeks were gaunt, and his jaw pronounced. There was evidence of a moustache and beard that was only just showing through on his pale skin and gave him an unshaven appearance. Recognition dawned.

'Oh my,' Joe said. The words came out in a hurry. He stared at the other man's outstretched hand and wondered if it was now too late to shake it.

'You know this idiot?' the shopkeeper joined in, putting his hand out to be paid.

Joe handed over a ha'penny without looking at the man or answering his question. The shopkeeper cashed up. 'So, do you?' he said again, before returning to his work when Joe gave a shallow nod.

'Little Jimmy.' Joe paused for a second, thinking. 'Little Jimmy Sutcliffe, isn't it? I remember you.'

The blue eyes brightened as Joe recognised him. 'Yes, though less of the little now. No one calls me Little Jimmy any more. James will do.' He smiled. It seemed forced, the corners of his mouth were still downturned. 'You do remember how we were

53

always at the front of the class back at school, and you pretended never to understand me?'

'Yes, of course. I'm sorry.' Joe wasn't sure he had been pretending, but didn't want to say so.

'You do remember, don't you? Old Fenning, used to put us next to each other in his classroom. His two brightest students he used to say, remember?'

'Yes.' Joe remembered, but rather differently. *He* had been one of Fenning's brightest students, but Little Jimmy Sutcliffe was not. His old teacher was always recommending further reading and philosophy to Joe. He had grown particularly fond of the old man. As a boy Jimmy always seemed entitled, from a rich family on the hill that looked down on them all. He expected to be one of Fenning's brightest and best, but really, he wasn't.

'I remember it, Jimmy… James.' He caught himself. 'We had some good years at that school. Before I had to leave.'

'I never really did understand why you had to leave.'

Joe nodded. He hadn't had time to tell anyone why he was leaving or where he was going to. He had only been there by the kindness of his Uncle Stephen who, because he had no children of his own, had decided to pay for Joe's education. That was until his younger siblings had needed schooling. His uncle simply couldn't pay for them all and so Joe had had to leave. After all, he had learnt all he needed to know, hadn't he? The local school would be fine for the rest of his education. 'We couldn't afford it, James.'

'Oh, that is rum.' He pushed his lips out and dropped his head. Joe wasn't sure if Jimmy was genuinely upset, or just humouring him.

'Don't frown, James,' Joe said, mimicking old Fenning. 'I did all right.'

Jimmy smiled again. Joe missed old Fenning. The man was a bright spark in a dark, cruel world and had always given Joe so much to think about. The master at his next school had been

54

unkind and unfair. Joe had withdrawn and found solace in books. He would have rather been at home, reading. Perhaps Jimmy *had* become Fenning's best student after Joe had left.

Jimmy shuffled, as the shopkeeper gave an occasional huff, making it clear that he wanted them gone. 'What brings you here in particular, Joe?' Jimmy asked. 'Oh,' he continued before Joe answered. He pointed to the newspaper that Joe was holding. 'I found a few old issues of that in Fenning's room once.'

'This?' He held up the paper. 'Fenning encouraged me to read it when I was at school, to learn about all walks of life he used to say. It's also interesting research for my newspaper work. I had no idea Fenning read it at the school.' Reading the newspaper would have been quite dangerous at such a school. He had only ever mentioned it in hushed tones.

'Oh yes, we found all sorts of things after you left. Best not to dishonour his memory with that sort of discussion though, may he rest in peace.' Jimmy sighed.

He didn't hear what Jimmy said next. He had never found out what had happened to Fenning after Joe had left the school. It had seemed like a different life. He wiped his eye with a handkerchief, passing it off as if he were wiping his nose. He didn't want to think of the old, kind teacher passing away. He wondered how it had happened, but he didn't dare ask.

'We could discuss our old school days and old Fenning sometime while having a drink,' Jimmy said, beaming at him.

Joe hesitated. 'I don't know, Jimmy. Sorry… James.'

Jimmy's eyes dropped to the floor. 'It would be fine to catch up. If you are busy, we could arrange a better time.'

'You're right. Why don't you give me your address, and when I've time, I'll be in touch.'

'Excellent. Just one second.' He patted his pockets. 'Here, do you have a pencil and some paper I could borrow?' The shopkeeper scowled as handed him a small notepad and a worn pencil. A few seconds later, Jimmy handed Joe a piece of paper. An address in Woolton. Joe could only imagine the large houses with their own estates, a good distance from their nearest neighbours.

'You know the area?' Jimmy asked.

Joe nodded.

'Good! Do pop by whenever you get a moment, won't you?'

'I'll try,' Joe said, cramming the piece of paper into his coat pocket.

'Whenever you get a spare second, we would love to see you up at the house. Just knock on the door and the man will let you in. That is whenever – the newspaper, was it? – whenever they let you free for socialising.'

Joe nodded again. He wasn't really listening. Jimmy brought back painful memories of a life he didn't really care for. Although he wanted to make more of himself, he didn't agree with how families like the Sutcliffes lived.

'What newspaper was it that you said you worked for?'

Joe mentally cursed for having mentioned it. 'Did I say newspaper?' It was a poor dodge and he knew.

'Yes, I'm sure you did.' Jimmy's smile didn't falter.

'That's right. Well, I er—'

At that moment, the welcome-bell jingled as the door opened and an older man, dressed in a tweed jacket, came into the shop. 'Good morning, Doctor,' the shopkeeper said. Joe thought he had been saved by the distraction, but Jimmy was still waiting.

'I'm a sub-editor for the *Daily Post*, James,' he finally conceded. Jimmy moved a fraction closer. 'It's not much, but it can be interesting, and it gives me a chance to write from time to time.'

'Fascinating,' Jimmy agreed, biting his lip in a thoughtful expression. 'I wonder—'

'I always enjoyed writing, I suppose.' If he could keep talking, he hoped Jimmy would get bored and have to leave. 'There were no jobs available when I started, I had to work my way up from the bottom. I'll work my way up to a top journalist one day. I've already talked to the editor about it.'

Jimmy was biting his lip, while scratching his head. Joe tried to gauge Jimmy's thoughts, but he hadn't seen Jimmy in so long, he didn't really know the man. The shopkeeper moved past them, tidying the shelves. He stopped in between newspapers to give the two men a very pointed stare, which he held for a few seconds, before returning to his work. He reorganised some magazines that the newcomer had disturbed. 'We should leave,' Joe said.

'I think that you would be interested in these.' Jimmy pulled out a wad of paper from his jacket and pushed them at Joe. They were a number of identical pamphlets, printed on a light, expensive brown paper. At the top of the page were the words 'Stop the War To-Day!' in block capitals. Joe sighed. Why would Jimmy be pushing these pamphlets on people? What was the war to him?

'You don't like them?' Jimmy asked. 'They are just the beginning, I asked for some larger prints to post on walls.'

'Why?' was all Joe could manage.

'Why?' A frown crossed Jimmy's brow. 'Because the war needs to be stopped before it even starts. It's not right. Britain should have nothing to do with it.'

'Right, that's enough of this. I told you I don't want nothing to do with this rubbish.' The shopkeeper stormed over to them and opened the door, politeness giving way to frustration. 'Out with you. Go on.' The door slammed behind them. A young woman was examining the vegetables on the greengrocer's stand. The doctor left the newsagent's and walked away. A horse cart rattled past, a cacophony of hooves and metal-clad wheels on the cobbles.

'You have to be careful, James. Protesting the war could see you in prison.'

'Yes I know, but—'

'It doesn't matter. You won't stop the war with these.' He shoved the pamphlets back into Jimmy's unresisting hands. 'People aren't going to listen to these. They'll either ignore them or be so disgusted with the sentiment that they will cause you trouble.'

'I thought you might understand...' Jimmy's voice was child-like, a squeak. His face puffed under that tuft of a moustache.

'I don't understand. These leaflets will not help, and I don't understand why you of all people would care. You will get arrested, or at best fined.' He couldn't help raising his voice.

'Old Fenning...'

'He wouldn't have wanted this,' Joe said. 'This is an incitement to riot. You're going to find yourself in a lot of trouble if you carry on.

'Fenning would have advised caution. He would say educate people about the war. Not to go all out on some kind of crusade. People are mad at Germany, and they'll be mad at you too. What good would you be able to do from a prison cell?'

'Th... that's...' Jimmy had developed a stammer from nowhere, and Joe felt sorry for him. 'That's w-why I w-wanted to talk to you, Joe. I r-r-read an article p-published by your p-p-paper. I w-wanted to ask if you could p-p-put me in touch w-with—' he took a deep breath '—Albert Barnes.'

Joe's heart sunk. This nervous man was trying to make a difference. He had read an article that asked questions about the war, and he wanted to speak to its author. All the time he had no idea that the person he was speaking to *was* that man. Joe felt ashamed at his anger, but he couldn't shift the feeling that Jimmy was wrong for this. It was as if he was searching for a place to exist, something to be part of, rather than having any real conviction. The army itself would have given Jimmy a sense of purpose. He had always gone from one idea to the next, without following it through.

Joe sighed. 'I'm sorry, Jimmy,' he said. 'I shouldn't have got angry with you. Albert Barnes is no longer in Liverpool. He enlisted. He'll be in France by now.'

'But why did he write the article, only to sign up?'

'Because he didn't, Jimmy. I did.' He didn't trust Jimmy, and he knew it was probably a mistake to tell him, but he hated lying. 'Don't you dare tell anyone, or I'll lose my job.'

'You?' Jimmy's eyes widened. 'Perhaps you can help me then.'

'Listen, Jimmy.' Joe gestured roughly at the pamphlets again. 'I could lose my job over this if anyone found out. We could all lose our jobs, or worse if we're not careful.'

'So you won't help me then?'

'I can't, Jimmy. I want to, but I can't. I disagree with the war too. We can both make a difference but turning people against you won't help.' He checked to see if anyone had overheard, while Jimmy examined his shoes. 'We shouldn't even discuss this here.' He put some distance between the two of them. The police could get funny ideas about two men talking closely on the streets. 'We'll talk again. But you must promise me something.'

'What?' Jimmy's voice was a whisper.

'You must not come by the newspaper.'

Jimmy nodded. A spark of light had returned to his eyes.

'If you do, Jimmy, people will ask questions. They will want to know why you're there, and that wouldn't end well for either of us.'

'How shall I c-c-contact you? If not at the newspaper?'

Joe didn't want Jimmy coming by his home either. That was another conversation with the family that he wanted to avoid, even if he could pass Jimmy off as a mad old school pal. He had never mentioned Jimmy to any of them. 'I don't think that you should contact me, Jimmy. I've too much to lose. Some of us aren't as well off.' It was cruel, but he wanted to make a point. 'I will contact you. I have your address.' He pulled the crumpled piece of paper out of his coat pocket and straightened it. 'I will keep this safe… until I need it.'

Jimmy was still as tense as he had been when they left the shop. A couple of gentlemen wearing long coats walked towards them, talking and swiping their walking canes with each step. They visibly perspired in the summer heat, their long moustaches keeping the sweat out of their mouths. They tutted at the pair of them, bemused that their way was blocked.

'Excuse us,' Joe said as he doffed his cap and dragged Jimmy to the side. He waited till they were out of earshot before talking again. 'You should go now,' he said, realising that he still held Jimmy by the collar of his jacket. He let go and brushed the other man's collar. 'We've been here too long, and I'm late for work.'

Jimmy finally put the leaflets away, carefully folding them in his pocket. 'Yes, you are right. Of course. I have things to do.' He took a big breath and reached out to shake Joe's hand. 'I will await your convenience, Joe. We shall look forward to having you up at the house, whenever you are free. No notice needed.'

Joe returned the gesture this time. It was a strong handshake, full of emotion. It was unexpected. Joe watched Jimmy walk away and felt a fool. He didn't think he would see the man again. They were from different worlds. From behind he could just imagine Jimmy having one of those long, tapered moustaches, and swinging a cane. Even if Joe did go to the Sutcliffes' house, he would feel entirely out of place, and his presence would serve no purpose, but to make him more anxious. Joe wanted Jimmy to succeed, to stop the war before any more needless deaths, but he would do things his own way. He would help to change public opinion. People could be made to see the war was wrong. He was sure of that.

Chapter 7

George was in a hurry, and he had left before breakfast. He would tell everyone later, of course, but he couldn't face their questions now. They might harm his already fragile confidence. He wore his best Sunday suit, which was reserved for special occasions. Today was definitely one of those. Tom had tried to convince him it would be all right, but he was sure that he would have trouble convincing the recruiting officer he was old enough. He hoped that they would think the two of them the same age.

Tom's eyes widened as he saw George. He was also in his Sunday best.

'Woo, look at you,' he said. 'Off to charm the girls in Belgium, are we?'

George wasn't in the mood for Tom's jokes, the butterflies in his stomach made him feel like being sick. It took all his effort to even speak.

'We'll be in uniform by the time we get out there, Tom.'

Tom chuckled heartily and patted George on the back with a couple of thumps. 'Don't be so matter-of-fact,' he said.

It was a ten-minute walk to Gwent Street, where they would find the local recruitment office.

'Did you tell your ma?' George asked Tom.

'Nah, she'd only worry about me, and what's the use in worrying her? I'm gonna do it anyway. What other option have I got?' An odd darkness crossed his face in contrast to his usually jovial attitude. 'Besides, you're with me, and she likes you. You'll look after me, won't you, George?' He laughed that familiar laugh, as George scowled at him. 'Did you?'

'No,' George replied. 'I left early to avoid it. I hope they'll think I just went to work.'

'Why not? I mean, ya old fella was in the army. Surely he'll be backing you?'

'I hope so, but I didn't want to find out. It's my decision, not theirs. A part of me was worried what they might say. I am under-age after all. I should wait, but I want to go now. I want to do my bit before I'm no longer needed.'

Tom gave George another pat on the back. 'Me too.'

On Gwent Street they met a group of men, chatting in excitement. Everyone was dressed smartly, in various brown suits, waistcoats and caps.

'What's all this then?' asked Tom, speaking to no one in particular.

A short man turned. 'We're queuing up, lad. Tha's the recruitment office.' His Lancashire accent was stronger and more rural than theirs. He had the look of a farm hand, with dried mud around his face and in the corners of his nails. 'Here's back, if you're looking to join.'

George heard the shout of a more familiar voice.

'Hello, lads!' Patrick smiled as he walked towards them, pushing through the crowd. 'What time do you call this? We've been queuing for a good while now.'

'We?' Tom asked, with a frown.

'Yeah. You didn't think I'd come alone, did you? The other lads are up front, waiting to go in. I saw you come round the corner and thought I'd come say hullo. Henry's keeping my place. He'll start worrying if I don't get back soon.'

'I didn't think you were signing up?' said George.

'What made you think that?' Patrick flashed his smile again. 'We couldn't leave Tom and you on your own, could we?'

'If you're about to be called in you had better go back,' Tom said, his usual good humour missing.

'Not gonna join us, lads?'

'Well now, cutting the queue wouldn't be a very good start to military life now, would it?'

'See you on the other side then, lads,' Patrick said, as he jogged back to the front, disappearing into the crowd. 'Don't want to be the last one in,' he called over his shoulder.

The queue took quite a while. As time went on George and Tom edged closer and closer to the recruitment office, and the single open door that would admit them to their new world. The queue twisted up the front stairs like a snake hunting its prey. Every now and then some unlucky men came back out and disappeared down the road in a hurry. Two of them passed George and Tom, muttering, '... 'king doctor. What's 'is problem anyway? There's nothing wrong with me. Who's 'e calling short anyway? I was looking 'im right in the face. Could have nutted 'im. Bastard.' They disappeared the same way as the others.

It didn't help George feel any less nervous. The sweat caused by the late summer sun was building up on his brow, and he wanted ever so much to scratch at it, but he knew it would only make him sweat more. Everyone else appeared happy to be there, excited, but he could only worry. Why were men being turned away? Would he have to walk in shame past the assembled men, hanging his head and trying not to notice the looks of pity? He lifted his cap and wiped a hand across his brow.

'Are you all right, George?' Tom asked.

'Yeah. I just keep thinking, what if they reject me?'

'Stop worrying. That'll only make them more suspicious.' Tom flashed his teeth.

'That's easier said than done.'

'I know. Just put it out of your mind. Remember what we agreed yesterday? Tell them you're almost nineteen. They'll fret that you're not old enough to go overseas and that'll make them forget you're not old enough at all.'

Tom had it all worked out, but George wasn't so sure. The army didn't send eighteen-year-olds overseas. George would have to train for a month, but so would everyone else. By the time they were ready to be shipped out it would be his birthday. They didn't have to know it was his seventeenth birthday. 'Shush,' George said. 'I don't want anyone to overhear you.'

'It's all right, George. It'll all work out. Just do as I said.'

Tom made George go first so he could back him up if anything went awry. They got in just in time to see another nervously walk through a different door at the back of the room.

'Next!' called a commanding voice.

Tom gave George a nudge in the back and he stepped forwards. The recruiting officer was sitting behind a table, wearing an army dress uniform. His cap lay on the table, facing the potential recruits, showing off its badge. The table was a simple temporary affair, placed there for the purposes of enlistment, draped with a white cloth, and paper piled up on top.

'Name?' the officer asked, without looking up from the forms. His accent was not local, but rather that of an educated, wealthy man. His manner made George even more nervous. George took off his own cheap woollen cap, folding it in his hands.

'George Abbott, sir.' George stared at the back wall of the room and tucked his feet together; his father had taught him the standard army way to be presented when he was a small boy.

The recruiting officer finally regarded him. 'Abbott, a good name, and you address me well.' He wrote a few notes on the form and looked up again. 'Do you know what arm and which regiment you are joining, son?'

'Army, sir. The King's Liverpool.' George beamed with pride at the name of his father's regiment.

'Good man,' the officer said. 'Let me sort out a few other things.' He stood and came around the desk to have a closer inspection. George kept his feet together and pushed out his chest, resisting the urge to salute. Somehow, he thought, that would be pushing it too far.

'How old are you, son?' The officer raised an eyebrow.

'Eighteen, sir. Nineteen next month,' he replied, as he had been practising internally since leaving the house. He was really two years younger, but they would never accept a sixteen-year-old into the army no matter how big and strong he was. He was still sweating and the questioning gaze of the recruiting officer made it worse. Neither of the men said anything for a few awkward moments. George hoped the sweat didn't show on his brow. It took all his mental strength not to reach up and brush it away.

The officer picked up the form and pen from the table and made a couple of fresh notes in black ink. 'Date of birth?' he asked.

George breathed for a second before replying, not realising that he had been holding his breath. He scrunched up his cap further in his hands. He would probably never be able to get the wrinkles out. 'Fourth of September 1895, sir.'

'Are you sure?'

He tried not to panic and ran a hand over his hair to help keep his breathing steady and give him time to calm down. 'Absolutely, sir,' he said.

'Very well, so be it,' the officer said as he ticked a box on the form and laid it back on the table, then grabbed his cap, placing it under one arm. 'Wait here.' He went out of the door at the back of the room. The sweat now dripped off George's brow and ran down into his eyes. He finally gave himself a chance to wipe it clear with his sleeve. He relaxed, but the stance felt forced. Why had the officer left? He turned to Tom for an explanation, but his friend just grinned back. Sometimes it was a welcome gesture, at other times it was infuriating. He was trying to help calm

George's nerves, but it wasn't helping. He wanted Tom to say something reassuring, but he just stayed silent. The other men in the queue didn't appear to notice his distress, and were quietly talking amongst themselves. 'What do I do now?' he said to Tom, losing his calm. The beat of his heart was thundering in his ears.

Tom shushed him with a wave of his hand. 'Don't worry, lad, He'll be back.' He nodded towards the door. 'Probably gone for his tea. Keep on as you were, nice and confident like.'

As soon as Tom finished speaking the officer popped his head back around the doorframe. 'This way, Abbott,' he said, beckoning George. George gave Tom one last long meaningful look, which was returned as a smile, and walked into the other room.

This room was slightly smaller than the first. A metal-framed bed was set to one side with cleanly pressed white sheets and various instruments laid out beside it. The officer handed him over to a male doctor wearing a white coat over his khaki and holding a notepad.

'The doctor here will perform some tests, to clear you for service,' the officer said before he left the room. George wondered if the officer was humouring him. He couldn't have believed that George was eighteen. Now the doctor would scare him off and they would have a good laugh. George would see this through, whatever may come.

'Good morning, son.' The doctor's tone was a lot friendlier than the officer's. 'Undo your shirt.' He was busy at the other side of the room. 'All the way down to the waist please.'

George quickly took off his jacket, laid it on the unused gurney and undid the buttons of his shirt. When it was down, it fell to the sides of his waist, held into his trousers by its tails.

Without warning, the doctor reached around and pressed the cold pad of a stethoscope to his back. 'Breathe in deeply, please,' he said. 'And out. Again, please... and again.'

He was polite, but he stood too close and there was a stench of stale alcohol on his breath as he too breathed in and out. As

George tried to put some more space between them, the doctor tutted and shoved him back. 'Stay still, son. This won't take much longer if you don't fidget.' He finished checking George's heart. 'If you could stand with your back to this, please.' With his hand he indicated a wooden standard against the wall with increments of height painted along one side and a wooden joist that came down to rest on the patient's head. He placed his notepad on the bed and examined George. 'Stand with your feet together, placing your weight on your heels. There we are.'

George did as he was bid and once again stared ahead, avoiding the gaze of the doctor who proceeded to gently bring the joist down to the top of his head.

'Now just take a deep breath and push your chest out, while still keeping your weight on your heels.' He picked up the notepad and pen again, making some notes. 'Hmmm,' he said after a moment. He crossed to the other side of the room, leaving George with the joist laying on his ever more sweat-sodden head, and pulled down a chart from the wall. It rolled down with a clatter and hooked on a spike that jutted from the wall. Various letters of differing sizes were printed on it, becoming smaller further down the page. There was a mirror next to the chart. George's reflection, distressed by the irregular surface, was not of a face he immediately recognised. It was tanned from hours working under the blaring sun. The reflection looked like him, but older, somehow more confident.

'Do you need eyeglasses?' the doctor asked.

George replied with a quick negative.

'Then could you please read the first line of the chart for me.'

George had no trouble reading the chart. The doctor nodded as George read each line, marking it on his notepad. It was the most confident George had felt in minutes. Although, he still felt as if the officer and doctor were waiting for him to crack.

'Very good,' the doctor said, bringing George out of his intro-spection. 'Just one final thing.' He then proceeded to push one of George's arms up so that it was perpendicular to his body and run a tailor's tape around his chest. George almost resisted being manhandled by the overly friendly doctor, but was determined to show that he could follow orders and stand his ground. No matter what, he would stand proud. If they didn't accept him, he would keep trying until they had no choice.

'Good,' the doctor said folding up the tape and putting it in the pocket of his overcoat. He then took George roughly by the jaw and opened his mouth. He moved George's head around so he could look at his teeth, as if George were a horse. Satisfied, he let go of George's jaw and returned to his paperwork. 'Now you just need to go through to the next room and hand the officer this form.' He pushed a piece of paper into George's willing hand and turned his back. 'Good day,' he said, finally.

George hadn't known what to expect; his father hadn't talked about army life much, except for drilling routine into his boys. Recruitment was nothing like what he may have dreamt; there was a lack of organisation that he, based on his home life, presumed all military life would have had.

Gripping the form, he went through to another room at the back of the house. This room was as bare as the first, like a village hall. A larger wooden desk sat at the right-hand side and another officer stood behind it. The man who had preceded George was busily signing a form. 'Good, now stand with the other men and await the oath,' the officer said, and the man joined a line of others waiting on the other side.

George handed the form to the officer who introduced himself as a magistrate. 'Confirm these details are correct and sign the attestation,' he said. 'Once you have taken the oath with these other men you will be given the King's shilling and will officially be a member of His Majesty's army. If you wish to change your mind, now is the time. Once the oath has been taken and the King's shilling received you will be bound to a minimum of three years' service or for the duration of the war.

'Next!' he shouted over George's shoulder.

George signed the attestation, while Tom walked into the room clutching his own paperwork. 'All good, George, as they say.'

The magistrate ordered them to line up. Patrick and their friends were nowhere to be seen. They must have already given their oath of allegiance to the Crown. He and Tom were so close to joining them.

'I told you it would be fine,' Tom whispered.

'Shh. It's not sealed yet. It was nerve-wracking back there. I thought that officer had found me out and decided to play a game with me. The doctor treated me like a prize horse. If I wasn't standing here with you, I'd think they were still having me on.'

'Odd. The doctor barely touched me. Took one look, made me read the letters, and shoved me through that door. Hold up, here we go.'

The magistrate had shut the door to the room.

'Where're Patrick and Harry?' George said in a hush. He hoped that the officer didn't notice his lack of discipline.

'I don't know. They must've gone, ended up in a different section. At least it means we won't have to put up with them out there.' Tom's voice was slightly louder than George's and earned a disapproving glance from the magistrate.

'Right, men. Raise your right hand like this.' He raised his hand to shoulder height with his palm facing outwards. 'Repeat after me, inserting your name one at a time in the correct place.' He picked up a piece of paper from the desk and began reading aloud, 'I...' He nodded to the first man in the line, who after a second's hesitation barked out his name in a hurry, and it stuck in his throat as if he hadn't spoken yet that day, 'Johnny Smith.' Then the magistrate nodded at the second man who was ready. 'Albert Jones,' he said. Every man along the line announced their name.

'George Abbott.'

'Thomas Adams.'

It took a few minutes for the assembled men to speak their names for the oath, and the magistrate carried on where he left off as soon as the last man spoke.

'Swear by Almighty God.'

'Swear by Almighty God,' the men replied in chorus.

The call and repeat carried on until every man had all said the final line, 'so help me God.'

The magistrate went down the line of men handing each the King's shilling and dismissing them. He got to George and said, 'This is the King's shilling. Take it and you are a member of the regiment.' He pushed a shilling into George's palm. 'Take this.' He then gave him a sheet of paper with his name and the name of the regiment on it. 'We will tell you when to report for mobilisation. In the meantime, you will attend training drill starting from Monday. Dismissed.'

George and Tom were now members of the King's Liverpool regiment. The enlistment felt like it had taken hours, stretching George's confidence to his wits' end, but in reality it had only been a few minutes. He had expected a sense of something new but he didn't feel any different. Tom grinned that grin at him and, taking George around the shoulders, said, 'That's that then, we're men now.' He laughed. 'Now to go home and wait, lad. I should probably tell my ma too.'

It was done.

Chapter 8

Joe had just woken up. He wasn't sure what time it was, but the sun glared in through the window. Last night at the newspaper had been a late night, editing more and more news about the war, and trying to get his anti-war message in wherever he could without Ed noticing. When he had got home, he was out as soon as his head hit the thin pillow. He hadn't even heard George leave in the morning. His brother had left before Joe had woken, which was unusual, as Joe was often disturbed by George. They didn't socialise or talk much – they hadn't since they were small children. One day, Joe would own his own home and bedroom.

Getting up early and reading was his usual morning pattern, but today he just got dressed. He tripped over George's boots on his way downstairs. He had done enough reading last night for a few days, and his head was still sore from the concentration.

Halfway down the staircase he heard raised voices coming from the kitchen and stopped.

'How dare you?' his mother shouted, just loud enough to be heard through the walls. Joe didn't hear the reply, mumbled as it was. 'How dare you?' his mother shouted again, loud enough to wake the house if anyone had still been sleeping.

There was silence for a few seconds, and Joe tried to relax. He daren't go further down the stairs, should anyone realise he was there.

'No, George. Not this time. You shouldn't have done this.' The anger in his mother's voice had more control this time. Then he heard an unexpected voice, that of his Uncle Stephen; a voice he hadn't heard in some time. He didn't visit their home often. His uncle was how his parents had met. He and Joe's father had served together and at a regimental dinner George's mother and father had been introduced. He had heard the story many times. Joe's heart raced as he thought of all the possibilities of what they were arguing about. He kept coming back to the same conclusion, and the thought made him sick. He hesitated, one foot on the bottom step and a hand on the banister. He dearly wanted to go upstairs and avoid the conversation, but his curiosity and his concern pulled at him. One day he would have to start confronting things.

'You're too young.'

The beating of his heart grew louder in his ears, and he still didn't hear George's response. Joe put his other foot on the stair, praying they wouldn't creak.

'Hello, Joe. What are you doing?' enquired a young voice, followed by the click of a closing door. She made him start. He had been so engrossed he hadn't heard his little sister creep up on him.

'Shush, Lizzie. Not so loud!' He waved his hands, but she only smiled in return and came closer. 'I'm just thinking. Why don't you run upstairs? And don't tell anyone you saw me!'

He was getting in the habit of lying recently, and he hated himself for it. If he told her what was happening then she would no doubt tell her parents at some point. She was too young to understand. By now, he could no longer make out much of the conversation in the kitchen. His mother was no longer shouting, but he could feel the tension as she moved around the kitchen. Still, his sister stood and smiled at him, craning her neck to see what he was doing, mimicking him.

'What are you thinking about? Is it to do with stairs?'

'It's not important, Lizzie. Now come along with you, up the stairs. Mum will be calling you down soon, and if you're not ready she will be upset.' Again he bent the truth to suit his needs, but Lizzie didn't need to know what was up – not knowing was better at her age. She would find out soon enough. She stopped smiling and stomped up the stairs, her curls bouncing with each step.

'Shush,' he said again, in a whisper up the stairs. He would rather not know himself for now. Once again, he was running away from things. If George had signed up for the army, it would rip the family apart. His sixteen-year-old brother was far too young to be going to war. The thought made Joe sick, and he rested his head against the banister, closing his eyes. No one was old enough to go to war. It didn't matter who they were. No one should have to kill another or be killed for their country. George was brave, not stupid, but Joe couldn't help but feel he had made the wrong decision. He felt guilty. Guilty that he had never reached out to his brother, and now it could be too late.

He went back upstairs, leaving the conversation behind. He wanted to be alone with his thoughts. As he walked past one door he could hear Lizzie singing softly to herself and the sound brought a warmth to his heart. She had a sweet voice, the voice of innocence. He re-entered the room that he and his brother shared, the two iron framed beds on each long wall, like a school dormitory. Kicking his shoes off, he fell backwards onto his bed with a creak of springs. A wave of tiredness hit him. He was tired with the world, with the constant conflict. He turned to the bookshelf that ran alongside his bed. His eyes fell on Tolstoy, amongst others. His collection was meagre, gathered from a second-hand bookshop in the city centre with what money he could spare, but the books were his. One day he would have his own library, full of books on any number of subjects. These took pride of place on the shelf, their battered covers only serving to highlight the quality of names presented on them. A couple had been given to him by his teacher, Fenning. They were both philosophy texts, to encourage him to higher thinking. Not today, he thought. Today wasn't the time to reach such works. He wasn't in the mood for opening his mind to possibilities and ideology. He was already weary of thought.

His spotted a copy of the *Labour Leader*. The same issue that he had used to help edit Barnes's article. He didn't usually leave the paper out, the writings of Brockway and the rest would not be welcome in this house. His father wouldn't appreciate them. Even his books were a risk. The newspaper was incriminating evidence when Barnes returned, and if he accused Joe of tampering with his article. Joe didn't want to think about the possibility now.

It was proving to be a bad kind of day, and it hadn't even really started yet. He was exhausted from work at the *Daily Post*, where others were leaving to join the war effort and everyone else had to gather round and work harder. Now he suspected that there was going to be some consequence of his editing of Albert Barnes's piece. Worst of all, was the news that his brother had signed up to go and fight – the very thing he was trying to convince other boys not to do. There was nothing he could do to stop that now. He could help others, but what good would that do if he couldn't even help his family? The least he could do was support his brother, give him confidence. He couldn't stop him going to fight – he would never listen to Joe, he never had – but, short of signing up himself, he could do everything possible to make sure George would come home.

He pulled out his notepad from the drawer next to the bed and began writing.

Dear George.

A door slammed downstairs, the kitchen door. With nothing short of instinct he jumped up from his bed and rushed to the top of the stairs. He was only just in time to see his mother's back. 'Come on, Lizzie,' she said and walked out the front door. His sister had gone back to listening at the bottom of the stairs, and now followed their mother from the house.

He rushed down the stairs to see what was happening, and peered out the front door. His mother and little sister were nowhere to be seen. Wherever they had gone, they had gone in a hurry. He decided not to follow. His mother had done this a couple of times before, but she would return later as if nothing had happened. He guessed that she just needed to calm down, and that Lizzie's presence would help her.

He turned back into the house and clicked the front door shut behind him. A moment later the kitchen door opened and Uncle Stephen walked out into the hallway. Stephen was a tall man, half a head taller than Joe, and always wore his uniform. Joe was fond of his uncle, but he wouldn't exactly call them close. He was a warm and friendly man, but the two of them had nothing in common. Joe had never been boisterous, or particularly adventurous, and his uncle was a classic example of what a military officer should be.

'Ahh, Joseph. Good to see you,' he said, in his clipped, proper accent. The sound of his voice reminded Joe of everyone at his first school, the sound of the upper classes. Uncle Stephen stood to attention, even in the Abbotts' small hallway. He always smelt of cigars and faintly of wool from his uniform. The smell that Joe always associated with the army. 'I don't suppose that you saw my dear sister on your way in, did you?'

'Only on her way out.' Joe almost stammered, feeling like a school child again, afraid of that new world. 'She didn't say where she was going.'

'Ah, yes. Well, I will find her. I can put all that expensive army training to the test and track her.' He winked, and moved to the doorway, easily gliding past Joe who was rooted to the spot. 'I'd best go and calm my dear sister down. She does tend to get upset so easily. I'm sure she will be all right, but I'd best go.'

He patted Joe, who had still said nothing, on the shoulder and said, 'Be seeing you.' With that he left, and Joe was alone again. Without the presence of his mother, sister, and uncle the house felt incredibly silent. He could hear his heartbeat thumping in his ears. Of course, the only other person left in the house was his brother, sitting in the kitchen for whatever reason. Joe decided that it really was time he knew whether his brother had done what he suspected. He wouldn't be able to put it off forever, and it was about time he had some courage himself. He finally had an opportunity to catch his brother on his own and have a decent conversation with him. To tell him how he felt. He would still write the letter he had started but for now that could wait.

With a deep breath he placed his hand on the door handle and walked into the kitchen.

Chapter 9

The conversation hadn't gone exactly as he had planned, but he hadn't expected his ma to storm out quite like that. It was good of Uncle Stephen to stay behind and give him some encouragement, but then he had left too. He hoped he would see him again before shipping out. He loved his uncle dearly. George put his face in his hands, elbows on the desk. He felt like crying, but a soldier didn't cry. A man didn't cry. He would remain strong for his mother's sake, but it was so difficult.

He heard the door click open again and looked up. He had expected his mother or Uncle Stephen, but it was his brother. He hadn't realised Joe was home. How much had he heard? Joe didn't say anything, but stood in the doorway looking sad. He always looked that way, some might say he had a sad face. George couldn't remember if he had ever seen his brother smile. At least, he never had with George in the room. Now, though, he looked as if he were about to break out in tears. It was a sentiment George shared, but how could he tell his brother that?

Joe opened his mouth, about to say something, but then was interrupted by the sound of their father's cane on the hallway tiles. 'What are you two doing moping around here?' he said, joining them in the kitchen. He was dressed in his work clothes, a woollen suit and bow tie. George knew that he so much wanted to be wearing his uniform, but his father would only ever get to wear it on special occasions. He wouldn't be joining George in France. 'Why aren't you down the dock getting work, and why aren't you at that paper of yours?' He limped to the table and lowered himself into a chair. 'Where's that mother of yours? She's normally here when I get home from work.'

George wasn't sure what to say. His father wasn't unused to his wife's bouts of sadness, but it wouldn't make him particularly happy to hear about another. Besides, George had something important to tell him, and he didn't want to put him in a worse mood. He was sure that his dad would be proud of him, and he would have to tell him sooner, or later. 'D—'

'She's just gone for a walk with Lizzie,' Joe interrupted, giving George a pointed look. He wasn't sure why Joe had interrupted. He always had to get in the way of things, ever since they were little he had been trying to get in George's way. But this wasn't the time; he was a soldier now and that gave him a certain sense of power.

'I've got something I need to tell you, Dad.' He took a gulp of air, remembering how his mother had reacted. He found it difficult to say what he wanted to. It should have been easier to tell his father, but he felt a strange sense of reluctance. Perhaps it was because of Joe's presence as well. He plunged ahead. 'I went to the recruitment office, up on Gwent Street. I went with Tom.'

His father didn't look up. He was flicking through the newspaper on the kitchen table, grumbling to himself with the turn of each page. George wasn't sure that he was even listening.

'He and I...' George paused again, trying to read his father's expression. 'He and I... well, we signed up. We signed up to the regiment, Dad. We wanted to go out to Europe, to France. We wanted to stop the Hun.' The words came out in a torrent, as if a floodgate had been opened. George thought what he had been trying to say was obvious, but the silence in the room had made him spurt it out. Joe sighed and sat down in another chair with a thump. He didn't say anything, but shook his head, then put his head in his hands. Their father carried on reading the newspaper. Nothing could change George's mind now.

'Dad?' George said, unsettled by his father's silence. He knew that when his father was silent, something was brewing. George thought that his father was going to cry out as his mother had done and felt guilty again. She had made him second guess his decision, but all along he had thought that his father would support him. Had he made a mistake? No, he couldn't have. He thought of returning to work on the dock and it made him shudder. He couldn't go through that again. His father's stories of the army sounded much better. It had made his father a man and given him so much pride. After all, that's how his parents had met. George wanted the same sense of belonging, to make something of himself. The dock had no prospect of advancement. Most of the men that worked there were twice his age and would never be anything more.

'Right,' his father said at last, in a low voice that always signalled he had made his mind up about something. He pushed the now closed newspaper to one side and looked at both of them, before settling on George. 'That's that then.'

Joe leaned forward on his elbows. 'If I had known—'

'You keep out of this.' Their dad didn't even look at Joe, but stared at George. The gaze was piercing, as if his father was trying to see into his very soul and guess his inner thoughts. His father had often told them off, but George hadn't seen his father look like this before. It made him shudder. 'You've made your decision then. I had expected you to wait a few years, but what's done is done.'

He couldn't have sat around and waited. What if the war was over before he got his chance? He couldn't live with the guilt of knowing he was here doing nothing and others were out there defending their country. He had always felt older than his years, which was perhaps something to do with being a younger brother and everyone he knew being older than him. Most of them treated him like an adult, except his brother.

'We could tell the recruiting office that they've made a mistake?'

'Don't you dare, Joseph. If he's taken the King's shilling then he's one of us now. He's a soldier, and there's nothing that can be done to change that. Besides, it's what you want, isn't it, George?'

George nodded. He thought about all the answers he could possibly give, all the different reasons. What would be the best thing to say? What did his dad want to hear?

'Of course, I always wanted to,' he said, and hesitated again. Why was it so difficult to talk to his dad? He felt like a child again. 'Now felt like the right time. When we got there, to the recruiting office, there was a whole line of other men signing up, including some I knew from school. I couldn't let them go without me. How would I feel sat here waiting? It wouldn't be right not to do my bit too.'

'Good, honourable reasons.' His father stood up and limped towards him. The click of the cane was deafening in the kitchen. He then put a hand on George's shoulder. It took all his willpower not to flinch. 'If it helps, I think you've done the right thing, son.'

'But he's too young.' Joe stood up and George thought that he was going to storm out again. Why was he getting involved? What was it to him if George enlisted? At least it would take the attention off him. 'How could they let him enlist? It's clear he's not old enough.'

'He's a grown man now, bigger than me or you, Joe,' their father said. 'He's an intelligent chap, that's what they've seen. They'll make him an officer in no time. And every man should do his bit. You know, I wish I was coming with you.'

'You're both mad.' Joe was pacing now, every bit as angry as he had been the other morning. He looked as if steam was about to burst out of his head, which had gone red.

'Don't talk to me like that, Joseph. I'm your father. Don't forget that you should be doing your bit too. If you weren't so selfish... What gives you the right to judge, Joseph? You, who won't lift his finger to help another.' Joe was frowning, furious, but he didn't storm out as he had last time. Still, their father didn't look at Joe, as if he didn't want to see him. Only George glanced between the two of them, oddly noticing how alike they appeared at this moment.

'No, Dad. People die in wars. Look at your leg! Do you want the same for George?'

'How dare you?' Their father raised his voice only enough to make Joe be quiet. It was a commanding voice he had practised for years. 'I was just one of the unlucky ones. Our George won't be. He's got a smart head on his shoulders. He's smarter than I ever was.'

'I have to go to work.' Joe moved to the kitchen door, but waited on the threshold. He gave George another sad look, slightly too long so that it became awkward, then with a sigh he left. George heard the front door close a few seconds later.

'When do you go?' his father asked, sitting again.

George didn't know the answer to that question. They would start training soon, he had been told, but technically he wasn't eligible to go out to Belgium yet.

'I don't know. The regulars have been mobilised, but I joined the territorials, the reservists. They haven't told us when we will be shipped out yet. I don't even have any kit.'

He handed over the form that he had been given after enlisting, along with the shilling that he had taken as part of the ritual of signing up. 'This is what they gave me. We'll have drill training and then when they need us we'll get our mobilisation orders. I'm not even old enough to go yet. They might decide to keep me back.'

'They won't. What did you tell them about your age?'

'I told them that I was eighteen, almost nineteen.'

'You gave them your actual day of birth, son?'

'Not the full date, no. I just changed the year by two and so to them I'm eighteen.'

'Very clever, half a lie rather than a full one.' His father's face became a brief smirk. 'Speaking of clever, or not, have you seen this rubbish they printed in the paper? All about the cost of war and encouraging lads to think about their decision before signing up. It's cowardice, rank cowardice if you ask me. Typical of the kind of nonsense that your brother gets up to at that paper. This Albert Barnes should be ashamed of himself. How could they let him write such a thing, let alone publish it?'

'It wasn't him, Dad. I overheard him say it wasn't. He's even signed up for the regiment. I saw him at the recruitment office.'

'Odd.' His father was back flicking through the newspaper.

George had a thought and rummaged in his pocket. He pushed the shilling across the table. His confidence was rising by the second, secure in the knowledge that his father was on his side. He could do anything with his father on side. 'It's not much, but there will be more where that's come from and I'll make sure it is sent here while I'm out in France, for you and Ma.'

'We don't care about the money, George. We get along all right. This isn't about money.' He shoved the paper aside again and looked at George. This time his eyes were full of warmth. Gone was the stare that made George feel tiny. 'This is about doing something right; doing something bigger than yourself. The money is yours if you want it, we've no right to claim it. You've done the right thing.'

Chapter 10

Frank leaned over and dropped a newspaper in front of him, as Joe was crossing out some lines on a piece of paper. It was that morning's copy of *The Times*.

'What's this, Frank?'

'You know what it is. It's *The Times*. What else could it be? Have you gone blind all of a sudden?' He cackled and Joe struggled not to give him a stern look that a school teacher might give an unruly pupil.

'You know what I mean, Frank. Why have you thrown it on my desk? I was busy working.'

'When are you not busy working, Joe? I don't think I've ever seen you stop. You're always in here before me, and still here after I've gone home for the night.'

That much was true, but often he was just reading, or trying his hand at writing. Every morning he would come back in and go over what he had written, then throw it away in disgust. The only way he would get better was to keep trying.

'It's a report on the British Army, Joe,' Frank said, bringing Joe out of his reverie by prodding the paper with his index finger. 'It's not looking good.'

He flicked through the first couple of pages. The grainy pictures of smiling soldiers and waving men at the recruiting offices were a stark contrast to the headlines and articles. Perhaps that was the whole point, Joe thought. The British Army had been heavily defeated at the small Belgian town of Mons, it said. They had taken over a thousand casualties and were on the retreat.

He set the newspaper down and took a sip of water from a glass on his desk. His throat had gone dry.

'Are you all right, lad? You look pale as a ghost.'

Concern and confusion was etched across Frank's face, and he could clearly sense Joe's discomfort. He took the newspaper back when Joe didn't reply.

'I just keep thinking of our George going out there.'

'I didn't think he'd shipped out yet?'

'No, he's not gone yet, but soon they say. With heavy losses like this, they will be sending them all over as soon as possible. See how many they've lost, and the war has only just started.'

'Well, wait, look here,' Frank said, prodding the newspaper and waving it in his face. 'It also says that the Germans suffered many more casualties, expected to be in the thousands.'

'Oh, and that means it's going to be all right, does it?' Joe felt ashamed at his outburst, but Frank was unconcerned.

'It's war, lad. There're bound to be casualties. But if we're inflicting more than them, then we will win. It's a simple matter of numbers. We've suffered defeats before and still won the war, and still looked good in uniform.' He smiled emphatically, but it had no effect on Joe.

'It also says here,' Joe said, grabbing the newspaper, 'that we're on the retreat.' He paused for a second, waiting for it to settle in. He had never thought of the British Army as 'we' before. The idea of nationalism was disconcerting. Perhaps the national pride was working its way into his psyche too. 'The British Army are almost as far back as Paris. That's something like... like a hundred and thirty miles from where they started. They're no longer helping Belgium, not anymore. The Germans far, far outnumber the British Army, even if they keep inflicting casualties, it's unsustainable.'

'Then they're gonna need our help, lad. You know it makes sense.'

Joe sighed.

'Come on, lad. I keep saying you'd look good in a uniform. There may be lots of them Germans, but they'll take one look at you and run away with their tails between their legs.'

He made a sound like a dog whimpering and ran around the desk. Some of the other men looked up, wondering what was going on, and Joe laughed.

'Carry on like that, and you'll get yourself shot,' he said as Frank sat down again, lazily draping his arm over the back of the chair. 'They'll shoot you just to shut you up.'

'Steady on, lad,' Frank said, all mock innocence. 'I have the very vocal cords of a tenor, me.' He burst into song, singing a couple of lines then stopping. 'Even the Germans will be rushing over to hear me. Hah.'

'I'd like to see that.'

He was being honest. It would be quite a sight, and perhaps show some semblance of peace. 'But, no, not for me. It's bad enough that our George is heading out there. I'll not be joining the army, no matter what they say.'

'Oh well, I didn't think I'd ever convince you, lad. You knows what you wants. Far more than I ever did.' He patted Joe on the arm, but this time it was as a sign of friendship, not in a playful manner. 'This is something I want. I reckon this is my last day, lad.'

'I was wondering how long you would last,' Joe said, not knowing what else to say.

'Then I'm off in the morning to take the shilling and sign an oath.'

He put his hand on Joe's arm again and turned his body gently so that he was looking into Frank's eyes. He was serious for a change.

'Will you do something for me, Joe?' he said.

'What?'

'While I'm gone… will you… will you look after all the girls for me?'

Frank burst out laughing again and pushed back on his chair, whilst wiping a tear from his eye with the back of his hand. 'You're a softie you, lad. Had you going for a minute.'

Joe tried not to get angry at Frank's ridiculing, he knew he was only joking. 'Oh, are you still here, Frank?'

'Hah! At least you have a sense of humour though. I'd be worried I might upset you otherwise.'

Joe didn't think that Frank would ever be worried about upsetting anyone, he was too free and easy. He acted like he didn't have a care in the world. Everything was a joke to him.

'You know you'll have to do all the boring work while I'm gone, don't you, Joe? Can't say that I'm sorry. I'd rather get away before it all piles up on my desk.'

'Yes, well your spelling is atrocious anyway.'

'Hah!'

Joe would miss Frank's laughter around the office, that was for sure, and he wasn't looking forward to the amount of work he would have to do. But that didn't matter. He felt like he was losing a friend, and who knew if Frank would come back? The office would be a lot quieter, and a lot duller without him. He would only have Mr Harlow's soft wheezing to keep him company on the long nights of overseeing casualty lists and reports from the front.

'Listen, Frank. It's my turn to be soppy now.'

'Oh, 'ere we go. I thought you were already being soppy. Is that not a normal state of affairs for you? You actually mean you're going to get worse? I'm not sure if I can take it. It's completely against my martial pride.'

'Shut up, Frank, and listen for once.'

Frank leant an arm on his desk and lay the side of his head

at an angle on his upturned palm, to show that he was listening, then smiled at Joe. 'Go on,' he said.

Joe tutted, wound up by Frank's levity.

'Just when you're out there. If you see my brother, you look after him. All right?'

'Ah, I was only joking. Of course I will. I'll take George under my arm and show him how a man in uniform behaves. Show him how to charm the ladies, since I seem to have failed with you. Hah!'

'If you ever find him somewhere he shouldn't be—' Joe ignored Frank '—you do me a favour and make sure you get him out of there. Get him to safety. All right? Do that for me?'

'All right, all right. You're so serious sometimes, I worry about you. You're going to end up very lonely sometime if you keep it up, you know? I won't always be there to cheer you up.'

Joe grumbled. He didn't need Frank to tell him that. Besides, it wasn't the point, he was asking about his brother.

'I can't promise anything, Joe,' Frank said. 'Who knows what's going to happen out there? I may never see him. He could be in a completely different regiment to me. But, I promise you I'll try to find him, and if I ever see him in danger then I will do what I can.'

'Good, that's all I ask.'

'You know, if you're so worried about him, you could enlist yourself and keep an eye on him? It would be the best way, you could do more than I could.'

'I don't think he would appreciate his older brother mothering him in the army. Besides, you know I'm not going to enlist, no matter how much you try and convince me.'

'Oh, go on. It'll be fun. You won't have a foil for your seriousness if you stay here on your own.'

'No, Frank.'

'Not even if I forced you?' He balled up Joe's sleeve in his fist, but it was gentle, and threatened to pull him off his chair. All the time he was smiling, the gesture lighting up his blue eyes. Joe tried not to resist, knowing that it would upset his friend.

'No, not even if I'm forced, Frank. You can't drag me round with you everywhere to keep you out of trouble.'

'Hah.'

A wheezing sound passed down the rows of desks, accompanied by the clop of heavy footsteps. Joe looked up just in time to see a puff of smoke and then Mr Harlow's round face peered out of the cloud.

'What on earth are you two up to now?' he said, shaking his head, glancing at where Frank still held Joe's sleeve. Frank let go quickly.

'Just chatting, Mr Harlow,' Joe said, trying to distract him. 'Sorry about the noise, you know how excitable Frank can get.' With that, he gave Frank a very pointed stare, who merely shrugged in reply.

'Hmmm,' Mr Harlow said, before taking another puff of his cigar. 'I knew I should have split you two up on day one. It's a wonder you get any work done at all, Gallagher.'

Frank mumbled something under his breath, but Joe didn't catch the words.

'I should bring my office out here, so I can keep an eye on you.' There was a glint in Mr Harlow's eye which showed that he was joking, but Frank just stared at the pile of work on his desk with a frown. 'At least I wouldn't miss out on the fun,' Mr Harlow continued, ignoring Frank. 'Do you have that work I asked you for?'

He could do that so well, Joe thought. Go from reprimanding someone to being their friend, then asking them for the work that they should have been doing. It was a well-practised management technique he had picked up somewhere. Joe couldn't think where he might have got such a thing; as far as he knew, Mr Harlow had been at the newspaper his entire life.

Frank shuffled through the papers on his desk, making what

was a mess into an altogether different type of mess. He found what he wanted between a pile of books and pulled it out, smiling to himself. The books clattered onto the floor. Without attempting to pick them up, he handed the paper to Mr Harlow.

'Here you go,' he said. 'I finished it this morning. Had I known you wanted it that desperately I'd have brought it you.' He beamed with pride at having not been found wanting by Mr Harlow and smirked at Joe who shook his head and scoffed.

'You should get that framed, Mr Harlow,' Frank said.

'Oh, why?' He frowned at the two younger men.

'It'll be worth something one day. The last article that Frank Gallagher, national hero, ever edited. It'll be priceless.'

'You're priceless, Frank,' Joe said, laughing.

'Another one leaving me.' Mr Harlow tutted and shook his head. 'Don't think that there will be a job for you here when you get back. I can't go keeping spaces for everyone that fancies their hand at soldiering. We've got a paper to run, you know. The owner said, "We have to support our brave men and boys," but what does he know about running a paper, eh?'

He stared for a few seconds, as if willing them to answer his question.

'Just you make sure that you get the rest of those articles ready to go for tomorrow's paper, all right? I'll have to go off and sort out finding someone to do your work, not that it's much. Still, someone's got to do it, even if it's a trained monkey.'

He walked off, leaving a cloud of acrid smoke in his wake. The wheezing grew quieter as his footsteps diminished into the distance.

'Well, I never. That was a bit rude,' Frank said shaking his head and trying to tidy his desk. 'He's never spoken to me like that before.'

'He doesn't seem very happy with you,' Joe said. 'Not his usual self anyway. What have you done this time, Frank?'

Frank's mouth opened in shock.

'Why do you always assume I've done something? I'm offended.'

'Because I know you, Frank. You're always up to something. What is it this time?'

'I'm not sure if you've suddenly developed a sense of humour, or if you're just being rude, lad.'

Joe fought the urge to smile. He enjoyed getting one up on Frank, but this time he wanted to know what was up with Mr Harlow. Usually, he fell over backwards to keep his staff happy. Joe had never seen or heard him have a go at anyone before. Nor had he heard him bad mouth the owner before. Something was definitely amiss.

'Perhaps it's just because I'm leaving,' Frank said. 'He's going to miss me around here, with stony faces like yours.'

Joe lost the fight and burst out laughing again.

'Frank, your world must be perfect, what with the sun revolving around you and everything.' He grinned at Frank, who bowed theatrically.

'I'm gone tomorrow, lad. And the sun will probably follow me too. This place is dark enough already.'

'It's not that bad, you're exaggerating. You're going to miss out on all the fun, Frank.'

'Aye, perhaps. I will miss the place. And I did really want to see that new Chaplin film. Guess I'll have to catch it on leave, if the army can spare me when it is showing. I suppose I'll let you come with me.'

'Thanks.' Joe rolled his eyes, but Frank didn't notice. 'Do you think, perhaps, that Harlow's upset because everyone is leaving. Not just you?'

'No, it's not that. Them other lot were useless when they was 'ere. I'm pretty sure he was glad to see the back of them.'

'How can you be so sure it was something else?'

'Well.' Frank leaned over to Joe's desk and then looked to see if anyone could be listening to their conversation. 'I happened to walk past Harlow's office yesterday.'

Joe felt like the two of them were conspiring. It was warm in the heat of the office. He pulled his collar open a little bit. He felt silly for it – there was nothing wrong with walking past Mr Harlow's office. He couldn't imagine what Frank was going to say, but it couldn't be that bad.

'And? Why is that important, Frank?'

'There was quite a heated argument going on inside. I couldn't make out the voices at first.'

'At first? You mean you stayed to listen?'

'Well, of course. Wouldn't you?'

'No, absolutely not.' Joe didn't even hesitate. 'What business is it of mine, what Mr Harlow may or may not be arguing about? Or yours for that matter.'

Despite the outburst, it brought to mind the time he had stood at the bottom of the stairs. On that occasion he had lingered too long, trying to listen to what his father and brother were discussing. That was none of his business either but it hadn't stopped him then. He tried to convince himself that because it was family it was different, but he knew he was lying to himself.

'Oh, will you take that rod out of your backside for one minute and just listen?'

'Wha—'

'Don't forget you're the one that asked me what I knew.'

'Yes, but—'

Frank wasn't listening and just kept talking. 'As I said before, Harlow was having a big old argument. Or, should I say, someone was shouting at him. It was more the other chap, thinking about it, but that's not the point.'

'Get to the point, Frank. Before he comes back and has another moan at you for not working.'

'I'm trying to, but you keep having to have your say. Just like always.' Frank sighed loudly, emphasising his frustration, before leaning in closer again and speaking in a quiet voice that only

Joe could hear. 'I think it had something to do with that idiot Barnes.'

Joe tried to hide his shock but knocked his glass of water off the desk as he jumped back from Frank's words.

'Damn,' he said, under his breath.

The water had spilled over some of his papers and he jumped out of his seat in horror. He picked up the papers in one hand and held them over the floor hoping the water would run off.

'Oops,' Frank said, not caring about the papers, or what might be written on them. Joe thought he could probably salvage them, but it would take some extra work. He picked up the now empty glass with his other hand, thankful that it hadn't shattered, and placed it upright on the desk. He then carefully pinned the damp sheets to the partition on his desk, clearing a space underneath them where the residual water might pool. He would find a cloth later, it was too late now. He set back down again, and self-consciously tidied the rest of his papers, attributing the accident to his lack of organisation, though his desk was a far cry from the state of Frank's.

'So, where was I?' Frank said, picking up the conversation and determined to ignore Joe's accident. 'Ah yes, why Harlow's in a bit of an old grump. Do you remember that article that Barnes penned before he left? You edited it, I think.'

Joe could only nod in reply. His mouth had gone dry and he longed for the glass of water that he had spilt on the table. He swallowed and his tongue felt like paper.

'You know the one, something about whether the war was just and all that rubbish. Just your kind of thing.'

'Go on,' Joe said, quietly, trying to pretend that he was eager for the rest of the story. 'What about it?'

'I'm coming to that. The other voice I could hear must have been the owner's, and whew, he did not sound happy at all.'

'How did you know it was the owner?'

'Well, he said that we have to "support our brave men and

boys"'. Frank put on an air of superiority and sat taller in his chair as he said it, as if talking down at Joe, who resisted the urge to laugh. 'So, it must have been him. I can put two and two together and get four, you know.'

'All right, Frank. I didn't mean any disrespect.'

'He was pretty angry himself. Probably could have heard him from here if you was listening. I think he said that Harlow would have to fire the man that wrote it.'

'You think?' Joe felt his throat constrict again.

'Yeah, well, his door's pretty thick, isn't it? Bit like him!' He laughed again and then looked around to see if he had been heard. 'Definitely heard something like that. Harlow tried to say he wouldn't do it, but the owner raised his voice again. I heard something break.'

Joe felt incredibly guilty and, worst of all, sorry for Mr Harlow. He was a decent man and didn't deserve the trouble that Joe had got him in. Still, he couldn't come clean, otherwise Mr Harlow would have no choice but to let him go. Then what would he do? With the war he might find some other work that other men had left, but without a good reference and a sacking hanging over him that was unlikely. There was also the fact that even though he had done wrong, he was still in the best place to have an influence on the war and to help people realise what it was costing them.

'Then he flung the door open and rushed out,' Frank carried on. 'He nearly bumped into me on his way out, but because he was in such a state he didn't really notice. It gave me a chance to pretend I was just walkin' past. Harlow just glanced my way as he closed the door. Didn't think much of it at the time, but after seeing him before… he must have known I overheard.'

Frank was being uncharacteristically sheepish.

'You don't think he thinks that I… do you?'

'What? I asked you earlier what you've done now.'

'I ain't done nothing, I told you that.'

Joe was joking, trying to take his mind off his fear, but Frank was no longer in the mood. It seemed that even Frank's moods could change as quickly as his.

'I meant, do you think he thinks I wrote it? Me?'

'No!' Joe denied it more forcefully than he had intended, and Frank jumped back in his seat. 'I mean, why would he? Albert Barnes wrote that article. You know he did. Why would he think otherwise?'

He was feeling desperate now and his words came out quickly. Frank didn't seem to notice.

'Yeah, but well, he's disappeared, hasn't he? He's gone off to the war. Why write an article saying we shouldn't fight and then go fight? Something's not right about that.'

'Could be he just wanted to question it and then decided that it was what he needed to do after all?'

He felt horrible about lying to Frank, but also that he now seemed to be condoning the acts of war. He was ashamed of himself. Ever since he had messed around with Albert's article he had felt ashamed. It had been a moment of madness, well intentioned, but madness all the same.

'Harlow can't think it was me, he knows I'm off too. Better sooner rather than later, I think. Before I get pushed.'

Joe was glad that Frank was too self-involved to suspect that it might have been him that had written the article. He didn't have anything else to say, so just patted Frank on the back as he stared into the middle distance.

After a few seconds the wheezing sound of Mr Harlow was back as he walked past.

'I thought I told you two to get back to work. Don't make me tell you again,' he said as he disappeared off out of the main office.

Chapter 11

George turned the corner of Lime Street, with Tom at his side. They had been training solidly now for a month, assembling in Prince's Park and drilling until they were exhausted, Corporal Campbell forever driving them further and further. Now, they had made the long walk through town from their homes, eager to be off. People lined the streets waving union flags and cheering as the soldiers marched by. He just made out the faces of his family before they were swept away by the crowd. The only one he hadn't seen was Joe.

The band led them with bugles and drums. It was inspiring. George couldn't help but smile at the feeling. Most of them were in khaki, but George, Tom and the others hadn't received theirs yet. Instead they wore the 'Kitchener blue' uniform that the War Office had thrown together for them.

The front of the station was an impressive sight, with a number of columns and two large arches chiselled out from white free-stone. On top of the columns a large iron-beam roof spanned the distance, curving over the open space. It resembled the sail of a ship, or a wave crashing over the building.

'Look at that, George,' Tom said. 'What a building.'

'I know.' George had sketched it many times when he got a chance.

'I've walked past so many times, but I've never had any reason to step foot inside.'

The boys had never travelled further than just up the coast. They saw a group of men in khaki heading into the station through the large pedestrian entrance arch, and with a tap on George's shoulder Tom indicated they should follow them. The arch blocked out the waning summer sun, and the noise of the station hit George. Not only were there groups of men in khaki, but messengers and train company workers rushed around. There was a strong smell of steam and oil, which almost caused George to cough. A whistle sounded, startling George as a train pulled off from a nearby platform, chuffing as it built up speed. Tom laughed at George's surprise. George saw a group of men he recognised, standing near an advertising hoarding. He waved Tom over with him as he walked in their direction.

'Morning, lads,' said Patrick, as usual working his way out of the pack to talk to George and Tom. 'Any idea where we're headed?'

'Hullo, Paddy,' Tom said with his characteristic grin. Patrick scowled in return, about to criticise Tom.

'Morning, Patrick,' George intervened. 'They haven't told us where we're going, but if you're here too they must have mobilised the whole regiment. They just told us to turn up, and here we are. I'm guessing you know no more?'

'Naw. We just been standing here like a bunch o' layabouts, waiting for an officer to come along. And there's been nae sign of anyone yet. The train lot have been looking at us out of the corner of their eyes. I don't like it.' The men walking past them, assembling goods and paperwork for the assorted trains in the station, were giving them sideways glances. They kept a wide berth.

'They're probably just a bit wary of us, Paddy. Ignore it,' Tom said.

'Or jealous,' Patrick countered, serious.

Tom chuckled but said no more as an officer appeared and

ordered Patrick's section to form up and follow him. Patrick waved them goodbye and joined his mates. A moment later their Corporal saw them, his permanent scowl etched on his face.

'What are you doing standing around here? Get on with you,' he said to George and Tom, his Scottish accent a stark contrast to the other voices. He ushered them in the right direction with an exasperated flap of his hands. George didn't hesitate and moved off in the identified direction, Tom at his heels. They marched down a platform, alongside a waiting train. The locomotive up ahead was painted in the black livery of the LNW railway and it puffed out steam, like a gently slumbering dragon. George couldn't see its name from where he was. The carriages were painted in a dark brown, with light cream around the doors, windows and roof. There were also a number of assorted box cars at the rear of the train.

'Here we go,' Corporal Campbell said, again ushering the two boys, but this time making them board a carriage. The rest of the section were already waiting for them in a cabin usually designated for the first-class passengers of the train but that today was full of soldiers, some of whom George recognised, some of whom he didn't. They were making enough noise to wake the dead and had there been any regular passengers on the train then they would surely have complained.

'Here ya are, lad,' said one of the other soldiers, a man from his section he knew as Bert, a thickset man, with fluffy black hair and a generous nature. Bert grabbed George's bags from him, throwing them to another soldier to stow at the other side of the compartment. They took Tom's bags too, relieving them both of their burdens.

Campbell tutted from the doorway and shouted, 'Sort yourselves out, soldiers. You're in the King's, not the bloody women's circle. Let's have some order in here.' As soon as the men calmed down and uttered a sullen 'yes, Corporal,' the Corporal sighed and slammed their door shut. The men grew excited again, chatting and joking amongst themselves, but with a careful eye on the door in case he came back.

George and Tom took seats across from each other in the cabin, joining in the general conversation from time to time. George could understand why the men were excited. For a lot of them, like George and Tom, this was their first time away from home, even the older men. They were going on an adventure. This train would take them as far as London, then who knew where?

'Off we go, George.' There was that flash of a grin, always bringing George back to home, reassuring him in an unusual situation.

George couldn't help himself and he grinned back.

'Not before time. We've been waiting long enough for this.'

The train pulled off from the station with a lurch and a whoosh of steam. One of the men fell on his backside. The other men laughed, before picking him up and plopping the red-faced soldier on a seat. George stared out of the window. He could see other trains being loaded up and holidaymakers boarding trains. The view disappeared as the train pulled into the man-made tunnel that ran under Edge Hill. George marvelled at the cut stone, the veins that ran through it. George pulled a bundle of papers from his pack along with a pencil and started sketching the line of the rock. The carriage filled with acrid smoke, and some of the men coughed as it grew more claustrophobic.

The navvies had blown out huge chunks of the red stone, and the seams could still be seen as the train moved past. It was impressive. George was amazed that humans had built it. Daylight cut through the surface at various point. As the train left the tunnel and turned, George had a view of the River Mersey running out into the Irish Sea. The tide was out and George could see the mudbanks at the side of the river, before the sun shining through the wrought iron of the Runcorn bridge obscured his view like the spinning of a zoetrope.

'What's the furthest you've been from home?' Tom asked, breaking George's observation of the outside world. He was drawn to it, finding the landscape rushing by and the beat of the train strangely mesmerising. Tom sat on the edge of his seat, waiting for George's answer like an excited child.

'We used to go down to Blackpool sometimes in the summer, but not very often.' George remembered his family's time on the beach fondly. He remembered playing with Catherine and Lizzie in the sand and sloshing around in the mud. 'We had some good times down there. The beach was beautiful, and the sea.'

'Aye. My old man used to take us to Wales sometimes, if we could get away when he was on leave. Which, as you can guess, wasn't very often. It would take us bloody ages to get there too.' He looked forlorn, gazing out of the window. 'It was a long time ago and all, when he was still alive.' Tom spoke in a whisper. George only just heard him over the noise.

It didn't take them long to get out of Liverpool, the train puffing along at a regular pace and clicking over the joins in the rails which gave it a regular rhythm.

'This is it, George,' Tom said, joining George in looking out of the window. 'No more milling about in the park, playing at soldiers. Now we get to the real work. We're off to war!'

Chapter 12

A group of soldiers passed Joe as he strode under the entrance arch at Lime Street Station. He moved aside so as not to get trampled, then jumped out of the way of a cart loaded with cases that was being pulled along by a porter. The station was a bustle of activity, and the smell of smoke clung to every surface. Goods were being stacked in wooden crates by sweating porters. The porters scowled at the soldiers that filled the station concourse when they thought no one was looking.

Instinct had steered his path this morning. Rather than heading into the paper, he had come here instead. He knew that the Liverpool regiment were shipping off, his brother with them. He was determined to keep an eye on his brother for as long as he could. He hadn't wanted to join in the parade, he disagreed with its very existence, but this was his way of saying goodbye, at least for the time being.

From his jacket pocket he pulled out a notepad, made from the cheapest paper he could find. The first chunk of pages had been torn out and thrown away when he had read back through the rubbish that he had written. It had left a rough edge of paper on the inside and some of the back pages were falling out. Editing the war article for the paper had given him incentive to write again, some inspiration that he had been lacking for a long time. That was why his subconscious mind had determined that he would come to the station rather than heading into work as usual. He wanted to write an accurate report of the men and boys heading off to war, knowing that not all of them would come back. There hadn't been a reaction to his previous piece yet, but he knew he was doing the right thing. Even if the piece wasn't originally his.

'Move it, lad.' An officer shouted at him as he led a line of four soldiers past the place where Joe was standing. Joe didn't hesitate to move out of the way again. It seemed the army always took precedence when there was a war taking place. The officer didn't give him a second glance.

Joe followed the officer, wanting to get a better idea of the man, the professional soldier. He was the only one of the group wearing a uniform. The other men were dressed in a mix of khaki and Kitchener blue uniform, with their own clothing to replace what they hadn't been issued. Joe opened a page on his notepad and in pencil wrote the words, 'Army cannot afford uniforms?'

He carried on scribbling more notes about how the men formed up, what they were travelling with and how many there were, until he recognised a face in a crowd of men coming his way. His younger brother was the image of their father, only younger and with a larger build. He hadn't seen Joe yet, as he was blending amongst the crowd, so he moved out of the way, careful not to draw any attention. He wasn't avoiding his brother, but he didn't think that his brother would want to talk to him right now. He was in his own, new world. The world of soldiers and camaraderie, and Joe wasn't part of that.

As the column passed him, he stepped backwards behind a concession selling newspapers, keeping his eyes on George the whole time. As he did so he felt a resistance against his heel and a grunt of pain. He turned to apologise.

'You?' the other man replied, oblivious to the apology.

'Hello, Albert. I'm sorry, I didn't see you there.'

'What are you doing here, Abbott?' Anger was stretched across his face and his bushy brown eyebrows were raised. The apology wasn't enough. 'You're not a soldier. Why are you here?'

Joe was confused. 'This is a station, it's not just for soldiers.'

'You know what I mean, Abbott. Stop trying to be clever.' Barnes pushed Joe in the stomach with a long index finger. The pain was sharp, but fleeting. He squashed his notepad away in the inside pocket of his jacket, not wanting to draw any attention to it.

He had to think of some way to diffuse the situation. Albert had never been this hostile before, but to say they had been friends would be a lie. In fact they had very little to do with each other, even at work. They worked in different departments and only knew each other in passing.

'I'm sorry for stepping on your foot, Albert. Truly, I am. I didn't see you behind me.'

'Do you think that's why I'm angry? Could be you're not a clever bastard after all, you're just stupid.'

He had the feeling anything he had to say would only make matters worse and make Barnes angrier, but he had to try anyway. He had a sinking feeling. He knew why Barnes was being aggressive towards him, and he knew that by asking he would only make things worse. But how could he know that it had been Joe? He was making a huge presumption. Joe knew though, that it was better to get it out in the open, than to try and pretend his innocence. Sometimes in life, you just had to take the plunge.

'I'm not stupid, Albert. I just don't understand why you're so angry with me. I barely know you.'

Barnes scoffed and poked another finger in Joe's sternum.

'I know what you did. Don't think I don't.'

There it was then. It was as he had expected. Barnes had every right to be angry with him, how could he not be?

'What do you mean?'

He couldn't help himself. Pleading ignorance had almost become a natural response; a defence mechanism. Barnes could probably see his guilt though, and Joe regretted asking straight away.

Barnes, frustrated, turned on the spot and blew out a violent puff of air from his lungs, as if he had been holding his breath. A small group of women, clothed in their Sunday-best tunic-dresses, walked past. One of them, a pretty woman with ebony hair that fell just below her shoulders looked at the two men in the corner before averting her gaze. Joe was trapped.

Barnes bunched his fists and relaxed, before turning back to Joe. There was less agitation in his body language, but his eyes still showed the flares of anger.

'You edit at the paper, right?' he said, in a near-whisper.

Joe nodded but said nothing. Barnes was almost on top of him and saying anything might risk making him angry again.

'An article of mine was published a few weeks ago, only it wasn't my article. That idiot Gallagher wouldn't have thought to change anything. I've seen him let basic mistakes pass through. Besides, I saw him on his way to sign up the other day, looking all proud of himself. He wouldn't say something against the war, even if someone told him to.'

More groups of people walked past, but they paid the two men no notice, not now that Barnes had lowered his voice.

'No, he wouldn't.'

'Which leaves you; you're the only other person who could have rewritten my article. The only other person with the means and the inclination to do something like that. No one else would bother. They would just get on with their job. Like you should have done.'

There was no way out now for Joe. He had to make his peace.

'I'm sorry, Albert. I wasn't thinking straight.'

'You're right, you weren't. Have you any idea how much trouble you have caused me? Not to mention the amount of trouble you're going to be in yourself. The least you could have done was change my name on the article. No, the least you could have done was stay well away. You could have cost me my job.'

He didn't think it was a good idea to mention that Albert had already cost himself his job by signing up for the army. Still, Barnes continued berating him.

'Why'd you have to change my article anyway? What gives you the right?'

'You were wrong.' It was a whisper.

'What?' Barnes, if it was even possible, moved closer to Joe.

'The stuff you put in the article. You had no proof. You made it all up from what you heard from other people. You were wrong.'

'How dare you? You can't stop yourself, can you?' Albert was furious, a vein bulged on his forehead. 'I'm the reporter, not you. You're just there to tidy things up. Judging by what you wrote in my place, you couldn't write a good article to save your life. You're nothing.'

Barnes pushed him with the palm of his hand with a force that surprised Joe. He fell backwards over a breadboard and landed flat on his back with a bump that forced the air from his lungs. The pain this time was lasting. He was too winded to talk. He just stared up at Barnes, exasperated, trying to force apology onto his face.

'You can't even stand up for yourself.' His eyes searched the station for something. 'Listen, I've gotta go,' he said. 'But when I get back, either on leave, or when the war's done, I'm gonna come and find you. Then, I'm gonna make you pay for what you did. Understand? You'll pay all right.'

'Hey, what's going on here?' A train station employee rushed over to where Joe sat on his backside, trying to calm his breathing.

'Nothing. Joe here tripped. Didn't you, Joe?'

Joe hesitated but knew it wasn't worth disagreeing. That would only make things worse for himself. He nodded, stifling a sob as his head throbbed. The porter frowned at Barnes, then helped

Joe to his feet. He thanked the man for the help with a smile, but the frown didn't leave his face. Joe felt dizzy and his vision was a little bit cloudy, but he felt better for being on his feet.

'Must be going now, Joe. Don't forget what I said.'

Without further ceremony Albert Barnes turned and strode off in the direction that the other soldiers were heading in.

'Are you all right, lad?' The porter was a kind old gentleman, and he dusted Joe down.

He nodded. It didn't hurt so much now. The porter, having to get back to work, left him to his pain. But first he handed Joe the notepad that had fallen out of his pocket when he fell.

He looked at the note he had made before. He would always fear the day that Barnes came back from war. Not knowing when that might be only made it worse. The butterfly of panic would always flare in his stomach every time he saw a man in khaki. Perhaps Barnes would forget by the time he returned. Anger had a way of dimming over time. Despite that, the worry wouldn't fade, and he wouldn't forget Barnes's anger.

Despite his wishes to help people, he had never intended to make someone so openly angry, and the thought truly saddened him. Some men were quick to anger. That was why war happened in the first place, but Joe had always believed that things could be resolved. This time, however, he didn't think Barnes would be welcome to any talking.

He stood still for a while, watching the soldiers depart and the station become emptier and emptier. The sounds and the smell of smoke waned as the trains departed. All the while Joe made notes in his notepad. Most of them weren't even about what he was seeing, but thoughts that went through his head about the injustice of the war.

He had initially thought that his confrontation with Barnes would discourage him from writing anything else. Instead it had spurred him on. He had never had so many ideas at once. He had come here to write an article about the boys going off to

105

war, but that wouldn't do it justice now. The focus of his thoughts had changed from how men interacted with each other, to whether man could ever have peace. He didn't think that Mr Harlow at the paper would like where he was going, but if the rest of the employees were going to go off and fight, then they would need him. Sooner or later he would have enough readership to get people to think about what they were doing. Sooner or later, someone would listen to him.

With a final sigh, he put his notepad back in his jacket pocket and left the now quiet station.

Chapter 13

The train pulled up at a station and hissed with steam. It hadn't been like their first journey away from Liverpool when the excitement had threatened to overwhelm them and the officers had to be on their guard. This time it was a more sombre affair. Their time guarding the London South Eastern railway in Redhill had dimmed their spirits. A few men were excited to be moved on, George saw the smiles and the glow in their eyes, but others were growing unsure of what they were supposed to be doing. He had used the time to explore and draw more landscapes, but like the others he was now growing restless. They were supposed to be out fighting the Germans in France.

Tom had slept for the entire journey. 'You've got to get as much sleep as you can, George,' he had said. 'You never know how long and how far they'll march you for when you're awake.'

He was right. When the lads were on duty they were required to do any number of backbreaking tasks, and Tom had developed a knack of sneaking a quick sleep in between any work. When he was awake, he was as wide-eyed and as keen as any of the others. Perhaps more so, especially after being given his stripe.

He woke now and looked for George with glazed eyes.

'Morning, Tom.'

'Mornin'. Where are we?'

'No idea. Yet another English town.'

'That's unusually pessimistic for you, George. It could be a nice town.'

'Sorry, Tom. I haven't had much sleep.' He couldn't sleep on the clattering, jolting train, no matter how hard he tried. He had taken to staying up and reading whatever he could find until exhaustion took over. Then he would wake a few hours later in a cold sweat.

'So, let's have a look at where we are then.'

Tom unfolded his long legs from under him and pushed himself up from the seat, disturbing another sleeping man.

'Easy, there!'

'Sorry, John,' he replied without looking.

'We're in Canterbury, lads. Look. It says right there.'

Martin was a small man, only just tall enough to sign up. Most of the other men made fun of him for his height, but he never seemed to mind. He pointed a finger in the direction of a station sign and the others followed his short, stubby finger.

'Canterbury, eh?' Tom mused. He thought it was under his breath, but George heard quite clearly.

'They're gonna make us pray before sending us out to fight Fritz.' Martin laughed, but stopped when none of the others joined in.

They all huddled round the windows, pushing into each other in order to get a view. Some of their initial excitement had returned and George was just as interested as they were.

'Is that the cathedral?' one man said. George couldn't see who it was, with his face pressed up against the cool glass. He could just about make out a stone structure in the distance. It wasn't like any building he had seen before, the large stones were rounded and cracked in places. One half of the building seemed to have crumbled and fallen away to dust. It had no windows, which he thought was odd for a church, but then he had never seen a cathedral before.

'It's not much,' another man joined in.

'That's not the cathedral, you idiots.' Tom was always the voice of reason. 'That's some ancient ruin. Pull your heads together.'

'Come on you lot, get off the bloody train.' Corporal Campbell walked past their compartment and banged on the door to hurry them up. 'Everybody off now!'

'I guess we're here to stay, George,' Tom said to him as they moved away from the glass.

George just nodded in return. He knew nothing of Canterbury, but he knew it wasn't in France. There were grumbles from the other men as they realised their situation. Some of the grumbles were from those men being woken up after having fallen asleep on the journey. George ignored them all, he just wanted to get to wherever they were going and settle in. The idea of yet another new home was unsettling. They were being moved around like cattle and all they wanted to do was get to the front. He followed Tom off the train.

The station was empty except for the loitering men in khaki.

The Corporal pushed his way through the crowd, swearing under his breath. When he got to the front of the group he turned around and shouted at them.

'Come on, you bloody fools. Form up, form up!'

The men moved into formation, four abreast, without talking. It was now almost second nature to them, and apart from a bit of shuffling they formed a column easily. It was enough to stop Campbell bawling at them.

They were led through the town, past the houses to their billets, where the numbers dropped off one by one, and in some places in pairs. The sun had started to set as they passed one small cottage by the railway line, with a thatched roof. The adjutant called out George's name with a clipped bark and carried on walking.

'Have fun, George,' Tom said as the rest of the column carried on.

George lifted the brass knocker and dropped it against the door twice. The door was painted a bright, royal red, with obvious care to detail. There wasn't a brush line to be seen in the thick, enamel paint. After a few awkward moments of looking off into the distance to see if he could see the rest of his section, the door opened.

'How do you do?' he said to the woman who opened to door, who was in her late middle years with greying hair. Her face was gaunt but turning to fat with age and she stooped over as she held the door handle.

'I'm Private George Abbott, I believe I am to be billeted with you.'

He held out his hand to shake hers, unsure of what else to do in the situation.

'At least you have a proper name,' she said, without taking his hand, or even shifting from her position. She appraised him with hawk-like eyes.

'I beg your pardon?' he said, trying to be polite and to emulate the conversation of a gentleman.

'I said, "at least you have a proper name", like His Majesty. Are you deaf?'

He shook his head, taken aback.

'Well, don't just stand there gawking. Get yourself inside, you're letting the heat out.'

With that, she withdrew inside the house, leaving him with only one option: to follow. He took off his cap and crossed the threshold.

Inside, the house was well decorated. Again, the white paint-work was exceptional and there were a couple of dark wood side tables with white porcelain vases on top. He put down his pack by the door after closing it to make sure that he didn't break anything, and rested his rifle next to it. The landlady had disappeared into the kitchen and so he took off his jacket and put it on a peg by the door.

The landlady came back out of the kitchen again and scowled at him.

'I guess you will have eaten.' She looked at his pack, still by the door and then back at him, a frown etched on her face. She didn't wait for him to reply. 'A proper soldier never leaves his equipment unattended. You'd best take that upstairs rather than leaving it there cluttering my hallway.'

'I'm sorry, I'll take it up right away, Mrs...?'

'My name isn't important. You shan't be here long enough to need it, if all is right.'

She walked up the stairs. George stood for a minute, exasperated. He hoped she was right. Lifting his pack back onto his shoulders and grabbing his rifle, he followed the ageing woman up the stairs. He couldn't work out why she was so hostile towards a man she had never met before. Perhaps she resented his presence in her house, but she must have volunteered as a billet for a solder? What was she expecting?

'You'll have my son's room, here at the end of the corridor,' she said as she led him along the upstairs hallway. It was narrow and his pack rubbed against the walls. No doubt she would complain about that too as soon as she noticed and he was careful not to leave any marks.

'Here.' She opened to door to a small bedroom with a single bed in front of a window. Clean white cotton sheets were wrapped around the mattress as if she were expecting a guest and not this soldier that she had scorned since arriving.

'You can have his room. He's in the East Surreys. Out in France, where you should be. If you were a proper soldier and not a terrier, that is.'

Ah, he thought – there it was. She moved out of the way of the door so he could enter. She wasn't resentful of having a soldier in her house, she was resentful because he wasn't a regular. It wasn't his fault which regiment he had been assigned to. Besides, they would all be going out to France sooner or later, or so he had been told. He hadn't been a soldier before the war and he wasn't as experienced as the regulars, but that didn't make him any less of a soldier than the others. The thought made him angry and as she turned to leave he dumped his pack on the wooden flooring.

'Don't make yourself too much at home,' she said and shut the door behind her.

He stared at the closed door, fuming. He was thankful that it now separated her from him, or who knew what he might have said. Things were going to be difficult enough as they were without rising to her attempts to unsettle him. She was being unnecessarily cruel, but that was her problem; he was determined not to make it his.

He sat down on the bed and tested the springs. At least the bed was comfortable. He pulled back the sheet to see what the bed was like and it was covered in only a thin woollen sheet. The springs poked through the mattress. In a way, it very much reminded him of his bed at home, but unlike his room at home there was only one bed. He didn't have the decorations he so much adored. He looked out of the wood-framed window and the view was of the railway. As he looked an express train screamed past, rattling the window and dislodging small particles of plaster dust that fell on him. The smell of smoke that he had grown familiar with over the past twenty-four hours rushed into the gaps of the window. The candle on the bedside fluttered. He couldn't ever imagine this being a home away from home.

He watched in the direction the train had gone for some time, wondering where it was going, and if another one would come past. When it remained silent he turned back to the room and thought about what to do with himself.

He heard a noise from downstairs and sat up on the bed, listening. The stairs creaked and the door handle started moving before opening. The intruder didn't even knock.

'Evening, George.' Tom's grin was a welcome sight. 'Thought

I would pop in and see how you were getting on.' He rolled his eyes, then nodded towards the door, indicating the landlady was listening.

'I'm fine, Tom. Just settling in.' He was determined not to give the landlady anything to pull him up on, or give him any hassle about. He hoped his time here would go without any further incident and he would soon be on his way to France.

Tom popped his head out of the door, then came back into the room with a satisfied look on his face.

'I think she's gone. We can talk properly now.'

'Good,' he said, with perhaps a touch too much venom. Tom didn't seem to notice.

'Listen, George, I haven't got long. She only let me in because she thinks I'm your CO.' They both laughed, but tried to keep it quiet enough not to alert the landlady.

'She'll be up in a moment to send me on my way.'

'How can she send you away? You're my guest.'

'It is her house, George. Be fair, she doesn't want any more soldiers than is absolutely necessary treading her carpets into the floorboards.'

At that second George thought he could hear the sound of floorboards creaking from outside the room and groaned openly. Tom took it to mean that he was sad that Tom had to go. He was, but that wasn't why he had groaned. He had groaned at the thought of being left alone with the old landlady.

'I'm staying in a house round the corner. There's a family there and they're not nearly as well off as this. It kinda reminds me of home, they don't have much between them. They're doing what they can to help me out, but I feel bad just being there, and I refused any offer of food. I had to get out of there for a bit to take the attention off me.'

'I'm glad you did. I've not been here long, but it seems like I haven't seen anyone in ages. Shame you have to go almost as soon as you got here though.'

'Well, I thought I would come and wish you a Happy Birthday, George. There won't be time tomorrow, while we're on duty. And, well… you only turn nineteen once.' He winked and George couldn't help but laugh. Tom always knew how to make him feel better, and an inside joke always helped.

'It's a shame I have to be here on my birthday,' he said.

'Not really, George. At least you've got a roof over your head. Think about that. There's lots of people that are worse off than us right now.'

'That's always true, I guess.'

'See, there you are, starting to smile now. That uniform will see you right. We'll be with the company tomorrow and you can forget about this place for a few hours while we do manoeuvres or whatever it is they have planned for us.'

'Why are we here, Tom?'

'I don't know, George, I really don't.' He shrugged and lifted a hand to George's shoulder, but thought better of it. 'I'll see you tomorrow morning. Sleep well.'

And with that he was gone. The door clicked shut behind him and his footsteps receded down the stairs. George hadn't been expecting that answer. Tom always had an answer for everything and could always put a positive spin on things.

He wanted to talk to someone, but there was no one there. The landlady had made it abundantly clear that she would be no source of conversation. Not for a lowly 'terrier' like him. Besides, he didn't know the woman. He was taking up her spare room. A spare room that he felt uncomfortable and alone in.

He carefully unwrapped his puttees, putting them to one side, then undid his boots and put the puttees inside. He lay down on the bed without getting underneath the sheet. There was no real need to, it was warm enough, but at home he had always felt reassured by his sheet before he drifted off to sleep. That wouldn't be the case here. This wasn't his bed.

He turned his head to the left and looked across to where Joe's

114

bed would be. He would never have thought it would have been possible to miss his brother, but he had never been alone like this before. Even if Joe had just been there reading to himself, at least George would have felt some kind of reassurance. He sat up on his arms and blew out the candle. Moonlight filtered in through the window.

He closed his eyes to try and force himself to sleep, but he knew that it would be a long time coming.

Chapter 14

Joe entered the building as usual, said hello to Stephen at the front desk, who was still there for now, then carried on up the stairs. Joe was in a good mood. Mr Harlow had allowed him to write a few small articles. It wasn't much, but there was hope, and things were moving forward.

At his desk he had acquired a pile of notepads and stacks of paper. On top of them all was that latest article that he had suggested to Mr Harlow. The editor hadn't been happy about it when Joe had told him what he wanted to write – he had shouted at Joe in the confines of his office, saying that the paper wanted nothing to do with such unpatriotic behaviour, that their owners would be unhappy – and now Mr Harlow had read the draft of it.

The draft was covered in Mr Harlow's handwritten notes, composed of his thick, blocky handwriting. There were plenty of crossings out, including a big cross straight through the first two paragraphs. Joe guessed he should feel lucky it hadn't just ended up in the bin.

He shuffled them into a drawer before anyone could notice that they had been left there for him.

He heard a noise behind him and turned.

'Ow!' a female voice said.

'Sorry, sorry,' he said to the woman.

'You have a habit of bumping into people.'

He looked up and recognised the face. It was the lady that had glanced at him in the station, as he had argued with Albert Barnes. She had a slightly round face, with pronounced cheeks, but she was incredibly pretty, and her eyes, the colour of which he couldn't make out in the gloom, had the light of intelligence that was immediately endearing. They looked blue to him, blue like the winter – but not a cold blue, they had an unnatural warmth. Her long black hair framed her face and helped it fit in with the rest of her figure. She smiled through her perfect lips, exposing white teeth.

Joe had to look away to make sure he didn't stare.

'Apparently, I do. I am sorry, truly.'

He saw Mr Harlow coming and his heartbeat increased further. What did he want?

'Ah, Miss Wallace,' he said. 'I see you've met our stalwart editor, Mr Abbott, already. Good of you to make your introductions, Joe.' He winked at Joe in a way that Joe thought was obvious, but Mr Harlow thought was conspiratorial. Joe struggled not to blush.

'How would you like to show Miss Wallace around, Joe?'

'Anne,' she said, still smiling.

He surreptitiously pushed the pieces of paper into a corner of his desk with a hand behind his back, hoping that none of them would notice. The smoke from Mr Harlow's cigar floated into his mouth and he coughed violently. His cheeks reddened.

'My pleasure,' he said. 'Which part of the building would you like to see first?'

'Good man, Joe. Miss Walla... Anne.' Mr Harlow smiled his sickly grin at Anne and flicked a dollop of ash over Joe's desk without realising. 'Anne is going to replace Albert. Not that anyone could replace him, of course. We all miss him round here, but the front called, eh, Joe?' He locked eyes with Joe who merely stared back. 'Dear Anne will be on a trial basis, of course. If we like her work, who knows? She might even be better than old Albert. After fighting the Hun he may have to fight for his job when he gets back.' He laughed a huge wracking laugh that made his substantial chins wobble in delight. When the others didn't join in he stopped.

'Ah, well, um, that's enough. Why don't you show her around, Joe? There's a good chap.'

With that he left, the cloud of cigar smoke following him.

Joe was unsure; he was no tour guide. What would anyone want to see?

'Where would you like to start?' he asked.

'Oh, I don't know,' Anne said, thinking. He could see the intelligence in her eyes. 'I've always wanted to see a real printing press. Let's see where all these papers get made.'

They walked through the rows of empty desks, the few occupants looking up at Joe and giving him a wry smile that he ignored. He wouldn't be drawn into their game. He knew what they were thinking and he didn't want to embarrass Anne. What would she think of him, if she caught him smiling back at them? To her credit, she said 'hello' to the others as they passed. It was met with mumbled replies. After they passed everyone, she spoke to him.

'Do you mind me asking?' Her sweet voice was a welcome relief to the thudded beating of his heart. 'What happened at the station?'

Joe tried to stifle his surprise.

'I'm sorry,' she said. 'I guess that it's my natural inquisitiveness. My father always said I ask too many questions.' With that she flashed a smile that made Joe immediately warm to her. It was self-deprecating in an obvious way.

'Oh, that?' he replied. 'It was just a little disagreement. It looked worse than it was.'

They carried on down the back staircase of the building towards the presses.

'Anne wasn't convinced. 'It didn't look like a little disagreement,' she said. 'That other man had you cornered. If that guard hadn't come along, I think he may have hurt you.'

'I had no idea you saw so much. You were walking away when I saw you.'

'What could we do? As young women, you're told that if you ever see a fight to stay well clear.'

'It wasn't really a fight—'

'I had to come back though, and make sure that you weren't hurt. By that time the guard was there. I'm not sure what I would have done anyway, so I went to join my friends.'

'I wish you hadn't seen that. It really was nothing.'

It was a lie, and she knew it. He attempted a smile at her, and she was kind enough to smile back.

'You still haven't explained what it was about, or who that other man was,' she said. For some reason he felt like he could be honest with her and it wouldn't cause any problems. She was unlike anyone he had met before. Their conversation felt natural.

'That was actually Albert Barnes.'

She looked suitably shocked, and he stifled a laugh.

'Exactly. The man that you are supposed to be replacing as he goes off to war. A more suitable fighter, I do not know of. He has the right temperament.'

He laughed again, and this time she joined him. It was a lovely laugh, not too high and warm, the kind of laugh that made you want to laugh more and hope it would never end.

'As you can imagine,' he continued, 'there are quite a few disagreements around here, particularly between the editors and writers. He didn't like an article I edited. That's all, but he rather took it to heart and threatened me.'

'What can have been so bad for him to threaten you?'

He stopped on the landing halfway down the flight of stairs.

The brickwork of the building made Joe feel claustrophobic, but at least here they were unwatched and no one would hear what he had to say. He looked into her eyes.

'You're going to think badly of me,' he said.

He didn't know why he said it. She had a way of opening him up that no one else had. With everyone else he was guarded, but to her he spoke his mind. Her eyes had a depth to them that threatened to engulf him, but he was happy to fall.

'I won't,' she said. 'I won't, I promise.'

'He had written an article about the war.'

'I see.'

'No, there was more to it than that.'

'Go on.'

'Well, most of it was wrong. He had no idea what he was talking about. It was all hearsay, none of it was checked.' He breathed after letting it all out in a torrent. 'He was saying all sorts of things, like the Germans are eating babies, and all kinds of other ridiculous things. I have no idea what he thought he was doing, but it was completely... wrong.'

'Never let the truth get in the way of a good story, Joe... or of selling a newspaper.'

He laughed, but it was half-hearted, a nervous reflex.

'I don't know why I'm telling you all this,' he said. 'I hardly know you, but I want to tell you everything.'

'Don't worry, I promise I won't write a story about you.' She smiled. 'I'm just curious. You seem nice, and that argument the other day didn't seem nice at all. You're... different. Most men treat me like a little girl. You are talking to me like... well, like an equal.'

For a moment she was distracted, staring off into nothing. Though he had only just met her, the thought of Anne being upset hurt him too. But her sadness disappeared almost as quickly as it had come.

'Surely that's not enough for an argument? Did you confront him about it? I wouldn't think it, speaking to you.'

'Oh no, that wasn't it. Not at all. No, it was somewhat worse than that. Well, you see, my job here is sub-editor. I'm responsible for reading through all the articles. I will have to read yours once you write them.

'Mr Harlow doesn't have time for reading all the articles, so he entrusts us to do that. We check spelling and grammar, that sort of thing, the usual stuff. But sometimes we have to make substantial edits.

'This time I couldn't let it pass through my desk, it was despicable.'

'So you edited it?'

'I edited it. Mr Harlow was busy that day, with all the news that was coming in about the war. He didn't mind what we were up to, as long as something was making the presses. I started off crossing out the bits that I thought were wrong, but by the time I had done that, there wasn't much in the way of article left. So, I had to add to it.'

'You shouldn't have done that.' She was right, but she was also shaking her head in sympathy 'What did you add?'

He didn't really want to answer. The writings of the *Labour Leader* and other papers weren't popular. However, it was about time something changed. He had already confided in her.

'I borrowed some lines from a few socialists. Fenner Brockway and the like. Not much, just some choice words. They were ones that had evidence too, unlike Albert's.'

She looked stern, her lips pursed and brow furrowed. He feared that he had blown it, and she would never to speak to him. He turned and continued down the stairs to the first floor where the machinery was kept.

'It was possibly a bad idea putting the article under someone else's name,' she said after a while. The rumble of the presses masked their voices from anyone else. 'You'll get in trouble at some point. Barnes must have taken affront to you changing his work. I guess it's easy to understand that he'd be upset.'

'What could I do?' he said, wincing at the petulant tone. 'I'll take whatever punishment Mr Harlow has to offer me, but I'm not looking fondly forward to Albert returning. I'm sorry for dragging you into it.'

'There was no need for anyone to behave like that. I'm sure you apologised. I'm not sure that I would have done any differently, in your shoes. In fact, I rather admire you for it.'

He nodded, not quite sure what to say, fighting the smile at the corner of his lips. She continued, and he was already fond of her warm, energetic voice.

'I think that I would have put my name on it though. Oh, well. I'm sure that when he gets back from the war all will be forgotten. Although I'm after his job…'

She smiled, to show that she wasn't serious, and he laughed a deep booming laugh he didn't know he was capable of. It felt good.

'So I'm not the only despicable creature around here?' he said, through laughs.

'I guess not.'

The presses were working away, as they walked down. The mechanical clattering was louder here, almost overbearing, and they had to talk a little louder to be heard. The air was thick with the smell of oils, paper and ink.

'So why is it that you want a job?'

She hesitated for a moment, unsure.

'Well, it's simple, I suppose. I wanted to make sure I got in before someone else did. With all the men off to war, women are going to be needed.'

It was such an intelligent answer. He was growing fonder of her by the minute.

'I would much rather be in a position where I can make a difference,' she continued. 'If I can, that is. Wouldn't this be exactly the kind of place where one could keep their ear to the ground on current affairs?'

He nodded; before joining the *Daily Post*, he'd had a very similar thought.

Walking past the presses, they glanced at the machinery as they went. Anne showed vague interest and said hello to some of the workers as they showed interest in her. Joe didn't attempt to describe anything, not knowing himself what each section did. There were printers and there were typesetters, big mechanical blocks that needed careful management and constant attention. That was all he knew.

It felt good to get the issue with Barnes off his chest, out in the open. He had considered telling Mr Harlow, but he either wouldn't care or wouldn't understand, and Joe would continue to feel dreadful. Though he still had the wait for Barnes' return hanging over him, he felt better for having told Anne. In a way it was good that she had seen what had happened at the station. Something occurred to him.

'Wait a moment,' he said. 'You didn't say why you were at the station. You weren't travelling anywhere. You wouldn't need a job if you were. You said earlier that you came back to see if I was all right.' His heart sank. 'Were you seeing your man off to war?'

She blushed. Joe thought the worst. Anne had been a welcome breath of fresh air, but now it seemed he had got the wrong idea. He cursed himself again and returned to feeling sorry for himself.

'Sorry, Miss Wallace. It was rude of me to ask. It's none of my business. Forget I said a word.' He walked off to show her the rest of the building, moving out of the oily stench of the press floor. She caught up with him.

'Don't be silly, Joe. I don't mind you asking questions. And it's "Anne".'

She flashed a smile at him, but this time he didn't feel as warm as before. He did feel silly. He always felt silly, just for being the kind of person he was. For always thinking about other people and worrying about them. He was a silly man, he had always felt that way.

She grabbed his arm and eased him to a stop.

'If you must know,' she said, 'it wasn't anything half as romantic as that.'

He stopped to listen.

'Now you're going to think me silly.'

She hadn't stop smiling even though he had just been rude to her. The situation was growing more awkward. This time she blushed again and waited for him to answer.

'I would never judge you, Anne.'

'You're kind to say so, Joe, but I think you might. The other girls... women I was with, well... it was their idea. They wanted to go down to the station and, well, you know what friends are like, when they suggest something you just tag along.'

He nodded, agreeing without reference. The only friends he had were few and far between, and they never did anything on a whim. He wasn't a natural follower.

'Well, my friend Sarah, the blonde – the others think of her as our sort of leader – she is always suggesting we do this and do that. Well, she had heard that the soldiers were leaving Liverpool on that day, going off to fight.'

She hesitated.

'Oh, you're just going to think I'm some silly girl.'

'I won't.' He urged her to continue.

'As we weren't doing anything important, on account of having no jobs or family, she decided that we should go down to Lime Street and just "see them". What exactly she was planning to do when we got there I have no idea. Perhaps she thought she could get herself a man. Though as they're going off to war that probably wasn't the brightest of ideas. She said she "likes a man in uniform". I guess I was just dragged along by the excitement of it all.'

Joe laughed another deep laugh, and a man working at the presses jumped up in shock, which only made him laugh the harder.

'See, I knew you'd think I was silly,' she said and blushed again, the red bringing warmth to her pale cheeks.

'I don't.' He had to force the words out between laughs. 'I don't. I mean I think the fact that you went to have a look at the soldiers is amusing, but I don't think you're silly. Actually, I think it's quite endearing. I was beginning to think you were all serious like me and only cared about questions.' He laughed again and smiled to show he was joking. 'I was worried that you may be waiting on your man to return from the war. Now I know that there is much more to you than that.'

Her cheeks were still red and there was now a hint of repressed anger to her eyes, and Joe felt guilty for laughing.

'Would you have been upset if I was waiting for a man?' she said, her voice almost a whisper.

Joe wasn't sure that he had heard correctly. Once again, it wasn't something he had expected her to say. Suddenly, it felt like they were on a playground bashfully glancing at each other out of the corners of their eyes, far away from the adult concerns of life and war.

Anne even stood awkwardly, trying not to meet his eyes. He thought he had better say something before she looked even more uncomfortable.

'I think that I... that that would be a little presumptuous,' he stammered.

It wasn't what he had wanted to say, but at least he had managed to say something.

'Usually, I would be annoyed if a man asked me such a question. It *is* none of your business. But there is something about you, Joe. I don't know what it is, but I will excuse you this time.'

She smiled again and everything felt all right with the world.

'This time,' was all she said. All she needed to say. The words and the smile were enough to calm his nerves. She took his hand in hers and led him away. 'Why don't you show me the rest of the building and find me a desk. It's hot and stinks to high heaven in here.'

'Of course,' he said as they walked off. Her hand felt warm and comfortable in his.

Chapter 15

George and Tom reported for training in the field next to their new camp. For the first time since joining the regiment in August, Canterbury had given the King's Rifles a proper field on which to train.

It was a crisp Monday morning, the autumn sun peeking its way through a group of clouds and evaporating the dew on the ground. In the new wooden huts they had been given, a few men who had overslept were being rudely awaked. They all turned out in full kit for the first time, even if some of it didn't fit properly and it was itchy as hell. Every man had a rifle and they finally looked like soldiers.

'Right, men. Line up along the tree line here.' Corporal Campbell waved them into place, rushing along the group of men and pushing some of them where they needed to go. 'Stand to attention. Come on, now. No, better than that, stick your chests out. Make like your old mums are watching. I've bloody told you enough times, see?'

Tom grinned at George, and he had to stifle a laugh. Campbell walked past them. 'Better, better,' he said, shouting for all to hear even though his section of men was only a few metres across, stood between the trees. There were other sections dotted around the park, each with an officer of their own. Some old men who had squeezed into their old uniforms were busy organising men around the park and barking orders as if they had never retired. The group nearest to George's had a retired captain with a series of medals pinned to his chest and a swagger stick clenched firmly under one arm, walking up and down the line of men shouting with a voice that was clearly past its prime. The Corporal was preferable to that old man; he was closer to them in age, not a toff, and would presumably be going out with them to Europe. Whenever that was.

'Right, men. Enough dilly-dallying. You, there. Stand to attention.'

The shout brought George back to attention and he snapped his view forward to the Corporal, but the command wasn't aimed at him. It was shouted at a scrawny, young man stood next to George in the line. George had seen him about the place but had not spoken to him before. He looked even younger than George. If boys like him were signing up then no one would suspect George.

Panic pulled at his stomach. If they found out his real age then he would be left at home while the older boys like Tom shipped out. He puffed his chest out and forced the fear down, willing confidence.

He heard a voice in the line behind him but didn't quite catch what it said. It was bound to be something crude and there was a small grumble of chuckling from the men around them. Campbell's head shot in the direction of the laughter, and he stomped over to them. George forced his gaze forward.

'P'raps you're wondering why this company is being led by a mere Corporal,' the man said as he walked along the line. 'P'raps you're too stupid to have even noticed.

'Well, let me tell you this. For starters, I'm not just some bleedin' Corporal, wet behind the ears. I'm not a fresh-faced Lieutenant straight out of officer trainin''

Some of the men snickered, and he stopped in his tracks to glare at them.

'No sir-ee, I've seen more sights and more combats that you can even count on your bloody fingers.' He resumed his pacing.

'No, you see, the staff wallahs were not expecting so many of you layabouts to sign up. They had no idea that any of you had a bloody inkling of martial pride in you.' The Corporal stopped dead centre and put on a show of appraising them. George had heard his father use the army slang for someone in charge, but he was sure the others would be confused. 'And, looking at you, I'm starting to agree with them.' He shouted the last line even louder.

'So they had to drag the likes of me from a well-deserved leave to babysit you bloody fools.

'You might think it's unfair that you got me, and I might think what did I do to deserve you lot, but let me tell you; we haven't even bloody started yet.

'You will address me as "sah!" and stamp your heel just as you would for any officer. Failure to do so will result in punishment. Do I make myself clear?'

'Yes, sah!' the platoon replied.

Campbell nodded and resumed his pacing, closer to the line before. As he walked past, George could smell the staleness of his breath. It was like the man had been eating nothing but meat for weeks.

'What this means is, that I'm going to need some section leaders, sharpish.'

He stopped in front of one man and stared him down. George could just about see from where he was, but the man seemed to bend backwards from the Corporal despite trying to stand firm. The Corporal started walking again, and George's eyes shot forwards. He hoped Campbell hadn't noticed.

'Right, now. Time to drill.' The Corporal moved aside. 'Anyone who falls behind will be punished. Anyone stopping to help another man will be punished. Any man refusing to drill will be punished and sent home as quickly as you can say "no". With this he smacked one hand into the other, then put his face close to the nearest man before continuing. 'Punishment will be in the form of more drill and then I will personally find you the most horrible task army life can give you and make sure you do it.' He turned away. 'I bet you all thought this would be easy didn't you? Take the King's shilling, lounge around in uniform making the girls swoon and then home for tea. Well, it's not. Army life is all about discipline. I've been lumped with you useless lot and I'm going to bloody well make sure that I mould you into something approaching a competent unit. We're going to show those other sections what we can do and go to twice the lengths they will. When they get tired, that's only halfway for us. Do I make myself clear?'

There was a grumble from the section.

'What's that? I said, do I make myself clear? Answer me properly, soldiers!'

'Yes, sir!' the men answered in a close unison with only a few voices falling behind and mumbling their assent.

'Now get running.'

'We're going to have to watch out for him,' Tom said to George as he kept pace alongside him.

'What do you mean?' George was trying to focus as much as possible on running. Campbell was shouting orders at the men to keep up and to push themselves harder.

'He's got something to prove, trust me. With the retired bigwigs around, he's aiming for a promotion,' Tom puffed. 'And we're just the tool he needs to get it.'

'I get you.'

'Just be careful, if any of us get in his way who knows what'll happen.'

'All right, all right.'

Tom was quiet for a few more moments.

'When do you think they'll send us to France?'

George thought if Tom put more effort into running than talking then he wouldn't keep stumbling over the uneven ground. He just wanted to get to the end of the run and talk about it then.

'I don't know. Just run, will you?'

Tom gave George a sideways glance and shut up.

*

George noticed the scrawny boy the other side of him dropping behind. It was getting worse and he was likely to trip the man behind.

'Come on,' George whispered. It came out louder than he expected, and the boy flinched. He was still drifting behind.

'Come on,' George said again, willing the boy forward.

'I can't!' he replied, exasperated, his voice weak and phlegmy, almost out of breath. He stumbled, about to break the line. George only had a second to think. He grabbed the boy by his left arm, using his strength to right him and pull him along.

'I have you!' he screamed at the boy, his own strength beginning to falter. 'You can do this, come on. We're almost there.'

He lowered his voice to a whisper. 'Focus on the end, look, you're almost done.'

The boy was back in line now, just.

George let go and the boy stumbled. Instinctively, he reached out to grab him again, but the boy pushed his arm away and charged ahead towards the finishing hut. He put his hands on his knees and puffed in great lungfuls of air as if he would never breathe again, before collapsing to the ground in a heap. The line reached him a few seconds later and came to a rest.

Corporal Campbell walked over and gave the boy a kick in the back to see if he was still breathing. The boy whimpered.

'What did I say would happen if you broke formation?'

The heap on the floor mumbled something, and Campbell gave him another kick.

'What's that, soldier?'

George went to stop the Corporal from his abuse, but Tom grabbed his arm, holding him back. 'It's not worth it, George, you'll be on a charge before we've even started. Let him get it out of his system.'

The boy had got to his feet now and was apologising to the Corporal.

'Once more round the park for you, and then you can practise digging a trench.'

The boy hesitated, but a bark from Campbell sent him on his slow, sloping way. He then turned to George. 'I saw what you did back there, soldier.' George puffed up his chest. 'I won't stand for that kind of thing, soldier. Not in my section. If you help him, I'll never make a soldier out of him. He's gotta suffer on his own, is that clear?'

'Yes, sir.' George's voice was a grudging mumble.

'And I'll have more respect out of you too, soldier.'

George repeated his response, louder.

'You'd best get on after your little friend. He's got a head start on you.'

Accepting his fate, he started jogging again, sweat already making his clothes wet through. During the short rest, the sweat had cooled in the fabric. It chafed as he ran off in pursuit.

When they got back the boys were exhausted, trying to get air into their lungs. The boy bent over, but George, standing up to open his lungs, gestured for him to do the same.

Both moved to a pile of boxes with a British Army stamp. Inside, laid neatly in rows, were various items, including an entrenching tool. George handed one to the boy. They begun digging and the spade-like tool was soon covered in thick mud and silt.

'What's your name?' George asked, now he had air in his lungs.

The boy looked up at George and hesitated. 'Fred...' he said, his voice a faint whisper through wracking breaths. 'Fred Madeley.'

'George,' he replied.

'Uh, nice to meet you,' Fred said, and went to shake George's hand, but thought better of it. 'Thanks for your help back there. I thought I was going to die, the pain in my chest was so strong. But you were right, I ran through it.'

George stared at Fred for a long moment. He looked out of place. He should be a clerk or something like that.

'Why did you enlist, Fred?'

'Why not?' He didn't look convinced by his own answer. 'I thought that it would be the right thing to do. You probably think I'm not cut out for it.'

George stumbled over a reply. 'No... no, that's not what I—'

Fred cut George off. 'And you would be just like everyone else. Everyone I've ever met thought I would amount to nothing, too weak and cowardly to be somebody. Well, I may need help from time to time, and I thank you for that, but I'm here to show them all that I can do this. You will see.'

George was impressed at Fred's newfound assertiveness. Perhaps the army was already bringing something out in all of them, a confidence. Who was George to tell Fred that he couldn't fight for his country? After all, wasn't that why they were all here?

Still, something was unsettling George.

'Just how old are you, Fred?'

Fred darted his head from side to side to see if anyone had overheard. He was almost shaking.

'Why do you ask that?' Fred said, putting more force into the entrenching tool and pulling a great lump of dirt out of the ground to deposit on one side. Sweat built up on his brow. 'What's age got to do with anything?'

George sympathised. 'I was curious, Fred. You don't seem that old. At least, not in a physical sense.'

'Not as old as you, no, probably not.' Again, he looked around. 'Listen, don't tell anyone will you?'

He didn't say anymore, but his eyes bored into George's.

'Why would I tell anyone, Fred? What possible reason would I have? Least of all an officer. I wouldn't want to lose anyone's trust.'

'Swear?'

'What? Oh, fine. I swear I won't tell anyone. No one cares, Fred. Look around us. If they did, they would have done something by now.'

'I'm sixteen, George. Sixteen. I shouldn't be here, but I want to be, all right? Don't judge me, and don't tell anyone else, I can do this. I don't need any sympathy, and I don't need a father figure.' He carried on digging.

George almost laughed at the thought of him being a father figure to anyone. Then another thought struck him: he had been thinking of Fred as a boy all this time, as if he were a child, but they were almost the same age. They were about as different in physical stature as it was possible to be, but they were both young.

'If it makes you feel any better, Fred...' George considered the implications of telling Fred his age, but one wouldn't tell on the other. 'I'm just seventeen.' George paused. 'Seventeen last month, mind.'

'You can't be,' Fred said. 'Stop joking. I mean, look at you. You're twice the size of me. '

'That doesn't mean anything, Fred. What's size got to do with age?'

The other soldier already looked older in his estimation, as if some weight had been lifted off his young shoulders and brought George and him closer together.

'I'm not telling you this to mock you. In a way, we're both vulnerable.'

Fred scoffed and gestured at George, disagreeing.

'What I mean is, well… we have to keep an eye out. To watch out for each other.'

'What on earth do you think you are doing?' A fresh voice cut into the conversation and they both turned, dislodging some of the freshly dug up soil. George stumbled in the moving mud, dropping his entrenching tool, but managed to regain his balance.

A Captain was striding towards them, a scowl etched over his raging features. He asked again, this time with less of a shout and more of a command. 'What on earth are you doing? Stop right this instant.'

George was the first to react. 'Sorry, sir. We only stopped for a second to catch our breath. We will carry on straight away… sir.'

The Captain's face was turning an odd shade of purple.

'That's not what I meant, Private, and you know it!'

George didn't know what to say. It appeared Fred didn't either. George hazarded a guess. 'Are we digging the trench incorrectly, sir?'

'Are you trying to be funny, Private?'

The Captain looked even unhappier than before. George was at a loss as to why, but he thought it best to try and resolve the situation.

'No, sir. Not at all, sir,' he said, forcing a tone of complete honesty.

'This is our training camp, Private!'

Realisation dawned. They weren't digging the trench incorrectly, they were digging where they shouldn't be.

'I'm sorry, sir. The Corporal ordered us to dig this trench, sir. A punishment, sir,' said Fred, before George had a chance to reply.

'Punishment? By the sounds of it, you well deserve it. You should accept it without comment, Private.'

'No harm was meant, sir.' The situation had gone beyond George, but he still tried to appease the Captain. They had just given Campbell even more reason to dislike them. George and Fred would not hear the end of this.

'I won't have a word said about any officer in this army, or any NCO for that matter. You can finish your punishment by returning that soil to where you dug it from. This time, do it neatly. When I inspect it later I expect to see flat turf on top and no sign of your idiotic trench. Is that quite clear?'

'Yes, sir.'

The Captain marched off back the way he had come.

George turned to Fred and noticed a tear at his eye. Fred, wiped his face with the back of his sleeve, sighed and picked up his shovel.

'Sorry, George,' he said. 'I should have kept my mouth shut.'

'Don't worry, Fred,' George said, joining in with the effort of refilling the trench.

Life in the army wasn't getting off to the start either of the boys would have wanted.

*

A series of wooden frames had been erected at one end of the field, like a hangman's gallows. Filled sandbags were hung from the joists with thick white rope. George waited at the back of a line of three men, each from his section, as one after the other they ran at the sandbag. Each man roared, enjoying the sensation.

The bayonet was easy to attach in a hurry and slid neatly over the barrel of his Lee Enfield rifle, clicking into place. It made the weapon feel even heavier in his grip, but, lacking ammunition, it gave it a certain power.

He let out a cry as he ran. For what, he didn't know, he was just caught up in the moment. It wasn't even words, just meaningless vowels, as loud as his lungs would allow.

There was an art to bayonet drill. Like his sketches. One movement, then another, each following on from the last. Thrust, pull, repeat. If it was wrong, you were more likely to harm yourself than the sandbag. George was still bruised from the last time he had got it wrong. His gut had taken the butt of his rifle at full pelt. This time he stuck the blade in smoothly, aiming for the middle. The shock of the blow was heavy and he had to get used to it. It threatened to push him away, but he held fast to the rifle. He had been told that the last thing a soldier did was lose his rifle; always keep hold of it and you'll have something with which to defend yourself.

The sandbag ripped along the seam and sand poured out. There was a whooping cheer from behind him. He didn't turn to receive the praise, knowing that the next man in line would already be charging the sandbag. He jerked his blade free and moved aside.

The absurdity of the situation hit him. They had been training for months now, and they were assaulting a fake enemy with real weapons. Perhaps the army didn't know what to do with them? There was no glory or honour in ripping open a bag of sand with a blade as long as his arm.

He much preferred firing drill. He was good at it too, only a few points away from getting his marksman's badge. The mechanical motion of pulling the bolt back, aiming and squeezing the trigger had a purity of form that he enjoyed. He hoped when they were finally out in France that they wouldn't need their bayonets. He had yet to see it in practice, but 'no one could get close to them' was what the regulars often said about the rate of British fire. George wasn't sure if they were merely bragging.

After drill, Campbell took them aside. He was unusually informal. He didn't order them to form up in fours.

'So as you bloody well know, I was roped into looking after you lot by command.'

There was no shouting, just an even, commanding voice.

'No one else was bloody stupid enough to take the posting, see.'

He stopped and appraised them for a moment.

'They've decided that there aren't enough officers to go around. What was meant to be a temporary situation has become bloody permanent. Too many of you idiots signed up, see, and now they need someone to lead you.'

He marched through the groups of men as usual. Their eyes turned to him as he went. 'What's going on, Tom?' George whispered.

'I don't know, lad,' he said back, not nearly as quiet. 'He's not being his usual self. That's for sure.'

'Well, the Captain, he spoke to me this morning he did,' the Corporal continued, either unaware of them or ignoring the infraction. They weren't the only ones whispering under their breath. Campbell was playing up the suspense and enjoying it. He stopped in front of them again and stuck his noise up in the air.

'He told me only this bloody morning, that I am to be made a Lance-Sergeant. That may sound to you like I am only a bloody acting-Sergeant, but it's more than that, see. I will be in charge of this whole platoon. That means orders comes down from me, and you bloody well listen to them too, see?'

To call it a surprise would be to lie. As far as they could tell he had only joined the regiment so he could work his way up the ladder. It wasn't unheard of for a non-commissioned officer to end up commissioned, but it took a long time. The Corporal was now one step closer. The Lance-Sergeant.

Officers were scarce. George had only seen the Captain a few times, when he gave them speeches. The rest of the time he kept to himself.

'What this means is—' Campbell hadn't finished '—that we need someone to take command of this little section of wasted potential.'

He made eye contact with one of the men, then walked straight up to one of the others and stared at him. He then swept his gaze around again, then moved on to stare at someone else, getting as close as possible without touching. Every man just stood impassively, waiting for him to move on. Some men he lingered on for longer than others, some he missed out. George was one of the latter.

'Now I know that some of you lot have been with us for a while,' the Lance-Sergeant said. 'But that's not what I'm after.'

He carried on his pacing. George grew tired of standing still.

'The man that will lead this section needs to have a good head.' He stopped in front of one of the men, shook his head and moved on. 'He needs to keep calm in the face of adversity, not to shy away from leadership, see. I'm not sure that there is such a man in this section.'

There were murmurs of dissent, and the Lance-Sergeant smiled a predatory, self-satisfied smile.

'Perhaps I was wrong. Could it be there's one of you that's good enough to lead? One of you might think he wants to lead, but that's not the same thing, see. Wanting does not get, only hard work and discipline gets. You'd have to be bloody stupid to think that just wanting to be an officer was good enough.' He stopped pacing. 'Who of you wants to be an officer?'

None of the men stirred, they just stared forward pretending to ignore him.

'Good,' he said, the smile back on his face. George felt uneasy, as if Campbell was about to attack.

'You're all learning, see. Now, which of you has a family history in the army? Whose wee daddies served before you ended up in this sorry excuse for a section?'

George put his hand up and felt a movement that indicated Tom had as well. It was a source of great pride that their fathers had served. It had also helped them settle in.

'Hmmm,' the Lance-Sergeant continued. 'Right then, which of you pampered lot's daddies weren't officers? Who didn't have that oh-so-wonderful privilege?'

Some of the men lowered their arms. He kept his up, the pain after exerting himself already burning down its length. He could drop at any moment.

'If you've got your hand up, stay. The rest of you get out of my bloody sight, you're dismissed.' He barked the last word in his usual manner. He walked amongst them again, tutting to himself the whole time. He was still enjoying the spectacle, the feeling of power that he had over them.

'No,' he said, standing in front of one man. 'You can go too.'

He moved on again, picking and choosing who would be given command of the section from the remaining men. Arms down, they were being dismissed one by one, until only a few remained.

If George was honest with himself, he wanted command. He wanted to earn a stripe, even if he hadn't said so before. He wanted it, not because he wanted to be in charge of the other men, most of whom were his superiors in age, and not because he wanted any kind of power trip or responsibility, but because he felt he had something to prove. He wasn't sure what he meant by that, it was an instinct. He had something to prove to Campbell, who had hated him from the start, and no doubt realised he was too young. He had something to prove to the others, including Tom, and even Fred, and he had something to prove to himself. However, what he had wanted to do most of all since the very beginning was to make his parents proud. Joe had made something of himself, but George had never progressed past being a dock hand. The army had offered a way out. He now earned a regular pay, his pay-book kept in his breast pocket like every other soldier. But a stripe would give him more. He had not expected his mother to take his signing up so badly, as both her brother and husband had served in the Boer War. He wanted to make her proud and show her that he could do this and do it well.

The man next to George slouched back to the billet, trying to keep his head raised, leaving behind Tom and a couple of others.

Some men didn't want the stripe, but others, like George, wanted it more than they could express.

The process reminded him of a cattle auction. The remaining men waiting to be picked by the farmer as his favourite and the rest being led off to slaughter.

The Lance-Sergeant stopped in front of Tom and stared at him for a long moment. George had no way of seeing what was in Campbell's eyes, but he did see him move off again. At no point did he regard George, and George was growing ever more frustrated at the situation. He was nothing to the Lance-Sergeant. Campbell had hated him since his first day. He was playing with him. He stopped in front of them both, and finally looked at George. But just for a moment.

'You,' he said, holding out a hand for Tom to shake. 'Well done, Lance-Corporal Adams, I've decided you've got what it takes to make a proper Lance-Corporal.'

George didn't know what to think. At the last moment the Lance-Sergeant had got his hopes up, then dashed them just as easily.

'Make sure you bloody prove me right, Lance-Corporal.' He took a piece of chalk out of his webbing and drew a 'V' stripe on the arm of Tom's khaki.

'That'll have to do for now, till we can get the quarter-bloke to sort out a proper bloody stripe,' he said, before walking away without further ceremony. He called back over his shoulder, his Scottish dialect cutting through the ambient noise: 'Now get the bloody hell out of here, you're all dismissed.'

Tom turned to George, a grin plastered all over his face.

'Did you see that?' Tom said, already knowing the answer. 'Tom Adams' army is one step closer, hah.'

He patted George on the back as they walked towards the huts. A couple of the other soldiers said 'Well done, lad,' as they passed.

'Lance-Corporal Adams. It has a nice ring to it,' George said, trying out the sound.

'I know, can you believe it? I didn't think he would make me a Lance-Corporal.'

'I can.' George did. He wasn't surprised. He had always seen Tom as a leader, and in a way he had always been the leader of their little group. George wished it had been him, but he forced a smile. 'Of course I can believe it. You're Tom Adams.' There was a touch of bitterness in his voice which he regretted immediately.

To his credit, Tom ignored it, flashing a grin at his friend again.

Chapter 16

Joe entered the office and went straight to work, smiling at everyone he passed. On his desk there was the usual pile of papers and notes he had accumulated during the week. A single white feather lay on top. He looked around the office. No one was looking in his direction. His stomach lurched. Where had it come from? Who could have put it there?

Who dared call him a coward? Many people had access to the offices. Anyone could have put it on his desk and he would not know who. Only two people, who weren't family, knew his thoughts on the war, Mr Harlow and Anne. Would they think him a coward? Joe didn't think he was a coward. Would they call him out this way, rather than speaking to him directly? Perhaps Anne had let slip to one of her friends by accident. Why here? Would they know where he worked? Had she told them that as well? His mind ran wild considering the possibilities. He hadn't considered Anne the type. She was wiser than that. Even though she liked to ask questions, she was always seeking information, not giving it away. Although he had only known her a short time, he trusted her.

Perhaps it was Albert Barnes? Had he told someone about the

article and asked them to get revenge? No, that was too far-fetched. Albert had only confronted him when he was about to ship out. Besides, this was too subtle for Barnes. It had to be someone else. Mr Harlow put things on Joe's desk, but usually work. Mr Harlow or Anne. Neither were likely.

'Good morning, Joe.' Anne's sweet voice rang out behind him.

He panicked and dropped a book on top of the feather, crushing it and hiding it from view. He turned in a hurry, hoping she hadn't noticed. Why had she snuck up on him? Did she put the white feather on his desk?

'What's wrong, Joe?' she said. Wrinkles of worry marked her usually soft face. She put a hand on his arm. It felt warm.

'Oh, nothing,' he said, forcing a smile. 'Nothing at all.'

Being that close to her felt fantastic. She had an aura that warmed him, and he could smell the faint scent of her perfume. He realised how close he was and jumped back, banging into the table.

'Ow.' He looked to see if anyone else had seen his mistake. Still no one looked up from their desks. She chuckled, but the look of concern was still on her face.

'Are you all right? You needn't be so nervous, Joe.' She reached out a hand and took hold of his. 'There really isn't any reason to be.'

He regarded her for a second, and she looked back. A worried frown crossed his brow. No, it couldn't be, not her. She had understood when he told her about the article he had written, she had been on his side. As far as he could make out she cared for him, perhaps as much as he cared for her.

'I'm sorry, Anne. You made me jump. I wasn't expecting you. I was in a world of my own.' He was lying and he hated lying to her, but he didn't know what else to say. He hoped that she didn't realise, but from the look on her face he couldn't be sure. He suspected there was a hint of annoyance, but he was being paranoid again.

'Why are you so anxious this morning, Joe? Are you sure nothing is wrong?'

It was almost as if she was pressing him to discuss the feather, leaning in closer, but how could she know? It couldn't have been her. He didn't like it, but he decided to bend the truth.

'Oh, it's nothing,' he said as he sat down. 'I'm just worried about my brother. Nothing for you to be concerned about.'

'Your brother?' Anne asked, tilting her head. It gave him the impression she was trying to reach inside his head and examine just what he was thinking. It was unsettling. 'Is anything the matter with your brother?' She sat at the next table.

'Nothing's the matter with him. Unless you mean his ability to run headlong into things without thinking first.'

He smiled at the thought, but Anne just stared back. 'Then why are you concerned?' she said, matter-of-factly. 'What has he done? Or, what is he going to do?'

'Well, that's exactly it. You didn't ask at the time why it was that I was in the station that day.'

'I had presumed that you were there writing a report or something of the sort. Newspaper business. I didn't think it was much to do with me.'

'Well, in a way you're right, I was trying to write an article. I think it was quite good, but Mr Harlow didn't send me down there. He didn't even know I was there. He doesn't really let me write copy, only edit. Well, it wasn't the main reason I was there, it was more a lucky coincidence of my being there.'

'Why were you there, then? Don't tell me you were there to have a look at the brave young men in uniform as well?' She smiled for the first time that morning, teasing him, and being self-deprecating. She knew full well the crime of such a thing.

He laughed. 'I guess I don't have quite the same tastes as you. I was there to see my brother. Or rather, to see him off.'

She nodded.

'Not that he knew it. I was there to see him onto the train, to wherever it was they were sending him.'

'He was one of the soldiers off to France? You didn't see him?' She had guessed where he was going.

'Yes, but... I had thought about speaking to him, wishing him luck. Telling him to look after himself. I gave up. I was too much a coward to approach him.' The word 'coward' made his stomach sink again.

'Why were you too afraid to talk to your own brother?'

Joe swallowed what he was about to say and hesitated. The conversation had escalated out of his control. At first he had been shocked to find the feather, and then his weak cover-up had been exposed and diverted onto something altogether more embarrassing. Embarrassing wasn't the right word. Why would he be embarrassed of his relationship with his brother? Ashamed? Perhaps, but that didn't cover it either. It had been fractious for many a year. They were two very different people who just happened to be born to the same parents. They hadn't shared much, other than a bedroom, since they were children. How could he make her understand that without appearing uncaring?

'I don't know,' he said. It wasn't what he had expected to say. She gave him an odd look. Was there pity in those pretty blue eyes? He hoped it wasn't that. 'We've never been close...'

'Why not?' She was now playing the role of counsellor. Had she read some Freud, or Jung? Sadly, he hadn't read much of either man's work. He usually read more political texts and novels. Could it be where she got her easy manner from, the slight incline of the head? Trying to put him at ease and get him to speak. What little he had read suggested that to be true, and it was working. Or was she being a good journalist, interviewing him and trying to get to his core thoughts?

He wasn't sure it was thanks to their efforts, or whether he just wanted to talk to Anne, to tell her his innermost thoughts and feelings. It was her, he promised himself, not any kind of, what did they call it, psychoanalysis?

'I don't know,' he said again, feeling stupid at his inability to form the ideas. Why could he always internalise things, but never vocalise them? Why was he so bad at speaking his mind, even with Anne, the one person that made him feel most at ease?

'You keep on saying that,' she said. 'For a journalist, there's a lot you don't seem to know.'

The comment was scathing, and he felt more stupid than ever. However, after an awkward moment Anne smiled, then seeing his expression burst into a laugh.

'I'm joking, Joe. You know I am, don't look so serious. You are too easy to wind up.'

Joe had flashbacks to his time in the office with Frank. She had filled his place quite well. Even better, in fact. She was a lot more attractive than Frank. He smiled back at her and let out a laugh.

'I'm sorry, Anne. It hasn't been a good morning for me. I do need a bit of humour sometimes.'

'But that's one of the things I like about you, Joe,' she said. 'Your passion. You don't do things by half. Too many of the lads around here are happy to just get by. You're not like them. You're much more focused, I guess. Not to mention, you're sweet. I've never seen one man care so much about anything before.'

He was flattered and fought the urge to blush. It was the first time that she had shown a real interest in him, and once again he was at a loss for words.

'I wish I could make my friends as passionate about things as you.' Her smile changed to a look of bored frustration as she stared into the middle distance. Only he would notice the change. She rarely mentioned her friends, except for that time she talked about why she was at the station. Perhaps that was what had had brought them to mind now. Regardless of the reason, he was thankful for the change of subject, for the distraction.

'What do you mean?' he said, clearing his throat.

'Hmm? Oh, my friends? Well, they're never dedicated to

anything. Unless they're trying to find men. It's quite frustrating.' She shook her head and smiled, but this time there was little humour in it. 'And that's the kind of thing that we're trying to put an end to.'

'What do you mean by that?' he said.

'We don't exist just for men, you know,' she said in a clipped manner.

He couldn't think what he had done to make her angry.

'I know you don't,' he said. 'Who is suggesting that you are?'

'Oh, not you. I'm sorry, I didn't mean to snap. It's just a frustrating feeling that you have no power. I was very lucky to get this job here, it means the world to me, and even then I feel like I only got it because I batted my eyelashes and Ed… I mean Mr Harlow fell in love with me.'

She stopped and covered her mouth.

'Don't tell him I said that, will you, Joe?' It was her turn to blush. 'I daren't think what he would say.'

Joe laughed then, seeing her face, regretted it. It was curious how she could go from fierce and powerful in one moment, to frightened about what one might think in the next.

'I wouldn't. It's none of my business how you got the job, as long as you're good at it. That's what's important, most of all. And you are good at it.'

'Thank you,' she said, blushing. He liked her vulnerability, there was something endearing about it. Although, he had also got a rush when she had been talking so forcefully.

'However, you still haven't explained what you were talking about just now,' he said, thinking that the conversation might bring her back out of her shell.

'Oh, well, isn't it obvious? I want the vote.'

Joe wondered why he hadn't seen it all along. 'You're a suffragette?' he asked.

'Yes. It's not our term, but yes. Definitely. The bloody newspapers can call us what they like, but we just want choice. Oops.'

Joe laughed. 'Go on,' he said, smiling, trying to reassure her. 'I want to know.'

'Yes, well getting work here was the first step of trying to force myself into a better life, away from relying on a man for my income. I also want the vote, and I've been trying to encourage my friends to help with the protests. As I've said before, they're quite useless.'

'I would say I know how you feel, but I don't, being a man and all. But I tell you this, I will do everything in my power to help you… if you'd like.'

'You're kind, Joe.' She brushed the back of his hand. 'I don't need the help of a man, that's rather the point. Besides, I'm not sure what you could do to help, but I appreciate the gesture.'

'How about this then? I would like to get to know you better.' He wasn't sure where his sudden confidence had come from. Perhaps it was the idea that they had shared values, or perhaps he was drunk on her beauty and intelligence. It didn't matter why. For once, he was proud of himself. 'I know you don't need a man, or perhaps want one, but perhaps some company? Would you, at some point, permit me to take you to the picture house, or even just go for a walk?' He had put his heart out there, and now he was waiting for her to stamp on it.

She hesitated. 'I think I would like that, Joe,' she said, a moment later. Then she noticed the clock that hung on the end wall of the office. 'Is that the time?' she said, standing up in a hurry and removing her hand from the top of Joe's.

'I have to be going,' she said as she collected her things. 'I'm sorry, Joe. We'll have to talk about this another time. I have to meet the others, and I cannot be late.' She grabbed her coat from the coat stand and threw it on, barely getting an arm in the sleeve.

'I'm sorry,' were the last words he heard her shout as she rushed out of the office. Just like that, she was gone. He had almost forgotten his worries, but in her absence they surfaced again. As he pulled over a pile of paper to start some work a book slid from the top and he saw the white feather. He knew he wouldn't be able to concentrate on work. He idly played with the feather, noticing its soft touch. Perhaps that was why it had been chosen; soft, weak, cowardly.

It couldn't have been Anne, he had to believe that. But, he realised now, he didn't know her at all, no matter how much it felt like he did. She had yet to make any mention of the fact he should be fighting. Why would she just leave it here for him to find? It didn't make sense.

It must have been one of the other women that had access to the office. There were a number of cleaners, and a couple of others who had replaced the men who had gone to fight. He was one of the few men left, and he would have to watch himself from now on.

Chapter 17

'I miss home.' George had to blow into his hands to get some warmth into them. The army hadn't provided any gloves. He almost looked forward to drill, to warming up his muscles and forgetting the cold. The billet was cold through, the only things keeping it out were the small glass windows at intervals along the length of the wall. The walls were a stained brown wood. There were gaps the mice crawled through. Someone had got a hold of some cloves and stuffed them into an orange, giving the room a strong smell. If Sergeant Campbell found out then they would be in trouble, but for a few minutes at least they didn't care.

George was lying on his side. He was so tired, but he couldn't keep his eyes closed. His mind wandered, thinking of everything – of home and wondering what the girls were doing.

'What d'you reckon we'll wake up to tomorrow? Them saying the war's over and telling us all to go home?' someone asked from the gloom.

'What a waste of time, I'd sure be annoyed,' another said from across the hut.

'I don't think that's how it works, Fred.' Tom was sat on the bed opposite George, smoking a cigarette, the pale blue smoke clouding around his head like a halo. Until now he had been gazing off into the middle distance, enjoying the smoke. His knees were pulled up to his chest and he scowled across at the younger soldier, speaking with a voice of authority. 'I doubt this war will be over by tomorrow. I don't think the Germans are going to pack up and go home for Christmas. It's serious, going by what the papers are saying.'

Fred dropped to the other side of his bed, kneeling on the floor and closing his eyes.

'What're you doing?' George asked, from the other side of the hut.

At first Fred didn't answer and George looked at Tom. He shrugged.

A few moments later Fred opened his eyes and in a small voice said, 'Just making a wish.'

George almost laughed but was stopped by the serious look on Fred's face.

'What're you doing making a wish for?' he said.

'It's a family tradition. Every Christmas Eve we wish for something we want. It's just something we do. I guess I miss them. It made me think of home.'

'What did you wish for?' Tom asked, feigning interest.

'I can't tell you. That's not how it works.' There was a slight upturn of a smile at the corners of his mouth, breaking through the seriousness.

'Are you wishing for the end of the war? So you can go home?' he asked.

'No, definitely not!' Fred replied, all trace of the smile gone. 'I don't want that. I want us to go to the front. I'm tired of waiting. Aren't you?'

'Definitely,' George muttered.

'To think they said it would all be over by now.' Fred was in full flow, and George was unused to hearing him talk so much. 'And we haven't even left the bloody country yet.'

George grimaced. Fred had picked up bad habits from the Sergeant, swearing whenever the mood took him.

'Oh, don't be stupid, Fred.' Tom had never quite taken to Fred. He thought the younger man would never make a soldier, that he didn't have any kind of martial bearing. George disagreed, and so Tom humoured him. 'That was all just newspaper talk. They always say things like that. You didn't believe it, did you?' He scoffed and took another drag of his cigarette.

'No, I guess not. I was just saying I'm glad they were wrong. I want to do my bit.'

'You will, Fred, you will.'

Fred beamed at that. Tom stood up and gave the smaller man a pat on the back, before walking out of the hut without a word. A minute later he came back with a bundle in his arms.

'I asked the post master to hold this back for tomorrow,' he said as he dumped a pile of parcels wrapped in brown paper onto his bed. He searched the room for something. The others were still in shock and confusion. Then Tom seemed to find what he was looking for. He vaulted over Fred's bed. He grabbed Fred's red football scarf, ignoring the protest, and wrapped it around his shoulders.

'There, we go!' Tom said, grinning at everyone. 'Gather round, gather round, lads. Christmas has come early!'

'Why've you got my scarf?'

'It's red and red is Christmas, right, Fred? The bishop back home always used to talk about wearing red at Christmas. Then he'd start handing out blessings. Don't worry, I'm only borrowing it, you'll get it back.'

The men from the other end of the hut crowded around Tom and his pile of parcels. They would do whatever he said. If he told them to jump off a cliff, George suspected they would. 'Now, get comfortable, lads. Find a place to sit, go on, there's plenty of room. Fred, budge up so Bill can get in next to you.'

'What have you got there?' one of the lads from the section said, slow on the uptake.

'Just take a seat and all will be revealed!' He flourished a parcel in one hand and held it up as if in mock surprise, then with a grin let it drop back on the bed and looked around the room at everyone assembled. They were like kids in a penny sweet shop, eager to see what Tom had to offer them, eyes wide and smiles large as they waited. 'Now that you're all here. I've got a surprise for you.'

There was a mock 'ooh' from the men and some of the others laughed.

'These here—' he pointed to the pile '—these are from the post master. I caught him this morning and offered him a hand.'

'Oi, that one's got my name on it, you thieving get!'

'Quieten down, Arthur,' George said. 'No one's been stealing, Tom will explain in a minute.' He nodded at Tom, hoping that he would get on with it, but Tom was enjoying himself too much.

'I offered to take the post for our section and I managed to convince him not to deliver it to you.'

'What'd you do that for?'

'So I could do this, you fool. It's Christmas. I was going to wait and surprise everyone in the morning, but then I thought, "The Bloody Sergeant won't let us have a Christmas."' They'd started calling Campbell 'The Bloody Sergeant' behind his back, due to his excessive use of the word. 'He'll probably make us march all the way up the Great Stour and back before we even get something to eat. Probably all the way to the sea if he's in a bad mood.'

There was a murmur around the room. Campbell liked to push them. He was determined that they would excel, be even fitter, and fight harder than a unit of regulars. Some of the men had wanted to give up, but Tom had managed to keep them going.

'At least we've finally got full kit and guns!'

'Shut up, there,' George said. 'Go on, Tom, get on with it.'

Tom grinned at him.

'I thought it would be something nice for you to have once we've shown the Bloody Sergeant that we can march as long and hard as he wants and go back for more. Then I saw how miserable you were tonight, thinking of the homes we've all left behind.'

Fred had closed his eyes again. George thought he saw a single tear roll down Fred's cheek, but he couldn't be sure in the flicker of candlelight.

'I've left my old mum behind,' Tom continued. 'And I don't know about you lot, but I can't help thinking of her.' Some of them nodded, others stared into thin air. George had left behind more than just his mother; there were his sisters, his dad, and even his brother. He wondered what they would all be doing on a cold night back in Liverpool, but it was painful to think of them all there and he the only one somewhere else.

Tom didn't wait for any of the others to join in. He was acting now as their superior, but also as the leader they all wanted rather than the leader they had. 'Well, you see, she's back home, and no doubt worrying about me, out here with you lot. She hasn't got anyone else. But the way I see it, there isn't much I can do for her from here, except for think about her. I'm sure the neighbours will invite her in.'

George smiled and nodded, knowing that his ma would drag Mrs Adams round to talk.

'I bet she'll think you lot are steering me down a wrong path, rather than making a man out of me.'

'I bet your ma will think you're off somewhere stealing apples and the Sergeant chasing after you,' George said, smiling at a shared memory.

Tom laughed. It was a good laugh, deep and powerful, unexpected given the mood. The kind of laugh that made you double up, trying get your breath back. Some of the other men laughed, not wanting to be left out. It took Tom a few seconds to get his breath back and compose himself.

'You're probably right, George. I will never live that down. It's a wonder that copper didn't find me and send me off to the army anyway.'

'Probably thought they was better off without you.'

'Oi. See this stripe?' Tom said, pointing to his arm, which at the moment had nothing on it. They all laughed again.

'Come on, I want my gift!' a voice called from the back.

'Fine, fine. Don't let me stand on ceremony,' Tom said, pausing again. 'Not like I was trying to do something nice for you.'

'Give it 'ere!' Arthur shouted, grabbing the parcel out of Tom's hand. The grab encouraged the others to go for their own, growing disappointed when a parcel didn't have their name on the front, before moving onto the next.

'Order, order!' Tom shouted, laughing along with everyone else. 'I'll hand them out.' He picked a letter out of Fred's hand, which made the young soldier look disappointed.

'This one's for you, Bert,' he said. 'And this one for you.' Picking up another and another, passing them to the correct recipient. George waited. After a couple of minutes, most of the men were sitting back against the walls of the hut opening their parcels, or letters from home.

Tom joined George who was sitting against the outer wall of the hut, from where he had been watching proceedings. The wall was cold against George's back, but it distracted him from the chill throughout the rest of his body. Something about it was unusually cosy. It reminded him of sitting by the fire at home, where he would have to sit on the floor in order to get anywhere near its meagre heat. Catherine would always sit on the floor next to him, as their parents took up the chairs and the other two squeezed in where they could. He missed his sister, they had always been the closest. Home felt like a long, long way away, but at least he had Tom.

Tom handed him a small packet, wrapped in brown paper.

'Thought I'd forgotten you, did you?' he said, all charm.

'No, not you.'

Tom's face was a patchwork of confused happiness. He shrugged and carried on unwrapping what Mrs Adams had sent him.

'I didn't think they would send me anything,' said George. 'Not that I really thought they would forget.'

'Of course they wouldn't forget. They love you... and they're proud of you. You're the second in command of Tom Adams' army! They should be giving you all the gifts in the world.' They both laughed. The cold wood chafed against George's back.

'That's just it. What could they afford to send?' He still held the parcel, whilst the rest of the section had ripped theirs open in excitement. He didn't want to break this moment. The moment of surprise and love that he felt. 'They don't have very much, why would they send me anything when they need everything they can get at home?'

'Who knows, George? Love can make people do strange things. Could be they knew you would be sat here brooding and thought you could do with cheering up.'

'Yes, well. I still didn't expect to get anything. They have other things to worry about.'

'Could be they miss you as much as you miss them? Have you thought about that?'

George nodded. The packet wasn't very large. Some of the other men had heavy parcels, brown paper ripped and across the floor. He unfolded his parcel, starting at one end and carefully folding it back. One piece at a time. Tom scoffed, but he carried on opening the packet in his own way. When the brown paper was undone, he folded it into one flat piece, and lay it on the floor next to him. He then placed the parcel on his lap. This was how he had unwrapped any present he had ever been given. He didn't want to rush. He took care because he wanted to prolong the moment. Taking longer to unwrap it made the experience even more special, more mystical, despite knowing who it was from.

Inside was a simple card container. The front was open. A couple of small white envelopes, addressed to him in the same way as the parcel, lay on top. The first envelope was written in his mother's handwriting: the practised, curvy script that was at times difficult to read. He put it on one knee. The second envelope was written in his brother's handwriting, the clear joined-up letters of a man who wrote professionally, simply addressed to 'George'. He put the second envelope into his coat pocket without looking at it.

Next was a metal tin. It was plain white with black script that spelled out the words 'Fry's Chocolate'. He smiled. His ma had remembered his love for chocolate. He didn't know how they had afforded it.

'Open it then,' Tom said, leaning closer over his shoulder.

George lifted the lid. On the inside of the tin was a postcard. The picture showed a ghostly bearded man, dressed in white robes, passing a tray of gleaming chocolate to a young man dressed in full khaki. On the back was a short message. *'To George, From Fry's Chocolate to the King's forces, with lots of love from your mother.'*

George ripped the foil this time and, breaking off a piece, gave it first to Tom.

'Thanks, pal.'

This time he went back to the letter from his mother, putting the tin of chocolate in his breast pocket, complete with the postcard. He would keep it close to his heart. The letter was written on several pieces of simple white paper. His ma loved to write and every time it went on and on, a stream of thought on the page. His brother had inherited that from her.

She wrote about simple home matters, what was happening on the street, what the neighbours were doing. He skipped most of it, it made him think of home too much. His father was as he always was. Catherine was trying to find work, and Elisabeth, in the way of six-year-olds, had fallen in love with a sixteen-year-old boy at the local church and wouldn't stop following him around. Joe and their father still weren't talking much.

George's father, she said, would not stop talking about George being in the army. She said all this and more. It was as if his mother had not known what to say, and so had run from one idea to the next. She could not believe that it had been so long since they had seen him. Almost four months, that had gone so quickly. They all missed him very much.

It was all too much for George. It had been bad enough before, but the letter brought memories of home. He tried his best to stifle a tear that rolled down his cheek by running his sleeve across his face. Whether through ignorance or through kindness, Tom didn't say anything. George folded up the letter, noticing the blotches where his tears had stained the page and put it in his pocket with the rest. There was a subdued silence around the rest of the hut now, as the other men treasured their gifts and read letters. Some of them looked warmer than they had done before, but George just felt cold. He decided then that he would start writing home, but what would he say?

At that moment the door at the end of the hut slammed open. The Sergeant stormed in. Everyone dropped what they were doing and stood, but they were too slow. Campbell bawled at them. 'What are you doing in here? Get those lights out! It's bedtime.' With a flourish he blew out the biggest candle and was gone, leaving them in the darkness.

There were a few whispers of ''Night, lad' while everyone scrambled for their beds. Reveille would be at five o'clock, even if it was Christmas Day. After that they would begin their usual four-mile march.

Christmas of 1914 was over.

1915

Chapter 18

He didn't come by Lime Street much, but when he did Joe loved the show of everything going about its business. It was busy by the station, with freight always coming and going. Sometimes he would just sit and watch. Today, though, he was meeting Anne, who had finally agreed to go to the picture house. She had suggested they go and see a new film that was being shown, and he had barely let her finish the sentence before saying yes. He hadn't even asked which film it was.

He was worried that his fondness of her had been too obvious. After all, she was a very astute and intelligent woman. It was one of the reasons he liked her. In their short time working together he couldn't get enough of her warm, endearing smile. He felt he could tell her anything. She would regard him with those fathomless eyes and then say something with conviction, something he hadn't been expecting, but something that made perfect sense.

Perhaps, he was getting carried away with Anne; not only was she intelligent, she was very modern, and was working towards a career. What if she only saw Joe as a friend? Could a man and a woman spend time together as simply friends? The world was changing, but he wasn't sure it was yet ready for that.

Joe had to grudgingly admit that the war was having some

positive influence at home. That women were now being allowed to work jobs traditionally considered suitable only for men was a good thing. Anne may just think of them as two friends that could spend time together enjoying the same things, but he hoped he was wrong.

He had suggested they meet inside Lime Street Station, as it had been the first place they had met, in a roundabout sort of way. She had laughed when he'd made the suggestion, and again it made him unsure. A steam engine blew its whistle as it departed, amongst a cloud of smoke. Joe looked up at the big clock face that hung above the concourse. As usual he was early, Anne wasn't due for twenty minutes. He decided to go for a walk, it would help calm his nerves.

He dodged through the traffic to cross the road and passed down the side of St George's Hall, built in a Greek style with white columns around its perimeter. It stood above Lime Street and St John's Gardens lay behind the hall. It was a small park surrounded by a stone wall and acted like the garden to St George's Hall as if it were a stately home.

Joe sat on one of the benches next to a flower bed. His father used to bring him and George here all the time when they were younger. The girls would come too sometimes. He would let them run and play in the gardens. Afterwards he would stop them and tell them of the memorial, its stone-grey facade towering over both young boys. Britannia stood on top, judging if they were worthy of inheriting the empire. Their father would sometimes tell stories of his time at war, but only when he was in the mood. Other times he would tell them to have pride in anything they did. The King's Liverpool regiment had fought for the country and had given everything so that the young, like them, would grow up in a free world.

George would ask question after question. Questions that their father would only answer if he was in a good mood. Those times he would laugh and talk of the heroism of the soldiers, other times his expression would grow dark and moody, and, picking George up in his arms, he would leave the park with Joe following behind.

Those stories had made Joe resent war. He had never felt that sense of martial fervour. The memorial was cold and forbidding and even as a child he couldn't understand why men should die for anything. It was so senseless. He also despised the look that came over his father's face. He hated seeing the darkness in his eyes. A look of remembering past horrors, of repressed nightmares. George had been too young to notice, but Joe had seen every tic of emotion and every cold bead of sweat that ran down his father's cheek. He had been haunted by sympathetic nightmares ever since. His father had too much pride to say anything to him, but Joe could imagine what he had been through. Joe's father thought that he had fallen too far from the tree. Their difference in personality had always been a barrier between them, while George had only ever wanted to make their father proud.

He met Anne in the station a few minutes later. He was puffed out from rushing to make sure he got back on time.

'Joe, are you all right?' she asked as he drew near.

'I, er, sorry I'm late,' he said, struggling to get the words out.

She wore a long black woollen coat, loosely covering a pale blue dress. The same dress, he suspected, that she had worn the first time he caught a glimpse of her. Her jet black hair was done up in curls that fell around her shoulders. She looked beautiful, so beautiful he was lost for words. He wore the same waistcoat and trousers he often wore for work and felt underdressed.

'You look beautiful,' he said at long last.

'Thank you.' She smiled at him, and turned from side to side showing herself off. 'I scrub up all right, I think. You look... you look like you're about to go to work.' She laughed, indicating that she was teasing.

'I'm sorry, I didn't think'

'Oh no, you look fine. You really should stop apologising.'

'I'm sor—'

He caught himself and they both laughed again.

'It suits you, really. I was just looking for an excuse to wear this. I don't get to very often. I can't really wear it at work, people wouldn't take me seriously. Just some middle-class girl with a dream of playing at journalist. We should get going. It starts soon.' She turned and took his arm, putting hers through his so that he had to form a crook she could hold on to. He didn't need to speak, a moment of quiet reflection to take in all of her was welcome. He liked her strength. She was confident and he liked it. Against his timidness it was welcome, and helped to bring him out of himself. It complemented her intelligence. When she smiled at him he could see all the knowledge and warmth in her eyes and he wanted nothing more than to stare into their depths.

'I've heard it's a delightful film,' she said, still smiling, enjoying the moment. 'It's called *Tillie's Punctured Romance*. Allegedly it's based on a very successful Broadway play. Isn't it amazing that we will get to see such a thing without having to step foot in New York?' She paused, gauging his reaction. 'Although it would be nice to visit someday. There's a young chap in it who's apparently kicking up quite a storm in New York. He's called Charles Chaplin, or something like that, I think.'

'You should write about it for the newspaper,' he said. Plays and films were so outside his experience, he felt he needed to say something. She laughed again, that laugh that in a few months he had come to enjoy so much. It was infectious. It made him want to laugh along with her, it didn't matter what they were laughing about. The rest of the world was a blur when she laughed.

Joe held the door of the picture house open for Anne and entered into the foyer. He was proud to be with her and, for some reason, wanted to show her off.

'Will you go and get the tickets, Joe? I need to use the lavatory.'

He nodded and let go of her arm, already feeling the loss. It was like someone had wrenched a part out of his soul. The tickets were being sold by a booth off to one side, opposite a similar booth selling confectionery. The amount of electric lighting in the foyer was incredible, he had never seen as much in one place. Oil lamps would not have had quite the same effect. The young man manning the booth handed Joe the tickets and took the money. Joe had managed to convince Mr Harlow to give him an advance on his wages. He needed it with the price of the tickets, which were simple paper stubs torn from a reel. Anne was waiting in the foyer. He loved the way she smiled as he got closer. He held the door open for her and they entered the auditorium. The light was much more muted and dim, and it took a few awkward seconds for his eyes to adjust. He daren't walk any further for fear of falling over. Once his eyes adjusted, he could see rows of seats lowering down as they approached the large screen at the far end of the room. A good number of the seats were already occupied. They pushed along a row of seats, apologising as they passed the other patrons. Joe stood on someone's foot in the gloom and apologised profusely.

'Why is it so dark in here?' he asked Anne.

'Atmosphere. Here we are.'

The seats folded down from the backrest. Comfortable rounded cushions wrapped around his body. Despite the curvature of the seat, Anne was very close to him. He could feel the warmth of her body and feel her breath as she leant over to whisper to him. 'We managed to get a good view. Well done,' she said. He could hear her smile even if he couldn't see it.

'With the size of that screen, I wouldn't think there was such a thing as a bad view.'

She chuckled softly beside him. The lights dimmed further, disappearing to darkness. There was a hum and crackle of the projector behind them. 'Here we go,' she said.

A white rectangle appeared on the screen curtain then changed to black again. It took a few more seconds for the film to start. He hadn't wanted to admit to Anne that this was his first time.

She was such a modern woman, he didn't want her to think less of him.

The main film didn't start straight away. Instead, the grainy image cycled through the projector, phantom lines and spots hovering across the screen. Eventually newspaper front pages began to appear, showing the big images and headlines of the large London papers. The *Daily Mail*, the *Daily Mirror*, the *Daily Telegraph* and various others, all explicitly condemning the actions of the 'Horrible Huns'.

Joe squirmed in his seat, trying not to get annoyed at the outrageous headlines he was seeing. They weren't new, but that didn't make him feel any better. The headlines were off-putting. There was some murmuring amongst the crowd, which only added to Joe's discomfort. Then the poster of Lord Kitchener was put up on the screen with the now familiar slogan, 'Your Country Needs You'. There was a great cheer from the audience, and Joe pushed himself further into his seat. The list of casualties flashed through his mind. He could only marvel at the number of names that he remembered. It made him feel nauseous.

Once the names had rattled through his head, he noticed that the film had started. The rest of the audience was laughing. From the rocking of the chair beside him he could feel that Anne was joining in. She lay the palm of her hand on the back of his. The little man on the screen did something silly and the actress, an older woman, looked at him, disappointed.

Joe was sweating, droplets running down his brow to build up on his cheeks where they sat, irritating him until he brushed them away. They itched and itched without end. It was as if he had turned ill in a matter of minutes. He felt his cheeks turn red. He wasn't sure if it was hot, or just his imagination. He shuffled in his seat, trying to get more comfortable and hoping to find more air, but it didn't help. He was getting angrier by the second, and he couldn't push away the mental image of the dead soldiers' names.

He had seen enough. The message at the beginning had done its work on him, but the opposite of what was intended. His body was rebelling against the easy, unwitting humility of the room and its idle viewers. Who were they to sit here and cheer for war, when they could happily sit by and watch a film without a care in the world? He wanted to be anywhere but in that room at this moment in time.

Anne sensed his discomfort and removed her hand. He shuffled more, but it didn't help. He didn't know what to do. He didn't want to leave Anne. What would she think of him? He wanted her company, but he was angry. He just wanted to be somewhere else, somewhere less charged. She leaned over and whispered, 'Have you seen this one before?'

He could see her looking at him through the dark, nervous worry etched on her face. Joe was the only person not laughing. What was wrong with them all? He tried to force a smile, but he was sure he could only manage a grimace. The sweat was back on his cheeks. 'No, I haven't,' he said. He couldn't focus on it. The war news had ruined his evening. 'I guess I'm not in the mood. I'm sorry.'

He could have lied, saying that he was fine, but she would see through it. In the darkness her brow furrowed, and she pursed her lips. He shuffled his backside on the seat again, which caused a squeak from the cheap cotton. Someone behind them shushed. Anne turned to see who, but Joe put a hand on her arm to stop her. 'It's not worth it,' he said, whispering. 'It's all my fault, I'm sorry.'

'You keep apologising, but I don't know why. What's wrong? Don't you like the film?'

'No, it's not that. I'm just can't concentrate. I guess my mind is elsewhere. Look, could we leave? I'm causing too much commotion, and you're not having a good time thanks to me. We could come back another day?'

'If you want to, I suppose we could rearrange. I wouldn't mind seeing the beginning again, I've missed most of it now.'

Joe never wanted to see the beginning again, to have to sit through the recruitment video. 'Yes, another day. You just tell me when and we'll come back. I promise I'll be more focused then. I might even laugh.' He smiled at her, and when she smiled back he relaxed a little. They worked their way back out of the crowd, awkwardly trying to see in the dark. There were a few tuts, but no one dared to speak. In the foyer, the staff looked at them in surprise. One man, presumably the manager going by the fact he was dressed in a freshly pressed suit, started in their direction. Before he could reach them, Joe ushered Anne out of the front door and onto the street. The cool air hit him and eased his nausea. The freedom helped put him at ease.

He couldn't help but notice the disappointment in Anne's eyes. She had been so excited about the film and kept looking over her shoulder back in the direction of the picture house. Not for the first time in his life he felt guilty, but he couldn't have stayed in there. It made him so sick. The recruitment film had made him think of his brother George, knee deep in the mud of France, and the claustrophobic nature of the picture house hadn't helped.

He took hold of Anne and looked her in the eyes, assertive for once. He brushed the back of his hand on the side of her soft cheek. 'I truly am sorry, Anne,' he said. 'I can't apologise enough. I didn't want to ruin a perfect evening. But I couldn't stay in there. I couldn't sit there laughing like everyone else, as if everything was perfect with the world. It just wasn't right.'

'Why not? What was wrong?' He noticed that she didn't pull back, or move away from him. Her closeness felt completely natural, and not for the first time he felt like kissing her.

'That war film, trying to recruit young men like me to fight. It's all so wrong, and the lies they print to do it. I couldn't sit there and accept it. It's not right.'

She finally pulled away, and all he felt was disappointment. 'You really are against the war, aren't you? I know you changed Barnes's article, but I didn't think you were this serious.'

'I'm a member of the No-Conscription Fellowship, Anne. Completely against the war and everything it stands for. I won't do anything to prolong it nor help to cause any more deaths to our lads, or the Germans.' He paused, expecting her to be shocked, but she just regarded him with a cool stare. 'I'd completely understand if you never want to see me again.'

'No, not at all.' His heart sunk and he almost turned away. 'What I mean is, that wouldn't make me not want to see you again. People like us need to stick together. I told you before that I admire you, and I meant it. You have strong beliefs and you stick to them. Like me, you want to make the world a better place.' She stepped closer to him again, not embracing him, but close enough that he could smell her hair, and it warmed him to his soul. 'I did so want to watch that film though.'

'I promise you, we will come back. You have my permission to drag me back if need be.'

'I will hold you to that,' she said, smiling at last. 'We had better go. People might start to gossip.' She gave him a wink and pulled him after her by the hand. As soon as he moved he bumped into something.

'Excuse me,' he said, as he let go of Anne and looked into the face of another woman, about the same age as Anne. The woman, however, was a different build to Anne; an inch or two taller and thinner of frame, whilst more gaunt around the face. She didn't look like she had forgone eating, more that she disdained the very thought of it. She was dressed in a shabby coat, and her cold eyes looked almost directly into Joe's, barely concealing a hatred that shocked him to the core. He thought he had possibly seen her around the office, but he couldn't imagine why she would hate him so, until she opened her mouth. 'This is for you,' she said, almost spitting the words at him. He looked down at her outstretched hand and in it she held a solitary white feather. He involuntarily started to reach for it but managed to stop himself.

'Coward,' she said, this time spitting in his face, and forcing the feather into his unresisting hand. She walked off at a brisk pace, before he could give her back the feather.

All he could think was where she might have got one feather from, but she must have already given out many others to men, like him, who she considered to be cowards. He reached up and wiped the spit from his face with a handkerchief that his father had given him. He wondered then whether the woman had been waiting for him. It was too much of a coincidence.

'Are you all right?' Anne asked, for not the first time that day. She put a hand on his arm and looked up into his eyes. 'Let's find somewhere where you can wash that off your face.'

'I'm all right,' he said, without meaning it. 'Although I don't think I'll ever be clean again. You know, over the years that's never happened to me. I've been bullied. I've been ridiculed. I've often been ignored, but I've never been spat on before. I'll have to be more careful I think, if this is how I'm treated when I am not outspoken.'

She moved in closer. 'Horrible woman. What was she thinking?'

'I know exactly what she was thinking. That I'm a coward. That I won't fight. Well, she's right about one thing. This war is bringing out a lot of new experiences for everyone. I wouldn't have met you without this war.' He smiled at her and crooked his arm for her to hold on to.

'Don't give up,' she said. 'Come on, let's get out of here.'

Chapter 19

The dock was like arriving at home for George. He guessed every port was similar, from the sounds of industry, to the smell of salt water, and the hard-worked look of the people. The thing that gave up the illusion was the accents. There was not a single Liverpudlian accent to be heard.

A group of men were manhandling crates from a ship onto a cart, and it reminded him why he'd signed up in the first place. Tom smiled, but didn't say anything. He knew exactly what George was thinking.

'Come on, lads,' he called over his shoulder and walked off.

A ship was waiting for them at the end of the dock, the white paint of its hull peeling back and revealing the bare metal framework underneath. It looked sick, the peeling paint like a rash on its skin. On the stern its name was painted: SS *City of Edinburgh*.

'She looks like she's got character at least, eh, George?' Tom said, grinning with enthusiasm. He had always liked ships, it was what had drawn him to work on the docks. George shook his head, not liking where this was going. 'Come on, let's see what the old dear has got for us.' Tom urged George forward. He had taken to his new rank without effort.

They walked up the gangway as they had done so many times

before. Many other soldiers were piling onboard, while the officers yelled at them to use every available space. There was straw all over the floor, which stuck together in globules of brownish, yellow muck. The stench of shit was everywhere and the men shied away trying to find a less fragrant part of the ship. George tried not to gag. Cleaning the ship had just involved moving the excrement around the deck. 'I'm not sure how long I can take this, Tom.'

'What? Don't tell me you've never been to a farm before?' He was still acting the officer. 'Jolly good show! Just pretend you're on a day trip, dear fellow.' He grinned his effusive grin and burst out laughing. George tried to glare at him but ended up exploding in a roar of laughter himself. The others looked over to see what they were laughing about.

'The likes of us do not turn our noses up at shit, George.' Tom pulled out a cigarette from his webbing and handed it to George. 'Here, this will help with the smell. It'll also calm your nerves. Go on, lad.' George had never smoked before, but now was as good a time as any. They were leaving the country for the first time, and he suspected today would be a day of firsts. He accepted the light from Tom as the match crackled and threatened to go out in the coastal breeze, then took a large drag. It burnt and he felt like his throat was going to close. Resisting the urge to let the smoke out only made things worse. As it reached his lungs he burst and blew the smoke in Tom's face. He felt like he was on fire. Tom laughed and patted him on the back as if he was helping to dislodge a tricky piece of food.

'Don't worry, it gets better after the first one,' he said.

They both tried to find somewhere to sit for the journey, so they weren't pressed up against everyone else. As the ship weighed anchor, steam bellowed from its funnels and mingled with the stench of excrement, forming an even more unpleasant smell. The passengers lurched with the ship as it began its journey, grabbing on to each other to steady themselves. George threw himself down on a steel cross section, opting to sit before he fell over. The swaying of the ship was already intense and it unsettled his stomach. He took another drag on the cigarette, feeling much better with each pull.

'What a fine cabin we've found for ourselves, George,' Tom said, sitting next to him. For once he wasn't grinning at George and stared ahead at the other soldiers. Rain started to fall and pooled between the railings. The deck resembled a straw-covered marsh. Another soldier pushed through the crowd to lean against the bulwark. He threw up over the rail, his body wracked in a violent spasm. No one moved to help the man. As he threw up over the side again, George put a hand on the man's shoulder.

'Are you all right, lad?' he said.

'Yes, I'll be fine. Never been on a ship before.' Despite the rain, the man wiped the spittle of his lips with the back of his sleeve. 'Thanks, though,' the man said, looking up at George. It was only then that George recognised him.

'No problem, Fred. I didn't recognise you in the rain.' He took his hand off Fred's back. 'I'd hardly call this a ship. More like a rust bucket.'

'Aye that's true, but she's got character all right.' Tom had joined them at the bulwark, still smoking despite the rain. He offered George and Fred a cigarette and they smoked together.

'I've never been on a boat at sea either,' George admitted.

'I thought you were both dock hands?' Fred was shocked, but then he already looked as pale as a man could.

'Oh, been on a boat, yes. But they were always moored up safe and sound. They were never like this. Never covered in shit neither.'

'How long do you think this will take?' Fred asked, keeping a hand near his mouth in some poor attempt to stem the need to throw up.

'You've got me,' Tom said. 'The way we've been going, it could be days. I don't know about you, but I'm bloody sick of all this

175

travelling. I just wish they'd sent us straight out there. Knowing our luck, we'll probably get there and be sent to some other bloody part of the country as far away from the front line as possible.'

Every word was interrupted by the swell of the water as the boat rose and fell, and Tom had to force it all out. The fact that he had begun swearing, like the Lance-Sergeant, wasn't lost on George. It seemed that it was the way most soldiers talked. He wanted to get off this boat as soon as possible, and if he could vocalise that, he would swear his head off too. At least the endless trains had been comfortable. He may have complained, but now he wished that he was back on a train, and not on this stinking, rusting boat. He wasn't even sure it would make it to France, as it crested a wave and fell forward, causing the confined soldiers to fall into one another. The seamen ran around checking parts of the ship and keeping observation over the waters. Every few minutes a crew member eyed the water with a frown. George had heard there were U-boats operating in the area, and they couldn't be too careful. A cruiser sped past them, on its way out to patrol the Channel and their ship rocked from side to side in its wake. George wasn't sure how much more of this he could take.

*

The ship was finally pulling into a harbour. They were in France. It had been a long time coming, almost seven months since they had signed up. They had been through a lot together already, but they had yet to fight. The war had reached a critical stage and the reservists were being moved to the front.

They were lucky, George thought. Some of the men he had spoken to before leaving Blighty were being shipped out to Turkey. They were going out there to fight the Ottomans, an altogether different war. He had signed up to stop the Germans rampaging through Europe, and he didn't fancy the heat of the desert. It was hot enough for him pressed together with other men in a ship on the channel.

As they sailed closer to the dock he could hear what he thought was the sound of thunder in the distance. The sky was clear and, apart from a slight gust of wind every now and then, the weather was quite calm. The closer they got the more obvious the sound became. Over the wind the dull crump of artillery was booming across the landscape and reflecting off the buildings that ran along the coastline. It was a rolling sound that didn't so much bang as provide a background din to the world. The workers on the dock didn't seem to notice the sound and George and the other soldiers disembarked. They just went about their work with their heads down. They didn't even acknowledge the soldiers.

It took George a few moments to get his land legs back; he rocked as his boots touched the firm surface and almost pitched over. A worker put out an arm to steady him. When George turned to thank him, he didn't meet his eye.

'Come on, George,' Tom said as he walked past.

They picked their kit up from the heap that had been loaded onto the dock and walked off after the rest of their section. As they walked away from the dock the smell of fish faded and was replaced with an overbearing scent of sweat and iron. The road ran off into the distance, and they didn't know where they were going. A sea of khaki moved in front of them and so they followed.

There were plenty of other people moving along the side of the road: some men carrying stretchers and others lying, groaning in the gutter. There were doctors, rushing about in bloodstained overalls, which were already turning from red to brown. They eyed the new men with an odd stare, somewhere between concern and suspicion. There were also nurses, but they were too busy to even notice them.

One of the men shouted at George and Tom as they passed.

'Good luck with the Boche, lads!' he said, his voice a hoarse growl. He was sat against a tree, one leg a bandaged stump and a bloody welt on the side of his face. He smiled a crooked smile at them as they waved. 'Give 'em hell!'

'Boche?' George asked Tom, who shrugged.

'It's French for the Germans,' one of the men in their section added.

'This lot must have been hit hard, Tom,' George said, looking around him at the carnage. He swallowed hard, feeling the bile rise in his throat. Some of the bodies were unmoving, others just groaned and groaned where they lay. There was one body that was frosting in the cold February air. How could that Tommy be so happy to see them when he was surrounded by this?

'Wrong place, wrong time, no doubt, George.' Tom looked like he was going to be sick, but he swallowed and colour returned to his face. 'I guess this is why we're here. This lot are going back to Blighty for treatment and they need us to hold the line for them until they come back.'

'We must have missed a big German offensive,' George agreed.

'Aye, the bastards have been putting up a big fight the last few months. Don't worry though, George. It'll all be all right now. "Tom Adams' Army" is here! We'll show them what for.'

He grinned his grin and it was at complete contrast to their surroundings, but George couldn't help but smile with him. They had been trying to get out to France for months, and now they were here. They had their work cut out for them, but it wasn't before time. The injured men by the roadside just affirmed George's decision to sign up. He would fight for them and he would fight for everyone still at home. He would fight because his dad couldn't and because his brother wouldn't.

*

Across the dock, their officers were waiting for them. The Captain and his adjutant were stood to attention and each of the private soldiers saluted as they came within distance, George and Tom amongst them. Some of the men were still pale from the voyage across the Channel, and George was sure that there were little globules of vomit on his battledress. He would have to make sure he didn't get close enough to an officer that they would notice and put him on a charge, but surely they would forgive him that? It had been a hellish journey. He had worked amongst boats for years, but never appreciated what sailing on one was like – and he had only sailed across the Channel. Some sailors were at sea for months.

He hoped that they would get somewhere soon where he could sit down and settle his stomach with a bite to eat and, most importantly, a drink. Despite having been out at sea, his throat was dry as a bone. But he couldn't wait to get the wetness of the sea out of his uniform. The air had been damp in the sea mist and his clothes had stuck to his body, chafing every time he moved.

The Captain gave them a small speech welcoming them to France and then he formed them up into fours. It seemed that they would be marching to the front. Even though they could hear the sounds of guns nearby, and some of the men around him flinched at every bang, the front must have been miles from where they were. George wasn't looking forward to the long slog. He remembered poring over the maps back home and the place that the British Army had managed to staunch the German tide was some distance from Le Havre.

They walked off, already weary despite not having moved far. George wasn't the only one who hadn't enjoyed the experience aboard the SS *City of Edinburgh*. Some of the other men from his company were dead on their feet, ready for bed. They would have to will themselves on, otherwise they would never reach anywhere to rest and would only get punished. It was this thought that pushed him on, despite the burning in his muscles and the chafing of his uniform.

After a few miles they stopped and the Captain pulled them

over to the side of the road so that some artillery could pass. They were just outside what once must have been a village. Farmhouses decorated the landscape, more pieces of masonry missing as they got closer to the front. Here, the artillery had grown from a background din, to a rumble, to now being on the verge of making the head swim. George had never heard so much noise. A few French villagers peered out of their houses at the stationary soldiers, then went back inside, shaking their heads. They wanted nothing more to do with this war. This wasn't a place where they would stop long, there was nowhere here to billet and every soldier that could be seen was moving quick step away. It was a miserable place.

There were less wounded men here, moving along the road in the search of safety. As they got closer to the front they saw more wounded landscape instead.

The artillery carriages reminded George of the horse carts at home, but instead of the carts with flat beds the horses were all attached to a limber that carried a heavy gun behind them. One horse slipped in the thick, cloying mud that caked the road and pulled the limber with it, the other horses in its wake. The artilleryman cursed and ran around the limber trying to right the horse.

The officers were nowhere to be seen to ask for orders, so George grabbed Tom and Fred's arms and pulled them after him, running over to the limber. Without saying a word, they put their shoulders to the limber and pushed, while the artillery man calmed the horse. The mud was cloying and thick, and made every footstep hard work, pulling at their muscles. The boys pushed and the limber pushed back. Fred cried out as his hands slipped on the wet surface and his body dropped. He landed face first in the mud and scrambled around until he found some purchase. The mud threatened to pull him down again, but he managed to get free and stood up, covered head to toe in brown muck. George looked away, trying to resist the urge to laugh, and put more force into the pushing.

Eventually, after more pushing and shoving, the sweat pouring down George's face despite the coldness of the day, they got the gun limber back on the road. The horses were distressed and whinnied at the artillery crew. It took them more time still to get them moving.

'I needed that rest,' Tom said wryly, leaning against a fence by the side of the road. The artillery had moved on and the NCOs had told the men to rest up while they waited for the officers to come back. Rain poured down in droves, making the mud turn into a thick bog.

'Right then, lads. Gather round, gather round,' the Captain said as he got back and stood on a slight incline to the side of the road. His adjutant, next to him, frowned. The hill was the only bit of green still left in the mud-drenched, boggy landscape, and George suspected that the Captain was not inclined to stand anywhere else, the height advantage was a coincidence. George couldn't help but compare the Captain to the old dock master, standing in front of the crowds and giving them their orders from up on high. He was a good man, the Captain, but he wasn't what George would call a rousing speaker.

'Right, now that I've got all of your attention,' he called out, before being interrupted by some movement from the men. 'Steady there, at the back.'

George saw Campbell push his way to the back of the assembled men, anger etched on his face, but he couldn't see what the problem was. The Captain continued regardless.

'Now, lads. We've some work to do all right. The top brass think that you're ready for it and so do I.'

A cheer went up from some of the men, but the rain still poured down on the rest. They'd been ready for almost six months already, George thought.

'We're to move up the line immediately and relieve some of our boys that need a bit of a break. It'll be the first bit of action for some of you, and I want you to make us proud. Let's show the rest of the army what the King's regiment can do.' With that final sentence, he climbed down off the hill with the help of his adjutant and the men went to find their sections.

Campbell pushed back through the crowd to the head of their section, rubbing his hands together, and with a smile on his usually dour face.

'That'll show them,' he mumbled half to himself and half to George.

They formed into fours without a word from the Lance-Sergeant and he looked on, smug and satisfied. His training had worked on them. There was no need for him to stand on an incline, his presence and voice easily carried across the section, and there were far less of them by now.

'Look, you horrible lot,' he said, by way of getting their attention. By now they were used to his manner. 'We've still got to get to the bloody front, see? So we're gonna march along this 'ere road, and then find our way on another bloody train.'

There was a distinct murmur and grumbling from the men, including George.

'Quiet, you bloody ingrates. You can march all the way there if you want, but you'll be too bloody tired to fight well, see? And I can't be having that. Form out!'

He barked the last command, and the men were quick to react, not wanting to be the last in line and receive a biting tirade from the Lance-Sergeant. At the next village along they found the train which they would be travelling on. It was nothing compared to the trains at home. George wondered that it could be called a train at all. Each carriage was made of sodden, wooden planking that was rotting and moulding in places. There was no platform for them to gain access to the carriages, so they had to climb their way up the side, putting one foot on the undercarriage and lifting the other leg up like climbing over a fence. The men already on the train helped the others up one by one.

The inside was covered with straw like a barn. It had been

used to convey cattle, before the army needed it. The corners smelt of urine, and there was a small metal bucket to one side. George didn't dare inspect it.

There were no seats for them to sit on, so the men had to sit on the floor. Those that got there first put their backs against the side of the carriage wall with their legs outstretched. The others had to sit, crouch, or lie where they could find space, and space was hard to come by once they were all crammed into the carriage. Once again there was no sign of the officers. George very much doubted that the Captain would travel in these conditions. He no doubt had a more lavish carriage to himself further up the train, or even a car in which to travel in comfort. With a lurch the train set off, smoke billowing down the side of the carriages and coming inside through the cracks and poor joins in the wood. Some of the men coughed, others fell over on top of each other with the sudden shift in momentum. George didn't think he would ever long for the boat that had brought them over here, but at least it was open to the air.

Once the train gained some momentum, the smoke drifted off and they were left with the rotten stench of the carriage again. Regardless, George breathed a deep breath, savouring the air.

Where they were going was anyone's guess, but the journey wasn't going to be an enjoyable one. George had seen just about enough of trains for one lifetime.

Chapter 20

George ducked underneath a piece of wooden lintel that ran across the entrance to the communication trench and stepped down into the mud. In the trenches, the soldiers were always ducking and crouching, trying to keep as low as possible. Standing up straight would give a German sniper the perfect opportunity to put a bullet through your skull, the soft cap scant protection. George's boots squelched, mud covering his puttees. The smell hit him immediately. It was like the smell of fresh, wet sand at the beach, as he remembered the beaches of New Brighton, but mixed with something else. Something that smelt like the rusting iron ships the he worked with on the docks. The smell permeated everything, filling the nostrils with rotting metal.

It very much reminded him of the smell of hospitals. He had been to one in Liverpool a couple of times when he was younger. He had escorted his father through the whitewashed walls, and the smell of blood and death had never left him. He had hated hospitals ever since.

He couldn't tell if the smell in the trench was from the abused, rusting ironwork, or if it was from the casualties this section had suffered.

They were going in to relieve one of the Irish divisions that had come in before them. He hadn't known what to expect when he ducked into their trench, but the soldiers were the same as the thousands he had seen so far. Only their regimental cab badges and their accents singled them out as any different.

'Ooh. Fresh fish,' the Irish soldier said at George's approach. When he spoke, it reminded George of Patrick. George wondered where his friend was; was he in France or still at home?

'We're here to relieve you, lad,' Tom said over his shoulder.

'That's all well and good, son, but we have to wait for the say so before we up and leave.'

The soldier was a Sergeant going by his stripes and he outranked both George and Tom. He moved along the trench in a crouch, careful to stay on the duckboards that kept the water in the bottom. He outstretched an arm and shook George's hand, then Tom's.

'Sergeant O'Connor,' he said. 'Most just call me Paddy. Welcome to Park Lane.'

He laughed and pointed up at a sign that hung on the entrance to the trench, which someone had painted the words 'Park Lane' on in lazy handwriting.

'One of the London lads here before us got a bit homesick. We thought it'd be poor luck to take it down. Damned if I've ever seen London, mind.'

George and Tom introduced themselves and the Sergeant led them back along the trench to where the others were sitting.

'Not that I'd mind getting out of here as quick as possible, the lice are killing me, but orders is orders and I've gotta wait for orders from the Captain before he says we can move out. Even if you have come to relieve us, like you say.'

'We have,' Tom insisted.

'Fair do. But we'll just stick around and introduce you to your new home for now if you don't mind?'

He handed them both a metal mug with a liquid in it that had been brewing in a larger tin above a stove. It smelled like coffee, but George could only just make it out over the smell of mud. The mug was nice and warm in his hands in the cold, and he just held it rather than drinking. The steam rose up around his head, warming his face and he breathed it in. It was a reassuring smell, comforting, but it had a slight tinge of petrol to it, a tangy metallic smell. The trench was a world of different smells, George mused. They would all take some getting used to, but the boys here seemed to take no notice as they poured more water from a petrol can into their stove and handed mugs around to the newcomers.

Rain fell around them and pinged off the corrugated metal sheets that lined the dugout. It hadn't let up for hours, and George wasn't sure he had ever seen so much rain. At times the Mersey would fill up and threaten to burst over the banks, but eventually it would subside. Here was only rain, and he had no idea where it would all go. The bottom of the trench was almost like a bog, a marshy, muddy mess that coated his khaki and stuck to his boots. The smell of damp only heightened the other smells.

He raised his eyes to the sky and the rain hit his face. He hoped it would end soon.

He reached around in his webbing and pulled out a sheet of writing paper and a small pencil. He stretched it out over a small earth ledge in the trench, careful to make sure that the surface wasn't wet. Small drops of water landed on the edge of the paper, but he couldn't prevent that. He was careful to wipe it away before it obscured the words he was writing. At first he didn't know what to say, but soon the words started to flow like the Mersey when the tide was rushing out. He tried to get everything they had been up to since he had last written home onto the piece of paper, but ran out of room. He had to keep it concise, the officers would censor most of it anyway.

When he was done, he folded the piece of paper and put it in his breast pocket next to the letter he had written to be sent home should he be killed. He would give it to the post master as soon as he got a chance.

He went back to the small dugout in his trench that they had put aside for sleeping and sat silently, gazing out over the trench, waiting for the inevitable German attack. He wasn't officially on duty, Tom was already snoring away next to him, but it took him some time to fall asleep.

*

George was woken by an itch on the end of his nose. Half asleep, and suspecting that a piece of his clothing had fallen on his face, he tried to slap it aside with a lazy hand. He jumped as his hand touched a firm, furry shape. His eyes hadn't quite adjusted and in the darkness he couldn't make out what it had been, until the shape moved again, and made a slight shuffling sound. The rat then ran across his legs not caring that he was there.

'Ugh!' He jumped up again, shouting.

The sound raised Tom who was asleep next to him in the recesses cut in the trench that the soldiers used for sleeping. He lazily came to, but the other men of their section were awake and alert straight away.

'What is it?' one of them shouted.

More rats sniffed around in the trench, hunting for food. Some of them were as big as cats, and possibly a lot more vicious. They hunted around in the meagre planks that they used for duckboard and disappeared into the bog at the bottom of the trench where wood was scarce. George felt embarrassed at shouting out.

'Just a rat, go back to sleep,' he said calmly to the other men, who looked at him with disdain. He could just about make out Tom's faint chuckling beside him, before he started snoring again.

Going by the light they still had a few hours until they were on duty, so George decided to try and sleep again. He lay there with the sound of the rats growing louder in his imagination. He daren't open his eyes for fear of what he might see, and every movement in the trench made him flinch. He hoped they would find something to eat and leave him alone.

*

The sound was harrowing. The artillery dirge on their arrival to France had been nothing short of terrifying, but this was worse. Much, much worse. They had grown used to the sound of artillery in their short time in the trench, but it had never been as loud as this. It sounded like every gun in France was firing, and firing in their direction. All hell had broken loose, and it brought to mind the description of the apocalypse that had been read out from the Bible, or at least what George imagined it would be like.

Before the assault every gun had been put into service to soften up the Germans and to cut through the wires that kept them from assaulting the enemy trenches. The army high command were determined to throw everything they had. This time the Germans were firing at them. The rifles, along with the rest of their brigade, had relieved the thirteenth brigade on the hill designated Hill 60, just south of Ypres. It was the first major engagement that George had been part of, but he felt like he had been preparing for it for months. The German counter-attacks had been fierce, but they had managed to fight them off time after time. But still the Germans kept firing and firing, determined to push the British back out from Hill 60 – but they had managed to hold so far.

Mud flew up and scattered around no man's land with each explosion, and with the rain, the site of the opposing trenches was heavily obscured from George. He couldn't see anything but the sheet of rain and muddy explosions.

The thing that was most surprising to George was that not only could they hear the shells flying overhead, but often they could be seen too, a silver blur in the sky. The bigger ones travelled slowly through the air, labouring until they lost altitude and landed on something in an explosion of brown mud and blood. Everything he had heard about the artillery on the way to the front had been true, but the reality was much more than his imagination could have come up with. The different types of shells made different sounds, and the more experienced soldiers could tell you which one was coming, and which way to run. George couldn't yet tell them apart.

Two machine gun pits in front of them fired, the guns seeming to chuckle in the dark, and spit hard rounds at the British troops. Men dropped as the guns strafed back and forth, only stopping to reload and then continuing the ceaseless attack. The Germans knew this ground well, they understood its strategic importance, with its views over the surrounding area, and they had brought all their available strength to this section.

George stole a glance along the horizon, careful to keep his head as low as possible. For miles around, the same sporadic light danced, showing the barrage that was taking place across northern France. The French forces to the south were being bombarded by their German counterparts, but the British were being hammered in their own sections. He couldn't imagine there being much ammunition left after this, but since he had got to France he hadn't known the artillery to run out. As far as he could tell they only stopped when they slept.

The Germans were coming at them up the hill, firing trench mortars to try and get at the British defensive position. They were forcing the Tommies to keep their heads low, but George and the others knew the need to fight back; they couldn't let them get near their trenches, or all would be lost.

He could see them through the smoke from the cordite, spiked caps glinting in the afternoon sun. They wouldn't attack in a desperate charge, but would use explosives to disorientate the defenders, then try to work their way up the hill, using the wreckage of the land as cover. It was fairly effective, but so far no German soldier had managed to make his way inside the British trench.

George leaned his rifle on the sandbag at the top of the firing step and sighted along it. With his eye closed he could move the rifle round searching for targets. A Lewis gun chattered intermittently along the trench from George's position, forcing the Germans to attempt to flank them.

George saw one German soldier get up from behind a barricade and run to his left in a crouch. He squeezed the trigger of his Lee Enfield and felt it kick against his shoulder, its crack a familiar sound in his ear. The shape of the German soldier lurched and disappeared from view, but George had no idea if he had hit him or had merely caused him to duck. The smoke that clung to the ground obscured anybody from view. One of the most frustrating things was not being able to clearly see your enemy. Before Hill 60, he had spent most of his time in the trench under threat of bombardment and snipers, waiting for the Germans to attack, but never seeing a single enemy soldier. The entire war seemed to be a stalemate. The front line fluctuated, but no ground was ever gained. They had done well to keep Hill 60 so far, but how long would it last?

The machine gun barked out again as more Germans tried assaulting up the incline. One of them stopped to throw a bomb towards the British trench. George leaned into the firing step again and squeezed the trigger. This time he saw a stream of red from his victim as he fell from view. A few seconds later an explosion rocked the place where he had fallen, obscuring the body from sight.

George thought it odd that he didn't feel anything about having shot the man. As far as George was concerned, he would have done the same had the situation been reversed. In the long downtimes he had often thought about how he would feel when it came to firing his weapon in anger. He had thought he would feel some disgust, but thanks to the heavy drilling the firing mechanism had become almost second nature to him. He could fire very quickly if needed.

He fired off two more rounds and his rifle cracked, causing the Germans below to duck. It was almost as if he was detached from the moment by distance. The German figures in the distance at the bottom of the hill weren't human, they were only his enemies.

There was a cry of pain beside him, and a thud as a body fell backwards. George didn't see who. He fired his last round and ducked to reload. Another soldier was crouching down with the prone figure in the gloom. 'It's a mess, lad. Someone help!' he shouted to George.

'Who's that?' George asked, jumping down from the fire step to help.

'Barnes,' he said. 'Someone help.'

George crouched down and the dark shape in front of him resolved into the prone form of Albert Barnes. He gave out a wet gurgling sound as his hands clutched his neck. The bullet had pierced an artery and he was trying to stem his own bleeding. His cap had fallen backwards into the mud and his eyes were bulging out of their sockets. Barnes stared back at George, a look of pleading in his eyes.

'Oh God.' A man behind George started muttering. 'Oh God.' He kept repeating the same words, insensible.

There was nothing that George could do. He kneeled, trying to get a better view of the wound, but bright red, arterial blood seeped out between Barnes's fingers. It ran down and mixed with the mud underneath the hastily erected duckboards.

George put his hand under Barnes's head, trying to support him. 'Stretcher,' he shouted, but no one moved. He shouted again, and finally heard the sound of running feet crunching away on duckboards. George didn't know Barnes well, only that he worked at the newspaper with his brother Joe. At least, he had before the war.

Barnes's eyes were boring into George's, as he tried to pull in lungfuls of air, eliciting a gurgle. He tried to say something, 'pain', or 'pay', George couldn't say for sure.

'Stay with me, Albert, we're getting help. Don't try to talk. Easy now.'

Barnes started thrashing and coughing. Specks of blood splattered over both his and George's uniforms as he begun to choke on his own blood. George knew that trying to clear the airway wouldn't help and calling for a medic was futile; by the time any medic arrived Barnes would be dead. So he did his best to calm the dying man, shushing him and talking to him as he grew weak and the light passed out of his eyes.

Until Barnes lay still, dead.

'Fucking hell.'

Tom leant over George at the dead private. Tom's face was white with shock and his characteristic grin was nowhere to be seen. George had no words for him and leaned back on his haunches in defeat. He put his hands to his face to cover his eyes, and realised they were covered in blood, which was already going brown. He was suddenly very tired, and he wanted to screw his eyes shut and close out the world. Other men were dying around him, but he didn't want to know. He didn't want to see it anymore. He screwed his eyes shut, but all he could see was the pleading look that the private had given him before he had died. He would picture it vividly for quite some time, and now he was scared to have his eyes shut at all.

'You there, Private.' The shout wrenched George's eyes open to see the Sergeant storming down the trench. 'What do you think this is, a bloody church? Stop praying and get up on your fucking firing step, Private. There's half of bloody Germany out there storming up that hill!'

George grabbed his rifle and jumped up, still careful not to put his head too far above the trench line. Now that the private had been killed he knew there was a sniper or marksman out there.

The Sergeant wasn't wrong, there were more Germans out there now, and they had managed to work their way further up the hill by another few metres. It was hard work, and they were being cautious, but they were making up ground. However, the more of them that pushed up the hill, the easier targets they became.

George pushed the bolt of his rifle forward and down and fired off two rounds in succession. The first winged an enemy soldier, causing him to dive for cover. The second caught another in the chest.

The Germans couldn't be allowed to gain a foothold on the hill, their orders had been quite clear: hold Hill 60 at all costs. The British had been desperate to move the line forward to this vantage point, and it was the first bit of ground they had gained in months. The 15th Battalion were the only men stopping it from falling back into enemy hands.

George also thought about the fact that if they didn't manage to hold on to the position, then he and Tom could lose their lives as the Germans invaded their newly worked trench. To him, that was far more important than some hill he had never heard of before.

But there were too many of them. Field-grey uniforms covered over half of Hill 60. Every now and then, they stopped on their charge to fire their rifles in the direction of the trench, trying to keep the defender's head down. The sounds of rounds cracking and thudding into their targets filled the senses. The Germans were eerily quiet as they advanced. And it was working. More and more men fell, crying out in shock and pain.

George kept firing his rifle, keeping up a steady stream of rounds as he had been taught, only stopping to reload the weapon after every few rounds. It was more efficient than packing the weapon full, which could cause it to jam. It was amazing how much he had learnt about soldiering in such a small time, but he still had so much more to learn. It was too frantic to see what

Tom was up to, but he could hear the crack of his rifle alongside him. Rounds whistled through the air around them in reply, and George heard one or two whip past his head. He closed his eyes for a second and prayed that they wouldn't hit him.

The German artillery still bombarded sections of the trench. George could hear the low whine and crump of the German shells. Their section could be hit at any moment. It wasn't worth worrying about, they wouldn't be around long enough to notice.

An enemy soldier had got up to about twenty metres from the trench, which was far too close for George's liking. His gun clicked dry and he stopped to reload.

The German stopped and pulled a stick from his belt. He leaned back one arm and balanced himself with the other in order to throw.

At that moment, Tom's gun cracked beside George. The German was hit in the top of the chest and was thrown backwards down the hill. The grenade, already primed, fell into the dirt. There was a slight delay before it went off. A few field-grey clad figures disappeared in a yellow-white flash. There were several more to take their place.

'Need more ammunition, here!' George shouted over the cacophony. He stole a glance around the trench to see if anyone had heard him, and noticed that reinforcements were coming forward down the communication trench, trying to thread their way through the bodies that littered the ground.

Three men wrestled a Lewis gun into position, and the loader immediately dropped to his knees to get the rounds into its firing mechanism. The chattering sound as it opened fire was a welcome relief to George.

He looked back out into no man's land and watched as a wave of German soldiers were mown down in front of the Lewis gun. They didn't stand a chance. They fell into a heap, and began moaning in pain, the sounds drifting up the hill to the British positions. Others jumped for cover, and many turned tail and ran back down the hill.

George fired his two remaining rounds into a couple that had tried to find cover, adding them to the field of corpses. He let the fleeing enemy go, having neither the ammunition nor the inclination to shoot them. The sky was growing dark and the Germans disappeared into its welcoming embrace.

*

'Gas! Gas!' the sentry shouted, passing the call along the line, before the sound became a choking cough. Everyone was up in seconds, if they weren't already standing. George didn't wait to see what the others did, he pulled back from the edge of the trench, looking out for the cloud of gas. Immediately, a faint smell of chlorine permeated the trench. They had managed to survive the night, expecting a renewed attack early in the morning, but this was something else. They had heard that the Germans had used gas in attacks further along the line, but their section had yet to experience it.

'Quick,' the Sergeant shouted in his Scottish burr, as he passed George. 'Wet your bloody handkerchiefs and put them over your mouth and nose. Get on with you!'

George didn't hesitate as he pulled a white sheet of cloth out of his webbing. He reached down and grabbed a rum bottle at his feet. Not caring whether it was still filled with rum, or had been used for water, he propped his rifle up and doused his handkerchief in liquid, quickly sticking it to his face. He passed the rum bottle to Tom and picked up his rifle again. He didn't want to be brought up on a charge for losing his weapon. He made sure the cloth covered his nose and mouth and was only happy when it cut out the smell of chlorine, to replace it with a hint of watery rum. It wasn't an altogether unpleasant smell.

He was lucky that he was positioned a bit further back from

the line. Other men hadn't been so lucky, or so quick to act. Some of them were already choking and pawing at their weeping eyes.

George reached for the nearest man and helped him towards the back of the line. The man was crying out and clutching at his face in immense pain. George could only pass him along to the rear and hope that someone could get him to a dressing station. Tom took the man and helped him back, before returning to face the attack.

The green-white cloud was spreading along the trench now, the wind blowing it the length of the trench rather than into it. That was what had allowed it to sneak up on them so suddenly.

'Bastards!' shouted the Sergeant, coming up behind George. The shout was distorted through his handkerchief. 'Using gas? This isn't even a bloody war anymore. It's a farce. Give me a gun and point me at my enemy, I'll be bloody happy!'

George didn't respond and the Sergeant ran along the trench to see what was happening. George watched the gas cloud drift and settle low on the ground. It didn't float up in the air, instead seeming to drift around the obstacles and barbed wire fences that littered no man's land. But that was no guarantee it was safe where the gas couldn't be seen. It poured over the edge into the trenches like a waterfall, dropping down to the duckboards. George resisted the urge to try and jump out of its way, hoping that it would only harm him if breathed in.

The firing step was covered by the green-white fog, and none of the assembled soldiers wanted to get any closer.

'If the Germans attack now, we're done for,' Tom said, from somewhere behind George. He had finished helping the wounded soldier to the rear. 'We can't see a bloody thing. For all we know they could be almost upon us.'

The Sergeant returned, a frown etched on his weathered face.

'Bugger,' he said, and continued when he saw Tom and George's expressions. 'The procedure for a gas attack is to move to the bloody flanks. But I've just checked, the wind is blowing the bloody gas into the trench at either end. So, we can't form up there.'

The gas filled the trench at a slow speed, so they were safe for the time being. However, the weight of artillery shelling from the Germans was growing stronger. The sporadic explosions around their positions suggested that the Germans had begun firing high explosives as well as gas. They would have to do something quick, or they would succumb to the gas, or be overrun by another German counter-attack.

'What do we do, Sergeant?' Tom asked, eyes darting around him for another explosion.

'I don't think we can maintain our position here, it's too bloody precarious.'

At that moment a mortar shell landed in a nearby section of trench, throwing up clods of dirt mixed with red, pink and khaki tatters of bodies. They all ducked instinctively. The trench collapsed in on itself cutting them off from the other end.

'Retreat,' the Sergeant shouted, turning towards the communication trench. He started grabbing the remaining men one by one and pushing them back towards their own lines.

'Get back!' the Sergeant shouted repeatedly, waving so that the soldiers could see over the sound of the shelling. 'Quick! Get back!'

'Listen, George, Tom' he said, quieter this time for their benefit only. 'There's nothing more we can bloody do here. This gas will kill us all if we stick around longer, and it's the bloody devil to fight in anyway. What are you waiting for?' The Sergeant grabbed George by the collar of his jacket and pulled him towards the communication trench. 'Get back, you idiots!'

George started running, Tom close at his heels. They didn't stop to see if the Sergeant was following, his shouting was being drowned out by the increased shelling. Shells fell around them as they ran, and they had to dodge an explosion as it landed to the side of the communication trench. It threw wet soil over them, and the sound rang in their ears. Their khaki chafed and scratched at their skin, but still they ran. Behind them they could hear the sounds of gunfire. The Germans were attacking. Whoever was left in the trench would be cut to pieces. The call to fall back had been a good idea. George hoped that the Germans would only find an empty trench full of the dead. It would be a hollow victory.

After the desperate run, the communication trench opened up into the perpendicular trench that, before mid-April, had been their previous front line. Other men were there, guarding the communication trench and awaiting any survivors. They waved George and Tom through as they got there.

Back in safety behind the front lines the men were finding places to sit down and rest their tired legs. They were throwing bits of kit all over the place to cut down on some of the weight that pinned them down. The officers were already moving through the ranks and ordering men to stand to in case the German counter-attack made it this far. The Sergeant moved past George and disappeared off down the trench. Nothing could kill that old bastard, George thought.

Tom spotted a rum bottle and grabbed it, hungrily filling his cup with water. The smell of the chlorine gas was still present in George's nostrils, but he would wait to clean his mouth of it.

He grabbed another soldier as he passed. The other man looked as they all did, covered in the muck and grime of the trench, with a faint hint of yellow around his sore eyes.

'We're looking for anyone from our section, can you help us out?'

'I think some of your lot are over there.' He pointed along towards a trench that ran perpendicular to the one they were standing in, a reserve trench. 'I'd try them if I were you.'

'Thanks, lad.'

George stopped. He recognised the other man, but only from belonging to another section in the same company as them. He was in the same section as Fred, and George realised that he hadn't seen the other boy since they went up Hill 60.

He pulled the soldier back by the arm before he walked away.

'Hey, lad. Do you know a Fred Madeley? I think he was in your section?'

'Fred Madeley? Short guy? Very nervous?'

George nodded. 'That's the one. Do you know where he is?'

'Yeah, he caught it. Got blown up by a shell over near Wipers.' He said it in such a matter-of-fact way, George was almost shocked. It was like he was reporting on the day's weather in Ypres, or telling him that the sun rose in the east and set in the west. 'Sorry, lad.' He didn't even look sad, or like he meant it. Fred was just another name to him. George let the other soldier go and he walked off, calling to his mates as he went, having already forgotten about George and Fred.

George sat down on a pile of dirt by the side of the trench and rested his rifle between his knees.

That was it then, another young life taken. George hadn't known Fred well, but he would have called him a friend. He was innocent, the same age as George, but somehow seemed so very much younger. He had so much to prove. He was brave, George would give him that. He hadn't deserved to die, none of them did.

George shed a few tears for a friend he had hardly come to know. He had seen many men die now, but somehow this one hit him the hardest. How would his poor family feel when they read that inevitable letter that told them their son, their underage son, had died fighting over a small stretch of mud and shit? How could they possibly know what their son had been through?

Chapter 21

Mr Harlow was waiting for them when they got to the office, a fresh cigar pushed between his fat lips, the blue smoke curled around his head giving the impression of a white tonsure. Joe had never seen Mr Harlow with an almost finished cigar. He must swap them when he headed back into his office so as not to be seen without a fresh one. It may have been a mistake arriving together, but Mr Harlow didn't seem to notice as he welcomed them.

'So, how are you finding things, Miss Wallace? It's been a few months now,' he said with his sickly smile. 'Anne.' He cut her off before she could correct him, remembering.

'Finest paper in Liverpool this is. Don't let them *Echo* lot tell you otherwise. We're right in the heart of the city here. Nothing passes us by.' He took his cigar out of his mouth and puffed a big whiff of smoke. 'Anyway, enough of that. I have a job for you.'

'Oh?' Joe said, excitement overcoming his usual quietness. Mr Harlow didn't even look at him.

'Yes, I think Anne has seen enough around here now. She needs to get out in the sunshine.' He smiled again and, just like that, Joe's excitement was crushed.

'Anne, I want you to go down to Knowsley Hall. You know where it is?'

Anne nodded. 'Yes,' she said.

'The Earl of Derby has kindly agreed to an interview. I want you to go down there and get as much exclusive information about his pals' battalions as possible. Can you do that?'

'We could both go, Mr Harlow,' Joe interrupted, relishing the chance to get close to Edward Stanley, the Earl of Derby, whom he had heard was against conscription. He gave Anne what he hoped was an apologetic look. 'It's a bit unfair to throw Anne in at the deep end. We could go together.'

Mr Harlow just gave Joe a stare, the kind of stare that a mother might give a child that had asked for too much, then took his cigar out of his mouth, puffed a cloud of smoke and placed the cigar back between his lips.

'I don't think so, Joe,' he said, and then he hesitated, perhaps searching for an excuse. 'I need you here. Lots of editing to do.'

'Mr Harlow. You know that's not true. Why won't you let me go?'

Mr Harlow looked angry. Joe had never seen him angry before. His eyes darkened and his lips tightened.

'Don't push the matter, Joe. I like you, but I won't stand for it.' He sighed as if telling off a naughty child. Joe had no idea if Mr Harlow had children, but at this moment he very much suspected that he did. He was treating Joe like one of his children. He didn't know whether to be offended or to be flattered that Mr Harlow might think of him in the same way as one of his own.

'You know full well why you can't go, Joe.' He hadn't yet finished having his say. 'After that last stunt you pulled. I had that article on my desk when the owner came in. I had to make sure that he didn't read a word. That would have caused a controversy. You might have lost your job.'

Mr Harlow had forgotten all about Anne now, who was stood to one side, occasionally glancing at Joe.

'No, it's better if you stay here. Don't want you embarrassing us in front of His Lordship, especially after all he has done for the war. I'll let you write, Joe. Just stay away from the war.'

That was exactly what Joe intended to do.

'It was bad enough when Albert wrote that article,' Mr Harlow said. 'The owner almost had my neck, I should have read it properly before I sent it to press, but I managed to talk him round, which was lucky for me and for the rest of you.

'Then he wanted me to do something about Albert. I said "What?" He said, "Sack the man, we can't have any unpatriotic writers writing for the newspaper, it wouldn't do." Well, I didn't want to, but he wouldn't listen. I told him it was a one-off but that wasn't good enough.

'I was all ready to do it, not that I've ever had to sack anyone before. But then Barnes himself came into the office and told me he was off. "I'm off to fight," he said. Well, I was shocked. I asked him "What the hell was that article about then?" and he just got angry. Said he was going to do his bit and he wouldn't be working at the paper anymore.

'It was all damned off, I tell you. Why would someone who had written an article about the realities of war then go on to be one of the first to sign up?'

Anne shot Joe a glance, but he kept silent. It was better for everyone involved that the truth remained unknown at the moment.

'Can't say I ever understood Albert much any way, but well, he's gone now so there's nothing that can be done.'

Mr Harlow looked sad. His cigar had almost burnt down to his lips in the time that he had been talking, and now he drifted off into silence, staring into the middle ground.

'I'll run what I write by you when I get back, Joe. And you could give me some tips?' Anne's smile was so sweet that Joe could only nod in response.

'Well, quite,' Mr Harlow said.

The mood had changed dramatically. Mr Harlow was known for wanting to be everyone's friend, but he wasn't usually so free with information as he had been just then. Joe felt guilty, and he knew that Anne thought he should tell him that it was he who had written the article, but what good would it serve? Mr Harlow was already angry with Joe for his proposed writing, telling him now wouldn't make things any better for anyone. Joe had suspected a sadness in Mr Harlow towards the end of his tirade.

'Mr Harlow?' Joe said.

'Hmm? Yes?' He had drifted off into a world of his own and was staring into the middle distance until Joe had said his name.

'Why are you telling us this, Mr Harlow?' Joe asked. 'Is there something on your mind?'

Mr Harlow pulled out the chair from what had been Frank's desk and sat down. He took a moment to compose himself, pulling heavily on his cigar and letting the smoke waft around his head. He seemed to enjoy breathing the smoke back in and smelling its foggy scent.

'I'm not sure it's my place to be telling you this,' he said at long last, refusing to look at them, but rather staring at the ground. 'I've had word from the war office.'

'What is it?' Joe pressed again, growing anxious for Mr Harlow to tell them what was wrong. He thought of his brother. All the things that might have happened to him flashed through his head. He didn't know what he would do if any of them became reality.

'It's Albert,' Mr Harlow whispered between clenched lips. 'I've just seen his mother… he's dead.'

At first Joe felt relief, then as soon as that emotion hit him, he felt guilt for being glad about what could only be bad news for someone else. How selfish could he be? It was possible that Albert Barnes had a brother too, what of him? He certainly had parents, a mother at least. What grief would they be feeling for their son now?

'That's horrible,' Anne said, filling the awkward gap of silence that had come about in Joe's introspection. 'Do you know what happened to him?'

203

Mr Harlow coughed and ran a hand across his mouth, then his head shot up, as if noticing them for the first time. 'Um?' he said.

Joe sat down next to him in an effort to try and bring them onto the same level.

'What happened, Mr Harlow?' he said. 'My brother is in the same regiment. I need to know.' He dreaded what Mr Harlow might say. What if they had come under attack?

'They are?' Mr Harlow asked. 'I haven't heard anything about your brother. They're stationed somewhere near Ypres. Albert was shot by a sniper. They say he died well.'

'My brother's all right then.' That was all Joe could think to say, and Anne looked at him. Mr Harlow sobbed a little to himself. He had never behaved like this before, and Joe didn't know what to do. Anne tried to comfort him, putting her arms around his shoulder and made comforting sounds.

'I'd always liked the lad,' Mr Harlow said after a few silent moments. 'Everyone is leaving. First it was Albert, then Frank. Soon it'll only be me left. I'd go too, but I'm not fit. They wouldn't have me.'

'That doesn't matter,' Anne said. 'We're not leaving are we, Joe?' She nodded at him, urging him to answer.

'Er, no,' he said. 'We're not.'

'You?' Mr Harlow said, looking up at them. He rubbed his sleeve across his face and started routing in the inside pocket of his jacket with the other hand. 'Didn't I give you some work to do?'

His voice had returned to its usual gruff manner, wheezing out each word. His face took on a harsher appearance, the pink wrinkles flattening out as he forced himself to pretend that he had not been momentarily weakened. After a few seconds, he found what he had been searching for and pulled out a cigar. Lighting it, he puffed what must have been a reassuring cloud of smoke out. Happy that things were back to normal, he stood.

'Do let me know how you get on with the Earl, won't you, Miss Wallace?' He turned to Joe. 'And you had better get on with whatever it was you were supposed to be doing.'

He walked away without waiting for either Anne or Joe to answer, and they looked at each other, bemused. Joe shrugged, he had worked for Mr Harlow for some time now, and he still didn't understand the man. It seemed that his moods were as changeable as the weather.

Mr Harlow spoke over his shoulder as he walked away. 'Oh, and there's no need to tell anyone about what I said about Albert. It's no one's business.'

'I suppose that that's my cue to leave,' Anne said, before grabbing her coat from the stand and running out of the door.

Before he could say anything, Joe was left on his own again. Albert would never be able to tell anyone about what Joe had done to the article, but now he didn't care; something had to be done to stop any more young men dying.

Chapter 22

They spread out into the village, happy to be free of the confines of the trenches. George stretched his legs; it was good to walk at a brisk pace again. Doing so in the trench could get you killed, if not by an enemy bullet then by a landslide that buried you. It was a horrible way to go. He had got used to crouching most of the time, the sandbags not piled high enough to cover someone as tall as George. He stretched his back and it clicked, but it was a good click. It felt good to stand upright.

They would need to find a billet. Other units were also being rotated from the front, and space would become limited. The first men out were always the first to get the good spots.

The nearest village was not unusual. There were ruined buildings everywhere, and the fields and roads were torn up with the movement of troops and material. However, there were still signs of life. A few dirty villagers walked past; some wheeled carts of hay, others churns of milk, some just wondered without purpose. They were a stark contrast to the soldiers that traipsed past. The villagers observed them from the corner of their eyes.

George's mud-covered khaki made him stand out as a soldier fresh from the trenches. You couldn't see the khaki underneath the thick, brown sludge. The itching from the lice that infested his uniform was so severe, that he would swear that others would be able to see them.

The section stopped at a cottage. Half of its roof was missing and there were several dislodged bricks in the wall, but it would still make a good billet for someone. They had to take what they could get out here, and it was better than the foxholes in the trenches. Anywhere was better than the trenches, even a farm knee-deep in manure. Despite that, they still wanted to make sure that they got the best. It would make a difference going back into the line once their rotation was over. A few good nights' sleep could buy you several extra hours of concentration on sentry duty, which in turn could save your life.

'There's room for four in here,' the Sergeant shouted from the doorway. 'Get on with it!'

The first four men of the section jumped at his command and ran to the cottage. Lucky bastards, George thought. If only he and Tom had been quicker, they might be sleeping under that roof tonight. They'd have to find somewhere else.

'The rest of you are on your own,' Campbell said, scowling in his usual manner before marching off into the distance between the villagers' houses.

Tom tapped George on the shoulder. 'Quick, lad. We'd best hurry if we want to find anywhere good. Before this bunch of layabouts finally works out where they are.' He pointed a thumb over his shoulder at the men behind him who were standing around, chatting amongst themselves. George stifled a laugh.

'I can use my stripe to get us in somewhere nice, just wait and see.'

Looking over their shoulders to see if they were being watched by the others, they walked off in the direction the Sergeant had gone. The road through the centre of the village was narrow. The gardens at the front of the cottages and houses had been cleared to allow heavy goods and artillery through at some point, and now tracks led through the grassy verges.

After a few houses, a wider path led away from the village and up a small hill. To the right-hand side of the hill was a copse of trees, and on the other side were fences that suggested a farm.

'Here, this way. Look,' Tom said to George, grabbing his arm for a moment and dragging him along. They were careful not to run, doing so might scare any locals, or get a reprimand from a superior that saw them.

One they had crested the hill they could see the entirety of the farm. The fields were ploughed in thick furrows down to the irrigation at the bottom of the hill, but there was little sign of crops growing. George had to admit he didn't know much about farming, but he had become quite intimate with mud. The fields looked like the rest of northern France that he had seen, water-logged, muddy and lifeless. The small ridges from the ploughing could almost be mistaken for little trenches.

The farmhouses themselves hadn't fared much better. They were just as ruined as some of the buildings in the village. Great clods of earth had been thrown up from the ground around them, and the bricks and stones that had been used to build lay in heaps. It was amazing that the artillery had reached this far back behind the line, but perhaps earlier in the war there had been some fighting here. It was hard to tell; one battlefield looked very much like another. It was possible that the BEF had come through here on their early retreats from the German army.

A large barn stood off to one side, and from the hill it looked to be less damaged than the other buildings. Perhaps the ever-present talk of the artillery's inaccuracy was unfair. That the barn was constructed out of wood made it even more remarkable. Its sides were painted in a deep brown-red varnish, and the tiled roof peaked in the middle.

'Perfect,' Tom said at George's side as they stood taking in the scene. 'That'll do nicely.'

They rushed down the hill, excitement almost taking over. A barn could be a warm place to get some sleep and some rest.

They couldn't have wished for a better place. The cottage at the end of the village now paled in comparison. George almost tripped on one of the ploughed ridges, not expecting the earth to be so hard, but he caught himself, trying not to reach out to Tom as he tripped.

The pair of them followed a well-trodden dirt path round the side of the barn, looking for the entrance, and hoping that seeing the other side wouldn't ruin their illusion of thinking the building was complete and unharmed.

There was a wooden door that hung askew on its hinges, as if it had been used often, but not maintained. It would still be good enough to keep the wind and rain out, even if it did wobble in the slight wind.

Tom reached out a tentative hand and knocked on the door to see if the farmers were home, or anyone was using it to shelter in. It wasn't fair to walk into someone's home unannounced, even if most of the village had been decimated and abandoned.

The barn door opened a little, and a face peered out. The face was grimy and coated in muck, but a white smile broke out amongst the dirt.

'Can I help you with something, mate?' the soldier inside said, still smiling at them both. It was more of a smirk than a smile. George couldn't quite make out the unit badge on the man's khaki, but there didn't appear to be a stripe. He was a private, just like George.

'We need somewhere to billet,' Tom said, indicating the barn with a wave of one hand. 'And this barn looks nice and big. Big enough for the lot of us to fit in there and be quite cosy.'

The private looked back over his shoulder theatrically, and then shook his head.

'No room at the inn, I'm afraid, mate.'

The door opened wider with a gust of wind, and George could see over the other soldier's shoulder. Despite the darkness inside it was clear there was still plenty of room. There was some straw packed in the corners that some men were fashioning into beds, but there was clear space on the floor to another side, and wooden rafters over one half of the barn that could be accessed by a short ladder.

'Lad, you've got to be kidding. There's loads of room in there,' Tom said, putting an outstretched palm on the door, holding it back in case the private tried to close it in his face.

'Are you doubting me, mate?' The smile slipped from the man's face and his thick London accent grew thicker. His cool blue eyes were piercing. 'Callin' me a liar, yeah? *Mate.*'

Forgetting the door, he stepped out from the barn and looked Tom straight in the eye. He puffed out his chest – it was an almost unnoticeable change, but George was used to men squaring up with each other. He'd seen it many times before on the docks. Most times it amounted to nothing, both men backing down before it could escalate, but sometimes the men would come to blows. Behind the private, a couple of his accomplices stood up and followed him to the door.

'Look, lad. We're just looking for somewhere to kip,' Tom said, standing firm and looking straight at the other soldier who was almost a head shorter than him.

'We didn't even know there was another regiment in this area,' George added, instead looking at the soldier's mates and watching them for any signs of movement.

'Yeah? Well I'm saying there ain't any room in 'ere.' The private didn't take his eyes off Tom, not even when George spoke. 'So why don't ya just sling your 'ook? Eh?'

'We'll keep ourselves to ourselves. You won't hear a peep out of us.' George knew it was futile, but he had to try nonetheless. 'We'll just find a corner and bed down for the night, then we can find somewhere else in the morning.'

'You're not listening to me, mate.' He put a hand on Tom's chest as if to push him back. Tom looked down at it, then back up at the private. 'There. Is. No. Room.'

Tom took a deep breath and seemed to stand up taller. He looked over at George. George had already resigned himself to finding somewhere else.

He almost walked away, but Tom wasn't appeased. He grabbed the wrist of the private's hand that was still lying on his chest and wrenched it sideways. The private didn't cry out in pain but rolled with the movement and brought up an arm. Tom was quicker. He clenched his fist and punched it straight into the man's face. He didn't have a chance to block, as Tom's punch took him off guard.

George reacted in a heartbeat, stepping behind the private and blocking the door of the barn from the other men, who shouted and rushed after their comrade. George now had his back to Tom, but he was confident his friend could look after himself. He on the other hand had at least three men to contend with, and he hoped that Tom would put out his man to come to his aid.

The first man that came at George was a small man, and he didn't have time to take in any other details. It was easy to dodge the first lunge as an arm went up, and George ducked to the side. The second punch was intended for his gut, but he caught it in his left hand and, rolling with it, lifted the small man off his feet and over. He landed on his back and let out an 'oomph' of expelled air.

The sounds of scuffling were still coming from behind him. George didn't have time to look, and see if Tom was winning. He filled the doorway, like some ancient defender of a long-forgotten castle gate.

The second man facing George hesitated. He was bulkier than his friend, but possessed a more cautious brain. He looked at George and sized him up, wary. George urged him on, wanting to get this, whatever this was, over and done with. He stopped short of beckoning the other man forward. He began to raise an arm to strike, moving forward, and George braced himself to block the blow.

'What the bloody hell is going on here?' The shout pierced through the sounds of scuffling and grunting. George spun round, forgetting his oncoming attacker and looking for the source of the shout.

Tom and the London private held each other by the scruff of their smocks, and with raised arms eyed the newcomers warily. Behind them stood another group of soldiers, with the Sergeant at their head.

'We're trying to get the lice,' one of the Londoners behind George shouted to accompanying sniggers.

Campbell looked fit to burst, and he stepped closer, looking for the man who had spoken. 'Don't get cocky with me, son,' he shouted back. 'I know exactly what is going on here, so you'd better stop right now.'

He walked past them all and into the barn.

'Adams, let go of that man right now. Abbott, with me. Now!'

Tom let go of the private and brushed himself down, straightening his smock and checking his webbing for any tears. The two men scowled at each other. George jumped to follow the Sergeant. The inside of the building was even larger than it had looked through the door, the design making best use of the available space. It looked as if it hadn't been used for any farming purpose for quite some time. What tools were still there were rusty and old. It was lucky that the fight hadn't gone further and into the building, otherwise there might have been some serious injuries with the shears and rakes that hung on the walls. It was quite a macabre scene, like a hideout for a human butcher.

Despite the rusty farming implements it was quite warm and cosy inside. There was enough old straw to fashion into beds for the men, as some of the Londoners had already been doing. There were also two layers to the barn, which would provide ample sleeping room.

'Yes, this will do nicely,' Campbell said as George walked up to him. He assessed the barn very much as George had done,

212

turning around on the spot and taking it all in. 'We will be able to fit the whole lot in here for a good few days at least.'

The Sergeant seemed to realise that George was standing there and his expression changed back from being impressed to one of annoyance.

'I expected better from you, Abbott.'

George was shocked. It was about the nicest thing Campbell had ever said to him in the months that they had known each other. He had always seemed cruel to George, never engaging in conversation and ignoring his ambition. Today was proving to be a very unusual day indeed.

'Sorry, sir,' were the only words George could force out between his surprise.

'Is that all you have to say for yourself? No witty remarks? No bloody mindedly thinking you are always right and that no one else could possibly be right? I know you've got a brain in there somewhere. I expected this kind of behaviour from Adams, but not from you.'

The Sergeant stopped short of knocking on George's head, but he was once again shouting into his face. It wasn't a parade-ground shout, he didn't want those outside to hear, but it was still loud enough to be aggressive and off-putting. George had become accustomed to it over the past few months.

'I… I don't understand, sir.'

'Of course you bloody well don't.'

George just stood, hoping that the Sergeant would explain himself. For a moment Campbell looked as if he was waiting for the same thing, but then he turned and begun counting off places in the barn.

'One… two… three…' He paused and turned back to George. 'That's the problem with you, Abbott. I've spent months trying to turn you into a bloody soldier. You might think I'm a horrible bastard, but I've been through this before. Nothing quite as bad as this mind, but I've seen men die. I had to make you bloody stronger, give you a chance to make it through. That's even more important now than ever, considering the hell that we're facing out there. At least you're good at listening.'

He stormed straight up to George.

'And yet, you're still trying to get yourself bloody killed!'

He didn't stop and walked past George to the open doorway, beckoning to the men outside.

'Right, I'm taking this bloody great barn for the King's.'

There were shouts of complaint from the Londoners, but the Sergeant continued unperturbed.

'You're welcome to stay if you bloody well want. It's up to you, but there are more of us than you. You can have one side of the barn, this lot'll take the other. And if I find you fighting again, I'll have you all up in front of a Captain. Now get on with you, the sun's going down!'

*

George sat with his back against the barn wall and his knees bent up in front of him. He had piled some of the spare straw in the corner as a bed and now sat on it with his greatcoat pulled over him to keep him warm. Fleas inhabited the straw and bit him, but they were nothing compared to the lice that already lived inside his uniform. At least they would all get a wash tomorrow and, he hoped, a clean shirt for the first time in months.

The wind buffeted against the outside of the building and squealed as it rushed past. It was a haunting sound, nothing like the horrible wailing of the artillery shelling, but disturbing enough to keep him awake.

Tom sat next to him in almost the same pose but smoking a cigarette. He had offered one to George, but he had refused it. He wasn't in the mood.

He hadn't been involved in a fight since school, and even then it was only a scuffle. He hadn't gotten into that kind of argument

214

as an adult and it depressed him. He couldn't understand what had come over him. The months of fear and doubt had burned brightly in a few moments of rage. He also didn't understand why the other men had acted like that, they were supposed to be on the same side. It had worked out in the end, and they were lucky not to be brought up on a charge. Campbell had been uncharacteristically kind. He just wanted somewhere to bed down for the night and didn't care to find a commissioned officer to report them to.

They sat this side of the barn, and the Londoners had taken up the other side. Each section looked at each other with nervous glances when they thought they weren't looking. There was a constant feeling of being watched. They were on the same side, but George couldn't find it in him to trust them, not after what had happened. He knew they'd want to get their revenge somehow. He guessed they'd get no sleep tonight after all. It was a good thing they had taken the side with all the rusty farming tools. At least they weren't in a trench. At least they were warm.

Tom blew a puff of smoke out and stretched his back out.

'Why did you do that, Tom? Why did you hit him?' George said to him, casting a quick glance over at the London Private, who was pretending to be asleep.

'I don't know.' He didn't look at George as he replied, he just looked at his feet. George wasn't used to Tom acting like this, and it was making him edgy. He just smoked his cigarette and brooded, refusing to look at George. He thought that Tom was embarrassed, but he had never known him to be embarrassed before. This was something else.

'We could have walked away,' he said, trying to keep the conversation alive somehow. 'Now look at the mess we're in.'

Tom let out a big sigh, as if he had been holding his breath for some time.

'I guess I just flipped. Look, I'm sorry.'

George looked at his friend, trying to understand him. He

looked sadder than he had ever seen him, and George couldn't remember Tom ever being sad, it wasn't in his character. He was always chirpy and ready for a joke. He wasn't sure he liked this new Tom at all. He needed Tom's confidence to help him through. Without that, what would he do?

'You don't have to apologise to me, Tom. Never. It's just that I... I don't understand. You're usually the first to stop a fight, to look out for people. I've never seen you lose your temper with someone like that before. You're not acting like yourself. I'm worried.'

Tom looked at him for the first time in minutes. His eyes were bloodshot, and George thought he could just make out tears in the gloom. He opened his mouth to say something, then looked away again, sighing and then taking another drag of smoke. The two of them sat in silence for a few moments.

'I don't know what to say, George,' Tom said. 'I don't. It got to me, all of this... this mess. Scrabbling around in the dirt, trying to survive, trying to fight the Germans so that they don't hurt our families. Then these idiots.' He swept a hand at the Londoners. 'These idiots act like we're on different sides, like we're not good enough for them. What, then, are we fighting for?'

It was George's turn to not know what to say. He just grunted instead. Hoping Tom would either continue or cheer up. Anything but silent brooding.

'I just flipped, George. I know it's not right, and I know it could have got us, and may very well *have* got us, into trouble. But in a way it also felt good.'

He looked up, his eyes boring into George's.

'I'm not ashamed to admit I'm scared,' he said, earnestly. He searched for another cigarette in his smock and with a click of flame he lit it.

'I think we're all scared,' George said, not wanting to look at Tom as he said it.

'Yes, you're probably right. However, I've never felt like this in my life. In the trench I feel like I'm out of control. I thought that my stripe would give me some kind of benefit, some kind of power, or set me out from the rest, but in the trench we're all the same. Just as likely to get hit by a stray shell or shot by a sniper. The Germans don't care if you're an officer. In fact, I'm fairly sure they seek us out. It's no good.'

He took another drag.

'When that private was squaring up to me I couldn't help myself. It was the first time that I felt like I had an enemy, not just some unknown soldier a few metres away across the mud.'

He gave George an apologetic shrug.

'For the first time in my life I felt in control. Like, I could do something and be in charge of my own actions. It was incredibly freeing. I'm ashamed to say I actually enjoyed it. Well, what I mean to say is that I didn't enjoy fighting him, but the sense of power, of freedom that it gave me. Though I'm glad the Sergeant turned up when he did. I don't think we would have lasted much longer against that lot.'

The others now appeared to be sleeping.

'You can say that again,' George said. 'I had three of the buggers to contend with, you only had one.'

Tom laughed, but it sounded hollow and distant.

'Yes. Thanks for having my back, lad. It always makes me feel better to know you're here with me. No matter what. We've been through a lot together, you and I.'

'We have, and I wouldn't have wanted to do it with anyone else. I'm so glad we signed up together. I couldn't imagine being here without you.'

Tom didn't need to reply, they just looked at each other and smiled. It was the first time either of them had spoken like this, and it felt good. Friends were important in life, and even more important when faced with adversity, the kind of adversity that war presented them with.

'Here, George,' Tom said at length. 'I want you to have this.'

He reached into a pocket of his webbing and pulled something out, something that glittered in his hand at the reflected light of the lanterns in the corner. After a moment's longing hesitation, he passed it to George. It was a lighter, one of the more modern ones that didn't need a separate flint and spark. Like everyone else in the army, George had taken up smoking. If you didn't beforehand, you would do afterwards.

'It was my father's,' Tom said. 'And I want you to have it. Should anything happen to me then it will remind you of me and could also be a lasting memory of my father.'

George knew Tom was lying, the lighter could only be a few years old at most, there were very few of them around. Tom's father died when they were young and it was far too long ago for this to have belonged to him. George regarded it in more detail, unsure of what to say. It was silver but had been blackened by soot and mud. There was an inscription etched into one side, but it had worn from use and he couldn't read it. It looked like German. Tom must have taken it from a dead German soldier during a raid.

'I don't know what to say, Tom. Thank you.'

He flicked it open and clicked the mechanism. With a satisfying *whoosh* the flame burst into life, casting more shadows on the walls around them.

Tom grinned at him. 'Fun huh, lad?'

George nodded back and put the lighter away in a pocket before anyone else could see it and envy him.

''Night, lad,' Tom said and rolled over to the left, pulling his greatcoat over him and snoring almost right away. George rolled the other way, but he didn't close his eyes. He lay there for a while in the ever-darkening barn, thinking.

Chapter 23

Anne stood over Joe's shoulder to see what he was doing as he ran his finger along the paper. She didn't say anything, but he could smell her perfume and sensed that she was there. He flicked another page and stopped, satisfied.

'Every time we get the casualty lists in, I have to check,' he said to her without turning.

'Why? I thought I'd let you finish,' she asked as she pulled a seat closer and sat next to him, pulling the paper gently towards her.

'It's become a kind of tradition, a ritual, I guess. I have to see them before they are printed. To make sure.'

'To make sure that none of your friends are on there?'

'To look for George. I don't know what I would do if I saw his name. I almost want to be ignorant of it, but I have to look. I have to make sure his name isn't there. It's odd, isn't it?'

'It's not odd. I understand. I often look at the names and wonder who they are and who has lost someone. Who the men were and what they were doing when they... when they passed.' She had been about to say 'died', but for a reason Joe couldn't guess, she had hesitated. 'George is your—'

'My brother. He is my younger brother.'

219

'Oh yes, you mentioned him before. Do you wish you could go out and look after him?'

'No, I don't. I wouldn't go out there for anything. You know I'm against this war.'

'Then why are you worried about him? If there is nothing you can do then what purpose will worrying serve? He made his decision to go out, and you made yours; to stay here and do what you can to stop people like him having to fight.'

He knew she was trying to reassure him, but it wasn't working. It felt like she was criticising him, but could it be he was just being paranoid? He watched her idly flicking through the pages of names, sometimes running a finger along a line, other times going back a page to see if what she had read was correct. The sheer amount of names was staggering, but it had become routine now, they were almost desensitised to it. It still didn't stop him worrying about George though. He didn't know what he would do if his brother's name ended up on that list, but he knew how he would feel. Guilty. Devastated.

'It's just that he shouldn't be out there.'

'Yes, I know,' she said without raising her head. He thought he heard a hint of impatience in her voice.

'No, what I mean is that he isn't even old enough. He shouldn't be out in France, they never should have let him go.'

'How old is he?' She looked up, done with the newspaper.

'Seventeen. Not even old enough to sign up, let alone be shipped out to France. I don't know what they were thinking.'

'Hmmm,' she said, and passed him back the newspaper. 'If he is anything like you, Joe, he's an intelligent man. Even at seventeen, I would dare say he's intelligent and shrewd enough to look after himself. If he's like you, he will be smart and brave enough to make his own decisions. He went out there, he fights because he wants to, and even if you disagree you should be proud of him that he is as strong in his convictions as you are.'

She was right, she had a way of always being right.

'I am proud of him,' was all he could say. He was; his little brother had grown up, and as Anne said, he was an intelligent man. He was a far better man than Joe. And Joe was always proud of him. Proud in the way that only a brother can ever be proud of another brother.

'You two are close?' she asked.

He had to think for a moment. He didn't know how he would describe their relationship, but close wasn't the word.

'No, not really. More's the pity. I think that's one reason why I worry about him so much. I never told him how much I care, and he's probably out there in the mud thinking that his family and his brother don't care one jot for him. It's not true, and it makes me worry to think that he might think that.'

'Why don't you write and tell him how you feel?'

'I do. I write to him all the time, whenever I have a spare moment, and something to tell him about. I've even written to tell him about you.'

She smiled, full of warmth, and put her hand on the back of his. He liked it when she did that. The closeness of her hand and the warmth of the gesture always soaked through him and took away his worries, if only for a moment. But his mood dropped again, as quickly as it had risen.

'But he never replies. I don't know if he reads them. I have no way of telling. I know he writes to our parents, to the family at large every now and then, but never directly to me.'

'Perhaps he is too busy out there? You have no idea what kind of chores and routine they have. What if he only has time to write one letter and so he choses to write to your parents?'

'I suppose that could be true.' He wasn't sure, he could imagine that the soldiers had plenty of time hanging around in between bouts of fighting. He didn't blame George for not wanting to write to him, he had never given him any reason to before now, and they weren't close. Joe just wished that they could be closer, he knew that somewhere deep-down, if given a chance, George would be the one person to understand him.

At that moment, Anne put a hand on Joe's sleeve, her eyes darting along the corridor. The sound of wheezing came closer, indicating Mr Harlow was coming, but it was much softer than usual. The big man stopped in front of the pair of them and just stared. His face was ashen and pale, and he gripped his cigar in a clenched fist that was so firm all the blood had drained away to leave a white blubber of flesh.

'What's wrong, Mr Harlow?' Joe asked as Anne stood up and went over to him.

'You look terrible,' she said. 'Come, have a seat. Sit down, sit down. There, good.'

She had pulled out her own chair and helped the large man into it. She had acquired a handkerchief from somewhere and was using it to mop his sweating brow.

'What's wrong?' Joe pressed again, eliciting a frown from Anne. He frowned back, sure that she too would want to know what was wrong.

'I... I received this,' Mr Harlow said, holding up a small chit of brownish paper, his voice only a whisper. 'It seems I am becoming the bearer of bad news.'

Anne took it from his hands and began reading, her eyes rushing across the page. As they got to the bottom of the telegram her eyes dropped and she closed them, pushing the paper to her breast. She took a deep breath.

'What?' Joe asked. Had someone close to Mr Harlow been killed in the war? He didn't think the man had any children that could be serving, and his wife was at home as far as Joe knew. It had to be a relative.

'It says—'

'Here,' Anne said, interrupting Mr Harlow and handing Joe the telegram.

'It says,' Mr Harlow continued, unperturbed, his voice still little more than a whisper. 'It says that the *Lusitania* has… It says it's gone down… almost everyone onboard with it. Almost all of them.'

'Oh dear God,' Joe said, and went to sit down himself. Those poor people. He didn't know much about the ocean liner, except that she was big. She was big and must have had a very large crew, not to mention the passengers.

'She went down yesterday afternoon,' Mr Harlow continued. His voice had become stronger, now he had found an audience to confide in. 'She was just off the south coast of Ireland. The telegram only came in this morning. Oh, God. My brother…'

He trailed off again and sobbed to himself for a few seconds, before pulling out another cigar from his jacket and lighting it with a whoosh of a match. Anne patted him on the shoulder half-heartedly as she stared off into the distance, lost in her own world.

'My brother… and his darling wife. They were both onboard along with their children. On their way back from holidaying in New York.'

Joe read the telegram. It said nothing about Ed's brother, only about the ship being sunk, and he said as much to Mr Harlow. Anne didn't even frown at him this time.

'No, no. You're right. I don't know. That telegram is just from a reporter.' He paused for a second, taking a long drag on his cigar. 'Listen, I want you two to do me a favour.'

He stood up and shook himself as if shaking off his melancholy like a dog shaking water off its fur.

'Anything, Mr Harlow. Please, what is it?' Anne asked, taking a step away from him now that he had stood up.

'It's rather more of it being your job, than a favour, but I want you to do it all the same. I need you two to go down to the pier head and to the Cunard offices. Find out whatever you can. As much as you can. There'll be lots of other people down there, asking about their families, some of them just enjoying the drama.

223

So, you'll have to throw your weight about as reporters and make yourself known to the staff. Then find out as much as you can for me.'

He stared at them as they stood still.

'Well? What are you waiting for? On with you.' With that he waved his hand at the door and strode off. He had exchanged sadness for anger much quicker than anyone Joe had ever seen before, and it threw him.

He gave Anne a look, then turned to get his coat from the stand. He daren't think how many grieving families would be down at the ocean liner's offices. Those poor, poor people. What must they be going through? He remembered when the *Titanic* had sunk. So many families from the city had had family onboard as crew, or heading to America to start afresh. The city was still reeling from it, many still struggling to make ends meet. How would they cope with another disaster?

Despite that he was glad. He knew it was terrible to feel this way, given the circumstances, but Mr Harlow had finally given Joe a reporting job.

Whether it was intentional, or just because he had been there when Mr Harlow had received the telegram, he didn't know. But he didn't care, at that stage he would've taken anything, and he was determined he would do the best job he could. Letting Anne out before him with a drop of his shoulder and a smile, he walked out of the office, head held high, feeling more important than he had ever done.

*

The Cunard offices were a ten-minute walk from the *Daily Post*, and by the time he and Anne had got there, Joe was sweating in the mid-spring heat. As they turned the corner a great baying noise overwhelmed them. Outside the Cunard offices and leading up to the facade of the brick building, men and women were gathered. It was like the early days of the war again when the recruiting offices had been overwhelmed. Except, rather than standing in orderly queues, excited, there was a great deal of shouting going on. Those that raised their voices reached for the building as if they were trying to gain the attention of some deity, and were being pushed back, unwelcome.

'What's going on?' Anne asked someone, as they joined the back of the crowd.

'I have no idea,' he said. Joe believed him.

He had expected a crowd of mourning mothers, wives and daughters, but what they had found was a scene of anger.

They pushed through the baying crowd.

'Excuse me!' He said 'excuse me' to each person that he and Anne weaved in between. Rather than a parting crowd he was only met with angry glances and resistance. He had to push harder to get through, and he grabbed Anne's hand to make sure that she didn't get lost behind him. The angry shouts begun to be directed at the pair of them, but Joe made a point of ignoring them.

At the front of the crowd, up a small flight of stairs to the building's entrance, a thick burly man was barring the way and pushing back the occasional troublemaker who grew overconfident.

A meaty fist applied to his chest pushed Joe back as he made to walk up the stairs.

'We're with the *Daily Post*,' Anne said. 'Please let us through.' The resistance fell back and with a rush they were through the crowd and into the reception area of the building. The baying crowd were kept behind them by the security men. 'What on earth is going on, Joe?' Anne asked from beside him, out of breath from their struggle.

'Who are you?' Another voice cut in, belonging to a young man, a couple of years younger than Joe. He strode towards them with a purposeful air, his head held high as he regarded them.

His greased, pitch black hair shone in the reflection of the electric lighting. 'How did you get in here?' His black suit marked him out as a clerk of some kind.

Anne took the initiative.

'We've come from the *Daily Post,* as soon as we heard the news,' she said, raising her voice so that no one else in the building would question why they were here, but the clerk didn't respond. 'Who are you?' he said again, this time directed at Joe who repeated Anne's repsonse.

'Ah yes, a most dreadful affair,' the man said, turning on his heels and beckoning them after him. 'Dreadful.' They followed at his heels as he carried on. 'You'll understand that none of the directors have the time to talk to the press?' They nodded, it wasn't a question. 'They are far too busy with the matters of business at a time like this. I, however, will be able to answer any questions you might have, on behalf of the company.'

Joe felt put out by the way that they were being dealt with, but what could he do apart from make a scene and demand to see the directors?

The clerk had led them to a small room off the central hallway that resembled a waiting room. Chairs lined the walls and a window let in a small amount of light from between the buildings. The white plaster was stained yellow where the waiting people had been smoking. There were a couple of newspapers on a small table in the corner, and Joe noticed a copy of the *Daily Post* with a sense of professional pride.

Anne took a seat, putting her hands on the knee of her skirt. 'What is going on?' she said. 'All those people outside, they seemed angry...'

The clerk gestured for Joe to sit down and he did, noticing the slight creak of the old chair. He took out the notebook from his jacket and began jotting down notes. The clerk glanced at it, but then found himself a seat across from them.

'The crowd?' Joe asked.

'Yes, it is quite odd I must say,' the clerk said, nodding at Joe. 'When we first heard the news we mainly had families coming to see about their loved ones, to find out what had happened to them. We did what we could of course, but things are all a bit confused at the moment, as you would understand.'

'Yes,' Anne jumped in. 'We have some questions to ask about that ourselves later.'

She wanted to ask after Mr Harlow's relatives.

'Hmm.' The clerk looked at her then back at Joe.

'May we ask some questions?' Anne pressed.

'Yes. Yes.' The clerk waved her request away with a well-manicured hand. He was determined that he would be in charge of the situation. 'It wasn't long after the families arrived when other people started to show up on the doorstep. Many of them angry, like you say, shouting all sorts of horrible things. At first, we thought they were blaming us for the sinking of the ship. I guess it's bringing back too many memories of the *Titanic*. Well, we learnt from that disaster without delay. No, it wasn't us that they were angry at. We still had to call in the security to keep them at bay, though. We can't have them making a mess of the building. We soon had a pretty good idea what they were angry about though.'

'And what was that?' Anne said. She was jotting down notes and didn't even look up at the clerk who only had eyes for Joe.

'Why were they angry, Mr...?' Joe tried, and the man continued without giving a name.

'Well, they're angry with the Germans of course.'

'Of course?' Joe stared dumbfounded at the clerk. What on earth was he talking about?

'Well, yes. Didn't you hear? I thought you two were reporters?'

The clerk shot an angry look at Anne.

'Oh, we are,' she said. 'Our editor didn't give us much information before he sent us down here. So you're going to have to be patient with us, I'm afraid, and help us piece together what is going on.' She paused, smiling at the clerk again. 'Our readers will be pleased to hear how helpful you were in representing the Cunard company.'

The clerk scoffed and grinned back. It wasn't a pleasant sight. Joe was getting frustrated at his refusal to answer Anne's questions or take her seriously.

'Now, hold on just a minute,' he said. 'If you don't start answering Miss Wallace's questions then we shall go and find someone else to talk to. Someone who might not be so inclined to agree with the Cunard company.'

The clerk looked shocked and opened and closed his mouth a few times before speaking slowly and carefully. He stared at Joe with narrowed eyes as he refused to look at Anne. 'The crowd are angry with the Germans because they sunk the *Lusitania*.'

There was a shocked silence in the room. The only sound was a faint clicking of a radiator in the corner as it cooled.

'You didn't know?' the clerk asked, and Anne shook her head. Joe could feel himself doing the same; this changed things.

'As far as we can work out the *Lusitania* was sunk by one of those German U-boats. Those people out there want retribution for that. That's what they're so angry about. I don't know what they expect us to do about it, we're trying to work out how many survivors there are at the moment, let alone condemning the Germans for this. That's something the government can do, surely?'

Anne nodded.

'How many people were onboard?' Joe asked. Something the clerk had said was worrying him.

'One thousand two hundred and sixty-six passengers,' the clerk replied, without hesitation.

Joe stared at him, and he looked straight back, unflinching. Joe was the first to give in, pretending to make a note in his notepad. 'And how many crew?' he asked, refusing to look at the clerk, who this time hesitated for a moment.

'On our manifest were six hundred and ninety-six crew of all ratings,' he said at length, clearing his throat afterwards in a way that was starting to annoy Joe.

'I make that out as one thousand, nine hundred and sixty-two onboard,' Anne added.

'Precisely.' Again, that little clearing of the throat.

Joe looked up again. Anne had gone white, if she could be any paler. The blood had drained from her face, and she covered her mouth with one hand. It was a large number of people to die, just like that, but the numbers were less than those in France.

'How many of those survived?' Joe plunged on, knowing already that he wouldn't like the answer.

'Well…' The clerk coughed. 'That's just it. We don't know as of this present moment. This is one of the reasons why the directors are all indisposed. We are trying to find out more about what happened, but as I'm sure you can imagine, reports coming through are somewhat confused and disjointed. As is to be expected.'

'A rough number perhaps?' Joe ventured.

'The only solid report we have is from the cruiser HMS *Juno* at the scene. Their telegrams mention that they believe only six lifeboats successfully launched.'

'Six?' Anne gasped.

'Yes, only six. But you must understand that you cannot print that as fact.' The clerk gave them both a stern look. 'We do not have enough details and cannot be sure of the facts until the entire area has been checked and the manifest cross-referenced. Why, even now there could be more information coming in that I am not aware of.'

'Of course,' Joe said, holding up an appeasing hand, palm outstretched, pencil between thumb and index finger. 'We're aware that this is only speculation at the moment. Anything we print will be appropriate.'

He thought about the previous articles he had written and

realised now that he was being dishonest. He would write and print precisely what he meant to. Some would try to use this article to rouse the rabble about the war, but he knew he couldn't do that.

'How many survivors does that make on the lifeboats?' he asked. 'How many can they hold?' He would instead focus on the human cost of the war, on both sides.

'It depends entirely on the type of boat, I'm afraid. The *Lusitania* was equipped with several types of lifeboat.'

'On average, then.'

'Say about fifty people per boat? Some can take more, some less.'

'So about three hundred people you would say?'

'If they were full, about that. Many would have perished in the cold conditions. The *Juno* stated that they found many afloat, drowned in the conditions, or frozen to death.'

Anne gasped again. 'How horrid,' she said, shaking her head. 'Those poor, poor people.'

'Three hundred, out of almost two thousand people,' Joe whispered under his breath.

'Early days yet,' the clerk tried to reassure him, clearing his throat.

*

Joe and Anne walked for some time in silence. They had left the Cunard building and the growing crowd behind. Joe didn't feel like saying anything, and Anne was quiet too, biting her lip in thought. The weight of the *Lusitania* disaster had hit Joe hard. It would affect the whole city in time, just as the *Titanic* had three years before. This time it felt so much worse. Perhaps it was because Joe was closer to it, old enough now to understand what it meant, or perhaps it was because it had not been an accident.

'How could they do such a thing, Joe?' Anne asked behind him, finding her voice.

He glanced over at her and saw the sadness in her eyes. He was sure it was present in his too. 'I don't know. I've been asking myself the same thing. How could anyone take another person's life? It's unthinkable.'

She sighed. 'How could they torpedo a *civilian* ship? With all those women and children aboard. The men too. They weren't soldiers. How could they do it? Why would they do it?'

'Perhaps they thought it was a naval ship? Who knows how much those U-boats can see under the water?'

'But the *Lusitania* was huge. They must have known what they were doing. It's horrible.'

'Yes.' He didn't know what else to say. They were at war with each other, and in war there were casualties. It was what he had been trying to say for the last few months. Perhaps now people would listen.

Anne shook her head again. They crossed a busy road, between the horses and carts. Joe didn't want to go back to work just yet, he wanted to get his thoughts right in his head before he had a chance to write down what he was thinking. 'They were defence-less,' she said, once they had crossed the road.

'Why does it matter if a man has a gun or not? Killing him is still a bad thing.'

'There were Americans on that ship too. They're not even in the war.'

'Oh, fantastic.' He stopped in the middle of the pavement. 'That means more men to throw into the war machine. America will surely enter the war now.'

'Isn't that a good thing? The war will end more quickly.'

'How can we know that? They didn't think it would last long at the start. Now they're going to start conscription soon. Why would they do that if they thought the war would be over soon?'

He didn't realise, but he had put a hand on her arm whilst

talking to her. He looked into her eyes and through the sadness he saw a flicker of determination flare. 'You still won't go? You'll stay with me?' she said in a whisper. 'I couldn't bear to think of you out there on your own.'

He didn't know what to say, he was dumbstruck. She had never openly voiced any kind of concern for him before. He pulled her close and hugged her. He didn't know why, but he wanted to bring her closer to him, into his world. She didn't resist and felt just right, like the missing piece of a jigsaw. As he had done at the picture house, he brushed her cheek, but this time he ran his finger under her chin and lifted up her head to look him in the eye.

'Nothing in this world will make me go to war,' he whispered. 'I will not leave your side, as long as you will have me.'

'I never thanked you for standing up for me back there.' Her voice was a whisper too, afraid that anyone might overhear them and break this moment. He kissed her then for the first time. Her immediate shock turned into reciprocation, and they held the kiss for a long, pleasant moment.

'You're a terribly forward young man, Mr Abbott. Whatever would your mother say?'

Happiness returned to her eyes and they laughed together.

He pulled her closer and she hugged him back, cuddling into his body. She fitted perfectly into the shape his arms made as if she were the other, missing, half of him. He felt that if she should ever let go that he would be incomplete again. He paused for a moment, smelling the sweet smell of her hair, then let go.

As she had when they'd first properly met, she took his hand in hers and led him away, but this time their fingers intertwined together.

Chapter 24

Soon it was their time to go back into the line. The orders had come down that they were to relieve another unit. Their rest was over. George could see the trepidation on everyone's faces, despite their best efforts to hide it. No one talked, they just stared. It was a look that permeated the entire army and at some point became disinterest. They packed up their belongings, removing any trace that they had been there, and were gone.

George was sad to leave it. Despite the trouble acquiring their billet, the barn had become a home for the past few days. It was always preferable to the foxholes in the trench where they grabbed a few hours' restless sleep.

Tom strode over to where George was forming up into the marching column. His face was downcast, with a heavy frown on his brow, and George could already sense that bad news was coming.

'I've just been to see the Sergeant, lad.'

George starting walking with the rest of his section and Tom fell in beside him.

'He says there's going to be an assault first thing in the morning. HQ want to make another big push to try and force the situation. They want us right at the front of it all, we're going in with the rest of the battalion, and the support of the entire artillery in this area. It's going to be a big one, I caught sight of them bringing shells up from the rear.'

'But we're only just going back into the line.'

'Aye, so they think we'll be fresh and raring to go. It's happening whether we like it or not, George.'

So much for that restless sleep. Even that was preferable to a full-on assault of the German trenches.

*

They walked, as was their orders. The artillery hadn't stopped firing. They had been carrying on for hours, pummelling the landscape into an unrecognisable mess. They were supposed to be laying down a curtain of fire in front of them, but some of the shells were falling short. George cursed the artillery under his breath. They had to slow their rate of advance to an even slower pace than the already painfully slow walk they were achieving.

'Steady there,' the officer shouted at one man, but George couldn't see who. The officer clutched his pistol, high out in front of him, in a way that showed he intended to use it, whatever the cost.

The artillery was a good screen, but George prayed that it would stop soon and leave them with the cover of darkness. If they were unlucky a shell could land right amongst the section. At least they wouldn't know about it.

They came to a length of wire. They had been told that the shelling would cut it, allowing them an easy way through, but as they got closer George could see that it was unaffected. Despite the orange flakes of rust and the disjointed angles, it was still intact. They would have to spend time cutting it themselves. Time they could ill afford.

A star shell went up, just ahead of them, and then all hell

broke loose. The Germans started firing trench mortars and they fell in the mud, throwing up great clots of dirt and body parts. George wasn't sure if they had been spotted, or if it had just been precautionary.

There was the crump of a change in air pressure around him, and a shell landed nearby. It blew dust at him, but he was unscathed. Men were still advancing in order, but he had lost Tom in the confusion.

'Tom?' he shouted, but he couldn't even hear his own voice. He couldn't see him in the darkness, he could be anywhere. He could even be one of the many bodies that littered no man's land. He dropped deeper into the shell hole, into the thick mud and stale water that filled it and now came up to his shins, soaking his boots. It stank of rot and decay.

There was a shape at the bottom of the shell hole, a body freshly deposited in the dirt. With fear, George turned the body over with one hand, keeping his other on the rifle. He was afraid of what he might see, Tom's lifeless eyes staring back at him. It was a struggle to get the body to turn, it was a complete dead-weight. He had to use his foot to help, but the mud pressed against him. It wasn't an honourable affair, but he wanted to find his friend, whatever the cost. If this was Tom he would at least try and return his body to their own lines. Once the body was perpendicular with the ground its centre of gravity shifted and it slapped back down into the mud causing ripples in the thick, scummy water. Dull, lifeless eyes stared back at him, just peeking out of the murky filth.

It wasn't Tom.

Thank God.

He pushed back in revulsion at the deed. He didn't know this man, but he had just kicked his body over. He crawled back up the mud backwards, unsure where he was going, but determined to get away from the body.

Another star shell went up ahead of them. In the light he could see some other men were advancing and not too far ahead. He rushed to catch up, slashing through the mud and grime.

A machine gun opened up somewhere to their right, the rattle deafening in the night. His section ducked. Some of the others weren't so lucky, and George could hear the puff and muted cries as they were hit. He could just about make out the machine gun from the muzzle flash. It didn't seem to be able to traverse as far as where he lay so he raised his head a little higher over the tip of the crater he was lying in. He couldn't see where the officer had gone; every man looked the same in the dark, whether friend or foe. There were some men moving in front of him in the direction of the enemy trench.

He moved his hand to get some grip and pull himself up out of the hole, but it went straight into the thick mud and almost became stuck. He had to use his other arm to pull it free, putting down his rifle at the same time. He was glad there was no officer around, otherwise he would be in trouble for that act alone, not to mention the fact that he wasn't moving forward in an ordered fashion. He picked up his rifle again and checked the firing mechanism. The bolt rocked back fine, but he doubted it would pass inspection. He hoped he wouldn't need it to before he got a good chance to clean it.

He ran after the other men, not caring about his orders, only intent on keeping up with them so he wasn't alone. They were pressing their advantage well and had managed to cross the ground to the first German trench.

He jumped in after them.

German soldiers were still defending the trench. The Brits were too close for them to bring weapons to bear so some men used bayonets to thrust at their enemies. A man lunged at George and he managed to parry the bayonet with his own rifle.

He grabbed for a club he had in his harness and swung it at the German. The heavy wood was wrapped in barbed wire and it hit the man on the temple. Blood sprayed across George's forearm. It was a brutal weapon, but it saved his life. He had taken it from the farm they had billeted in and added his own barbed wire as he had seen other men do to similar weapons. Bayonets were too long to wield in the close quarters of a trench brawl.

Panting from the struggle he searched for his next target. A young German saw him, his mouth dropped open and he turned and ran. George let him go.

The others were dealing with the remaining Germans. There was still no sign of Tom.

The trench was in a lot better condition than the trenches they were used to. The duckboards were about a foot deeper and the walls were reinforced in a way that George hadn't seen before. Apart from that it appeared almost the same as the British trenches. Both sides had pretty much the same conditions in which to suffer. There was a lot less mud, but it wasn't a place that someone would want to call home. And still, the Germans had left it to get out of the artillery fire. That same artillery fire that was now falling down amongst the British.

'Someone tell those fucking gunners to pack it in!' a voice shouted over the din.

The officer turned on him but said nothing to reprimand him.

'We'll have to head back,' he said at length, looking unsure about it. The officer had still yet to fire his pistol in anger, but he couldn't argue that they were in a precarious situation. They had lost too many men and were in danger of being fired upon by their own artillery. If and when the gunners stopped firing, the Germans would counter-attack from whatever safety they had gone to. There weren't enough men left in the section to hold on to the enemy trench and the officer had come to the same conclusion.

'There's nothing for it, lads. We can't hold this trench with what's left of us,' he said again, confirming George's suspicions. 'Come on, let's get back over that wall. On with you.'

There was some groaning from the men, a couple of whom had only just crawled into the trench from no man's land.

'You can't be serious?' one of them said. It was the same voice that had complained about the gunners.

This time the officer looked fit to burst.

'Of course I'm serious,' he shouted at the man, still brandishing his Webley revolver. 'We're heading back to our own trenches, now get on with it.' He gestured back out into no man's land, but the private was not done.

'We can't go back out there, sir.' He spat the title out, and stared at the officer. 'We only just got through it the first time.'

'We can't stay here either,' George said, stepping between the two men. He didn't know why he did it, but he was keen to stop any fighting between their own men. The private, should he survive the raid, would no doubt be up on a charge, and the officer might push matters to make sure he saved face in front of the men. George didn't want either. The officer gave George a nod.

'The private's correct. We can't stay here. Good soldiers that you all undoubtedly are, once Fritz comes back we will be outnumbered. There's nothing here for us, the raid has failed and I would rather take my chances out there—' again he pointed at the gloom between the lines, '—than take my chances with a German counter-attack. They'll have their backs up after this, that's for sure.'

In small groups they climbed up the parapet and back into no man's land, hoping to use the early morning darkness to their advantage. The German machine guns had been silenced, so George ran for it. In the darkness it was hard to tell which way was what. A few minutes later, after squelching through mud and dodging barbed wire, George rolled into a trench, his small group behind him. The trench was empty save for a few dark shapes moving about at one end.

'Let's go check it out,' he said to the man next to him, fearing they may have ended up back in the German trench.

'They're Lancs! Look at the badges,' someone shouted. 'Thank God!'

The dull glimmer of bronze shone on their sleeves as another Very light flare went up in no man's land. George ducked further down into the trench as another shell hit no man's land just off to one side. The artillery was still heavy here, and as he moved towards the Lancashires in the next trench a shell went off in a communication trench behind him, throwing thick mud and dust up into the air. The men that had been there were now gone, and the trench itself had partially collapsed. Some of his group moved to try and dig them out, but George knew they were already gone.

Instead, he carried on in the direction he had been travelling, moving closer to the small group of Lancashires. They were from the same battalion, so they must be close to their own lines. He asked the first man the way back to their unit, but the man just stared back at him, unblinking eyes staring out from the dirt around his face. George thought about shaking him, but realised there was no point. He didn't know where the man's mind had gone, but hoped it was better than this place.

The other couple of men were helping a wounded man down to the bottom of the trench and George moved up to see if he could help. He reinforced another man, by putting his back against him and making sure that he didn't slip in the mud. They managed to lift the man to the ground, groaning with the movement. He lay on the fire step, out of the mud and drainage at the bottom of the trench.

As another Very light went up, George caught a glimpse of the man's face. It was pale despite the muck and sweat that covered it, and an intelligence showed in his eyes.

'Joe?' the man said suddenly, trying to get up. The other men pushed him back down. 'Joe Abbott?' he continued, quieter, unsure of himself.

George was shocked. He hadn't heard his brother's name in

239

over a year. In the dark, muddy hell of the trench his brother had been far from his thoughts, but here was this man that had mistaken him for Joe. He couldn't believe it. There was a family resemblance between the two brothers, sure, but they didn't look alike. George had lost weight and grown gaunter during his time in the trenches. He realised he must now resemble his brother more, Joe always having been the thinner of the two.

He moved closer to the stricken soldier, trying to work out who he was, while the man still repeated his brother's name, each time more quietly than the last as his strength was leaving him, his energy almost spent.

Another shell exploded nearby, causing them to duck as the shrapnel and debris flew everywhere. The change in pressure hurt George's ears and the whomp of the explosion caught him. It took all his willpower not to drop his weapon and put his hands to his ears.

The other men had pushed themselves back against the trench wall, avoiding the worst of the blow. But one had not been so lucky; the trench wall no longer existed in that section and half his body was buried good in the mud and slime that had fallen into the trench. No one moved to uncover him. It didn't matter any way. A large chunk of his torso had been ripped open and his arms lost; he would bleed out before anyone could help him. George tried to blink away the image, but when he closed his eyes it was still there. It always would be. He'd seen enough horrors to last a lifetime.

A Very light flew up into the sky highlighting the grisly scene in its off-white glow.

'Frank?' George said, as the face in front of him became clear, then disappeared as the Very light blinked out. It was always difficult for their eyes to adjust as the light kept changing at every opportunity, but George had seen enough.

'Joe, it really is you,' Frank replied, his voice a hoarse whisper that George had to lean closer to make out. One of his fellows had gone off to fetch a stretcher-bearer or a medic and had left

George more room to kneel next to Frank's prone form, as he lay along the duckboards.

He fumbled in his pocket and then drew out what he was searching for. Flicking open the silver casing, he sparked the lighter, bringing it closer to Frank's face.

'Hey, mate. Don't you care about the gas?' the soldier opposite him said, and George ignored him. Yes, a stray match could set off some gas or explosive, but there had been no sign of gas being used on this section. They were safe for now. He used it to illuminate the man's face, to check that he recognised him. It was Frank Gallagher, from Joe's work. Perhaps a little bit thinner and less lively, but it was the same man. He had that almost pockmarked face that showed signs of teenage acne. George didn't know him well, he had only met him a few times. Everyone looked different in khaki, but some faces you didn't forget.

'If you're going to waste that flame, Joe, at least gimme a fag,' Frank said with a cough. At least he still had his sense of humour. George pulled a packet out of his webbing and put a cigarette between Frank's lips, with care, making sure it stayed in place. Then he lit it, the end glowing red hot in the darkness.

'Thanks, Joe,' Frank said, between clenched teeth, expertly keeping the cigarette in place whilst talking, even in his wounded state.

George thought for a minute. Frank still believed that George was his brother. In his state, would there be any point to telling him otherwise? George didn't like the idea of lying to someone who was on the edge of death. They were all on the edge of death out here.

Then a thought occurred to him. If Frank thought he was Joe, then it was possible that Joe was out here too. Perhaps he was lost out in no man's land, wherever Tom had gone. He had no choice but to plunge ahead.

'Sorry, Frank, but I'm not Joe,' he said, repositioning the cigarette in Frank's mouth, then lighting one of his own.

'What do you mean, "not Joe"?' Frank's voice was growing ever weaker. '"Course you're Joe, I'd recognise you anywhere, lad. Now's no time to develop a sense of humour.'

George took one of Frank's hands in his, to rouse him.

'I'm not Joe,' he said again. 'I'm his brother. I'm George. Do you remember me?'

Frank brows furrowed despite the glassy look taking over his eyes.

'George?' he whispered.

'George Abbott,' George urged.

'George... I remember you. You're Joe's little brother. What are you doing here? You don't work at the newspaper...' He trailed off, growing delirious with his pain.

'Where is that medic?' George grumbled, looking around at the others who in the darkness shrugged almost imperceptible shrugs. He tried Frank again, growing more desperate.

'Frank, we're not at the newspaper. You know where we are. My brother, you know my brother.'

'Joe, my good pal Joe.' Franks eyes lit up at the mention of Joe's name.

'Yes, Joe... my brother.' He had taken Frank by the shoulders without realising. 'Is he here, Frank? Is Joe in France?' He shook Frank's shoulder and felt guilty as the other man groaned with the movement. He was losing consciousness, but something still held on.

'Joe? In France?'

'Yes, Frank, is he here?'

'Don't be ridiculous. I never could get Joe in khaki. It wasn't his colour.' He began laughing, a dry, wracking laugh that plummeted through his entire body, shaking him where he lay. Despite the obvious pain, it was a good laugh. Frank had always had a good laugh. George leaned back on his haunches and let out a huge sigh of relief and built-up pressure. He had almost been holding his breath.

Joe wasn't in France.

That small fact brought him immense relief. He couldn't imagine his brother in this place. In the mud and blood. In this hell.

'Your brother is still back at the newspaper, doing my job for me. Y'know he wouldn't fight.' He coughed, and the corners of his mouth darkened. It was a couple of tense, worried seconds before he spoke again. 'I'm starting to think he was right.'

'Don't worry, Frank. Everything's going to be all right.' He had no idea if it would be. Frank was fading fast, but he had to say something, something to keep his mind on the future and keep him fighting. 'The medics are on their way, lad. Just you wait.'

'I reckon this is my last day, lad,' Frank croaked out from his blood-drenched mouth. The sound was a whisper, but he spoke with a forcefulness that made the blood dribble even more.

'Don't say that, Frank. The medic is on his way.'

Someone tapped George on the shoulder, but he didn't turn.

'He's gone, lad.'

The voice was quiet, respectful, by his side.

George straightened. He didn't know Frank well, but he knew he was a good man. He did what he could to smarten him up and moved him out of the mud. It wasn't fair to let a man die like that. He closed his eyes and said a prayer for his brother.

After a few moments he went off to find his section.

*

The day was turning to light as they found their own section of trench. It had been a long night, and every man was tired, strain etched on their faces. The officers were busy tallying the dead from their own units, working out who was missing from those who were present.

In the late afternoon when the sun was already beginning its downward slope, a figure slipped into the trench and dropped down in front of them. Everyone jumped up, but George recognised the silhouette.

'Tom? Tom Adams, is it really you?' He hugged his friend as if he hadn't seen him in years, squeezing the air out of his lungs in a big bear hug.

'Easy, easy, lad. That hurts,' Tom said, pushing George away. For once he didn't have a grin on his face and it unsettled George. The other men drifted back to their dugouts and those who were repairing the trench started digging at the loose earth again.

'You're hurt?' he asked, checking for the signs of a wound, before he was again pushed away.

'No, George,' Tom said.

George gave his friend a shrewd look, expecting him to be playing the hero.

'No,' he said again, with more force. 'I'm fine. Honestly, I'm fine. Leave off, will you?'

'All right. I'm just glad to see you is all. I thought the worst.'

'I know, George, but I'm all right, see? Look.' He twirled on the spot, and then grinned at George, but it seemed forced. There was no humour behind that grin.

'I can see. But where have you been? I couldn't find you out there. I searched and called, but you had gone. You couldn't have gone far.'

'I didn't,' Tom said. 'I er, I got a bit lost once all the guns started firing. I couldn't hear anything in the noise.'

George wasn't sure, but he thought he saw Tom force back a shudder.

'That machine gun was giving the men around me hell, George. I ended up in a shell hole once it opened up. One of the explosions must have forced me in there. I… I didn't know I was in it until I was in it… if you know what I mean?'

George was confused, he had never heard Tom sound so uncertain in all the years they had known each other. Since they had met he had been the very epitome of calm and controlled. The man standing in front of him now was an altogether different man. Not just because of the mud and blood that stained his skin and khaki, but in the way he talked. It wasn't the fact that he talked like a soldier, it wasn't that at all. Actually, he was no longer talking like a soldier but more like a frightened little child, telling his mother about the monster under his bed. In all his life, George had never imagined Tom Adams being that small, scared boy, but now it was the only image he could picture.

Tom grinned at him again, trying to overcome this barrier that had come between them all of a sudden, but it didn't work. Something had changed in their relationship.

'What happened after that, Tom?' George asked, trying not to pity his oldest friend. 'I must have strayed some distance away from you once the Germans broke loose. Apparently, I was nowhere near you.'

Tom didn't answer but patted his webbing. Once he had found a cigarette he put it in his mouth and gestured for George to help him light it. George passed him the lighter that he had kept in his webbing since Tom had given it to him, and Tom snickered at the memory. 'Thanks, lad,' he said, and handed it back.

'Keep it,' George said, hoping that he hadn't said it with too much anger. 'I don't smoke half as much as you, and… it belongs to you. I was just looking after it, right?'

Tom squinted at him, then put the lighter away without another word.

'So what happened?'

'Not much, lad.' Tom sat down on the firing step and took another drag from his cigarette. 'I didn't leave that shell hole. I mean, how could I?'

He paused for George's judgement but seeing the blank expression George forced onto his face, he carried on.

'How could I go anywhere? That machine gun was ripping the ground to shreds. Little tufts of dirt kept dropping on me every time it fired. When it shut up, I went to move, and bang, it opens up again, traversing back and forth, dropping more spots of dirt on me... and worse. Those lads out in the open didn't stand a chance.'

'I know, I saw them,' George conceded, not wanting to bring back the memory, but having little choice.

'If I'd have left that shell hole, it'd have been nothing short of suicide. Call it whatever you want, but I was in no position to help with the raid, I was pinned.'

George knew what Tom meant, as he too had been pinned down inside an altogether different shell hole. But he had found his way out, hadn't he? Tom could have done the same.

'There was another lad inside the hole with me. He looked younger than you, but he wasn't afraid. He was just like you, he was. He got up right to the edge of that shell hole, grabbed his Lee Enfield and faced the enemy.'

Tom stopped and took a deep breath and a drag of his cigarette before continuing.

'Next thing I know,' he said, 'he's falling back into the hole, face first, or at least what's left of his face. The machine guns caught 'im and gone clean through his hat. There was nothing left of the poor lad to recognise him with. His own ma wouldn't have known him from the rest. There was no way I was gonna join him in the bottom of that hole without the top of my head.'

He took another long drag and George sat down next to him on the firing step, unable to look at his friend's face anymore. The sorrow there was too heartfelt, and George could empathise. His mind flashed back to the corpse he had found in his own shell hole. How had that poor man died? He shook his head to clear the image and Tom took it as disagreement.

'Well, many others would have done the same, lad,' he said. 'I know you're a hero and you'd have run off to beat the whole German army on your own, but there was no way I was getting out of that shell hole. So I sat there.'

'That's not what I was—'

Tom ignored him.

'I sat there all night, listening to the sound of the guns firing and my own heartbeat hammering in my ears. After a while it started to get quieter.'

George wasn't sure whether he meant the sound of the guns or his heartbeat.

'Once the machine gun had finally given up I chanced it. Guessing that you lot had probably made it back by then, I crawled back through the mud and dirt. It took what seemed like hours, and at one point the machine gun opened up again. I pushed myself down as far as I could go, right into some poor old sod's earthly remains. The stench was awful, and I don't know how long I lay there for until it stopped firing again. The I crawled on, rolled over the edge of the trench and there you were, as if an angel, staring back at me.'

'It's all right, you're back now.' George patted Tom on his back. 'Let's get a brew and some kip. We'll be back on duty once the sun goes down.

Tom nodded and together they went off in search of some of the petrol-tinted tea that was so common in the trenches.

Chapter 25

Joe sat on the bench overlooking St John's Gardens, Anne at his side. The grass was covered in leaves of various different colours: browns, yellows, and some still held on to the green of summer. They blew around in the air, swirling in patterns this way and that way. Every now and then a strong gust would force one bunch of leaves at another, attacking them with a crunch. He shivered in the chilly air and pulled his coat tighter around him in a vain effort to warm himself up.

'They're saying it won't be long now. The military act will come soon. Conscription.'

He spoke, trying to break the silence between them. It wasn't an awkward silence. Anne was enjoying the park as much as he was, but he enjoyed it more when they were talking.

'Who're saying that?' she asked, staring off into the distance at the trees whose leaves were slowly falling to join the others on the ground.

'The No-Conscription Fellowship are quite sure it's imminent. Parliament are definitely heading that way. Especially after that registration day they had in August. I still regret having to sign that document.'

'What else could you do?'

'I could have thrown it away. I'm sure they would have sent me another one to fill in though. Or worse, sent the police around.'

They sat in silence for a while. Anne moved closer along the bench, and Joe put his arm around her, thankful for her warmth in the cold autumn afternoon. The smell of her, that close, was intoxicating. It took over his sense so much that he almost forgot what they were supposed to be doing.

'We're late, we had better go. Are you sure you want to come? It'll just be my parents and us, my sister Catherine will be out, and Lizzie has been under the weather. I think, in some way, that will be even worse.'

'I'm sure.' She leaned in to him and they cuddled closer. 'I want to meet your parents. Although it's nice to just sit, and be.'

'We can stay if you want? I can't think of much better than sitting here with you.'

He smiled at her, and they kissed. It struck him as amazing how natural that felt now. At first he had been awkward and nervous around her, but in a few short months they had grown closer and closer. Being with her felt like the most natural thing in the world, and he wondered how he had ever managed without her. For the first time in his life something gave him confidence.

'No, we can't,' she said. 'Your parents will be waiting, and I don't want to anger them before I've even met them.'

He couldn't imagine how she could anger anyone, and smiled.

Often, he would walk home, taking in the sights and smells of Liverpool and composing himself before interacting with his parents, but he didn't want to have to make Anne walk all that way. They caught the tram from the city centre up the hill and just under half an hour later they were on his street.

Joe put his hand on the front doorknob and left it there for a moment. He took a deep breath to calm his nerves and breathed out. Anne noticed his hesitation and put a hand on his back. 'It'll be all right,' she whispered in his ear. He nodded and turned the iron doorknob.

The door opened to the familiar smells of his home, and he walked straight in.

'Home sweet home,' he said to Anne, smiling as best he could. He resisted the urge to go straight upstairs as he would have done if he were alone and instead walked towards the kitchen.

'Joseph, is that you?' his mother's voice called from inside.

Go on, Anne mouthed at him, and he pushed open the white painted door.

'Hi, Mum,' he said, as she turned around to face him. 'I'd like you to meet Anne.'

His mother shot up straight away from the chair she had been sitting in at the table and rushed towards them. Joe was taken aback by the movement, but his mother took Anne in a big embrace and hugged her with warmth.

'Anne?' she said. 'It's so lovely to meet you. At last.'

She eyed Joe and feigned anger.

'I don't know why he has been keeping you from us for so long. He's probably ashamed of his humble upbringing. Still, you're here now and it's lovely to meet you.'

'Oh now, Mrs Abbott. I don't think Joe has been keeping me from you. We've both been very busy at the newspaper, what with the war on.'

A look crossed his mother's features that he didn't quite understand. Was it anger? Confusion? Regret?

'Joseph doesn't tell us much about it, I'm afraid. When he's here he's sleeping, when he's not, I presume he is at the newspaper with you.'

She stopped and put a hand over her mouth.

'Oh, where are my manners? Please, please have a seat. I'm not used to having company. I forget myself.'

She pulled out the chair she had been sitting on further from the table and proffered it to Anne.

'Thank you,' Anne said, as she sat down. Joe sat down next to her and studied his mum. As usual she was keeping herself occupied so that she didn't have to meet the frustrations and disappointments of her daily life.

The front door banged shut, followed by the sound of a walking stick on the wooden floorboards of the hall. Joe's mother's face dropped.

'I was just preparing some tea for the family. It's not much, but I hope you'll stay?'

Anne looked at Joe, uncertain, and he shrugged. 'I'd love to stay,' she said, smiling at Joe's mum, and patting Joe's hand.

The kitchen door creaked open wider and Joe's dad's footsteps signalled he was walking in. The walking stick appeared first, followed by the gaunt figure of his father.

'Oh,' he said, upon seeing Joe and Anne sitting down, and stopping in the doorway.

Joe shot up straight away, not liking the feeling of being sat down in his father's presence and the lack of control it gave him. He knew that his father didn't like the idea of men lazing around; a real man should always be busy doing some task or another. Joe guessed that it was army training. The devil makes work for idle hands.

'Dad,' he said. 'This is Anne, my…'

He paused, not knowing how to introduce Anne. They had never spoken aloud about what they meant to each other. He had just assumed that she was his girlfriend and that they were in a relationship, but now that he was put on the spot, he hesitated. He could feel Anne's eyes on his back, waiting to see what he would say next, but he was frozen.

'Good afternoon, Anne,' his father said, saving Joe from his hesitation. He breathed a sigh of relief. His father didn't even seem to notice his consternation and carried on speaking despite him.

'So you're the woman that's going to turn our Joseph into an honest man?' He walked around the table click-clicking his cane against the floor, his every step the visage of pain in his eyes as he scowled. 'Let's get a proper look at you.'

The smell of food wafted through the kitchen as Joe's mother turned to Joe's father, holding a stew pot in her hand. She frowned in his direction.

'I'm nearly done cooking, Alfred. Leave poor Anne alone and find your place at the table. She's intimidated enough as it is without you giving her a parade once over. She's turned out delightfully, so why don't you just leave her be?'

'Sorry, dear,' he said, and eased himself into the seat at the head of the table, inching slowly down so as not to jar his injured leg. This was one of the few times when Joe's mother resembled the famed Northern Woman that was in absolute charge of her husband. Where, with a few choice words, she could force her husband to do her bidding. He couldn't understand why she wasn't like this more often. Perhaps her upbringing had caused her to be more timid, but most of the time she acted as if she was her husband's servant. So many times it had upset Joe enough that he had wanted to do something about it. Ultimately, he had yet to find a way to save her from his father, if indeed she needed saving at all. He still believed that, under that patina of fear, she loved his father dearly, and that separating her from him would do more harm than good. If anyone was capable of doing such a thing, should it be needed, then surely his Uncle Stephen would have done something by now.

'So, Anne. How do you know our Joseph?'

His father was busy sticking a napkin into the collar of his shirt. It was something he always did, and something that always drew a sigh of frustration from his wife. It wasn't that he was a messy eater, but that he was fastidiously clean. Not a spot of food was allowed to touch his clothes, otherwise he would march himself away, or as close to a march as was possible given his injured leg, and change. Life in the army must be hard if it was always like that, and not for the first time Joe felt for George out at the front.

'Well, Mr Abbott—'

'Call me Alfred…'

'Joe and I met at the newspaper.' She smiled at Joe and he couldn't help but smile back, until he caught his father's expression of mild annoyance.

'Oh yes? Did he write something about you? About your family or something? You're dressed very finely. You must come from a very good, upper-class family.'

'Oh, no. Not so high and mighty.' She blushed, her cheeks going a ruby red through her pale skin. 'That is, I mean to say, my family are all very good people, but you might call us middle class at best. My father is a teacher, and so was my grandfather and his grandfather, as far back as I can remember. It's so good of you to welcome me into your home.'

'Ah, so that's how you come to speak so proper? As for me, I've got my lovely wife to thank for that. You should have heard me during my army days.'

Joe thought that his father was about to go on and tell one of his army stories, but instead he stopped and stared into the middle distance, remembering. Joe was shocked by how open his father was being with Anne. He had already taken a liking to her, and Joe couldn't blame his father for that. He was thankful that Anne had said teacher, and not school master as her father really was. He wasn't sure what his father would make of that, although he seemed to be warming to Anne.

'My mother also made sure that I learned to read and write well, as well as to speak. She didn't think anyone would take me seriously otherwise. She had quite… unusual ideas. She couldn't help but fall in love with my father, but she runs the household.' She blushed again.

Joe couldn't help but marvel at the similarities between himself and Anne. He had never thought to ask her about her family before. He had been so immersed and absorbed by her, he hadn't had the time to think about the world around her. He had often wondered what had brought her to the newspaper, she was more than capable. Not many of their peers could read and write half as well as she could. He had the luck and benefit of the education that his wealthy uncle had paid for, and he guessed Anne had a very similar situation. He would ask her about it sometime, if the opportunity arose.

'That's all right, love,' Joe's mother said, setting a bowl of Scouse in front of Anne, and then Joe. The smell of the beef stew hit Joe's nostrils and he felt warm inside. The smell of the local specialty always reminded him of happier times, of when he was a child and the prospects of work or the threat of war weren't things he was conscious of. Of course, they had never served it at his school, the dish was too far beneath them. 'We don't care a jot about what class you're from in this household. We're all the same, flesh and blood.'

Joe's father made a 'hmph' sound.

'I've been helping some of the Belgian refugees we took in with their English,' Anne said. 'It's so satisfying being able to help them in some small way.' Anne, growing more nervous, shot a glance at Joe for support.

'We met at the newspaper, Dad. As in, Anne now works with me at the newspaper.'

'A woman? Working at the newspaper?' His father appeared shocked, which was surprising in itself.

'A woman with a job?' his mother countered, with a twinkle in her eye. 'What a modern and fantastic world we are living in. Don't stand on ceremony, love. Dig in.'

She sat down at the table with her own bowl of Scouse, after giving her husband one.

'Well, with the war on,' he said, 'we've lost a lot of the male workforce. Anne has been a great help, and more and more women are taking up the work as the men go to the front. We need more help trying to make people see sense.'

He knew that what he had said had been a mistake as soon as he saw his father's expression drop. He had been enjoying the food, lapping it up, but now his spoon dropped back towards the bowl as he stared at Joe.

'I suppose you think this is acceptable?' he said, emphasising the last word, looking at both Joe and Anne.

Joe chose his next words with care, not wishing to elicit any further anger from his father. Over the years he had got used to thinking before speaking, otherwise he found himself in trouble.

'I do,' he said. 'I think it's more than acceptable, it should be standard. I wouldn't be surprised if, after the war, women find themselves in more positions of responsibility.'

'I don't mean that. I mean this anti-war talk you've been publishing. Men should be going out to fight, as is their right in all that is good and normal, and women should stick to what they know best. They're needed in the war effort too.'

'I don't know what you mean.' Anne's brow furrowed, and she wouldn't break her stare with Joe's father. In that moment Joe admired her, she was so strong and confident. That moment alone summed up everything he had come to love about her, and why he just couldn't keep away.

His father was not to be talked down.

'Men, good men are dying out there. Why should anyone be any different? If we refuse to fight, then we will lose this war. Then what? Do you fancy speaking German, lass? I'm afraid I'm not very good at it!'

'There are other things that help the war effort. A man needn't fight to help us win this war.'

'True enough, but do you really think writing articles for a newspaper amounts to that? What good is it doing? Especially that paper you two work for.'

He scowled at Joe, who thought he could see actual pity in his father's eyes. It shocked him.

'The kind of newspaper that would publish defeatist and anti-war statements? How, precisely, is that helping the war effort?'

Anne opened her mouth to speak but shut it again. She was

struck by Joe's father's final comments. She didn't know what else to say. She had made her argument and he was having none of it. She was trying to get Joe's attention, but what could he do? What could he say that he hadn't already that would change his father's mind?

'The best way to stop more men from dying is to end the war,' he said.

'And how do you propose you're going to do that, Joseph? Hiding away in that warehouse of yours writing little articles with your friends?' There was real venom in his father's voice.

He didn't raise the fact that apart from Anne he didn't have any friends, not since Frank had gone out to war.

'I didn't say I was going to do it on my own.'

'Hmm, I don't doubt it.'

His father's tone angered him. They would never see eye to eye. He didn't even know why he was trying, but he wouldn't back down from his stance, not now, not ever. That was what having morals was about. Believing in them without question. It was almost religious in fervour.

'Millions of men are dying, and for what? We have to do something to stop it. It can't go on, Father. Otherwise there will be no one left to fight. What happens when the only soldiers left are the old and the infirm?'

'And I suppose you think that you're going to be able to stop it?' His father's fist banged on the table, emphasising key words, as he stared at Joe, his gaze unflinching. He had an iron, soldier's stare, and Joe forced himself not to break it while his father continued speaking.

'You don't have a clue, Joseph. Even with all your education, your book learning and your newspapers. You still don't have a clue. Other, better men than you have tried to stop wars. The ultimate truth will always remain. The only way to win a war is to defeat your enemy. To stop your enemy from winning the war, you have to stop them wanting to fight.'

He sighed and broke his staring match with Joe. He looked at his wife, and at Anne as if seeing her for the first time, then sighed again. 'Do you think that if we stop fighting, that the Germans will just lay down their arms and go home?' he asked.

Joe hesitated. 'I think that they may, given the chance,' he said with caution.

His father's fist hit the table again, and he strained in his seat as if wanting to stand up, but he was struck down by his injured leg. 'Then you're an idiot! If we lay down our weapons and walk away then they will have won. We won't have saved lives, we will have caused many more innocents to die. The only thing stopping them from walking into the French countryside is our boys at the front. Admitting defeat will only give them time and confidence to produce more arms, more ammunition and carry on their advance. They won't put down their weapons any more than we should.'

The room was deathly silent. Both Anne and Joe's mother had stopped eating at his father's outburst, their cutlery left forgotten on the side of their setting. They stared at him, concern on their face. Anne had never met his father before, but his mother had seen him angry plenty of times. However, neither Joe nor his mother had seen his father quite like this, ever. It had been an impassioned speech based on experience of fighting, and Joe was speechless, but he still couldn't bring himself to agree with his father.

Anne was blushing. He guessed it was because she was embarrassed.

'Can we not just enjoy this food?' his mother asked across the table at her husband with a stern look on her face. 'I had to queue up to get that beef, and I want to enjoy it while it's still warm.'

'Oh, I'm sorry, dear,' his father said. 'Of course.'

He started eating again, staring at his bowl, and making motions to show he was indeed eating.

'It's delightful, Mrs Abbott,' Anne said, trying to break the awkward silence that had arisen around the table in the aftermath of Joe and his father's argument. 'My mother's cooking doesn't come close.'

Joe's mum beamed at her. He had never seen her so happy. He was sure Anne had mentioned that her family had a cook. He wondered what it must be like to have someone to cook for you at your whim.

'You're too kind, love. It was the best I could do on short notice. Joseph didn't tell me you were joining us until this morning. This was the best beef I could get once I had got to the front of the queue. It'll do, but it's not the best. These food shortages are getting worse and worse.'

'It's completely my fault, Mrs Abbott. I forgot to tell him I could make it.'

'It's no one's fault, love. Just a matter of circumstances. We're just happy to have you here with us. It's an absolute pleasure to meet you.'

The rest of the meal continued in silence, as Anne sneaked glances at Joe, and he tried his best to smile at her and reassure her. He almost wished he hadn't brought her here, but she would have had to meet his parents at some point. Especially if they wanted to get married, which he hoped was a distinct possibility.

After they were finished, the plates had been cleaned up, and his father had retired to the front room, Joe decided that they had had enough for the evening.

'I'm going to walk Anne home, Mum.'

His mother nodded and gave Anne big hug.

'I'm sorry for tonight,' she said. 'Please don't be a stranger, you brighten up our house.'

Anne was flattered by the comment, and at a loss for words. So she nodded and said her goodbyes.

Outside, the mid-autumn evening was cool. There was a slight breeze as there always was in Liverpool, focused up the hills that surrounded the river Mersey. Stars were beginning to peek out from the heavens and only a few clouds darkened the already blackening sky.

Joe took off his coat and wrapped it around Anne as they walked up the hill with slow steps.

'I'm sorry about tonight,' he said. 'About my father and the awkwardness.'

'It's all right. You don't need to apologise. Knowing how passionate you are, I could only imagine that your father would be the same. You both have very strong opinions. It's just a shame that they seem to be polar opposites. I think it's good for you to have someone to play devil's advocate. It keeps you in your place.'

She smiled a cheeky smile at him, and he forgot his seriousness, laughing.

'I think you're mocking me.'

'Only slightly.' She smiled again. 'Your father isn't entirely wrong, you know.'

'I know. But I also know that I can't condone taking life. No matter how well mannered others think it might be. We only have one life, and so many are being cut needlessly short.'

'If you can't take another man's life, then you could always do something else to help. They're always asking for stretcher-bearers, or medical orderlies. That way you would be helping people, not killing them.'

He stopped dead in his tracks. She sensed his lack of motion and turned around.

'What difference does it make?' he said. 'Whatever I do will condone and continue the war. It's all part of the "war effort". The best thing I can do is oppose it, then perhaps people will start to listen and understand that it's wrong. Do we have to argue about this? I've had enough arguing for one evening.'

'I'm not arguing, Joe. I'm just worried about you.'

She started walking again, eager to get home before the night got too cold, and too dark. 'Very soon they're going to make everyone fight, and what will happen to you then? At least if you chose another path you would avoid that.'

'I don't know,' he said as he followed. 'I guess I will have to cross that bridge when I come to it. There's no use worrying about it now and spoiling the time we have together with arguments. I'm sorry.'

'I keep telling you not to apologise, you don't need to be sorry for anything. I'm an adult, I can argue with the best of them. Let's just enjoy our time together, before the world explodes.'

He turned her head to face him and kissed her. He thought she might resist, but instead she leaned into him and pulled him closer. He held her close for a few minutes, feeling her warmth against him and drowning in her scent. He wished he could hold on to that moment forever, but he knew that it wouldn't last.

Chapter 26

The door to the estaminet jingled every time someone entered, and each time some of the soldiers inside would start at the noise, their eyes darting around for danger. George had got used to it, and for some unknown reason, its quaintness reminded him of home. The same couldn't be said for the others. One man had once asked the owner to take down the bell, but the little couple that owned the place had just stared at him, uncomprehending. The soldiers in the cafe had laughed at him and told him to sit down. Instead he had left, rather than be humiliated. A little French went a long way out here, and not for the first time George wished he had bothered to learn some. Tom claimed he was fluent, but George was sure that every word out of his mouth was nonsense, and he had never heard him speak it to a Frenchman.

Tom took a drag on his cigarette and blew smoke out in George's direction, who tried hard not to cough. He still hadn't got used to smoking, and the estaminet was heavy with it. Smoke hung around the ceiling like miniature clouds.

'Ah, it's good to be back in civilisation,' Tom said, between bouts of smoking. For the first time in what seemed like months, his characteristic grin was plastered back on his face, and it made

George smile to see it. He nodded his assent and took another swig of the pale Belgian beer. It was nothing like what they got at home, but it was pleasant. It had more kick to it than the beer back home, and he had seen more than one man drink too much of it in the short time they had spent in the town. Some of them had been late for training, with terrible hangovers, and the Sergeant-Majors hadn't been best pleased. So far, George had managed to avoid punishment, and he now took each sip with care, trying not to drink the stuff like it was water.

'I'm just glad we didn't have to wrestle for a billet again,' he said.

The town had afforded far more places to billet than the village they had been assigned to before, and they hadn't seen any sign of the Londoners since their last encounter. Their section had been billeted in a disused warehouse, which the sappers had come in and prepared for use. For the first time in almost a year they had bunks to sleep in, and a healthy supply of rations. For the first time in months they had clean clothes, and they had managed to get rid of the lice. It had only been a few days since they had been brought out of the line, but it felt good.

'You can say that again, George. I thought that bloody barn would be the death of me.'

George couldn't help but smile at his friend's swearing. They'd both picked up some of the traits of soldiers, the language being one of them. 'Good thing the Sergeant came along when he did, I say. Still, he's gone and left us now. He thinks he's too good for us, that one.'

The officers and NCOs had their own estaminets further along the road, where they could socialise with men of their own rank and backgrounds. This one was for the rank and file, and if you didn't already know when entering, you could tell from the smoke, the smell, and the bawdy singsong that went on in the corners – not to mention the run-down appearance and the peeling walls. In this town it was lucky that it still had a roof.

George spared a thought for the poor couple that owned the place, who cowered behind their bar, scared witless of the British soldiers. At least they would be thankful for the income it brought them. On occasion French soldiers came in, and their faces lit up as if they were being saved, but the French were few and far between these days. They often found their own places to drink and relax and were often in different parts of the line.

'You're just jealous, Tom,' George said, smiling at his friend to show he was joking. 'Don't worry, you'll soon be able to go up the road and drink with your people.'

They both laughed and drank some more. George started to think that perhaps they were already drunker than they had thought. At least they weren't singing yet, or worse. Some of the men from the section had got drunk and hitched lifts into Poperinge to see the sights. Word was that the main attractions were a number of choice brothels. There weren't a lot of women left near the front line, and those that were had to work for their upkeep. It wasn't something that George wanted to think about, and he didn't doubt that the best women were kept for the officers. He couldn't imagine the poor souls that provided their services for the men like him. He didn't fancy trying to find a way back to his billet afterwards either.

The door jingled again, taking George's mind out of the gutter. As all eyes turned to the door, a man he recognised walked in, surrounded by a couple of other lads from a different regiment.

George leaned over to Tom and poked his arm.

'Ow, whaddya do that for?' Tom slurred, his voice loud enough to be heard over the din.

'Shh,' George said. 'That man that just walked in, I recognise him from somewhere, but I can't place where.'

'Him?' Tom looked over, with bloodshot eyes. He took another drag of his cigarette to calm himself. ''E's from the one fifth. Look at his sleeve. Fine bunch of lads, but not as good as Adams' Army. Hah.'

George thought for a moment.

'One fifth? Wasn't that where Patrick and Harry ended up? Wonder if he knows them?'

'Why don't we find out?'

Tom stood up before George could stop him by dragging his arm back down.

'Hey, lads.' He waved. 'Why don't ya come and join us? Plenty of room over here for a bunch o' Scousers.'

The three men looked at each other and shrugged. Picking up their glasses from the counter, they came and sat with Tom and George. George shuffled to the side as they sat down, giving them more room, but instead making it feel like an interrogation panel. He tried to shuffle his stool back without them noticing.

'All right, lads,' the obvious leader of the pack said. His long face had a pale complexion, made even paler by his black hair. He spoke out of the side of his mouth, as if telling you a secret. A scar went from the opposite side of his mouth up to his ear. 'One for home?' He raised a glass to emphasise the toast.

'I'll drink to that,' Tom said, and took a long swig of his drink before the others could catch up. They all laughed together.

'Name's Edward. I haven't seen you lads in here before.' He shook both their hands, introducing the other two men as Stan and Bill Flannigan, brothers. On closer inspection they looked remarkably alike, not quite twins, but close enough to know that they were related. Except one of them had a heavy, broken, boxer's nose. Going by his broken-toothed smile, he wasn't afraid of a fight.

George wondered at the consequences of two brothers signing up at the same time. Would he and Joe have fought well together, if things had been different? He very much doubted they'd be sat at the same table enjoying a pint together with strangers.

'We only got up here the day before yesterday,' George said before introducing himself and Tom. 'Took us some time to get our bearings.'

'I didn't even know you Rifles were out here. Thought you were still back home. We've been out here since February. We were freezing our arses off back then, I don't mind telling you, but it's even worse now. This winter is gonna be bloody terrible.'

'I fuckin' hate winter,' Stan added and the others laughed at the obvious in-joke between them.

'We must have come out here only a few days after your mob then,' George said, trying to be a part of the conversation, whilst wanting to steer it in the direction he intended.

'A couple of our mates were serving with you.' Tom jumped straight in, in his drunken state lacking the tact the George was trying to employ.

'Oh right,' Edward said. 'Well, we are the best battalion in the entire bloody army.' They laughed again, still good-natured despite the provocative statement.

'I wouldn't be too sure about that, lad.' Tom grinned back at them, enjoying the banter that they had been missing in their time in the trench. It was almost as good as having Patrick and Harry there, but it wasn't quite the real thing.

'I fought with some of your lads at Loos,' George said and regretted it. The faces of Edward and the Flannigans dropped to their drinks, the good-natured conversation dissolving.

'Aye, that was a bad one,' Edward said after a long, awkward silence. 'We lost a lot of good lads in that one. The Hun took a heavy toll, for sure.' The three of them took another drink and Edward sighed. 'No doubt we'll be back down the line again soon, and back into the shit.'

Edward drained the last of his drink and waved the young waitress over. She wasn't much more than a teenager, and, George guessed, the owner's daughter, but still many of the men eyed her with lust. Her blonde hair ran in ringlets down her shoulders, and she had wide, scared eyes. The owner of the estaminet looked over at his daughter, and a frown crossed his features, before another soldier at the bar took his attention.

265

'Five more beers, *s'il vous plaît*,' Edward said, his eyes still on the table. 'Or whatever you call them here.'

He didn't speak again until she returned with the glasses of smooth blond liquid, frothing just at the top.

'Let's drink to better times, lads. Soon, we go back into the line, but now, we drink!'

He beamed at George and Tom, then pressed the glass to his lips. He purred in enjoyment at the taste of the beer, overdoing it slightly and letting some drip down his cheeks, which he wiped off with the sleeve of his smock.

Tom wouldn't be appeased. He had gained focus in the conversation and the topic brought him to the edge of sobriety.

'Do you know anything about our mates, lad?' he asked. 'Paddy and Harry. Have you seen them about? Know anything about them? You must have seen them.'

Edward and the others stared with blank expressions; no recognition crossed their faces, and once again they just looked at each other and shrugged. 'Sorry, lad. Those names don't ring a bell.'

'Sorry,' George said. 'Their surnames are O'Brien and Williams, both privates as far as we know.'

Edward slowly put down his fresh glass and looked at the Flannigans, then down at his glass. He took a long drink, refusing to meet George's eyes.

'Old friends of yours, were they?' Edward said at length.

George nodded, noticing Edward's use of past tense for his friends. 'What happened?'

'I'm sorry, lads.' Edward looked to the Flannigans for support, but none was forthcoming. 'Paddy was it? Private O'Brien got it up around Ypres during the summer. I wasn't there at the time, but you hear things, ya know? He never came back from a raid. Most of his section did, but said that they hadn't seen him on the way back. Your other friend, Harry? He went pretty mad. Was desperate to go out and find the other lad, the Sergeant had to stop him and hold him back.'

266

Edward sighed.

'All the fight went out of him after that. He didn't speak to anyone and kept himself to himself. He was blown up along with half his section at Loos, it was a wonder we got any of them out of there, they were pretty roughed up. Look, I'm sorry, lads. I truly am.'

Tom put his head in his hands, covering his eyes. George wanted to put out a hand to console him but knew it wouldn't help. He wanted someone to do the same for him, but also knew that it wouldn't take the pain away. They had lost their friends, and hadn't even had a chance to say goodbye. It felt like he had been shot through the heart. Butterflies flew around in his stomach, and he felt sick. It was his and Tom's fault that they had signed up. They had died, but Tom and George were still here. It seemed unfair somehow, and he wished he could do something now to have made them stay at home. They didn't have to come, they signed up to be with their mates and they hadn't even been assigned to the same regiment.

Tom stood up with a dragging of wood on the floor, and the chair fell backwards. He didn't try to catch it, just let it fall. He walked away from the table without saying anything, whilst fumbling to light a cigarette. The door jingled again, as he wrenched it open and walked out.

George was unsure what to say. 'Sorry,' was all he could manage, as he too got up and crossed the room. The cold hit him as he opened the door, and he pulled his greatcoat around him. It was trying to snow, small specks of white floating around in the air, but never quite seeming to make the ground. He searched for Tom in the darkness. There was no electric lighting. He saw his silhouette walking down the main road already several paces ahead of him.

'Tom,' he shouted. 'Tom, wait for me.'

The figure didn't stop, but he was sure it was Tom; there was no one else around. No one but a soldier would dare venturing out in the darkness and the cold, and the rest of them were drinking their night away in the estaminets.

He ran to catch up with Tom. Once, the exertion would have left him out of breath, but after months of training he was fit enough that it was little effort. He reached out to Tom's shoulder to drag him back and stop him, but Tom shrugged him off.

'Leave me, George.' He kept on walking. 'I just want some time to myself, all right? Just some time.'

George stopped, unsure of what to do. He hadn't seen Tom like this before. The change in character scared him. He didn't want to leave Tom alone in the dark, but at least he was walking back in the direction of their billet. He was left with the choice of going back to the estaminet or going back to the billet himself. The hour was quite late, and he was getting tired, although it felt good to be free from army life if only for a few hours. He stood there in indecision, his head moving from side to side, up and down the street as the snow fell, as Tom's silhouette disappeared off into the distance.

He didn't much fancy going back to the estaminet and explaining to Edward and the others what had happened. He had only just met them and knew it would be awkward; in fact he hoped that he never saw them again. On second thoughts, he had had enough to drink. He didn't like the prospect of waking up at reveille for another training session for the next big push with a splitting hangover. An early night might do him some good.

So, he would have to follow Tom, even though he had asked to be left alone. George would leave him alone, following at a safe distance. At least that way he could make sure that Tom made it back to the billet.

*

George ducked under the wooden joist to get to where a small parapet was cut out from the firing step, having just come back from the latrine. He could still smell the stench on him. The on-duty soldiers often used the parapet as a space to get out of the rain, and today was no different. Except this time, it was the threat of snow sticking to your face and reducing your body temperature down to a dangerous degree. Tom was already huddled there with his coat wrapped under him and his knees brought up to his chest. George handed him a brew, which Tom took, nodding at him and saying nothing, before sitting down next to his friend. Tom hadn't said much to George in the few days since the estaminet, except for the odd 'good morning', and other pleasantries. Tom hadn't been cold towards George; he just didn't seem to have too much to say at the moment. Speaking of cold, it was too cold to speak now, and George didn't dare open his mouth in case his teeth began chattering again.

George didn't feel much like talking either; he had received a letter that morning with the usual Christmas bar of chocolate, but what he hadn't been expecting was the news about his sister. He had shed what tears he had left for Lizzie, when he realised that he could only just picture her face.

Tom didn't drink the brew George had handed him. Instead he wrapped his fingerless-gloved hands around it, rubbing them against the warm metal for added heat. All the while the rain fell down amongst the duckboards. At least for once the rats were nowhere to be seen, George thought. George passed Tom a piece of creamy brown chocolate.

He said something in reply, and George didn't quite hear.

'Hmm, what?' he said, clamping his jaws back together in an effort to keep the cold in.

'M… M… Merry Christmas, I said.'

George hadn't even thought about it. Today was just another day in the trench as far as he was aware. Another day of mind-numbing dullness as they sat around in case the Germans decided to attack. Even the British officers wouldn't be made to issue an attack order in this cold. He very much doubted that the Germans would try to either. He would bet that half the artillery guns were frozen shut, there would be no shelling to prelude an attack.

At that moment, there was the crump of a bang further up the line. A shower of brown snow fell over their trench and George shook it off him. A couple of machine guns opened up on either side, but stopped as soon as they realised there was nothing to shoot at. The explosion could be someone with a trench mortar getting bored.

'Merry Christmas, Tom,' he said, smiling ruefully.

Chapter 27

A woman in a beige winter dress pushed a heavy perambulator down the street and past him, the dust of the road turning the hem a blackened-brown. Joe caught a glimpse of the child inside, wrapped up safe in the white cloth coddling, not a care in the world, or any inkling of the horror that was going on. He wondered if this child would grow old enough to be forced to fight in the war that was even now consuming thousands of lives. It was supposed to have been over before it had started, but two years later it still dragged on with no sign of a conclusion. They had said it was supposed to be over by Christmas, a cliché, but they were just closing in on their second Christmas without any sign of it ending. Would that child someday be on the end of a German charge?

He shuddered at the thought.

How could such a young woman have had a child during a war. Was her husband not out fighting? Perhaps he owned an estate somewhere and only his staff had to go to war. She had looked well off.

What business was it of his who went to fight or not? He was against the very idea of the war in the first place. If he had his way, no one would be fighting.

He walked up the road to his house. The neighbours glanced at him warily, but wouldn't show outward aggression. He knew that they had already disowned his family. His mother hadn't told him, but he could see it in her expression and what she didn't say. Even Mrs Adams next door had begun avoiding the Abbotts. It made Joe sad to think that he had caused his family to be pariahs, but it wasn't his fault. People could make him an outcast all they wanted, but his family had nothing to do with it. They had tried to talk him out of it enough.

Even Anne didn't feel safe coming to his house any more. Some of the neighbours had been aggressive towards her for associating with him, and her parents were not keen either.

The family were all in the front room as he entered the house, and only Catherine looked up as Joe walked into the room. His mother was wearing black and was dabbing her eye with a handkerchief. Joe's heart sank. What had happened? Was it George?

Catherine jumped up from her chair and headed off Joe at the door. Pulling his arm, she took him into the hallway, and to the bottom of the stairs. She hugged him, laying her head on his chest. They weren't close, but she had never been a distant older sister to him.

'I'm so sorry you have to find out this way, Joe. We couldn't find you earlier.'

He rubbed a hand across his face. He had dreaded this day for so long, he didn't know what to do.

'How did it happen?' he asked. 'Was he in an attack or… what happened?'

'What?' Catherine stood back. She put a hand to her mouth in sudden realisation. 'Oh, George? No, it's not George. Oh, Joe.'

She reached for him again, but he pulled away.

'It's Lizzie. Her cough… she had an infection in her lungs.'

His legs gave way underneath him and he landed on the bottom steps of the staircase. The wood creaked in sympathy.

His little sister? He couldn't believe it. He shook his head and fumbled for the banister to pull himself back up.

'There was nothing they could do.'

He pulled himself up and pushed past her, wrenching the door open and rushing out into the street. He had lost his only connection to this family and he wanted to get away. What had Lizzie done to deserve this? He had always feared for his brother's safety – he was in constant danger – but Joe had never imagined that someone so young would be taken from them. He couldn't come to terms with it. It wasn't right. He had to walk and think. He didn't know where his legs were taking him, but he went anyway. He had to clear his head.

*

'Joe, where have you been?' Anne asked as he walked into the office. She drew him to one side. 'Without Mr Harlow here to protect you, you have to be careful.'

Joe didn't say anything. He didn't feel like talking. Anne just took it as his unwillingness to listen.

'You know that the owner is suspicious of you. With all the other men your age and older gone off to fight, he's wondering why you won't.'

'You know, and he knows why.' Joe shook his head.

'Why don't you agree to go and do some menial task?' Anne asked, imploring. 'It will keep you away from the war, and it will stop the authorities from harassing you. Will you not consider it?'

Joe looked at her, and at first said nothing. How could he make her understand his principles, and everything he believed? He often thought they were so alike. Before the war had taken over their lives and forced them to this, they had been. They could talk about philosophy, and politics, but now, now everything had changed for them. She was so concerned for him that he almost

273

wanted to weep. He knew that he wasn't being fair to her, and that by associating with him she would be ostracised. But even for her, he couldn't change his views.

At times like this he often wondered if religion might be an easier way. So many people found solace in faith. For many of the other conscientious objectors, religion was a huge part of their argument, and for the most part, from what Joe could tell, their argument got a lot more recognition from those in a position of power. To say it was easier for them would be unfair, but it seemed as if the Quakers and the like were more understood than those that just refused to do any harm. If they had no religion, what was their problem?

But then Joe couldn't bring himself to resort to religion either, and he was certain he couldn't lie about it. The way he had learnt at school had been unusual as far as he could tell from his conversations with others. His teacher, old Fenning, had often talked philosophy and had told the boys to make up their own minds about things.

Joe had decided after many hours reading scriptures and essays that he could find no solace in religion. He liked the moral messages, but they should be human messages, not just attributed to religion.

'I'm sorry, Anne. If I were to do that I would be a hypocrite. Anything I might do that would benefit the war effort would be to condone the war. I can't support them in any way. It wouldn't be right. If I can provide for the war effort then I can go and fight and I'm not prepared to do that.'

Anne just stared, biting her lip. She was unsure what to say, opening her mouth once, then closing it again. Then with determination in her eyes, she ploughed ahead.

'Can't you see why you're not giving them much choice?'

'There's always a choice, that's what this is about. We should always have a choice. They cannot force us to go to war to fight for things we don't believe in.'

'Don't be obtuse, Joe. You know exactly what I mean.'

Her lips pursed. She frowned at him in frustration and all he could think about was how pretty she was. He knew she understood, but he also knew that she was conflicted. He couldn't quite understand it himself. She was on his side and against it all at the same time. Perhaps it had been her that had put the first white feather he had ever gained on his desk all those years ago. Perhaps it had been her subtle way of trying to encourage him to do what she saw as the right thing, without having an open conflict with him. An open conflict like they were having now. He could imagine her being tactful like that, trying to save his feelings, in her own special way. He felt a little anger himself now, but it was dangerous to think like that. He had to stop himself before he said anything he regretted. He had already made her angry by just being honest. He could never control what he said around her. She had a way of opening him up like a key. At times he loved her for it. This was not one of those times. He decided to stay silent.

She carried on the conversation for him.

'The tribunal will not end well,' she said. It was like she couldn't face him, to look him in the eyes and say what she knew to be true. Not because of any embarrassment, or lack of conviction, but because she couldn't bear the look of pain that he knew dropped onto his face at her words. 'They will call you a coward. You know they will.'

'I know,' he whispered, wishing he could just take her in his arms and hold her, but she wouldn't not thank him for it, not right now, not while they were having this conversation and she had things that needed saying. 'It will be up to me to convince them that I'm not a coward.'

'They won't believe you.' This time he could see the pain on her face that no doubt matched his. She held his gaze. 'They'll only see that you refuse to fight, and see that as cowardice. I can see why they would think that.'

He was speechless, and didn't know what to say. His expression must have changed because Anne hurried to continue.

'I'm not calling you a coward,' she said with almost no pause. She almost reached out for him but stopped herself. 'Just that I can see why they would think that you are. The men that want to fight have gone. The only ones left to judge you are the ones like you, who won't be involved, or those too old to go and fight.'

Now she put her hand on the back of his.

'The men that are too old to fight will hate you. They will envy your chance to fight, and hate you for not embracing it. Surely you can see that? They will not listen to any other story.'

Joe hoped with all his strength that she was wrong. The tribunals had been set up to help people like him, hadn't they? They had to see that it wasn't cowardice that stayed his hand, but the fact that he didn't want to, *couldn't*, harm another man. He couldn't think of anything more hideous than that.

Then it occurred to him: if not wanting to hurt your fellow man was cowardice, then so be it. If they would not believe him or understand his values then he would try and educate them. If he still failed then he would pay the price. But nothing would make him go to France, not even to find George. He would stand by his principles whatever may come.

'Look, I don't want to talk about it anymore,' he said. 'We've had this argument before. It never changes. Can we not argue for once? Today of all days.'

He hadn't meant to be rude to her, but his heart was breaking and he wasn't sure he could hold it together. He didn't want to think about the war for once.

'What's the matter with you, Joe? You've been acting strange since you walked in. More distant than usual.' She stared at him, as if trying to penetrate his inner thoughts.

'It's nothing,' he said.

'Don't be like that, Joe, you know you can tell me anything. What's wrong?'

276

'It's Lizzie,' he said.

'What's Lizzie?' Anne looked confused.

'She's… she's gone.'

With those words the floodgates opened. Tears rolled down Joe's cheeks unchecked. He didn't care who saw him, it didn't matter anymore. Years of pent-up rage and frustration came forth at his closest sister's death. He had held his emotions in check for so long, but he couldn't any longer. She had been so young, so full of life until a few short weeks ago. He blamed himself. Perhaps he should have tried to bring in more money to the household and if he hadn't caused his family to be outcasts, then they could have got her more help. It was all so sudden. He sobbed and tried to wipe the tears away, but they were too many.

Anne still stared at him, and he saw one tear drop down from her eyes to run down her cheek.

'I'm so sorry, Joe.'

She was still so pretty, even with tears in her eyes. He didn't reach up and wipe them away, but instead pulled her close to him. He didn't care that they were supposed to be working, or whether the owner would have anything to say. All he wanted to do at this moment was to hold Anne close to him, smell her hair and forget about anything else.

He hadn't had a chance to say goodbye to his sister, and he couldn't imagine losing Anne in the same way. The thought brought on more tears.

He would never let her go.

1916

Chapter 28

Joe read the casualty lists for the newspaper and his heart almost stopped. The news coming in from France was growing worse and worse. Despite the conscription, the British Army had thousands more casualties. The latest assault was being labelled as a success, but the roll of the dead was bigger than any he had seen before. He ran a finger along each line of text as his finger blackened from the ink, but he couldn't see a 'Private. Abbott, G.' and for that he was thankful. With Lizzie's passing, Christmas had been non-existent and the family was close to breaking point. Joe felt it would only get worse, and he hoped for George's safety. He was due home on leave soon, but it was likely to be cancelled as it had several times before.

He was also thankful that there were no other names he recognised either. He looked around and the rest of the office was almost empty, only a few of the older men working at their desks. There were also women working away, but Anne was out somewhere working on an article. He had been so absorbed in his own troubles, he hadn't paid attention when she had told him. He knew she was doing something along the lines of gathering reports of the war, but to her it was just a job. She hadn't seemed to notice, or was too aware of his worries to pull him up on it.

He thought of all the boys and men that had lost their lives in this latest battle and that they were now just names on a sheet of paper. How many mothers would be receiving letters from commanding officers telling them of their sons' bravery in the line of duty? How many mothers would receive more than one letter on the same day? He knew his mother feared that day more than anything, but at least she would not receive one for Joe.

At that moment he also felt guilty for the thought. What right did he have to be glad that he wasn't there? What made him any more special than the soldiers who were giving their lives? Education? That was unfair on the other men. Just because he had received a better education that should not single him out. No, what made him different was that he was willing to fight for another cause. He would fight the government and the military so that those other men could come home. So that they could have the opportunities that he had.

He finished scribbling down some notes on a piece of paper in front of him and put the pen to one side. He pushed the most recent letter he had been writing to George underneath the pile so that no one would read it in his absence.

Anne would come to meet him soon, and he had taken the time to compose his notes. It had taken him a few drafts to get it right, but he was somewhat confident he knew now what needed to be said. Even if he wouldn't use the notes in the military tribunal the very act of writing them out had helped ease them into his memory. It wasn't a rousing speech, he wasn't capable of awe-inspiring oratory, but he was happy with the points he was trying to make. He had applied for exemption, and all going to plan it would be granted.

Anne walked into the office from the stairwell and smiled over at him. For once she didn't put her hat and coat on the stand, but instead walked straight over to him. She lay a hand on his shoulder.

'Are you ready?' she asked, eyeing the notes in front of him.

He grunted in reply, rested his ear on her hand and relished the warmth there. If he could, he would have stayed there for the rest of eternity. Knowing that wasn't possible, he stood up and retrieved his jacket and tweed hat. They left the building arm in arm for what could be the last time.

*

The town hall stood magnificent at the end of Castle Street looking along the road as if in judgement. Like many of the other buildings in the area it was made from a pale grey stone that had begun to go a blackish-brown from the soot and smog of local industry. The top of the building was a dome, on which Minerva sat holding a spear and staring down at the street.

Joe and Anne entered via the main entrance to the front of the building, which was housed in the middle of three arches underneath a series of columns. He held the door open for her letting her inside first, with a smile. She gave him a knowing look, suspecting that he was trying everything possible to hold off the inevitable. The tribunal could not be avoided, but he wasn't going to run at it with open arms.

Inside the building many people went about their business. Clerks rushed about holding sheets of paper and telegram notices, ignoring the newcomers. A man sat behind a desk looked up at them, smiled sweetly, then continued with his work without saying a word and seeming to forget that they were even there. By the desk there was a sign with notices attached detailing various meetings. One stated, 'Military Tribunals – Main Hall, First Floor'.

'I guess we know where we're going then,' Joe said, trying to elicit a response from Anne. She just smiled, put her arm in his and walked them up the staircase. The interior of the building was painted in a brilliant white. Red marble columns held up the first floor high above Joe, and a grand staircase stood in the middle, lined with a red carpet. It broke into two further staircases that rose from a landing that housed a stone sculpture. He leaned in to Anne to get a waft of her smell, and he smiled at her reassuring scent. The building made him think of some stately home. It was exactly how he imagined the inside of Little Jimmy Sutcliffe's house looked.

Joe stopped in the corridor at the top of the staircase. His heart was hammering inside his chest and he felt as if he wanted to be sick.

'I just need to use the toilet,' he said. 'I won't be a minute. Will you wait for me here?'

There was a lavatory to one side and a man walked out. Anne nodded and stepped to the side, so as to be out of the way of the people coming and going along the wide corridor. Joe pushed the heavy door and was at once in the lavish lavatory. He guessed the town hall had a lot of visitors, some of them very important people, so it paid to have running water and well-kept facilities.

He checked and he was alone, alone with his thoughts. He hadn't needed to use the toilet, he just wanted some time to compose himself and to calm his nerves. He had no idea what to expect from the tribunal. He was thankful that Anne was here with him, but he would rather be anywhere else. He had the sudden urge to run away and glanced over at the nearest window. The top panel only opened a crack; it wasn't enough for him to fit through, and what would he do once outside? He could fall the single storey to the ground and hurt himself. There was no escape that way.

He put his hat down on a shelf and ran a hand through his hair. The room's single, shining mirror reflected his image back at him. The electric lights shined off the glass surface and made him realise how unkempt he appeared. He ran a tap and, using the water, he tried to smooth down his hair, but it was being particularly stubborn that day and kept flicking back up.

Instead he tried to straighten his suit, but because he was so

284

nervous it just felt uncomfortable. In the end he gave up. They would have to do with him as he was.

He walked back out of the lavatory to where Anne was waiting for him. He tried to force a smile at her, but the feeling of nausea returned and he had to cover the grimace that crossed his face.

'Ready?' she asked, with a bright smile. He could stare into those eyes for hours and always feel better.

Together they walked down the corridor towards the hall at the end. He opened one of the heavy doors and held it open for Anne to walk through.

There was a crowd gathering inside. The military tribunals were open to the public and he had no doubt that people would travel far to hear the gossip about these so-called conscientious objectors. He wished he was here as a journalist, but he was the one on trial.

Anne smiled at him again, squeezed his hand, and took an empty seat to the right-hand side of the aisle.

In the middle of the room was a table, and behind it were five empty chairs. He walked to the front of the spectators' chairs and found himself a seat.

The tribunal panel filed in a moment after Joe had sat down. The first man, Joe recognised as a representative of the Lord Mayor, Sir Max Muspratt, although he couldn't remember the representative's name. He was a large bald man, who wheezed as he sat down at the table, and looked disinterested with the whole thing as he regarded his own nails. The Lord Mayor would be too busy advising the war council to attend these meetings.

After him came an elderly man in the dress uniform of a Captain. He was a gaunt man with a serious face. Despite his muscles turning to fat with age, the wiry frame of a soldier could still be seen beneath. His black moustache was neatly trimmed, greying at the edges, and wobbled as he introduced himself and the other men at the table. He was too old to be a serving officer but must have been dragged out of retirement for this.

With him were the clerk in charge of paperwork, a local councillor, and a Quaker from the factories over the water. Together they would be judging Joe and the other men.

A couple of men were called up before Joe. Both were arguing on religious grounds, and Joe grew more nervous as he heard their cases. Sweat ran down his temples and collected around the collar of his shirt. He grew very uncomfortable as it went on, but he had no choice but to stay where he was sat.

As the second of the two men was excused from military service and requested to do work in support of the war effort, the clerk pushed his glasses up his nose, shuffled his papers and looked up.

'Next,' the Captain said to him, in a loud voice used to having commands obeyed.

'Joseph Abbott,' the clerk called.

Joe stood up and turned to walk along the row of seats. As he did so he caught a glance of Anne out of the corner of his eye. She smiled encouragement at him and nodded, urging him to be brave. He walked out in the centre of the hall and stopped a couple of metres in front of the tribunal, feet together and eyes forward in what he thought, with a certain sense of irony, was very similar to a parade stance a soldier might take.

'Please state your argument for exemption in front of the military service tribunal,' the clerk said to him over the top of his glasses, in a bored voice.

Joe cleared his throat with a clenched fist over his mouth. He hoped that he didn't seem half as nervous as he felt. They would see the sweat running down his face. It was a hot day, he hoped they would put it down to that. He had to speak up at last, he couldn't play for time any longer.

'I wish to appeal for exemption from military service,' he said, 'on moral grounds.'

There was a hush around the room as people reacted to his statement. It could have been part of his often overactive imagination, but he suspected that at least some of them were already judging him. He had a long-standing relationship with paranoia. Sometimes it was oddly comforting, other times he remembered how much it isolated him from the rest of the world.

'What are these "moral grounds" of which you speak?' asked the Captain, all blustering moustaches.

Joe tried to compose himself. He fingered the folded-up sheet of paper in his pocket, trying to recall his argument. His mind had gone blank in the stifling heat of the main hall. The tribunal panel stared at him, already beginning to wonder if he was just stupid or mocking them.

'The moral grounds, sir?' he said, unsure how to continue.

The Captain nodded at him, frowning.

'The moral grounds are that I cannot do harm to another man.'

The clerk began scribbling notes.

'Are these moral grounds religious, Mr Abbott?'

'No, sir,' he said, after a moment. 'I do not consider myself religious.'

'So I can enter into the record that you have no religious objection to the war?'

Joe considered his answer.

'You may,' he said.

'You have a brother serving out in France, do you not?' the Captain asked, already knowing the answer.

'Yes, sir, I do. His name is George.'

'And you would rather leave him to do the fighting and cower at home?'

'Not at all, sir.'

'That seems to me very much what you intend to do.'

'As I said, sir. Not at all. It is precisely because my brother is out there in France that I am doing this.'

'He is willing to sacrifice himself for King and Country, unlike you.'

'His sacrifice, sir—' he said the honorific through clenched teeth, his patience thinning, but knowing that he had to remain calm if he was to have any hope at all '—his sacrifice will serve nothing, but to break my mother's heart.'

There was a loud gasp from the assembled crowd.

'Some of us must stand up against this needless war. There is no longer any hope of victory, only death. I wish more than anything that my brother will not lose his life for no other reason than vanity.'

'How dare you!' The Captain half stood from his seat before the Quaker talked him back down.

'I'm afraid, Joseph,' he said, glancing sidelong at the Captain as he spoke, 'that you are not yet qualified to talk about the merits for or against the war.'

Joe started to protest, but he held up a placatory hand, palm outstretched.

'We are not here to discuss whether the war should be happening, or should not. We are here to discuss whether you should be fighting in it, like many of our fellow countrymen, or whether you have any reason by which to stay behind. Such is the letter of the law.'

Joe nodded, the argument dying on his lips. The Quaker gestured to his fellow panel members to continue. The Captain was still red in the face, and he blew out his moustaches before continuing.

'What would you do if a German walked in that door right now and tried to attack you?' he asked.

'I'm not sure, sir. It is hard for one to know what one would do in the heat of the moment.'

'Would you retaliate?'

'I don't think so, sir.'

'What if he tried to rape your mother?'

'I don't think that is a likely scenario, sir.'

'Hypothetically then, what if a German was trying to rape your mother? What would you do?'

'I would try and stop him, sir.'

'Would you not shoot him?'

'Certainly not, sir. I would not take a man's life.'

'No matter what he did to you?'

'No matter. I could not take another man's life.'

'So you are a coward?'

Someone in the crowd jeered.

'No, sir. I stand before this tribunal, despite my very best wishes of being somewhere else.'

His response did not have the expected reaction, and the Captain frowned.

'You dishonour us, as you dishonour all the brave boys out in France.'

Joe didn't know what else he could say. He had made his case, but it was as if they didn't care. Something in the back of his mind told him that they were going to refuse him exemption no matter what he said. So he remained silent.

The tribunal took his silence as agreement.

'You're a coward, sir!'

Joe didn't answer. There was no way that he could convince them that he wasn't a coward. By refusing to go and fight he was a coward in their eyes. No amount of philosophy or principle would change their minds. Still, he couldn't let it lie.

'Your honour, this isn't a matter of cowardice. I would not be standing here if I were a coward. I would have run away.'

'Lies! Outright lies. How dare you lie to us?' The crowd grumbled in sympathy with the judge. They had already condemned him as much as the judge. 'If you stand there and say you have no religious reason for not joining our brave boys in France, then you must be a coward. It is as simple as that, young man.' He gave Joe a stern nod, as if he were telling off one of his children.

'You want complete exemption? Therefore you say you will not accept any service in France, whatsoever?' the clerk asked, interrupting the Captain's outburst.

289

'No, sir. I will not.' Joe held the judge's gaze, determined not to back down.

'Then you leave me little choice. If you will not so much as lift a stretcher, then you will spend the rest of the war in prison. You will have an opportunity to report for military service. If you continue to refuse then you will suffer the consequences of your actions.

'Based on the declaration of no religious objection to the war, and working in the letter of the law, I am left with no choice but to order you to report to the local barracks for service within the army.' The clerk in charge of proceedings brought a stamp down onto a piece of paper. With that final bang it was all over. He had been dismissed. The tribunal had forgotten all about him, men were moving around and the panel themselves were discussing the next case, whilst the clerk shuffled and organised his papers. They had decided his fate in only a matter of minutes and without listening to his case. How could he have lost so spectacularly? He had been mentally planning his arguments for so long that the tribunal itself was a short disappointment. It wasn't supposed to have gone this way. Not for the first time, he thought that he should have claimed religious grounds after all, but as soon as he thought it he knew that he couldn't bring himself to lie.

They called the next man forward, who shuffled past Joe, trying to catch Joe's attention with a downcast look on his face.

In defeat, Joe turned and walked away. Anne caught up with him outside the main hall and grabbed hold of his hand.

'What am I to do now, Anne?' he said, not wishing to look her in the eye lest she see his inner turmoil and disappointment. He felt on the verge of tears in horror and frustration at his impossible cause.

She didn't answer right away, but just rubbed her thumb over the back of his hand, trying to comfort him.

'You could lodge an appeal?' she suggested.

He shook his head.

'You heard them in there. They didn't take me seriously for one moment. They would laugh me out of there if I tried to appeal. I'm afraid I'm somewhat of a lost cause.'

'Not to me, you're not,' she said, throwing her arms around him and hugging him close. He breathed in the scent of her hair and it helped to relax the sense of fear that was rising within him. 'You have to keep on fighting. I know you, you won't ever give up. Don't let this small setback defeat you.'

Chapter 29

Liverpool was different. George could tell from the moment his boot touched down on the stone of the platform. His newly issued steel helmet clattered against his back as he stepped down from the train.

The hubbub of the station had disappeared since the last time he had been here, and there was a sombre, melancholy air to the place. He also felt that the station was darker, but that could have been the winter gloom, or his mood. People were still catching trains, but no one smiled, and they were seldom in pairs, or in groups. Even he was on his own for once. Tom had been left back in France. His leave was due soon, but George's had come through first. It felt unusual to leave Tom and the others behind. They were a sort of family to him now, and he missed them dearly. As for his real family? He couldn't say. Of course he missed them, he always would, but the experiences he'd had over the last eighteen months had driven a wedge further between them. His mother still wrote regularly, but he had less and less to say in reply, as his life grew further and further away from something they would understand.

Leaving Lime Street, he didn't go straight to the family house. It didn't feel right just going home as if nothing had happened.

What would he find there? Would it now feel cold and empty, with the gaping absence of his baby sister? He would prefer to put off that experience for now and keep the memory of his former home as pure and untouched as he could. He could still imagine walking in the door and seeing Lizzie bobbing along, the curls of her hair whipping against her small shoulders. Then he remembered why he had come.

Instead of going home, he went first to St James' cemetery by the Oratory chapel. He knew it well, they had played nearby as children, a lifetime ago now. It wasn't far from his family's house. He had even at one point sat and sketched out the Doric style chapel and drawn his own imaginings of what the finished cathedral would look like. He walked all the way there. He wanted to see his home city as he had before, walking the streets and feeling the cobbles under his soles. As many things had changed as had stayed the same. The streets still had the same names, but the people looked different. Civilians, as he thought of them now. The sombre atmosphere was not exclusive to the station, the whole city felt oppressed and it wasn't just because of the overcast sky. There were fewer horses and carts on the roads, and an extra motorcar here and there.

St James' cemetery was up on one of the hills towards the south of the city. A perfect place for a view of the Mersey. He stopped before going in and looked over at the river he hadn't seen for well over a year. At least that was still there, he thought. From here, one could see the site of the Liverpool Cathedral, but it seemed, like so many other things, the war had halted its construction. He had missed the funeral, as he had been unable to get even compassionate leave at the time, so short were their numbers. His mother had explained what had happened in the letter she had sent him. It had been the first time he had sobbed since before the war. He still kept the stained paper in his webbing with all the other letters, including the unopened ones from his brother.

He walked into the cemetery through the wrought iron gates, past the Oratory that he remembered from his childhood, and down into what used to be a quarry. Hundreds of gravestones stood in rows. Some were white, others had moss and other things growing on them. One or two of them were even cracked.

He found the grave under a small elm tree at the back corner of the quarry, as expected from his mother's description in a letter. Both the rich and the poor made use of St James' cemetery, as the largest place to bury the dead in Liverpool. Being poor, the Abbotts had to find a space for Lizzie at the back of the quarry. Although, his mother had written that Joe's friend Anne had been kind enough to donate a little money to help find a better plot, and a nice gravestone. He wondered who this Anne was. Had she filled his place in the family?

At the moment the gravestone was just a simple wooden one, much like they gave to the soldiers they had to bury out in France. George had thankfully never been on grave-digging duty, but he had seen enough of the heaps of mud in his time. The graves were sometimes indistinguishable from the muddy fields, but the soldiers knew they were there. How could they forget? They were told they would get stones later, but he wasn't sure. The front line didn't move much, but when it did it often uncovered the graves, and when an attack had settled down, they would have to be buried all over again.

He knelt down nearby, not ashamed to get dirt on his uniform. There were no officers around to pull him up on it, and he didn't care. This was a private moment. The earth was still fresh over her grave. The grass had yet to make its way back over. There wasn't much soil, just a small patch about a metre long. She had only been a child, and she shouldn't be buried; she should be back at her home living her life, unaffected by the illness that had taken her. The small grave could have been one of the many he had seen out in France, even given its size. One of the ones for which they hadn't found much to bury. He shook his head, trying to banish the thoughts. This situation was heart breaking enough without thinking of France. He closed his eyes, but he could just see the freshly dug graves again, row after row.

'I thought we might find you here.' It took him a second to recognise his sister's voice, and he jumped up in surprise. 'I'm sorry, I didn't mean to startle you,' Catherine said, smiling at him like it was a private joke. She looked older than he remembered her, much older, and he wondered if he had aged as much in the time. She had lost the chubbiness to her cheeks which were now gaunt, giving her the look of the malnourished, and she had grown her hair longer, which straightened out the curls. He wouldn't have recognised her if she had not spoken.

'Catherine,' he said, searching for anything more intelligent to say.

'The very same.' She smiled, and he finally got a sense of a face he recognised. 'Gosh, it's good to see you, George. You look so different, not just because of the uniform, but almost taller.'

'I'm not the only one,' he chuckled, but it felt forced. Thankfully, her replying laughter was more natural, and she came closer to get a better look at him.

'No, it's not been a kind year.' She didn't elaborate further, but placed a flower she had been holding on top of the grave. 'We had thought that you would come here before heading to the house. It's a shame you didn't manage to make the funeral. It was a wonderful service. The others will be along in a minute.'

As she said that, he heard more footsteps on the path through the cemetery. His mother and brother were coming towards them. If he thought Catherine had looked older then that was nothing compared to his mother. The death of her daughter had diminished her in stature and in health, and Joe was holding one arm as she carefully covered the grass. She wore a black mourning dress, and her hair was greyer than it had been before. He had never thought of his mother as an old woman until this moment.

His brother looked the same as he had always done, perhaps a little sadder, if that was even possible.

'Dad?' he asked Catherine, at his side.

She shook her head. 'He's at work. He won't come up here. To him, she's gone and that's that.' She paused, welling up and wiping a tear away.

'My George,' his mother said, coming closer. She put her arms around him, and tried to pull him closer, but she had such little strength. He relented slightly and hugged her back. He couldn't remember the last time he had embraced her. 'You've grown. God, it's good to see you.'

He let go of her and stood back, helping to support her with one arm. His brother opened his mouth to speak, nodded slightly and held out a hand. 'George,' he said, as George grabbed and shook hands. It was a strangely awkward gesture, but it was what he had come to expect from Joe. He had been about to say something, but George had no idea what.

The atmosphere was awkward. George felt uncomfortable standing there with his brother staring at him. He so much wanted to ask Joe what he had been about to say, to form some connection between them. It had been a long time coming, but he couldn't think of the right words. France had taken it all out of him.

'I thought we could say a little prayer for our Lizzie,' Catherine said. 'Before we head home and get you settled in.'

He didn't think he would ever be settled here again. Almost two years of living somewhere else, sleeping in mud and rain, made even this situation feel too comfortable. He couldn't imagine living back inside a house again, confined by those walls. 'That would be nice,' he said. 'I'm sorry I couldn't make the funeral.'

The others nodded, saying nothing. What could they say that would change anything? They all stood in silence. George took his hat off and doffed it under his arm, and Joe did the same, focusing their vision on their shoes. He could hear his mother's lips moving as she silently prayed. He tried to think of words, but once again they wouldn't come. As he closed his eyes, his mind wandered back to France, to the mud, the blood, and the constant explosions.

*

George had spent a few days back in Egerton Street, but as little time as possible in the house. Being under that roof felt confining, he wanted to see the sky and to always get his bearings. The house was silent as he had expected without his little sister to fill it with her singing. His mother wanted to speak to him all the time and mother him, and he couldn't take it. To avoid the house, he left in the morning as he used to, and walked. He walked wherever his feet would take him, alone with his thoughts. Perhaps after the war he could use the money he had earned to travel, to go and see as many landmarks as possible and draw them. Perhaps then he could make some money by selling landscapes. That possibility seemed a hundred years ago at that moment. He had to leave Liverpool today and report back to the army. He couldn't wait any longer; if he did they would court-martial him and he could end up in prison, he had a duty to do.

He also couldn't avoid his family any longer. Each chair was occupied that morning, except for the small wooden chair where Lizzie would sit that was left purposefully empty. He had decided that today he would join them, one last time before he went back to the front. They sat in silence, as they often had, eating their meagre breakfast. They looked at each other from time to time, as if daring the other to start a conversation. He knew that he would have to break the silence soon, but he didn't want to break their hearts yet, not when everything was so peaceful for the first time in what seemed like years. Even his father seemed quietly content at one end of the table, though he was still avoiding any contact, conversational or otherwise, with Joe at the other end.

'I'm leaving today,' he said, his voice like a gun in the silence. 'I have to report back.'

'Oh, George,' his mother replied. She sighed heavily and put some plates down. Then she walked over to him and raised his chin with her hand, as she had done when he was a boy. She wiped some food from the corner of his mouth with a cloth. 'Can't we keep you for one more day?'

'Orders are orders, Ma. If I don't head back today, I'll be in for it.'

'Leave him be, Jane. He's got a duty to do.' His father didn't look up from the paper. 'They'll be missing him at the front.'

Joe scoffed loudly and put his cutlery down. Once again, he opened his mouth to speak, but this time he was interrupted by Catherine.

'Don't start,' she said to Joe, in a whisper. 'Can't we just enjoy this moment together while it lasts?'

Joe looked at her for a few long seconds, then gave a shallow nod. 'Of course.'

'Well, it's about time that there's some good news, at least. I didn't want to tell you before, it didn't seem right.' Catherine beamed, talking directly to George. 'I'm getting married.'

He nearly choked on some oats but managed to catch himself. Catherine had been after a husband for quite some time. He would provide a way out of the Abbott household to her own home. 'That's fantastic,' he said, meaning it. 'Who is he?'

'He works down at the docks with Dad. We wanted to get married before he shipped out, but didn't have the money. So we'll do it when he comes back on leave. Then we can get our own house and start a new life together. After the war, of course.'

She was so happy it was infectious. George felt himself smiling, despite the fact at the back of his mind he wondered if the wedding would ever happen. He hoped it would, for his sister's sake, and it would be one less mouth to feed for his parents. His father must have arranged for the two of them to meet.

'We,' Joe said, 'that is Anne and I, are thinking about using the room to house some of those Belgian refugees.' It was their father's turn to scoff, and he turned the page of the newspaper with a louder rustle. 'It was more Anne's idea, of course.'

Joe smiled a smile that George was completely unused to. The change in his brother was quite dramatic, and he could see that this Anne meant a lot to him. Unfortunately, he hadn't had time to meet her during his leave. Next time.

'You will have to come back for the wedding. It won't be the same without you.'

'I'll see what I can do.' He didn't want to let her down, but he was entirely at the whim of the army. If he could return for her wedding he would, it would give him something to look forward to.

He finished his breakfast and put his cutlery down. He had run out of time. He looked at each of his family in turn, taking them in and storing their image in his memory, then stood. 'It's time,' he said. 'I'd best go and catch my train.'

Both his mother and sister jumped up and hugged him, both lingering in a way that was both heartfelt and made him want to stay that little bit longer. His father finally looked up and bid him farewell but was otherwise unmoved.

He picked up his things and went to leave the house as he had done two years ago. This time, however, he knew exactly where he was going, and what he was getting into. There would be no marching band on his way to the station this time, no ceremony. He would walk there on his own, taking in the sights of Liverpool one last time. He didn't know when he would be back. It could be another two years.

The only one that followed him to the front door was his brother. Joe reached out a hand again, and he grasped it. The handshake lasted for a few seconds longer than was comfortable, and George felt the urge to pull his brother towards him. He didn't know if he would see Joe again. There was so much he wanted to say to him, but the words just wouldn't come, no matter how hard he tried. Words just weren't enough.

'Well, Joe,' was all he could think of. 'Goodbye for now.'

Chapter 30

The artillery shattered the morning air, as shell after shell was thrown over no man's land towards the German lines. Explosions that blossomed like new trees across the landscape, appearing at random fashion, never growing in the same place twice. One thousand and five hundred guns were said to have been brought together for 'the big show', and their munitions peppered the landscape. Some shells fell well short of their intended targets. Their aim was still inadequate. George remembered the damage it had caused to their own troops time after time. Or perhaps it was that the very idea of artillery was to put down a curtain of fire, to make sure the enemy kept their heads down. No one had ever told George which it was, and so, with bitterness, he attributed it to the former.

The bombardment had begun in late June as the guns were brought forward and the soldiers were busy training and practising for what the officers were calling 'the big show'. They had moved along to a place called La Citadelle de Dinant, or The Citadel, to begin their preparations. The bombardment had proven to be a big show. A light show casting flashes across the landscape in an apocalyptic diorama.

Then the battle of the Somme river had begun, and still, almost a month later, it raged. The first waves went in and yet more men went to the front. But still the King's Rifles sat; they had been moved up to a reserve trench, but no further, waiting for their chance to take part, growing more and more nervous about their prospects. The other Liverpool regiments had gone in before them, with some of their companies being moved forward at a time to reinforce the others. But as of yet, George's section hadn't been called on for anything other than relaying the odd message or helping to reinforce the trenches that the French who had occupied this section had left in a sorry state. Some of the others were growing restless. The heavy work of reinforcing the trenches and building firing steps, which had taken all summer, with the boiling sun falling down on them threatening to melt them in their itchy cloistering khaki, had not been enough for some.

George had to admit, at one point he would have been restless too. He remembered the time back in England when they had all wanted nothing more than to get to the front. Now something had changed. He wasn't sure what it was. Perhaps it was that the trench work had been exhausting and had not allowed his brain any time to think of other matters, or perhaps it was the fear of going back into the fight that stopped him. The fear that he had tried to repress, but was always there, just under the surface, waiting to come up and take over his body.

They had sat in that reserve trench, spending hours on repair, hours to recover for most of July, while the other battalions had been thrown at enemy positions in order to try and gain some ground. So far they had failed to take Guillemont village, despite effort after bloody effort. But now it was the Rifles' turn. This was not some raid to pass the time in the hope of capturing German prisoners, but an actual assault. One for which they had been preparing for over a month now, to the point that George could go through the battle plan in his sleep. That was, if he got any sleep.

The order had come down the line via a series of carrier

pigeons and messengers that they were going to move to the forward trench and therefore the front line, to relieve the 30th and 35th divisions, fourth army. They had been waiting almost a month to join the fray and tempers were on edge.

The artillery barrage had been going on for some time before dawn. A constant presence since the most recent battle of the war had begun. More guns had been brought forward and more shells. The dull crump of shells hitting the earth, and the whine as others flew overhead, was overpowering. A whizz-bang flew overhead and exploded somewhere behind them. The British Army may have been firing everything it had, but the Germans were giving as good as they were getting. It was a wonder no shells hit each other in the air, George thought.

The idea was to hit the German positions and keep their heads down, stopping them from being prepared for another attack. The miles of wire that crossed no man's land were also supposed to be cut, but from where George crouched in the trench he couldn't imagine it was doing much good. The shells were landing far too close to their own lines, and soil was dislodged to land amongst the duckboards as each shell hit the ground. A big explosion went off to their right and he ducked, fearing the end.

The din of the shelling had become background noise to George, he had been in the trench that long. He still ducked and flinched every time an explosion went off, but he feared the end of the shelling more than he had feared the sound when he first came out to France. The absence of artillery fire would mean that they would soon be going over the top and another big push would finally be under way.

The others didn't even flinch anymore. Tom often told him not to worry about it, but now he sat with his back to the parapet and stared into the middle distance, the whites of his wide eyes just visible through the muck that coated his face. Another explosion went off in a nearby trench and George could hear screaming. One man was asking to be put out of his misery, but no voice answered him. Tom still sat there staring at nothing. George couldn't imagine what was going through his friend's head.

There was an eerie moment of quiet as the bombardment abated and the explosions stopped. The only thing that landed on the plains of the Somme at that moment in time was the summer sun. Within seconds the officers made themselves known, coming out of their dugouts and walking along the trench to the front. Each officer took to the head of their sections and put a whistle to their mouths. On synchronised watches they blew their whistles and disturbed the calm of the Belgian countryside.

It was also penetrated by the sudden shouts of men charging up the ladders and over the firing step into no man's land. They shouted encouragement to each other and the officers joined in too, reminding them of their orders and the importance of an orderly charge. Any man who tried to overstep the leading man was shouted back into position and they advanced at a good pace.

George was one of the first up, following in Tom's footsteps, making sure that the two of them kept together. He had lost Tom in a raid before and he wasn't about to do so again. This time they had over a year's experience of fighting and trench raids to help them. Or at least, that's what George hoped. He couldn't help but think that experience and training hadn't helped some of the men they had lost along the way. They had been planning this one for months, and the King's regiment had had a few weeks behind the lines preparing the raids in formation, whilst trying to avoid the sight of the German air reconnaissance planes. But now when it came down to it, their preparation didn't count for anything.

It was difficult to see much with the new steel helmet they had been given, it only added to the sweat that was pouring down his face and it slipped with every movement. He could understand why they had been given them, but it would take some getting used to. Although he couldn't understand why it had taken so long. He had seen the damage a bullet or shrapnel could do to an unprotected head. Too many had lost their lives that way. He shuddered at the thought.

The silence in the absence of weapon fire didn't last long, as almost as soon as they were over the parapet a machine gun opened fire from a German trench. From their new aeroplane reconnaissance they had known that it was there, but the officers had chosen to draw it out, while a section had the express orders of attacking it direct. That didn't go too well for them as a direct assault was akin to suicide. George watched as the guns traversed their way and the bodies fell. A trench mortar fell close by and the first of the guns was silenced. It wouldn't be for long, but it would buy them precious time to get closer to the enemy trenches. There was a wall of noise that they were assaulting into, walking across no man's land with an arrogance that lacked fear. Explosions threw up mud and dirt everywhere, and rifle rounds whistled past. The assault was breaking in parts, as some men began to run towards the enemy and others ducked for cover. Their fine order was becoming a mess, and the weight of opposing firepower wasn't helping.

As it had done on every previous occasion, their training seemed to go out the window. There was no order to this madness of war, and the officers seldom had any time to think or react to the changing situations that they were presented with. They just had to advance and hope that everything would come together as planned. This time, as usual, it wasn't coming together.

George moved across no man's land, keeping as low as possible. His pace was a little more than a walk, but not a run. He didn't want to get too far ahead of his comrades, that way lay disaster, but he also didn't want to fall too far behind. They would need his help and moving too slow made it easy work for the snipers and machine gunners. It was also hot wearing khaki at this time of year, even if it was early morning.

The Germans had known they were coming. They would have spotted their aeroplanes, and also used their own to see the training that the men were doing behind the front line. As soon as the British artillery had stopped and the assault had begun in earnest, the Germans had opened up with everything they had.

Still, the British advanced, hoping that by sheer weight of numbers alone they would overpower the German defenders.

Tom moved alongside George keeping low and ready. The rest of their section was scattered around the debris of no man's land around them, picking their way through the mud and bodies. Men fell every few seconds, dropping into the early morning darkness, and no one stopped to check them. To do so would be suicide. The machine guns stopped every few seconds to reload or cool down, and the attackers would use this opportunity to push further forward.

A whizz-bang landed a few metres away from them with a loud crack. Mud flew everywhere and George's vision was covered with wet brown. His ears stung from the noise and he could feel the pressure pressing in against his brain. He banged his knees as he fell, and he cried out, but couldn't hear his own voice.

When his senses cleared he found that he had fallen into a shell hole, or ditch in the ground. It was deep enough for a man to crouch in without putting his head over the edge. He couldn't work out how he had avoided being hit by that shell, it was so close, but he seemed unharmed, except for the headache he now had. Tom had been by his side. He searched with desperation, hoping to find Tom's reassuring grin, to see him jump up and lead them to safety as he had always imagined. There was no grin.

Neither was there heroism. Instead Tom sat deeper down in the shell hole staring back into the middle ground – at what, only Tom could tell. His eyes were unfocused and distant and his face was set hard in determination. For once, George couldn't tell what was going through his friend's mind. Tom had grabbed hold of George's arm in the fall but didn't seem to have noticed, he just stared at whatever world his mind had placed him in. It took a hard shove from George to get him moving.

'Huh, what?' he said, as if waking up from a deep dream.

George punched him on the arm, with a quick jab.

'Come on,' he said. 'Now's not the time for lying around. There's a war on.' He tried to imitate the Sergeant's Scottish accent, but it was no good. He tried a grin but was sure it was more of a grimace. 'The Germans are over there and we should be after them. We're dropping behind the rest of our boys.'

Tom still didn't move, he just stared at George, as if looking straight through him. Then after a few seconds he swallowed and smiled at George. It wasn't his usual grin, much more forced, like a grimace, but it was a start.

'You're right, of course, George. I was just, er… in a world of my own.'

Tom reached out a hand to help George up and over the crater's edge. Together they helped each other out of the trench, using the other for support. Once out of the crater they leaned forward on their bellies so that they could crawl forward.

George didn't dare look at the quagmire that had become of the land between the two trenches. He feared he might spot friends amongst the dead. He felt Tom shuffle up beside him, breathing slow breaths near his ear.

'We'll have to stand up if we want to get at the enemy, lad,' he whispered. There was a wobble in his voice, like when speaking the first words of the morning.

The artillery was still falling over no man's land. The wind was blowing some shells wide, but George suspected that the main reason they were falling short was due to the lack of accuracy of the guns. They were supposed to be moving forward to cut the German wire and take out any machine gun nests, but they were just falling all over, clods of dirt and sometimes body parts flying up into the air. It was difficult to see just what was going on.

The artillery drifted over their section again, and George pushed his head down into the dirt. After a series of deafening explosions, he raised it again to assess the situation, and to find the rest of his section.

The Sergeant reared up in front of him.

'What do you two think you're bloody doing?' he shouted over the din of battle, standing before them like a god, the early morning sunrise lighting his features.

'Wondering which way is forward, sir.'

'Don't give me that bloody cheek, Abbott. I'd expect it of Adams, but not from you.'

He reached down and helped haul George to his feet. The sounds of warfare were still around them; machine guns coughed every few seconds, and the combined shells of both sides flew back and forth. George wasn't sure that it was safe to stand, but he didn't have much choice. He squatted down behind a barbed wire fence, waiting for the Sergeant's orders.

The Sergeant reached down to help Tom up. Tom took his time to accept the Sergeant's hand and worked his way up onto one knee.

At that moment there was a crack, like the sound of breaking wood. And then the landscape burst into bright white light as the Germans sent up a Very light. The Sergeant pushed Tom back down as bullets whistled their way.

The Germans had spotted them. He could hear each round thumping into wood or plinking off metal. One grazed the top of his steel helmet and dazed him.

He could make out the muzzle flash of a machine gun spinning their way. The bullets traversed across the ground. Somehow George could see them hitting the ground; they looked like pebbles skimming off the surface of a lake.

He heard the thuds first, then turned to look at the Sergeant. His body wracked and danced with each blow. In a fraction of a second, George was up and leaping at the Sergeant. He hit him around the waist like a rugby tackle, and together they rolled into the shell crater that George had left only seconds before.

Tom crawled in after them, scrabbling after the Sergeant.

'Fuck, fuck, fuck,' he said repeatedly.

He rolled the Sergeant over, who was now covered head to toe in dirt. Blood was pouring through two exit wounds in his chest. The bullets had managed to miss his heart, and he was still conscious, but the blood was bright red.

He gritted his teeth and moaned in pain. George tore some cloth from a pocket in his webbing and pushed it against one of the wounds, trying to stop to flow of blood. It wouldn't clot, and the Sergeant was losing a lot of blood.

'Don't, it's no bloody use,' the Sergeant coughed. Blood rimmed his lips.

'We have to try something, sir. To stop the bleeding and get you back to our lines.'

The Sergeant tried to shake his head and failed. Instead he grabbed hold of George's hands and held them together.

'You make sure you survive this bloody war, Abbott. You hear me?' An iron grip took hold of his smock seam and pulled him down closer. He could smell the Sergeant's breath, tinged with the iron of blood. 'You bloody hear me?'

'Yes, sir,' he whispered.

'Truth is, sir…' He hesitated for a moment before continuing. 'I always got the impression that you hated me, sir.' He was trying to take the Sergeant's attention off his wounds and keep him talking.

'You're a bloody idiot, Abbott.' Even bleeding out in the bottom of this shell hole, the Sergeant's will was relentless. He glared at George through the pain of his wounds.

'I was trying to teach you Abbott. To be a good soldier.' He coughed again and went silent for a few seconds. George thought he was gone, but then he spoke again.

'I needed to be harsh on you. Otherwise you wouldn't have lasted a minute out here. I knew what we were up against. You lot had no idea. You were all bloody civvies. But I always had faith in you.'

309

The Sergeant's face wavered in George's vision. His eyes had watered up, and he blinked them dry. The hand holding George's smock eased off and dropped to the Sergeant's chest. Without thinking, George moved back in respect.

Tom pawed at the Sergeant's wounds. It was no use.

'Don't, Tom,' George said. He saw the desperation in his friend's face. He felt it too, but he had seen enough death now to know what it looked like. He knew the smell of iron and blood well enough.

'He's gone.'

'He saved my bloody life. He can't be.' Tom breathed deep, sucking in great lungfuls of air in shock, and sobbed. His face was covered with the Sergeant's blood, bright red, as if he had been painting. He sat back in the trench and put a hand to his mouth.

George stuck his head up, looking for any sign of the enemy, and trying to decide what their next step should be. He moved closer to Tom to talk to him, edging forward on his knees as the khaki scratched at his skin.

Tom's eyes shot over his shoulder and back at the signs of fighting in front of him. He was like a caged animal looking for an escape route. His gaze wouldn't stay still, his eyes kept moving away. He didn't even seem to see George crouched next to him in the shell hole.

'We have to find a way forward,' George said, almost unable to hear his own voice.

Tom didn't respond, and George wasn't sure if he hadn't been heard or if Tom was ignoring him. He repeated himself and still nothing. Tom kept turning his head. At one point he looked straight at George, but his eyes were unfocused, they didn't register George, but seemed to stare straight through him at some unknown vision.

George gave his friend a friendly punch on the arm, trying to drag him out of his reverie. Tom started at the punch and fell back into the shell hole, cowering. His eyes darted from side to side for some threat, despite being surrounded by them. George leaned closer to catch Tom's gaze, but he just stared right through him as if he wasn't there.

Tom's hand relaxed and the rifle slid out of it, easing down into the bottom of the shell hole, where the mud sucked it up.

'Tom, your rifle,' George shouted over the din. Tom didn't answer. He didn't even seem to hear George's words. He would be brought up on a charge for losing his rifle, but if they stayed in the shell hole much longer they would come under enemy fire, or worse.

George tried to raise Tom out of it, grabbing both his arms below the shoulder and shaking him as vigorously as he dared. Tom roared, pushing him back. George almost tumbled into the muddy bottom of the shell hole. He stood up on his haunches.

'No. No. No,' Tom said, shaking his head.

His fight or flight instinct kicked in. He pushed George again, forcing him out of his way and climbed to the top of the shell crater. He didn't stop there.

'Tom, what are you bloody doing?' George called after his friend, unprepared to leave the relative safety of the crater. 'Get back here!'

Tom didn't turn, he didn't stop. He climbed out into no man's land and started running. He dodged the explosions around him like an athlete, dodging this way and that. George shouted after him, but he disappeared into the distance out of sight.

George kneeled there, mud coating his khaki. He was in shock. Tom had always been there for him, and now he had gone. Just like that. In a way it was worse than the others. At least they had had no choice in the matter. Tom had upped and left of his own accord, without even a thought for George. He looked up. The specks of dirt and debris in the air fell on his face like raindrops.

He had to decide what to do. He could either press the assault on his own, hoping that some of the others had made it to the

German trench and he could support them. Or he would have to return to his own trench and face the consequences.

He looked around. He was so very alone. No man's land was littered with corpses and the debris of the last two years of war. The Sergeant still lay where he fell, staring at George as if in judgement of his decision. There was no way George could continue on his own. His section had been decimated. He was the only one left. They had come all the way from Liverpool together. The only way he could honour their memory was by surviving. He would have to return to the trench, there was nothing for it. He picked himself up, not noticing the mud that slid off his khaki. He picked up both his and Tom's rifles in his blood-drenched hands and climbed to the top of the shell crater.

As quick as he could manage, he jogged off back in the direction of his own trench.

Chapter 31

He was sitting in the front room of his house when they came for him. Anne sat next to him and held his hand. She hadn't said anything in minutes as they had both descended into silence, expecting the inevitable. Joe had been living in fear ever since the tribunal, knowing that he had no choice but to do anything except what they told him to do. He had not been made an exception of, and he was answerable to the law. He suspected that they hadn't even read the appeal that he had spent hours crafting when he was supposed to be working at the newspaper.

He had known they would send for him soon. It had taken longer that he had expected, and a cruel streak in him suspected that they were toying with him, punishing him further by making him wait.

In his left hand he clutched a piece of paper, crumpled by his semi-clenched fist. In his other he held on to Anne. She should be working but had refused to leave him. The piece of paper was his enlistment papers, ordering him to report to the Knowsley Park barracks for training.

He was supposed to have reported on Monday. It was now Tuesday, and like every other conscientious objector who had

313

refused military service, he fully expected them to send the police round to arrest him. It was, after all, the law.

A black shape moved past the front window, casting a shadow in the front room, and there was a knock on the door. Joe started in his seat, even though he had been expecting the knock. Anne tried to soothe him, but he jumped up in agitation. There came another polite knock on the door, perhaps thinking that the first hadn't been heard, but how could it not have been?

Joe walked out to the hallway and opened the door. A young, but well-presented policeman stood on the threshold. Joe had met him before, in his work for the newspaper, but he couldn't recall his name in his worried state. He cursed himself; he was normally so good with names.

'Hello, Joseph,' the policeman said. There was a sullen look on his face. 'I'm here to take you in, I'm afraid. I'm sure you know why.'

Joe nodded.

'Just give me a minute please,' he said.

The policeman didn't respond, he just turned away and stepped down the street.

Anne was by Joe's side, and he pulled her close. He breathed her in, not knowing when he would smell her, or feel her warmth again. He held the hug as long as he dared, unsure of when the policeman would interrupt them. He could wait, Joe decided.

'I will come back soon,' he said. 'They can't force me to be a soldier and they cannot keep me against my will.'

He could feel her gently sobbing against his chest.

'I know,' she said between breaths, 'I know.'

The policeman coughed politely, and Joe let go of Anne. He used a thumb to wipe a tear from her eye and smiled at her even though he didn't feel it.

'I have to go now.'

He kissed her, with more force than perhaps he had intended, but she didn't pull back. As soon as they stopped kissing he felt an absence, an absence he didn't think he would ever be able to fill.

As he stepped out of the house, the policeman grabbed him by the back of the arm and started leading him down the street.

'You don't need to do that. I won't run away.'

'Fair enough.'

He let go, and they walked the rest of the way in silence, the policeman's heavy boots clicking on the cobbled streets. It struck Joe as strange. Here were the streets that he would walk on his way to work, and here he was being led down them to a place he didn't want to go. How much things had changed in these past few months. The horses and carts still clattered past, but the streets were much emptier. There were no men of his age, only the elderly.

The people he passed, some of whom he knew well, looked at him with barely contained hatred. He could feel them all judging him as he went. A women spat at him, and he wiped the spit from his eye with the back of a hand. The policeman didn't step in to stop their jeers. What could he do? They were treating him as if he were a murderer, as if he had committed some more heinous crime than simply refusing to harm his fellow man.

He hoped that someday, through his actions and through others, they would understand. He didn't bear them any ill will. It was a changing world, and he hoped it was for the better.

The police station and bridewell was a square brick building that stood on the corner of Campbell Street and Argyle Street. There was a huge lion's head keystone hanging above the entrance, to instil a sense of fear in all prisoners brought underneath its arch. A small tower looked out over the street as if it was a watch tower.

The policeman took Joe in under guard and signed him in with the Sergeant at the desk. The jail was old, and the air smelt musty. There was a sense of damp in the old bricks. The policeman opened up one of the seven iron doors that closed off the cells,

315

and escorted Joe inside. There was a shelf to the back covered in a thin mattress, and a faint smell of asphalt and sick.

'I'm sorry for having to put you in here, Joseph,' said the policeman.

'It's all right. You're just doing your job.' He sat down on the mattress. 'You can call me Joe. Only my father calls me Joseph.'

He liked the policeman, there was a kindness to him that was becoming unfamiliar in this new world Joe found himself in.

'In the morning I will take you to the barracks,' he said, shutting the door behind him.

He was alone for the first time in months, and he had never slept this far from anyone. Until the war George had always been across the room from him, and even since he could often hear his parents snoring from their bedroom. It was going to be a long, silent night.

*

Joe walked along to the barracks unsure of what to expect. He had grown up around soldiers and some of them, like his Uncle Stephen, could be friendly, but they could also be dark and aggressive if wronged.

The policeman walked along behind him, making sure that he went to the barracks. He didn't come too close but walked in line several paces behind. He made it clear that he trusted Joe, but that it was his duty to make sure.

Joe walked into the barracks through the front door, unsure of where he should report to. His father had never prepared him for this. Perhaps he had thought it would be natural. Soldiering would never come naturally to Joe.

Inside, an army officer was doing some paperwork. He was too old for military service, much like the officer at the military tribunal, but not as grey, or turning to fat. He was still a fit man, and as he stood Joe could appreciate his commanding presence. The man towered over Joe by almost a head.

316

Joe passed the officer the enlistment paper that he had been sent and the officer took it with a frown. He scanned the paper and then crumpled it up in one hand.

'You're late,' he said. His voice was a bass rumble, warming. The officer reminded Joe of his uncle. Not just because both were officers, but there was something very similar in their mannerisms and body language. He held himself up well, straight-backed, and stared straight forward, regarding him with a cool air. Joe supposed that was the way that all officers were trained in the army. Although his father was a very different man.

'Be late again, and I'll put you on a charge.'

The officer was used to giving commands, and hadn't noticed that Joe had not yet spoken, nor apologised. Not that Joe had any intention of apologising.

'You'll need to go to the Quartermaster Sergeant later to get your uniform. For now, you'll just have to train in your civvies.'

'I won't wear it.'

Joe's voice came out like a squeak, and he cringed. It was the first time he had spoken that day and his voice had been weak and pathetic. It wasn't the determined resistance he had been aiming for.

'You'll do what you're told.'

The officer's demeanour changed. He stood over Joe, his face red. His eyes were as hard as steel, and he no longer reminded Joe of his uncle. He reminded him more of his father now.

'There is no will and won't in the army,' the officer shouted. 'In the army you do as you're told. Without question. If you don't then people will die. It's as simple as that.'

He strode to the back of the room, then turned around when Joe didn't follow.

'You're also expected to follow an officer if he leaves a room. Come on, will you?'

For some reason Joe followed. The officer's voice had a strong effect on him. He would have to fight his battles another way.

317

They could shout at him all they wanted, but they couldn't force him to fight in their war. Even if they dragged him all the way to France then he would sooner die than fire a weapon at another man. They could dress him up in their uniform, but he would be no more a soldier than his mother was, or his sisters were. He would object every time, in his own little way.

On the green behind the barracks building there was a group of around forty men in khaki, busy drilling. As Joe watched, the men squatted down with their hands on their hips, then raised themselves up. They then put both arms up, leant to one side and then the other. This was all led by a man at the front, facing them. The men were all of varying ages; ageing men who had been brought in as part of the conscription act, and boys who had only just turned old enough to be considered.

As the officer strode out, he called to them, his voice booming across the green.

'That's enough Swedish drill for now.'

They all stopped what they were doing and stood to attention.

'Time for bayonet drill. Get to it.'

The group of men began jogging in lines to the end of the green, and the officer turned to him with a red face, nostrils flaring.

'Fall in, Private Abbott!' he shouted.

Joe refused to run. He couldn't remember the last time he had run anywhere and he wasn't about to start now. He didn't want to be here, and the best way that he could think of frustrating the officer was to only obey some of his orders. Joe also got a perverse pleasure from it. He was in charge of himself, not the officer. So he walked after the group of soldiers, plodding along at his own pace. The officer eyed him all the way, his frown growing deeper every second.

By the time he reached the group, they were already engaged in bayonet practice. Something about the very nature of the act seemed archaic to Joe. In groups, the men charged sacks that

318

were suspended from wooden joists. Each man stood with his legs spread apart, then shouting at the top of his voice, he charged with his rifle and attached bayonet out in front of him. It seemed to Joe that each man was trying to shout louder and charge harder than the previous man, and the officer was shouting them on, going through each procedure with a clipped growl.

They were like animals, Joe decided. Each one was trying to be the best of the group. He was sure that if any women were present then they would be trying even harder to impress. Some men didn't look as interested as the others, but they still joined in. It was mindless destruction to get them into the war spirit and it made Joe feel sick. These were only sacks, but the aggression was still horrifying. Would these men be as forceful and deadly if they encountered a German soldier? He didn't doubt that they would.

When the last rank of men went through the drill the officer walked over to Joe, with a wooden mop handle in his hands.

'Your turn, Private.'

He raised his hands to pass the mop to Joe. It had a bayonet wrapped at one end. Joe guessed that the private soldiers only got a working rifle when they had passed a reasonable level of training. As Joe had already missed the few days' training that these men had had, then he wouldn't be given one. He was glad that there were still rules and regulations. At least this wasn't complete madness.

He didn't take the proffered mop from the officer. He had no intention of taking part in this barbaric practice. He didn't expect the officer would go to the effort of forcing the mop into his hands and running him towards the sack himself.

'No,' he said as calmly as declining a cup of tea. He didn't feel calm, but he had practice of forcing his voice to be steady.

'That's "no, sir" to you, Private!'

The recruiting officer was right up in Joe's face, and he had the hilarious urge to kiss the man in reply. It would simply be a matter of defiance and jest, but he rather suspected that it would only make him angrier.

'I am a civilian, not a private.'

'You are while you're in my drill ground. Now get on with it.'

'You will have to make me, sir. I am no soldier, and I will never take a weapon against my fellow man.' He looked over at the drill group who had started their routine again. 'Nor against a piece of sacking.'

The officer shook his head. His frown deepened and the corner of his mouth curved up. He scratched behind his ear, then turned to his recruits as if thinking.

'Look, lad.' He leant over and whispered, his mouth only a few inches from Joe's ear. 'Do you want to go to prison? You do know that's what will happen if you refuse to follow my orders, right? I'll be forced to court-martial you. It doesn't have to be all that bad. We need all the men we can get, and I'm sure a clever lad like you will work his way into a cushy job.'

'I'm sorry, but no. Thank you. I am of the opinion that the war is wrong and will not permit myself to take part in any way.'

'Then I'll not have you in my unit,' he shouted, for the rest of the men to hear. Some of them stopped in their drill to see what was going on. A quick glare had them back on their way.

'I have no use for a man that will not fight. You're a danger to us all.'

'I'd be a danger to you, even if I put on your uniform.'

The officer frowned at him, then stepped back.

'I'll process the court martial myself, and you'll be hearing from the war council. Now get out of my sight!'

Joe turned around and walked away as calmly as possible. For once in his life he wanted to run, but he wouldn't give the soldiers the satisfaction. He didn't know where he would go next. He wanted to see Anne, but he supposed he should tell his parents what had happened. He didn't know how much time he would have, or how much longer he would be free. He hadn't expected to get away from the barracks that easily, but the officer mustn't think he was worth the effort. He would make the most of his time before they sent him to prison. First he would send a letter to the No-Conscription Fellowship, telling them of his experiences, then he would go and see his family, and then to find Anne.

Even with the prospect of prison hanging over his head, for the first time in his life he felt truly, wondrously free.

Chapter 32

'He's back. He's back!'

'What?' George jumped up from the alcove he had secured himself in their rudimentary dugout and tried not to bang his head. 'What are you talking about, Cragg?'

Private Cragg wouldn't stand still, almost jumping from toe to toe in agitation as he rushed into their trench line, almost upsetting the brazier that they were using to brew some tea. The others glared at him, as they rescued their tin cups from the sodden ground.

'Sorry,' Cragg said, as he passed each man to get to George. 'Sorry. Sorry.'

He turned to look at George who was almost a head taller than him, and he was almost out of breath. George felt like slapping him around the face but kept his hands at his sides.

'Calm yourself down, Cragg. What's the matter with you?'

'I'm sorry, Abbott. I came as quickly as I could. I was up at HQ when they came in. It took me some time to get away, but as soon as I could I came straight here. I thought you'd want to know.' He tried to get all the words out in one go, and sentences merged into one.

George put his hand on the lad's shoulder and breathed deep,

322

encouraging Cragg to do the same. It worked and after a moment he was calm enough to speak.

'He's back, George. They've found him. They found Tom.'

It took all George's composure not to run off and find Tom for himself. He had been holding back all this time, wondering what had happened to his friend and frightened if he did anything he would make it worse. Besides, he had a duty and that duty was to remain here in the trench should he be called upon to fight.

'Where?' was all George could say, and the word came out as a whisper.

'He was hiding out in a nearby village. Some Military Policeman found him there when he was off duty. Still had his khaki on 'n' everything. Stupid bugger.'

George grabbed Cragg by the collar of his tunic, lifting the smaller man off the ground.

'Don't say another word,' George growled into his face. To their credit the other men carried on brewing their tea, ignoring the confrontation. He gripped harder, his knuckles going white through the lining of dirt, and he tried to calm himself. He didn't know if he was angry at Cragg, or angry at himself for not going after Tom. He'd left his best friend to wander through no man's land, while he hid in a shell hole. He was the true coward. Cragg stared back at him, eyes bulging in shock, and George felt guilty again. He released his grip and set the other man down.

'Where? Where is he now?'

Cragg's mouth moved, trying to form words, then stopped. He tried this a few times, before deciding to keep his silence.

'I'm sorry,' George said, a whisper. 'Tell me where Tom is… Please.'

'I don't know, Abbott. All I know is they've locked him up somewhere, awaiting the Captain's judgement. I came as quickly as I could…'

'I know, I know. Thank you.'

George pushed passed him and walked down the trench. He could feel Cragg's questioning gaze boring into his back. He squeezed past the waiting soldiers, some brewing, others snoring in their dugouts. He hadn't been ordered to leave the trench and he knew that doing so was a dereliction of duty, but he didn't care. He had to see Tom, he had to know what had happened in the shell hole out in no man's land. He had always relied on Tom's strength of character, and Tom had always told him when he was being stupid or did something rash. This time, however, Tom wasn't there to stop him.

Men moved up and down the reserve trench going back and forth about their tasks. George ignored them all.

A hand caught him on the arm, arresting his march. He almost shook it off in his haste but turned to reprimand whoever had dared to stop him.

'Where do you think you're going, lad?'

George looked down at where Corporal Owens' filth-covered hand gripped the arm of his tunic, then back up at his face, regarding him with cool eyes. He was an older man, in his early thirties, hair turning to silver at his temples. He had the calm demeanour of a former school teacher or doctor. He was always so patient. Sometimes it was infuriating. Owens let go.

'You've heard then?'

'I have, Corporal. I was just on my way—'

'Why?' Owens interrupted him.

'Why, Corporal? I don't know—'

'That's exactly what I mean. Come now, Abbott, there's no good running off all guns blazing. Being around here should have taught you that much, not to mention your experience. Do you even know where you are going?'

George shook his head. If he was being honest with himself, he wasn't sure. All he had known was that he had to act. He had to do something.

'I didn't think you did. Rushing off isn't going to help Tom one bit, or yourself for that matter. You have to calm down and think. What are you going to say? What are you going to do? This isn't being very smart, and I thought better of you, lad. Give yourself five minutes to think.'

He couldn't wait any longer; unlike the Corporal he wasn't patient. He needed to act and soon, otherwise the guilt would eat him up.

'But if I don't go now—'

'Nothing will change in the next five minutes. Do you honestly think decisions in this army happen that quickly?'

It was so easy for him to say, but what did he know? Tom needed him. George stood as if any moment he was about to leap, his body wouldn't allow him to stand still and he kept looking off down the trench.

'Look at me,' Owens said, with force, and even with George's willpower it was hard to resist the command. 'There is nothing you can do, especially in this state. You have to accept that.'

He didn't know what to say. He couldn't give up, he would never give up on Tom as Tom would never give up on him. The Corporal had taken his arm again, and he thought about breaking free from the grip, but knew it would only make things worse. He didn't know the Corporal well, as he'd only been with them a few weeks. Another one of the endless promotions and reassignments to stem the thinning ranks. For all he knew this man could turn angry at any moment, and even though George didn't want to hear it, he suspected that he was trying to help him.

'I want to see Tom. We go a long way back.'

The Corporal's mouth turned down at the corners and his eyes grew softer.

'I know you do. Perhaps the Captain will let you see him, perhaps he won't.'

'I need to know why.'

George didn't know what he meant by those words, but they had come to him out of the corner of his subconscious. He needed more than anything to speak to Tom. To ask why. Why had he given up? They were all in this together. Why had he run? What did he hope to accomplish? Why had he left George to die? Bitter anger flared for a moment in his mind, but he forced it back under the months of torment and mud with all his other emotions.

'We all do. We all do.' Corporal Owens sighed, and let go of George's arm once again. 'Just promise me that you will stay calm? Anger and rashness will do you no favours in front of the Captain. I can't afford to lose another good man. Be polite and put your case before the Captain. Then whatever you do, accept his decision with good grace. Promise me, and I will cover for you here.'

'I will,' he said, and left the Corporal behind in the reserve trench.

*

George stepped up to the officers' dugout at the end of a diagonal run of reserve trench.

'Private Abbott?' said an officer, coming out of the dugout. The Captain's adjutant was a short, thin man who didn't look at George as he addressed him.

He nodded, not knowing how the officer knew who he was. The Corporal must have warned them of his arrival.

'Go on in. He's expecting you.'

'Thank you, sir.'

The adjutant lifted up the gas sheet for the dugout and admitted him.

George walked in. An officers' dugout was an easy place to be out of place and to make a mistake which might cause pain further down the line. A soldier always had to be on guard, never at ease.

The Captain leant over a desk, writing on a sheet of paper in

326

waning candlelight. The candle fluttered at the inrush of air as George entered. The Captain finished writing what he had been writing. After a few awkward moments he sighed, put his pen down, and looked up in George's direction.

'Private?' he said.

'Abbott, sir.'

The Captain regarded George, then leant back in his chair, took off his spectacles and rubbed his eyes with the back of his hand. He must have been in his early forties. His hair was going bald and greying at the sides. His eyes had crow's feet. He had a slight hint of greying stubble on his chin and cheeks that indicated he hadn't shaved in a while.

'Ah yes. Jennings told me all about you.'

George guessed that Jennings must have been the Captain's adjutant.

'Please do have a seat, Abbott. I can't abide talking to people stood above me.'

George pulled out one of the wooden chairs from the table and plonked himself down, his webbing clattering. He was too exhausted to sit with care, and it felt good to be able to sit on a real chair. His backside had never quite got used to sitting in dirt and mud.

The Captain poured himself a drink, but didn't offer one to George. He became aware of how dry his throat was, but it wouldn't be appropriate to reach for his water bottle in the Captain's company, so he waited, licking his lips to try and force some saliva into his parched mouth.

'Do you write home, Abbott?' the Captain asked, after a sip of whatever it was he was drinking.

'Home, sir? Yes, sir. As much as I'm able to, sir.'

He cringed at his own overuse of the word 'sir'. But the Captain didn't seem to notice.

'That's good. I would very much like to write to my dear old wife. However, I spend most of my time writing these.'

He held up the sheet of paper he had been writing on for George to see, then put it back on the table.

'It's a crying shame to have to write so many letters to these poor families. It's a wonder we have any time for actual soldiering. Once I've finished writing the day's letters and dispatches I'm no longer in the mood to write to my dear wife. I wouldn't want to worry her with all the details. What on earth would I say to her, Abbott?'

'I don't know, sir,' he said, honestly.

'Too right, Abbott. Too bloody right.'

The Captain stood up with a creak of wood on wood, and paced over to a cabinet on the wall, pulling out another bottle of dark brown liquid, which he brought back to the table.

He took a moment to pull out the cork and pour a measure. The liquid glugged into the dirty glass. George licked his lips in thirst but knew that the liquid wouldn't do anything to quench it. The Captain didn't pour a second glass and sat sniffing the drink. George would have to find himself some of that water that always carried the faint hint of rum, thanks to the rum bottles it was transported in, when he got back to his trench.

The Captain breathed in deep and put the glass back down on his table with a clunk.

'It's not good, I'm afraid, Abbott,' he said at length. 'Not good at all. Corporal Adams was found miles from the front line without his rifle. While I sympathise with the soldiers, this simply won't do. What if every man in khaki put down his rifle and walked off?'

George didn't say a word; anything he did say would only serve to incriminate his friend further. He was angry at Tom too. His oldest friend had left him in the middle of no man's land during an assault. There were too few of them as it was, without Tom running away. They could have pressed some kind of advantage, but when it was just George left, he was lucky to be alive.

'We wouldn't have much of any army left if that happened,

Abbott. Then the Germans would walk all the way to Paris after surrounding the French forces. Then what, Abbott? Then what? The Channel is only a short distance to cover. They'd be marching down Whitehall by next Wednesday. The war might not be going exactly to our initial plans, but it's still infinitely preferable to letting the Germans do as they please. Think of what they would do to the women and children. The stories from Belgium are bad enough.'

The Captain became more animated as he spoke, emphasising each word. The signs of lack of sleep pulled at his features.

'I'm sorry, son. It simply won't do. If we let one soldier get away with it then there will surely be more to follow. We've few enough men as it is these days. You're one of the original lot, aren't you? Came out with us in 1915?'

George supposed he was, though he had never thought about it that way. He had come over with the regiment, despite being new to soldiering then. Most of the lads alongside him in the trenches these days had come over since, to plug the gaps as it were, and conscription had helped with that.

'Yes, sir. I was in Canterbury with everyone before the war. There's not many of us left now.'

'Indeed, there's precious few of you left. The lads we're getting through now are barely trained.' He paused for a moment, reflecting. 'Adams was with you in Canterbury as well.' It wasn't a question, the Captain knew well who was who out of his men.

'Yes, sir. That's why I want to see him, sir. We go back a long way. Lived next door to each other before the war.'

'It's no good. I can't afford to lose more experienced men like you and Adams, but HQ will want to set an example to the other men. I will put in a recommendation, but there is very little possibility that they will take it into consideration.'

'I just want to see him, Captain,' George said, a whisper.

'Hmmm.' The Captain put his hand around his jaw and considered George for a moment. 'I'm sorry, Abbott. Now isn't a good time I'm afraid. He's about to go up in front of the court martial. As much as I may wish to, I cannot allow you to see him.'

'Sir—'

'No, Private. That's quite enough on that matter. You'll have to forget all about Adams and get back to the trenches. That's all there is for it now, I'm afraid.'

It wasn't callous. The Captain gave off the air of a caring uncle, and he very much reminded George of his Uncle Stephen. The strain in his eyes showed that he wanted to help George, but that regulation and principle wouldn't allow him.

George stood up and threw a quick salute.

'I will be going then, sir,' he said, then turned to walk away. 'Thank you for your time.'

'Abbott?'

He stopped in his tracks and half turned, not wanting to look the Captain in the eyes lest hope take over. The Captain had stood too and was holding his glass between two hands, staring into its depths.

'I am sorry, son.' That was all he said, before turning his back on George, indicating that he was dismissed.

George pushed his way back through the gas curtain, and nodded to the adjutant, his will deflating all the while. He didn't know what he had expected. Most officers wouldn't have given him the time of day, but the Captain had been different. If anything, that had made things worse. He could handle it if the Captain didn't care, but he seemed genuinely upset, and that made George wish even more that he would do something. It was no good. He was restricted by military regulation. The same regulation that had Tom in solitary and was about to have him up in front of a court martial.

There was nothing that George could do, and not for the first time since coming to France, he felt useless.

Chapter 33

Walton Prison was a heavy presence, as Joe walked towards it trying not to glance around like a frightened animal. His heart was beating in his chest, but he wouldn't let the sensation overcome him. He was terrified, but so too would those men be, out in France forced into a war they shouldn't be fighting. It was the least he could do to show them respect and prove that he wasn't a coward after all. For some reason the authorities had let him arrive on his own, even though he had resisted the tribunal as much as possible. He wondered if they were looking for an excuse to send the police after him, expecting him not to turn up at the prison under his own volition. He had heard about the games of cat and mouse the police liked to play with conscientious objectors and suffragettes.

Some of those who disliked him for his objection to the war could be quite aggressive towards him, policemen included. He had had to keep his head down since it became public knowledge. Perhaps it was better that he would be locked up for some time, if only to keep him away from such people. But then he wondered what the other inmates would be like. What were their crimes? There must be some much worse than objecting to the war.

He had come alone and carried no personal belongings. He had been told that he wouldn't be able to take anything in with him, should anything be used to break out, or as a weapon. Anne had wanted to accompany him to the gates, but he had flat out refused. He didn't want her anywhere near this place, and he wasn't sure he could have kept it together had she come with him. Instead they had said a tearful goodbye at his home before he had left, walking all the way to the prison to collect his thoughts. His mother had hugged him, Catherine too, but his father had left without a word. There were only the three of them left now in a house that had once housed five. And soon Catherine would be gone too. Of course, he would miss her wedding while in prison, but there was nothing he could do. It brought a tear to Joe's eye to think of them all, and he brushed it away with a finger. He wouldn't allow himself to walk inside the prison with a tear in his eye. He had to remain strong, otherwise who knew what would happen?

From the outside, the prison was like some kind of medieval castle. There was a towered archway that led off from the main road, like a barbican. Joe could imagine a portcullis hanging overhead, its spikes facing down at the unwary, but instead two heavy wooden doors barred his way.

He reached one fist up and knocked, as heavily as he dared, on the smaller door inside a larger door. After a few uneasy seconds, just as he thought about knocking again, a slot slid aside with a creak of wood on wood. Cold eyes peered out at Joe, but the man the other side of the door didn't say a word. Remembering, Joe reached around in his pocket searching for the piece of paper that was his order to attend the prison. He held it up.

'Joe Abbott,' he said. 'I'm to come inside and be held at your convenience. I would ask you to open the door, but I would rather forget it and leave.'

He flashed a grin that he didn't feel, but the eyes just stared back until Joe, embarrassed, coughed into the same fist that had knocked on the door.

The slot closed again, but Joe knew better than to feel any hope at that sudden action. With a further creak the smaller door opened back on its hinges, giving way to a slim view of the courtyard across the threshold. A thickset man obscured that view as soon as the door opened fully, the man with the cold, dead eyes that had stared at Joe through the viewport. Joe had half expected him to be wearing chainmail and a tabard, a sword scabbarded at his hip. Anne was right, he did read too much. He smiled and laughed under his breath at the thought. The other man gave him a sideways look, his breathing slow and controlled, just about discernible even over the distance between them.

He took Joe in a rough grip under one shoulder and hauled him inside. He let go and turned, methodically shutting the door behind him. The gatekeeper may have been a man of few words, but he appeared to be fastidious about his work. He took care to replace each bolt in its lock before turning back to Joe.

'You'll have to see the chief warden.' His voice was pitched higher than his frame would suggest. Joe had expected a deep rumble, not a such a high-pitched voice, and it took all his willpower not to laugh again. He didn't suspect that the man would put it down to being nervous, or if indeed that was even a concept within his ken.

'After you,' Joe said, and the big man pushed past him towards the main building. He reached out a meaty hand, grabbing Joe under the arm again, and pulling him along with him.

The main building was even more castle-like than the entranceway. Two big red brick towers were joined by a central archway and building, with white stone bricks used to represent the crenellations. In its day it may very well have been magnificent, but now it was an oppressive edifice staring down at Joe in judgement. Thick black smog had coated the stone in a layer of grime that gave lie to the medieval impression it was trying to give. A chimney stack sat atop one tower, giving out faint black and white smoke and the smell of a fire drifted through the air to congeal with the smog. Joe felt like a pauper being dragged to a dungeon.

The main door opened and another warder stepped out. The

gatekeeper pushed the paper he had taken from Joe into his hand and let go of Joe's arm. He walked away.

'Goodbye,' Joe muttered under his breath, already feeling alone before he had even stepped foot in the prison.

'Abbott, eh?' the new warder said. His deep voice was more what Joe had expected from the gatekeeper. Joe wasn't sure if it was a question or a statement. He had Joe's name in front of him, so Joe nodded, already suspecting that his mouth might get him in trouble here.

The warder just glared at him and waved a hand at the door. 'Get on, then,' he said.

Joe put one foot inside the door and was met with darkness. The inside of the prison was dim, and full of stale air. His eyes took a second to acclimatise to the difference in light.

The warder moved behind him and blocked out the sunshine. Joe felt a force on his back, and his trailing foot caught on the doorframe. He fell. He tried to put his arms out to arrest his fall, but the floor rushed up to meet him. His face smacked into the cold concrete, and splitting pain rushed through his head. The room went even darker for a second before his senses reasserted themselves. His nostrils were overwhelmed with the smell of the place, a thick cloying staleness that reminded him of his old school. His only other notion was of the sound of laughing from behind. He rolled onto his side.

The warder towered over him and laughed, a deep booming laugh that rocked his whole body. 'I didn't think you would go down so easily,' he said, in between fits of laughter.

Joe rubbed his head, trying to soothe away the pain, but it was a constant stinging in his temples. He put out a hand for some help to get up, but the warder ignored it. His laughter had died down now, but he still smirked.

'Pick yourself up, coward,' he said.

*

Minutes later, Joe was being led into his cell. The heavy metal bolts slid back and the door opened for him. Of course, he had no control over when the door might open or close, and he was sure any attempt to get in the way would only result in another 'fall'. He didn't remember being that clumsy.

The cell stank of rusting iron, the pallet in the corner had seen better days, and the only piece of metal that looked as if it had been maintained was the grey painted door. Even still, flecks of paint dropped off when it moved. As he was shoved inside he was met with an even stronger smell, the smell of piss and shit. He gagged at the stench. There was a small metal bucket in the corner of the room.

He turned round to face the warders, so many questions on the tip of his tongue, but they remained unspoken. He willed them to say this was some kind of joke, but he knew that it was futile; this was his new home. He hadn't even seen any other prisoners yet. Was he to be kept isolated? Away from any other human contact, with only the warders as his occasional company?

'What are you waiting for?' the larger of the two warders asked Joe. He looked like a brute, someone Joe would expect to see working down at the docks, hauling cargo. Far from laughing at Joe again, he was back to scowling at Joe as if he smelt of something indecent. Perhaps, he was just scowling at the smell in the cell. He had a broken nose. From the way he held himself, Joe could very well imagine this man being some kind of boxer. His black hair was cut close to his skull, the same way George's had been after he had enlisted in the army. Joe wondered why the warder wasn't out in France. He was of the right age, despite his weathered appearance.

'I…' Joe started, confused. 'I don't know what I'm supposed to do.' It was true. Prison had always been so far from his thoughts that he had never thought about what happened to someone when they were imprisoned. He was sure that his time would be spent in this cell, but the warder seemed to want something, otherwise they would have closed the door and been gone by now.

'Take off your clothes.'

'Pardon?' Joe was incredulous.

'You didn't think you'd be able to wear civvies in here did you?' The warders smirked at each other, then back at Joe. 'Who knows what you might have hidden in there.'

The bigger of the two men stepped inside the cell, closer to Joe.

'Now take them off,' he said. 'Otherwise I will have to do it for you.'

Joe did as he was told, not wanting to be asked again by the big man. He started with his shoes, undoing the laces and kicking them towards the door. He had had enough of the men for one day and he didn't want the warder closer than was necessary. Who knew what he might do if he had to remove Joe's clothes with force? In seconds he was down to his underwear, his clothes a brown pile on the floor next to the door. One of the warders bent down and picked the pile up.

'We'll look after these while you're here,' he said and left Joe alone with the big warder.

Joe sat down on the pallet, feeling the cold of the cell even more by the barred window.

'What shall I wear?' he asked, growing tired of the way they were treating him, and no longer caring what he said. At that moment another warder arrived, carrying a bundle in his arms.

'There you are,' broken-nose said, as the other warder entered the cell. 'What took you so long?'

The new warder grunted in reply. 'You know why.' He passed the bundle to the other warder and left the room again. Joe wondered whether all the warders were in a permanent bad mood, whether this was just their manner, or whether they were unhappy at having to deal with him. It could be the latter. He sat back further on the pallet and wrapped his arms around his body, trying to find more warmth.

'Here.' The broken-nosed warder put the bundle he had been given down on the side of the pallet. 'You can wear this if you want to wear something.'

He smirked at Joe showing semi-rotten teeth, and it was an expression that Joe could only describe as being pure evil. The warder was taking some kind of perverse pleasure in his suffering. If this was what the warders were like, then what would the prisoners be like? Joe shuddered and it was nothing to do with the chilly breeze that permeated the cell.

He sat the bundle of clothes on the pallet and reached out a hand. He stopped abruptly when he saw the colour of the cloth. It was a khaki colour, the same colour he had seen George wearing before he set off to France. He recoiled, realising what the warders intended for him.

'What's this?' He didn't want to ask, fearing the answer, but he couldn't help himself.

Again he was met with that predatory smirk.

'This? Oh, this is your uniform, coward.' The rotten breath hit Joe like a hammer. The warder was far too close for his liking. There was only one person he liked being that close to him and she was miles away. Small victories.

'It's not… not what I was expecting.' He was playing for time, trying to think, but also willing the warder to go and leave him. He hoped this was all some sick joke, and soon the prison chief would come and put him out of his misery. He knew that he was lying to himself, but he had to cling on to something. The warder was still enjoying his distress. He picked up the tunic and held it out for Joe, much as a tailor might to someone trying on a new suit jacket.

'Ya see, you're a military prisoner, right? So there's only one appropriate uniform for you.'

They'd even gone to the trouble of putting the regimental badges and pins on the tunic. This wasn't just some khaki they had got out of storage, it was the King's regiment uniform. What was worse was that they wanted him to put it on.

'You only need put this on, and you can walk out of here at your pleasure.' The warder still smirked. Joe was lost for words. He couldn't think how to formulate his argument, to make this overbearing bully of a man understand. It had been his problem all along.

'But… that's the reason I'm in here.'

Broken-nose laughed out loud in that booming volley that Joe was becoming ever so familiar with.

'Of course it is, coward. I know exactly why you're here. You're too scared to go and fight the Hun.'

'I'm not…' He thought better of it.

'You're too much of a coward, when there are people like me that would love to go out there and get stuck in. To show Hun what we're made of. If only I had your eyesight, I'd happily go out there and fight.'

The warder reached for Joe's head and he pushed himself back against the wall in fear. The touch didn't come and the warder just boomed with laughter again.

'See, you're just a coward.'

Joe got angry for the first time, and he stood up and crossed to the other side of the cell to put some distance between himself and the warder.

'I may be intimidated by larger men, but I am no coward.'

The two men watched each other and rounded the cell, like two boxers waiting for the initiating blow. Joe was at a disadvantage because he wouldn't be the one to attack, and the warder knew that. He smiled with confidence at Joe who kept moving to keep away from him. The cell was too small to put much distance between them. To an observer the situation would have seemed hilarious. Joe, a scrawny, thin man dressed in only his white underwear, circling the big, bruting warder. He had no chance.

'I don't want to fight,' he said. 'I've come here because fighting is the last thing I want to do. I will defend myself if necessary, but I won't fight.'

'All you have to do is put on that uniform and you're free to go. I will open up every door for you and forget about you. You'll be warm, at least.'

'This war is wrong. I can't help but think that. Nothing you say or do to me will change that. I've already had enough abuse and derision for my opinion. Nothing will change it.'

He was back by the pallet now, the movement had brought him some warmth, but the cold breeze was sapping his energy. He sat down and the warder stared from by the doorway.

'This war is wrong,' he repeated. He looked down at the floor unwilling to meet the warder's judging gaze. 'It's even turning us against each other. Men are dying, and no one has yet given us a good reason for why. Go out and fight if you want to. I'm not stopping you. But I won't lift a hand to kill another man. I'm no murderer. Even if you will lock me in prison. If that's what needs to be done to keep me from killing other men, then so be it.'

The warder grabbed open the door and walked into the corridor.

'Just remember, you only need put that on.' He pointed at the uniform. 'And you're free to go.'

With that, he closed the heavy door behind him, which fitted into its frame with a loud clang that reverberated from the uncoated walls and was deafeningly loud in the confined space.

Joe, exhausted after his short time in prison, lay down on the pallet and stretched his legs out. He closed his eyes, willing his heart to stop beating so fast, breathing in deep. In, and out. Without the knowledge that he was in a cell, the cold breeze that kept blowing over his skin and raising goosebumps would make him think he was lying down outside. He shivered where he lay. Some time later he fell asleep.

Chapter 34

George walked inside the rudimentary cell and nodded to the military policeman on duty, who shut the door behind him. Tom was curled up in a corner on the pallet they had given him for a bed. He still stared at the floor after George had entered. George stood opposite, as there was nothing to sit on, and coughed. Still Tom didn't respond.

'The Captain finally relented and gave me permission to see you. After the third time of asking. Begging more like,' he said after a few awkward seconds. 'He warned me against it actually, but I had to come.'

George was trying to fill the silence, and he was sure that Tom didn't care for what he said. He finally regarded George.

'Thank him for me, George,' he said. 'God, but it's good to see your face. The old Captain was right though, you shouldn't have come. You shouldn't see me like this.'

Tom's skin was pale, even against the white walls of the room, and there was a sick pallor to him. There was a few days' growth of beard on his chin, and the black stubble made him appear a lot older. His eyes were drawn, and the youthful exuberance was a distant memory.

'I had to come, Tom. You know I did. I couldn't live with

340

myself if I didn't. You're my oldest friend and I couldn't leave you in here to rot on your own. Everything's going to be all right.' He wanted to reach out and somehow comfort his friend, but he had no idea what to do. This situation was unprecedented.

Tom looked George in the eye and burst out laughing. He rocked back and forth on the pallet he was laughing so much.

'What?' George asked, put out.

'You…!' That was the only word Tom could say between laughs.

'What do you mean, "me"?'

'You know what, don't be daft, lad. You trying to comfort me. Don't get me wrong, I appreciate it. It's just… it's just that it's usually me saying things like that to you. "Don't worry, Georgie, everything's going to be all right." Look how much this place has changed us. I'm locked in here and you've grown up. Oh, don't look at me like that!'

George tried to be impassive as Tom had sensed his unhappiness at the implication.

'It's a good thing, George. Trust me. You don't want to rely on me anymore, it's not healthy. It's time for you to take charge. "George Abbott's Army" always had more of a ring to it.'

He flashed that all so familiar grin for the first time in months, but through the black stubble, and alongside the pain in his eyes he looked like a different person.

George suddenly felt an anger he had never felt before. It rose up within him and made his head hurt. The outside world felt distant and distorted.

'I'm the one you fucking left behind, Tom. So don't give me that. We could have pushed that attack if you had been with us, but instead you left me to die. Don't make out like you're some fucking martyr for my cause. It's not fair!'

Tom's mouth fell open and he stared at George. Then his head dropped and he stared at the ground.

'I'm sorry,' he said. He sounded like a chastised child, and

341

George knew that he could never maintain his anger at Tom. It still stung, but they had been through so much together.

'Oh, it doesn't matter, Tom. Does it? I made it back in the end.'

'No, you're right. I shouldn't have left you. I just… I… I just couldn't take it anymore. I didn't even think. I felt trapped. My head was buzzing, and my heart was hammering in my chest. I no longer saw you, and I no longer saw the explosions and gunfire. I just saw a means of escape, and I ran.'

He sighed a heavy sigh and looked up at George. His eyes were red with tears, but his mouth stuck in a line. He was still angry, but angry with himself.

'I know it's a terrible excuse, but there it is. I can't explain it any better than that. In my fear I was blinkered to reality and I fled. I'm a coward and that's all there is to it.'

George sat down on the pallet next to Tom and shared his view of the opposite wall. It was an unremarkable wall, with white paint peeling to reveal the brickwork underneath. He could imagine how staring at it for hours on end in confinement could drive a person insane. He closed his eyes and shook his head to banish away the thought.

They both sat there for a while in silence. What Tom was thinking, George had no way of telling, but he could hear him breathing away. He didn't even know what he was thinking himself. He had been angry at Tom, worried for him, and every other emotion he could think of. He didn't know how he felt now, seeing him in this state. He tried not to think about what was going to happen.

'Where did you go?' he said, forcing his mind away from the dark path it was leading down.

It was an honest question, but Tom made a confused 'hmm' sound from next to him. George got the impression that trying to change the subject had only annoyed Tom more.

'Where did I go? Why are you asking that? What difference does it make?'

'I just want to know. I'm curious. You disappeared without a word, and then the whole time… well, the whole time I was worried about you. I had no idea where you were, and I couldn't leave my post for fear of the consequences. So where did you go?'

Tom didn't answer straight away. He shuffled in his sitting position on the bed, but George still couldn't look at him. After a few moments, Tom sighed and spoke.

'At first I had no idea where I was going,' he said. 'I just wanted to get away. It was like my vision had gone blank and I just ran blindly. Kind of how I imagine a blinkered horse might feel. It took me quite some time to get my sense back and realise what I had done.'

'After that, I stopped in a clearing and tried to get my breath back. I didn't know where I was, but I was somewhere behind the lines. I knew if the military police found me I'd be in a lot of trouble, so I decided to keep running.'

He sighed again.

'It wasn't very clever, and it certainly wasn't very brave, but I think we've already established that I wasn't particularly thinking straight.'

'Then what happened?' George asked, determined not to bite and give his opinion on Tom's actions. He could feel Tom observing him, his eyes boring into the side of George's head, wondering where he was going with this.

'Well, lad,' he said. 'I wanted to go home. To see my ma. It's been too long.'

George nodded in agreement.

'But there was no way I'd be able to board a boat at Le Havre, or anywhere else for that matter without a correct form. I was trapped between the enemy and our own army.

'So, I thought I'd go back to that estaminet we drank in near Ypres. That village was nice, and if I only had a few hours before they found me I'd want to spend it somewhere like that. And, I thought I'd see if I could try my luck with that pretty serving girl. She was a real looker.'

George could hear Tom's smile in his words and he laughed. Something of Tom's old self shone through at that moment and they shared the laugh together. It reminded George of better times, back home in the Grapes, even on the dock, where Tom's carefree attitude had got them through the working day and they had often laughed together with their friends. Then the war had come along and changed all that. Now Patrick and Harry were dead, and it was only Tom and George left. He no longer felt like laughing, and his lips straightened at the thought. They had lost so much, and he could dwell on that for hours. He tried not to. The only thing that made any difference was thinking about what the war had brought to the other people of Europe. George and Tom had lost a lot, but at least their families still had their homes. Out here, the same could not be said. In the villages they had billeted in and fought over, the houses were but ruins. Who knows what would have happened if they hadn't stopped the Germans from advancing further?

'So,' George said, breaking the silence and his morbid train of thought. 'Did you find her? Did you have any luck?'

'I wish! The bloody place was closed.'

They both laughed. It felt good to laugh. George couldn't remember the last time that either of them had laughed like this. The war had always been in their thoughts and in this cell was the first time that it had felt distant, as if it was now happening to someone else. The laughter died out as George realised that he would soon have to return and face the war. He couldn't hold it off for much longer. Tom too lapsed into silence. The only sound in the cell was the sound of their careful breathing. Not even the outside sounds of war penetrated the walls of the cell.

'Hey, George,' Tom said after a while of them sitting in silence. 'You know I'm not going to be around much longer, right?'

George didn't know what to say. They had both been thinking

it all along. The charge for being absent without leave was one of the most severe the army had. He just nodded, trying not to dwell too much on the fact. He sighed involuntarily.

'I reckon Joe is right, ya know,' Tom continued.

It was an odd comment, and George wasn't sure where it had come from. George hadn't mentioned his brother in months. In fact he didn't think he had since they had been out in France. He had kept the contents of his mother's letters to himself.

'How do you know? What do you mean?' he said.

'My ma tells me. She writes too, ya know.'

Tom gave George a punch on the arm.

'Don't be stupid now. You know exactly what I mean. Don't try and hide from it. You're always running away from your problems.'

George couldn't bring himself to point out the irony of that comment. He frowned and pursed his lips, letting Tom continue.

'I reckon your brother's right. He always had more sense than you.'

George stood up from the pallet. There was a defiance in Tom's eyes, and it scared George. He had never spoken to him like this before.

'What are you talking about?' he shouted, his anger at Tom for leaving him coming back, and adding to the anger he felt at hearing his words. 'What's wrong with you?'

'There's nothing wrong with me. I've finally seen the truth. We shouldn't be fighting this war. Sooner or later you will realise that for yourself.'

George heard movement outside the room, and a shadow crossed the outline of the door. He heard a key being put into the lock, and then it opened with a click.

'Time.'

The military policeman didn't enter the cell. He just stared at them both with an air of thinly veiled contempt. George could see now why they were so hated by the other soldiers. How could they take any joy in what they had to do? Yet some of them seemed to enjoy it, more than was natural.

Tom had gone back to huddling in the corner, holding his knees up to his chest. He rested his head on the wall beside him and refused to meet George's eyes.

'Just go, George,' he said. His voice didn't falter. 'You shouldn't have come.'

'But…'

'Goodbye, George,' Tom forced, with finality.

'Bye, Tom,' George whispered as he turned to leave.

He walked out of the cell, using all his willpower to not look over his shoulder. Yet another metaphorical corner was turned in his life. He would have to live life without Tom. As he left through the front room six other privates were being instructed by the provost martial. They stopped as he came near, eyeing him with suspicion. Two of them he recognised from his company; they had known Tom. The other four he didn't recognise. It occurred to him then that according to army regulations it required six volunteers for a firing squad. He wanted to scowl at them, but what good would it do? He couldn't understand their decision, like he could no longer understand his oldest friend. Why would they volunteer for such a duty?

He left the building as quickly as possible. He no longer wanted to be a part of this. He had other duties to attend to.

*

George stormed down the trench, barging one private out of the way. He didn't say sorry, he just kept on walking. He wiped a hand across his cheek, smearing more mud across his face. Tears threatened to fall, but he wouldn't let them. He was angry, not upset. He couldn't allow himself to be upset.

'Woah, what's got into you?'

Corporal Owens grabbed him by the arm, arresting his charge.

346

George almost lashed out, but he caught himself; he liked the man.

'What happened up there, George? What happened?'

'Tom.'

'He's what's made you so angry? You look like you're about to go off and fight the Germans all by yourself.'

'I've thought about it.'

'Come on now, sit down or something. Tell me what happened.'

George sat on a small ledge in the mud by the side of the communication trench and breathed. After a minute or so, he was calm enough to relate to Owens what Tom had said.

'I don't suppose he was trying to be rude, George.' He gave him that fatherly look which George was fond of, showing that despite it all Owens still cared. 'He was just trying to make it easier on you.'

'Easier?'

'Yes, easier. He's probably scared witless. He didn't want you to have a difficult goodbye. Not amongst all of this. He wasn't trying to be rude, and I'm sure that he certainly cares about you. Probably too much, if truth be told. Arguing with you, well that was just his way of making sure that you left the room, and that you didn't try and do anything drastic to try and save him.

'You see, he wanted to make it easier on you, by making you angry at him, and, if only for a short while, by making you hate him.'

George put his head in his hands, covering his face with fresh mud. He didn't care about the mud, he just wanted to shut the outside world out. He didn't understand what was happening, and too much had changed. He wanted to run away, but knew he wouldn't get very far. For the first time he could see why Tom had run. It was an instinct, left over from their days as wild animals. George could feel the same sensation now, and it was only his self-pity that stopped him from bolting.

Owens pulled George's arm away, revealing his face.

'Come now, George. Let's get back to work fixing these trenches. It'll take your mind off things. Best to keep busy.'

Owens hauled him up with a hand under George's armpit. He gave him a pat on the back, and together they forced their way through the muddy trench back to their section.

*

George sat and forced his back against the wall of the trench, feeling the cool wet earth behind him, and closed his eyes. The morning sun coming over the horizon lit the back of his eyelids an angry red, but it was the mere effort of closing them that was calming and relaxing. He didn't close them for sleep, but to tempt his mind to somewhere else, anywhere else but here. Somewhere birds sang, unaware of the war that was going on around them. It was amazing that they were still here despite the devastation to their habitats.

A shot rang out in the distance. It reverberated around the nearby trenches and across no man's land, an eerie power in the still quiet of the morning air.

George couldn't be sure if it had been one shot of a sniper picking up a target, or the shots of the firing squad ending his oldest friend's life. Gunfire was always present in the trenches, echoing through the morning gloom.

It was about the right time, he told himself.

A single tear fell down his cheek.

He hadn't cried for another man since Fred had died, and that was right at the beginning, when it still affected him. Every time since, he had just become more and more numb, until now. Now he had lost everything, and he shed a tear for Mrs Adams who had lost the only thing left in her life worth living for. He knew the news would devastate her. But she would have to know at some point. He vowed then, if he ever got home, he would be the one to tell her about her son. To tell her that he wasn't a coward, that none of them were. This war had done strange things to all men, and Tom had been brave for signing up in the first place. They had never expected it to be an adventure, that was a lie they told themselves, but none of them, not one, was a coward, despite what the army said. He would fight now to prove them wrong, to live out the war and tell everyone what had happened to them so that they might understand the horror of this war.

That determination was all he had left.

Chapter 35

A heavy clang awoke Joe from his troubled sleep with a start. He rolled over onto his side and looked in the direction of the sound to see a warder placing a tray in the middle of the floor. The warder nodded at Joe and withdrew. Joe hadn't seen that particular warder before, but he supposed there must be a whole staff to guard the inmates that he wasn't yet familiar with. He doubted he ever would be either. Whole shifts would come and go and he might only ever see a fraction of them. As for being familiar, he didn't ever expect that he might strike up anything like familiarity with a warder. The only ones he'd had any close encounter with so far had seemed to despise him as the coward they thought he was.

He took another look at the tray without moving. Brown slop sat in one embossed section, that had small pieces of what Joe guessed was meat floating in it. It reminded him of his mother's Scouse, but without looking as rich, or as appetising. A dark brown sliver of bread lay on the other side of the tray. He neither felt like eating, nor felt like moving at this moment in time. The food wasn't drawing him. Instead he rolled back over, clutching his arms around his body again and tried to sleep.

He didn't know how long he lay there, rolling and flitting,

unable to find any perfect kind of sleep. Either from the cold, or from having too much free time to think and letting his mind run wild, he never found anything approaching normal sleep. Sounds came and went, at times he thought he was snoring, at others all seemed silent. It was an unusual experience, each shiver dragging him from the precipice of sleep.

Eventually he rolled over, determined to give up on the concept of sleep. He was tired, oh so tired, but he felt that he'd had enough of that pallet, and his faculties were returning to him through the fog of his mind. He had no idea how long he had slept; without a clock to go by, he didn't even know what time of day it was. He sat up on the bed and leaned back against the wall. Pale light shone through the bars, casting a slight shadow across the floor.

A tray still sat on the floor in the middle of the room where the warder had left it. Only this appeared to be a different tray. The dimensions were a little different, but enough that Joe could tell the difference, and the food on top was a different colour than before. A pang of hunger hit him as a sharp pain in his stomach. He felt like he hadn't eaten in weeks, but it couldn't have been that long?

At that moment the door to the cell opened. Joe caught a glimpse of outside his cell. A warder, the one he hadn't recognised who had brought him his food before, stepped inside.

His head was at an angle, regarding Joe as a mother or teacher might regard an unruly child. Joe felt ashamed, sat on his pallet in only his underwear. It was worth noting that sitting anywhere else like that may very well have had him in a not so dissimilar cell. The indecency was quite a shock to him, and he could feel the warder's eyes judging him. What a pathetic man he had become.

Other men had done far worse for their principles. Some had even died, he had to remind himself, but it was so difficult to remember such things when the cold was like a bayonet in his brain.

After what felt like a very long time, but was in fact only seconds, the warder sighed when he saw the tray at his feet.

'You can't keep letting your food go cold,' he said, still looking at the tray. His voice was soft and calm, again reminding Joe of a teacher. He didn't need to raise his voice like the other warders he had met, and there were no outward signs of aggression from the man. He picked up the tray and moved it outside of the cell, out of sight.

'You'll have to eat at some point. You can't go on starving yourself. It will do no good.'

Joe didn't answer. He didn't disagree with the words, but he was feeling too weak to even lift his head. How could he explain that he had fallen into a dark state of slumber and melancholy, and had somehow missed the food? They might be assuming that he was on some kind of hunger strike, but that wasn't it.

'Look at you,' the warder said, continuing as if Joe was unwilling to walk. 'You're shivering and malnourished. None of this will do any good, you know?'

He patted a hand on the uniform which still sat on the pallet next to Joe, untouched. The warder stared at the wall, thinking, then without another word walked out of the cell.

The door was left open and Joe arched his head to see more of the prison. He had seen little of it in his time here. He was worried that the four walls of the cell were all he would see for the remainder of the war, and it was already beginning to drive him mad.

He wanted to run. He didn't know where he would run to, but he had the impulse all the same. He almost laughed at the idea of running naked through the prison. He had been running his whole life, from one thing or another. He had always run from the responsibility of his actions. He shook his head, trying to regain focus. Had the prison cracked him? Was he wrong all along? No. He couldn't believe that. Despite what he did and what he meant to the world, taking another life was always wrong, and this war was the pinnacle of that. In here, all he had left was his principles, he wasn't about to throw them away for that little.

So why did he want to run away? Was it just that primitive fight or flight reflex? He stood up from the pallet, and took a step forward. He realised for the first time how weak he was, and his body almost collapsed underneath him as he stumbled closer to the door.

The warder returned and regarded him again, perhaps wondering where Joe thought he was going. He didn't enquire, thinking better than to ask an obvious question. He had left the door to the cell open after all.

'Er… take these.' He handed Joe a pile of folded grey cloth. 'Don't tell anyone I gave it to you.'

'I c… couldn't, even if I wanted to,' Joe scoffed, then felt guilty. He didn't want the warder to feel he was ungrateful, so he tried to smile. Instead his teeth chattered together as a sudden shiver took hold of him.

'Well, quite,' the warder said. 'Probably best that I didn't tell you my name. They… the others that is… they still want you to put on that uniform. Whatever their opinion, it isn't right to force a man to freeze to death. I'll dispose of the khaki, as long as you promise to put that on, and not say a word to anyone, should they ask.'

'I p… p… promise.' It was hard for Joe to get the words out through his chattering teeth. It made him feel a fool, and a child for not being able to control himself, and he clamped down on his jaw. He walked back to the pallet and put the uniform down. He dressed quicker than he had ever done before, pulling the trousers on and tying them, then putting on the grey woollen jacket. He did it all with his back turned to the warder, for some reason feeling the need to hide this act of dressing from him as much as possible. Even though he had spent how long now in his underwear, he was still determined to have some decency, and some kind of standards. They could think whatever they wanted

353

about his objection, but he was determined to be as smart and well presented as possible.

'Better?' the warder asked when he was dressed.

Joe nodded, already feeling warmer than he had done in a long time. The wool didn't make much difference, but it was a more than welcome difference, and he no longer felt as exposed.

The warder picked up the khaki uniform.

'Good. I'll take care of this and with luck, you'll never see its like again.'

He went to walk away, but hesitated.

'Look,' he said, and Joe was struck with how young he was. He must have been about the same age as Joe, in his early twenties, but the marks and lines on his face suggested a much older man. 'I'm not saying I completely agree with what you're doing.'

He moved to the door, to see if anyone else was nearby, his brow furrowed. He came back to Joe and the expression on his face changed to something softer, as if a decision had been made and he had relaxed. He let out a deep breath.

'I don't completely agree, but I do admire what you are doing. There are a lot of criminals and cowards in here, and you're not one of them. I know a coward when I see one, and I've met lots of men with no principles. The reason I took this job was *my* principles, to make sure people were obeying the law. I don't feel I need to do that with you. You're no threat to me whatsoever. By your own admission you'd never hurt another man. So throwing you in here is just cruel, and I'll never understand that.'

He shook his head and grumbled at himself.

'I've probably said too much. But, well, you need to look after yourself in here. These other men, they're all criminals and thugs. There are even murderers in here. Some of them are ex-army, or troublemakers. They won't like you, and they won't like what you stand for. So you just stay out of their way, all right?'

Joe nodded, not knowing what he could say to appease the warder. He was overcome by this simple act of kindness, by his admission that Joe wasn't wrong. It was helping his conviction, but it also threatened to bring a tear to his eye. He sniffed it away, trying to pass it off as another shudder of cold.

'I will try and look out for you, but I can't do much in front of the other warders. If they notice anything is wrong, I could lose my job. I've got a family back home, just as I'm sure you have. They need feeding, and I need this job. But I will do what I can. I'll bring you some paper so that you can write to your family. Not much mind, but I'm sure they'll be dying to hear from you.'

Joe knew that wasn't true. His family wanted nothing to do with him after he had refused to sign up. 'Thank you,' was all he said, unable to meet the warder's gaze. His words were a whisper, a croak from a small voice, like the first conversation of the morning, but actually caused by the humility and sorrow in his thoughts.

He realised then, with a pang of guilt, that he hadn't written to George in quite some time. What would he think? Would his brother think that he had forgotten him? George must be in some horrible place, far worse than this. At least Joe had a roof over his head to keep the rain out. If this warder could get him some paper and something to write with, George would be the first person he would write to. Then he would write to Anne, but what would he say? What could he say to her that he hadn't already?

He noticed then that the warder had left something else for him on the bed. A bundle of letters was tied up with string, and with what little strength Joe had, he pulled the string open and ripped open the first letter. It was from his mother, telling him of the usual stuff from home, as if he hadn't left. There were several more from her, and he devoured them all, soaking up the words as if he hadn't read for a long time. The last one was from Anne, and he couldn't open it quick enough. He missed her more than anyone, and both delight and dread filled his mind as he started reading it. He wondered why she hadn't been to see him, but the answer was clear: she too was in prison, where she had been incarcerated for protesting. It didn't say where, it was a simple letter as it was perhaps all she had been allowed to write. He read it a few times to make sure. She finished off by saying that she missed him and signed it with all her love.

'Now you're properly dressed,' the warder said, breaking Joe from his thoughts. 'Perhaps it would be a good idea if you joined the other prisoners for some food. You look like you desperately need something to eat.'

'I think… I think that would be good.'

'Remember, not a word about anything I said to you before.'

The warder led Joe out of the cell, a surprisingly strong grip reaching around his arm, long fingers joining up.

*

The canteen, or so Joe likened it, was a large room on the ground floor of the prison, in what could only be described as an annex. High windows filled the room with a filtered light that splayed dark shadows across the benches and the tables were arranged in lines. Some prisoners already sat at the tables, most of them in the dark spots, talking quietly amongst themselves. Some of them glanced in his direction as he passed, now on his own as the warder had left him.

He joined the queue of waiting prisoners that led to where the food was being given out from great metal troughs. All the men waited, with impatient tapping of their feet or shuffling. Joe didn't expect conversation, he was just happy to be out of his cell. The dining hall wasn't much warmer, but the open air was far more welcome, and it felt a vast expanse compared to his cell. He moved along the queue, breathing in the air and the smell of warm food, patient.

There were no trays for the food, they could be used as

weapons, or for some other insidious task that Joe could only wonder at. Instead, small zinc bowls were used to portion out the food. He took an empty one and moved along. The man the other side of the counter lifted the ladle and dished up a serving of the brown sludge. It splattered over the bowl and dripped down its sides, spotting Joe's hands. The soup made his stomach rumble in anticipation. At least it was edible, he told himself. Hunger had a strong way of making things palatable. Some of his school meals had been little better than this.

He picked up a spoon and turned to leave the queue. As he turned he hit an object behind him and the soup splashed across the front of his prison uniform and onto the man that had been standing behind him.

'Sorry,' he said in a meek voice, and shook his right hand trying to dislodge the broth.

The man grabbed Joe's wrist in an iron grip and dragged it upwards. Joe had no choice but to look the man in the face.

'What the fuck do you think you're doing?'

He bawled at Joe with a mix of stale breath and spit. His eyes were almost bulging in his anger. Joe's broth had covered the other prisoner's uniform, turning the grey wool a brown sludge. Joe hadn't intended to spill his food, despite his brain telling him otherwise he had wanted to eat it, but he knew he would pay for that, somehow.

'I… I'm sorry. It was an accident.'

The bully dug his nails deeper into Joe's wrist, causing him to cry out in pain. He was certain he could feel blood dripping down his arm.

'A fucking accident? Are you serious?'

'Yes. Why would I spill my food?'

'Nothing you do is by accident, coward. You're a piece of work.'

So this prisoner knew him then. Joe tried to recall any memory of having seen this person before, but it was no good; he was sure he hadn't met him outside of the prison. That only left one thing, word of mouth. The prisoners must have heard about him, but who from? The warders? Would they tell the prisoners that a conscientious objector was coming into the prison? He knew they had wanted to torment him, but would they actually talk to the prisoners? Word must have got around some other way. The man had stood behind him at the counter on purpose, waiting for him to do something stupid, and he had got what he wanted. Joe regretted not being more careful.

'I don't know what you're talking about.' It was a poor defence, but it was all he had. The other man was stronger than him, and angry. He would have to be careful not to infuriate him more. 'I just want to sit by myself and eat. I mean you no harm. Here, I will help clean up the mess.'

He searched around for something with which to wipe down the front of the other prisoner's uniform and saw nothing. Instead he bunched up his own sleeve around his free fist and started scrubbing the man's front.

'Never mind that,' he said in his deep baritone voice. 'Ger'off me!'

He pushed Joe's hand away and let go of his other. Joe cradled his free hand and began rubbing at the wrist with thumb and forefinger joined. There was no blood, it had been a psychosomatic response. His wrist still hurt though, that was every bit as real as the situation he found himself in.

'I'm sorry,' he said again. 'What else can I do?'

Before the other prisoner could respond, the warder from earlier on came over.

'What are you two doing?' he shouted at them. The aggression looked strange on his face, like he was forcing it, and Joe flinched away from him.

'Get to a table now, or you'll be put in solitary. No talking in the line!'

He ran off to deal with another prisoner who was complaining about the food.

Joe was going to have to watch his back in here. He suspected there were a lot of rules, and no one was going to tell him what they were. He was going to have to find out the hard way.

'Shit,' he said under his breath.

'What did you say?' The other prisoner hadn't left him alone as he'd hoped.

The fist came out of nowhere, cracking him in the nose. He felt blood burst out of his nostrils, this time for real. He fell back with the blow, dropping the zinc bowl. He reached out to arrest his fall. Groping, his hands felt another man passing behind him in the queue. He had no choice but to put his weight against him, or he would hit the floor.

'Oi,' the man shouted and pushed him away.

Joe dropped to one knee and rested himself on one hand, thankful that he hadn't fallen flat on the floor. He was still vulnerable but at least he wasn't prone. His knee was in the pool of broth and it soaked into his uniform. The hot liquid burnt, but he didn't have time to move away.

The big prisoner threw another punch in his direction, and Joe threw up his other arm to protect his face. The blow hit him in the elbow and jarred his shoulder. The prisoner was far stronger than Joe was.

The was a lot more noise in the dining hall now, and Joe could hear shouts of support for the prisoner, and jeering in his direction. Where were the warders? Why weren't they stopping this?

'Fight back you coward,' the prisoner shouted in his face, spittle flying as if from the maw of a rabid animal.

He punched Joe again. This time he didn't have a chance to raise his arm. His head cracked and he felt his nose break. He could taste the cold iron of blood in his mouth as it ran down his lip. He began to feel disorientated and the room spun. The big man wouldn't stay still in his vision. He blocked out the electric light from the ceiling, and the words streaming from his mouth became unintelligible.

Joe tried to stand, to do anything to get away, away to safety. He felt hands push him back down again, and he slipped in the broth, spreading his knees to leave him sitting as if in prayer, head bowed in pain. Another series of blows hit him, but the pain seemed distant. He fell onto his back, and lay, groaning. He tried to form words, to appeal to mercy, but his tongue filled his mouth and his lips were swollen.

He became still. He had given up.

After a few painful moments, fearing more blows, the shadow above him disappeared. He felt strong arms grab him under his armpits. The motion hurt him almost as much as the punches had and he groaned again. Someone tried to speak to him, but he couldn't make out the words over the sound of his heart beating in his ears.

Instead, they satisfied themselves with dragging him away from the scene.

1917

Chapter 36

George was so numb from tiredness, he felt like he was already dead. He was having some kind of existential experience, looking outside of his own body. It felt weird and unnatural, and he couldn't shake the feeling of not quite being alive. Had he already been killed somewhere else in this war and his mind was yet to keep up with the information? Would the increasing numbness become eventual blackness, nothingness?

It was painful to keep his eyes open, the tears stung and every time a light passed it hurt even more. He stared into the distance, on watch for the enemy, blinking his eyes as often as he dared, to clear the strain, but to avoid them closing for good. Keep them open he must, or he would be shot like so many men before him. The fear of falling asleep made him sick to the stomach, the odd full feeling that accompanied fear and belied the fact that he hadn't eaten well in years. It gave him the curious need to burp.

He had never felt so lonely and scared in his life. He needed someone he trusted, someone that cared for him, to tell him that everything would be all right. But where would he find such a person? Not here in the trenches, they had all gone. He was the only one from Canterbury left now.

The battalion had moved back up the line towards Ypres again, and leave into the towns and villages in the area had been sparse. They had been too busy preparing for the next series of assaults to think about any downtime. George and the other lads that had been around for a while were well versed in the army's tactics by now, and they'd been thrown back into the trenches to get ready.

Almost every face around him now was new and unfamiliar, and even the brown muck of the trenches had failed to diminish their youthful facade. They all appeared young to him, even the ones that had been born before him. They had not seen as much as he had, they were yet to be reborn in war.

While he was on duty, keeping watch, they all huddled around the trench, trying to keep out of the mud. Every man stared into the middle ground and no one acknowledged each other, ensconced within their own private hells. Men came and went, bringing the rum ration round, and bringing post. A runner brought news to a nearby officer, then ran off in the other direction past George.

There was a crack that reverberated in the silence of no man's land, followed by a heavy thud. A body dropped in front of George, swelling the mud at his feet. Its helmet rolled off and bright red blood mingled with the brown earth. No one else moved. The cold lifeless eyes of the runner stared back at George as if imploring him for help. He shrugged. Another fallen soldier. He had been foolish enough to put his head above the parapet. In the trench you either learnt not to do it by seeing someone else get shot, or you learnt it the hard way.

After a while a pair of stretcher-bearers came by to take the body away. Where they took them George didn't know, and he no longer cared. He just sat there smoking and waiting for word on the next big push. The French had often buried their dead in the walls of their trenches; he'd once had the misfortune of having to dig them up to repair a trench.

There was a tap on his shoulder and he turned. It was Private

Sutcliffe, getting ready to go on duty and relieve George. He could tell by the downturned corners of Sutcliffe's mouth that showed through the brown fuzz of his growing beard that he wasn't happy about the prospect. Being on sentry duty was long and boring, one of the most hazardous positions to be in, but everyone had to take their turn. George had been told that the private was an old school friend of Joe's, but he had never broached the subject with Sutcliffe. There hadn't been time.

George nodded his thanks to the small, grumpy man, and slid himself out from the sentry position. He handed the trench periscope to Sutcliffe and walked away. Very few words passed between him and the other men from his section now. What was there that could be said? He could remember the last time he'd had a drink and a joke in a local estaminet. Other soldiers still visited them, but not him.

He rubbed a hand across the stripes on his sleeve. Sergeant. It was something that he had wanted for so long. He remembered a time that seemed like too long ago now, even though it was less than two years, when he had been angry at Tom for getting a stripe ahead of him. He had wanted to write home and tell his parents how well he had done, so that they would write back and tell him how proud they were. It wasn't that they weren't proud, he knew they were, he had just craved the recognition more than anything, he needed it to keep him going. Now it had actually happened, he expected it would just be a footnote in one of his letters, should he get time to write. Now he had been promoted it felt hollow, empty.

It wasn't that he didn't want it. He knew he would be a good leader. Hell, he had lived long enough through this to be one of the most experienced men in the regiment, even at only nineteen years old. He had spent over a year in the trenches before he had got the chance to go on leave. He hadn't been allowed since. He had even missed his sister's wedding, and she would probably never forgive him. This was the only life he knew now, and he would teach the other soldiers his craft.

It was that it felt hollow. He hadn't been angry with Tom because he had been promoted ahead of him, he had been angry because he had been promoted without him. It had separated the two closest of friends, and that had worried George at the time. Now that he had been given this stripe, it only served to further highlight how far apart the two friends had grown. Here was George still in the land of the living. Tom was gone and forgotten for most, buried in the mud of Flanders. He hadn't even been buried with the other brave lads who had given their lives for this war.

Only, he wasn't brave. That's what they had said, right before they had shot him. God only knew what they had done with his body.

George threw himself into the nearest dugout, and wrapped his arms around himself, too tired to think any longer. He wished he had his greatcoat to keep him warm, but he would have to make do. His eyes stung and his head hung heavy with a dull ache. Despite it being summer, the area was cold and the sky was overcast. In a few short hours they would be taking part in another assault. This time they were hoping to overcome the mistakes of the previous battles. George was determined that he would at least try to get some sleep. He rolled over and lay on his side, closing his eyes and slept a restless sleep until just before dawn.

*

They were up and out of the trenches as they had been many times before, rushing up the ladders over the parapets with as much haste as they could manage. George led his section up the incline that led from his trench up to the German lines. They had a slight advantage of being able to fire down at the British, but they wouldn't be able to see them. Not just because of the shelling, but because the early morning was covered in a heavy mist, which gave the scene a haunting, lonely feel.

The British advanced behind a creeping barrage. It was deafening. George could feel the pressure of every bang and thump of the guns pressing against his ears. The constant low rumble gave him a headache. He thought he had seen as much shelling as he could imagine, but with every fresh assault the artillery seemed to bring forward even more guns.

They advanced slowly through no man's land, under orders not to get too far ahead of schedule lest they fall under their own guns. The going was hard, and the overcast sky, bringing increasing rain, was turning the ground to thick mud that clung at their boots.

The section had been well prepared. They knew the area well from their days surveying and raiding this section. They moved forward, using the cover as best they could, quickening the pace when they could, and spreading out to make sure that they weren't easy targets.

George passed along the railway line that led from Ypres off to the west. He had been told to keep it to his right at all times on the way to their first objective. If he kept an eye on it, they wouldn't get lost in the mud and the featureless expanse between theirs and the Germans' lines. He had been lost before out here, and it was a more terrifying experience than the assault. He could just make out the hill through the mist and mud-flinging explosions. The Frezenburg Ridge was their first objective, and they had to get there as soon as possible. George slipped in the mud but righted himself with the help of his Corporal.

Corporal Harlow was by his side, moving and keeping alert as they had practised. When Joe's old boss had first joined them, George hadn't thought much of him, but he had proven himself well and worked twice as hard as any other man to be the best soldier he could be. He gave George a tug forward and carried on up the hill.

The artillery was crossing the first German trench, and George crouched down, expecting fire to come against them at any second. As they slogged up the hill, taking mud with them, they pushed through the broken wire and found the German trench empty.

With a quick gesture, he ordered his men to keep moving up and over the trench. They didn't have time to stop and inspect the trench, the reserve sections would have to deal with that. They had to get moving even though they had made good progress thanks to the cover of the barrage – the rain was growing stronger.

He jumped down into the trench, noticing the run-down state of it, and with help from Harlow, he climbed up the opposite side. The German trenches he had seen before were in much better condition than this one, but he pushed the thought from his mind, intent on his target.

He climbed to the top of the ridge, already exhausted. His uniform was chafing at his skin as the rain soaked through and his feet were getting new blisters from the slog through the mud. His head was splitting.

From the incline he could see a bit further than before, but the mist was still hampering their advance. The artillery died out gradually as the army began to fall on their objectives; they were on their own now.

There were some sounds of shouting up ahead and, through the mist, George could make out a group of Germans falling back. Field-grey figures blurred into the grey mist, but a line of soldiers formed a rear guard. Without thought he dropped to one knee, pulled back the bolt on his Lee Enfield and shot the nearest man. The round took him in the shoulder of his firing arm and he fell back to the mud. The Germans returned fire, and he heard a cry of pain behind him.

Following his example, the rest of his section begun firing at the rest. They let the runners go. Shooting a man in the back was frowned upon, even out here.

George pulled himself back to his feet and continued the advance.

Rounds zipped past them, and a few unlucky men beside him dropped to the ground. In the cacophony of war, he didn't hear their cries. The section didn't stop to see if they were fine, or go back for them. Their orders were clear: keep moving. They had to clear enough ground for the reserve battalions to be able to reinforce them. They had already advanced further than George had in the entire war. He had never been this far into Belgium.

There were more trenches the other side of the ridge. Like the British, the Germans had reserve lines, and unlike the forward lines, they weren't empty.

They came under a heavy weight of fire a few metres from the trench as the mist cleared enough to get a good line of sight. George and his men advanced in an ordered fashion, firing their weapons when they got a clear shot and using the cover of the ruined ground to keep them out of sight for as long as possible.

The German trench ringed a farm which had been fortified as a defensive position. Machine guns opened up around it, and more men fell into the mud. No crops or animals were left to the farm, long since obliterated by war, and it now resembled a small castle. There were shouts, explosions and gunfire all around. His ears rang with pain at the sounds. They didn't have enough men to attack the farm, but if they could get to the trench then they would have some relative safety until the reinforcements arrived. He didn't dare check the time. He knew they were too far away.

One of his men jumped up and threw a Mills bomb towards the trench. As he released, a sniper put a bullet through him, and he collapsed like a marionette that had had its strings cut. It was a brave act, in a desperate situation, and George would make sure he got a commendation.

A few Germans jumped out of the trench and ran towards the farmhouse. A few seconds later, there was a thud as the bomb went off. Body parts cartwheeled in the air and the firing from that part of the trench died out. It was now or never.

George jumped up from behind the barricade he had been crouching behind and shouted his men to fall in with him. He ran as fast as he could towards the German trench, the weight of his gear adding to his momentum. He didn't check if his men were with him. He thought about attaching his bayonet, but didn't have time. A machine gun was still firing rounds into the ground below the ridge.

He jumped down into the trench, his feet landing on hard wooden duckboards. His boots prevented him from jarring his ankle. A small group of German soldiers were moving along to reinforce the trench. He fired one shot along the trench, then another. It was more difficult to miss than hit.

More men followed George into the trench. Some had bayonets attached and grappled with the few Germans that were left. George didn't look to see what happened to them. As an officer he had to assess the situation. The trench was a mess, blood and body parts mingled in the duckboards. A young German lay against the firing step, groaning in pain. He had lost both legs, and would die from a loss of blood in seconds. One of George's men leant down and put him out his misery with a quick round. The groaning stopped.

Corporal Harlow came up beside him, in a crouch. The German machine gunners were still firing on them, but they were safer now in the confines of the trench. The Germans could only come from the flanks or assault them directly. There was no communication trench in this section, for which George was relieved.

'We've secured this part of the trench, Sergeant.' Harlow's voice had lost some of the wheeze he had had upon enlisting, but he was still out of breath like the rest of them. 'But I'm not sure how long we can hold it for. That farm is pretty well fortified, and we've lost too many men.'

The Corporal put George's thoughts into words, and he nodded. They would have to try and force something, or dig in. The fog wasn't helping things.

He had an idea, but it was dangerous.

'Corporal, when I say so, throw a Mills bombs towards that machine gun pit from along there.' He pointed to an alcove in the trench closer to the farmhouse. 'Don't put anything above the trench.'

Harlow nodded and moved to obey.

'Now!' George shouted.

As soon as the bomb went off, the machine gun went silent. George pulled himself up to get a better view of the situation. The fog was easing off, but was still thick in the valley below them. Fierce fighting was taking place all along the line, but the other nearby sections were pinned down as they were.

He ducked down back into the trench, avoiding the bullets that whistled past his head. Dirt tumbled down into the duckboard after him, and the sandbags threatened to fall, lurching on the apex of the trench wall.

The usual sounds of warfare filled George's senses: the crack of rifle fire, the chatter of machine guns, accompanied by the dull crump of explosions, but there was a new sound permeating the landscape, an uncomfortable sound that was always just on the periphery of hearing. A low resonance rumbled through the earthworks of the trenches that reminded George of the sound of distant thunder. Unlike thunder it didn't stop, but carried on resonating, until it was joined by the whir and hum of a mechanical engine.

All of a sudden, the rising sun in the morning sky was blocked out by an immense shadow across the trench, and the sound grew in intensity with the added high creak of gears. George could smell thick engine oil, much like that used on the ships back home, and he got the sense of a massive machine lumbering over him.

It didn't fall but lurched over the gap in the earth in which George was hiding, and then was gone, light falling back into the void.

He crawled up after it, at first kneeling on the firing step and then using his hands to claw his way up to standing. In his curiosity he just about dared to pop his head up and risk a view into no man's land. The machine was rumbling away from him in the direction of the fortified farmhouse.

It was a great land-ship, painted in an olive green that almost helped it to blend in with the landscape – if only it had a bit more muddy brown to it. George had heard rumours of these land-ships or tanks from when they had been used further up the line, but he had never seen one for himself, until now. The sound was deafening, and for the first time he admitted to himself that he had been terrified by it. He was relieved to see that it was on his side.

On each side of the tank, a gunmetal grey cannon protruded. It looked ridiculous, like the side sails of a tall ship. Every so often one of the cannons recoiled and shot a round at the German defences.

It was a lumbering machine, but the sight of it gave them hope, and clearly terrified the Germans. It fired its cannons at the farmhouse and the concrete sandbox that housed the machine gunners collapsed in a shower of grey dust. Germans started to pull back from the farmhouse. Moments later another land-ship crawled across the trench they had taken and the men cheered.

George went back to organising his men. He ordered Harlow to take a section and hold one end of the trench while he took the other. They couldn't get much further with the men they had. They would have to fortify the ground they had taken before the inevitable German counter-attack. George had seen it before at Loos, and by the Somme river. Even with the land-ships roaming their lines, the Germans would come.

George would have to hold out until the reinforcements arrived.

Chapter 37

Joe awoke with a start, and almost screamed. Pain forced him back down against the bed, or whatever it was he was lying on. Every slight movement elicited another peal of pain, and he tried to lay still. Even shallow breathing ached.

He had been having a terrible dream, and that had woken him suddenly. He was being beaten by meaty fists. A group of men wearing khaki uniforms surrounded him, jeering, and joining in with the barrage of blows. He couldn't get away and they kept laughing at him. It wouldn't stop, each laugh had brought more pain as the men crowded in. He couldn't take any more, and then he had woken up. He knew now that despite the horror of it, it was real. Some parts of it were the fiction of his mind, such as the khaki and the large leering grins of the men beating him, but the pain was glaringly, horrifyingly real.

He could only move his eyes from side to side without feeling pain, using them to search for where he was. He didn't recognise the room, but the barred and shuttered windows reminded him that he was in the prison. He closed his eyes, succumbing to the weight of his eyelids as his body told him to rest so that it could repair his wounds.

He was as safe as he could be in the prison, there was no point trying to make an escape or alert anyone. If they thought he was asleep at least they would leave him alone. They had beaten him to within an inch of his life. That must be enough now? It would have been a warning of some kind. He wasn't sure against what, but they must have known that pointless violence would serve no use here. Although, they were already in prison, what did they have to lose? He wasn't even sure these kinds of men would think that far ahead.

He opened his eyes again, feeling vulnerable and scared. The cell was still empty, still grey, and still cold. He rolled over onto his side and was hit with a wave of pain. His whole midriff felt like it was on fire, as if he lay on hot coals. He reached again for the comfort of lying on his back with an arch in his spine borne from pain. He lay there for a long time, panting and trying to claw air into his damaged lungs. After some time, he started to feel more human. The initial shock had almost overwhelmed him, but the pain was starting to numb now that his body had woken to it.

He finally felt able to try and stand up. He rolled his legs to the side of the pallet, grimacing at the pain, and grinding his teeth together to stop from crying out. He let his legs dangle over the side of the bed as he sat up. He inspected the bruises on his body, all an angry purple poking through his pale skin. Some had patches of red and even yellow, all were sore. He pushed himself up on both arms and onto his wavering legs. He had an overbearing need to urinate. The urge had never been so strong before and the constriction of his bladder only added to the pain in his body.

He stood, straining, and almost pitched forward. There was still enough strength in his limbs to keep him upright. He took one tentative step after the next, moving towards the bucket in the corner of the room. As he walked muscle memory returned to him and he became more fluent.

He dared not look at it. The smell of the standing water was enough to turn his stomach, so he turned and eased himself down. The metal was cold against his backside and he jumped away from it. He decided he would have to be quick, like jumping into the sea on a cold spring day. Those cold waters of the Irish Sea would be a welcome alternative to what he faced now. After a few seconds he grew numb to the cold.

At that moment the cell door opened with the clanking of the heavy lock, and the jangling of keys. He almost fell with the shock

*

The warder led him down the narrow walkways, and down two flights of stairs to the main concourse. The prison was expansive, and Joe was sure there were parts he would never get to see. The warder pushed him along, prodding him in the small of the back, and Joe had to force himself not to cry out in pain. It took immense effort not to stumble, but still his walk was a tumbling gait that only just propelled him forwards rather than downwards.

Eventually they came to a warehouse that doubled as a work room. In it, other men were working away at long reams of beige cloth, pulling it towards them and then working with their hands. Joe was forced into a metal chair by a large hand that pushed at his shoulder. The chair squeaked with the physicality of it, but Joe was used, by now, to the abuse. The bruise on his shoulder was but a new one to add to the rest on his battered, purple body. Everything hurt, but it hurt so much that it had dimmed to a constant numbness.

A number of tools lay on the workbench before him, each designed, as far as he could tell, for stitching and sealing the beige hessian material together. He picked up a pair of scissors from the bench, and marvelled at them. He thought it odd that they would supply them with what was essentially a murder weapon. Several big warders stood at intervals along the walls, keeping an eye on the prisoners. He wouldn't get two yards without being stopped by one of them.

He could always kill himself, but what would that prove? How far he had fallen; the thought would never have crossed his mind but a few months ago. Now, it was there at the back of his mind, like a whispered command, just to see if he could get away with it. The depression had hit him hard.

He ran his thumb along one of the blades; the scissors were blunt. He could see, out of the corner of his eye, the other prisoners struggling to cut the hessian.

'Get on with it,' the nearest warder barked at him.

'Get on with what exactly?' Joe whispered, unable to speak at a higher volume. His larynx craved water, to abate the dryness and the crackling cough that seemed always on the edge of occurring.

'Sewing, lad,' a voice at the next workstation said. Joe looked over to see who had spoken.

'Don't look at me,' the voice hissed again, and Joe's head shot back to his own workstation. 'If you look at me, they'll think that we're talking.'

'We are talking,' Joe said.

There was a pause.

'Well, yes.' The speaker sounded confused by Joe's statement. He knew he was stating the obvious, but he didn't care anymore. 'We are talking, but they can't hear us if we speak quietly. It will be obvious if we're looking at each other.'

'What are we supposed to be doing here?' Joe wanted to get straight to the point, he was tired and fed up. 'I thought this was prison?'

'Shh! Quieter.'

One of the warders walked down their row of desks, and Joe made it appear as if he was inspecting his materials, which, in a way, he was. When the warder was gone, the other man spoke again.

'They put you to work in prison. Everyone knows that.'

Joe supposed he had never thought about it. The prison wasn't somewhere he ever thought he would end up. He waved the end of the hessian at the other inmate.

'So what's this for then?'

'That? That's for cutting.'

Joe wasn't sure if the other man was being deliberately obtuse, but his manner was frustrating him. He talked with more care and tried to phrase his question to get the answer he had wanted all along.

'What, then, are we cutting it for? What are we supposed to be making? Bags? What for?'

'Bags, aye,' the other said. 'What did you think we were making?'

Joe was silent.

'They're for sandbags of course. What other kind of bag do you think they need thousands of at the moment?'

Joe put down his tools. He turned to the other man, no longer caring about the warders and what they might do to him. The other inmate was a thin man, but not gaunt through lack of nutrition like Joe. No, he was thin of nature. His oval face was framed by a neat black beard and centred with a moustache, that on the outside would have had more care taken of it. The man's skin was deathly pale, and Joe wondered if his was the same. He shuddered at the thought. There was an intelligence behind his green eyes that looked on in shock.

'What are you doing?' he hissed, and his moustache wobbled on the top of his lip.

'Absolutely not.'

'What?'

'There is absolutely no way that I'm making sandbags for the war.'

The other inmate sighed and rolled his eyes. 'Look, we're all just trying to get by. Get out of here alive, you know? Just pull your weight and we'll all be fine.'

377

Joe shook his head. He had had this argument many times before, but his conviction had never faltered. He had gone further with it than many people thought he might, but he could go further still. To object was to object.

'I'm a conscientious objector, surely you've heard?'

The other inmate looked around to see if they had been spotted. A warder was moving in their direction but hadn't noticed the two talking yet.

'We all are,' he said leaning closer to Joe.

Joe was shocked. He was lost for words and just stared around, dumb. The warder had noticed him and was rushing over.

'Don't be a fool,' came the concerned voice from beside him. 'Just sit down and get on with it or you'll make it worse for all of us. Please.'

'I can't,' he whispered. 'You know I can't. I'm sorry.'

The warder grabbed Joe by the arm, wrenching it around behind his back almost pulling it from his shoulder socket. He whelped and held back a cry of pain. His bruises stung with the exertion of his muscles. He couldn't hold that position for long without breaking down.

'What are you doing?' the warder shouted. 'Get back to work.'

'No,' was the only word Joe could get out of his mouth in spite of the pain from his arm.

'No?'

Joe grunted an affirmative and stared as defiantly as he could at the warder.

'Fine.'

The warder pushed him along the aisle of benches. Every other man had stopped to watch, and the warders shouted at them to continue. Joe's arm was stuck in the arch of his lower back, and the warder's iron grip gave him no room for comfort. He pushed him in this fashion all the way through the prison and back to his cell. Another warder opened the door, and Joe was pushed inside. He tripped over the doorframe and landed on his outstretched arms. The shock of the fall jarred his right wrist and he clutched it with his other hand, breathing in through his teeth in pain.

Neither warder moved to assist him, and he lay there on the floor with sore knees and wrists. He knew they didn't care about him, but he couldn't work out why they were so hostile towards him. There must be far worse people than he in this prison. Perhaps they were treated worse.

'If you refuse to work, then you will spend all your time in here,' the warder who had brought him back said. 'You will eat here, you will sleep here, and you will also defecate here.'

The other warder grinned at the last statement, and Joe looked away.

'You will have no contact with other prisoners, this cell will be your entire world. You have already refused to put on your uniform and leave the prison. You are one of ours now. That means that by refusing to work, you refuse all other concerns. Is that clear?'

Joe didn't answer, what was the point? They could do what they liked to him.

They stepped out of the cell, leaving him prone and closed the door behind them. The heavy clang shut out the sounds of their walking away, and left Joe alone with his thoughts. He had always found solitude less tiring than being around others, but the only way he could describe his current situation was lonely. It was a paradox of conflicting emotion within him. For the first time in his life he longed for the company of others. He sat on the pallet. A tear rolled down his cheek and he wiped it away with the back of his hand as he stared after the closed door.

*

Joe's life became monotonous. He sat in his cell, back against the wall, and stared at the door. He didn't stare and wait for it to open, it was just the only difference in the cells walls. He counted the rivets every now and then, playing mathematical games in his head. After a while even that grew tiresome. Often he slept, allowing himself to drift off into a dream world where things were much better than here. Other times he just sat and listened. He could, on occasion, hear a faint tapping against the pipes that ran up the walls of the prison. He guessed it was Morse code, but he had never bothered to learn it. So, he liked to play games trying to think what messages the other prisoners were trying to send to each other and inventing his own codes and ciphers.

Every now and then a slit in the door opened and food was pushed inside. He left it where it lay, unwilling to touch it, despite his ravenous hunger. He had heard of other prisoners going on hunger strike and had decided that it was the only way he might be listened to. Every other way of being heard had failed him and refusing to eat was all he was left with. They weren't taking him seriously. To them he was just a coward, but he would show them. He had no fear. Fear wasn't it. He hadn't wanted to do it. He had refused food before, but that was in self-pity, not as an act of defiance. Now it was different, he had been left with no choice.

He didn't know how many days it had been when the door opened again. He had thought that it would never reopen, that they would leave him there forever to starve and waste away. So, it came as a shock while he sat on the bed staring at the closed door yet again, that it opened up and in stepped a warder.

He wasn't surprised to see that it was the kind warder who had brought him his prison uniform before, and who had taken him to eat. He looked down at Joe's uneaten food and sighed, for Joe's sake.

'What have I told you about eating?' he said. 'I know the food's not great, but you'll need to eat something sooner or later.'

'No,' Joe replied, making sure that he looked the warder in the eye, and raising his voice as loud as he dared. 'I'm on strike. You can tell the others that. I'm not eating until I'm released. Unlike some others, I'm not happy to just sit here and wait till the war is over. That's not what this is about.'

He felt sorry for shouting at the kind warder, but what else could he do? The other man's mouth hung open at Joe's words, and he looked around to see if anyone had heard. He shushed Joe, coming closer to the pallet bed.

'Look, I only came to bring you this.' He handed Joe a sheet of paper and a pencil. 'I can't force you to eat, but if you write something on that, I'll make sure it gets to your family. It's the only thing I can do for you. As for the rest, well, I'm sorry but you're on your own.'

He did genuinely appear sorry, and he sighed again as Joe stared at him.

'Quickly,' he said, gesturing to the pad. 'You'll have to write something now. I don't know when and if I'll be able to return. The other warders are already growing suspicious.'

Joe stared at the blank sheet in his hand. For once he had no idea what to write. On his desk at work he had paper after paper covered in words that he had written as easily as breathing, but now he was pushed he couldn't think. Every word dripped out of his memory as if he had forgotten language altogether. What could he say? There was nothing new in his life, except for solitary confinement, and his family would only worry about him if he told them that.

He scribbled a quick note to Anne, telling her there were other conchies in the prison and suggesting she might write an article about it. He cursed his handwriting. When he wrote at pace, even he couldn't read the words, and he hoped that those who received the letter would understand.

Next, he wrote to his mother telling her that he loved her with all his heart and that he would see her and his father soon. He said that he was sorry that he had caused them pain, and that he was sure the neighbours would forgive them soon.

Scribbling as fast as possible, whilst the warder hovered over

381

him, he saved the last bit of paper for George. Again, he was unsure what to say. He couldn't tell George anything that he had been through, that wouldn't be fair on him. The only thing he could think to say was that he could not wait to see him again. Upon finishing, he folded the paper in half and passed it back to the warder.

'Please make sure that gets to my family. They will know what to do with it.'

The warder nodded and made for the door.

'I will try my best to help you again, but I can make no promises.'

'Thank you,' Joe said, as his stomach rumbled and he shivered at the same time.

The cell door banged shut, with a terrible, final waft of cool, outside air.

Chapter 38

George had been in France for over a year since his last and only leave. He had been granted permission to head home many times and have some rest from the war, but something had always come up. There always seemed to be another big push, where leave was cancelled, or another raid that he had to be on. There was even that one time when a member of his unit had been caught trying to smuggle German contraband out of the country and the entire unit's leave had been cancelled. They had never forgiven him for that; many of them did it, but it was stupid to get caught. The man responsible had got quite a beating from those most affected by the cancelled leave, one that he wouldn't forget, but at least he had kept quiet about it.

Most of the other men in George's section had started to call him unlucky, and made sure that they weren't scheduled to be on leave at the same time as him. Some of them even bartered for it, and he laughed at them for their superstition.

He wasn't unlucky, he mused, sitting with his back against the wall of the dugout, absent-mindedly running the cigarette around his mouth. If luck even existed, he was the exact opposite. He was lucky. He was still alive. He had been through over two years of this war and he was still alive.

383

He grabbed his rifle from beside him and started cleaning it, first dismantling the firing mechanism and removing the bolt. One of the things that had kept him alive so long was having a well-maintained and always ready to fire weapon. The other thing, he supposed, was luck. Not that he believed in anything so fancy anymore. He had seen far too much pain and suffering to believe in any kind of higher power anymore. Those that had been disabled and maimed by the shelling and explosives were the truly unlucky ones.

He was the only one left of the lads from his school that had come out here. You might call that lucky. But then it could be the lucky ones were the ones that had seen the end of war. Wherever they were, their suffering was over. They were now at peace, Tom, Patrick, Harry, Fred, and the rest of them. There would never be an end to this war, not until they were all gone.

He reassembled his rifle and glanced along its sights, checking they were still true. He got up and searched for his haversack amongst the trench. He was due for leave, and this time they had assured him that he would be sent back to Liverpool for a few days to see his family, to see how they were getting on, and to discuss the things they had said in their letters. He was terrified. He was no longer terrified of the shelling, and warfare, but he was scared of going home. He hadn't been there in so long, he had no idea what to expect. Last time had been an unhappy experience. His mother would end up crying again and he couldn't handle that. His father would beam at him in pride. And his brother, well, that was another story. He had no idea what to say or even think about his brother anymore.

They would ask him questions about the war, about what it was like and he wouldn't be able to answer. There was no way they could understand, it wasn't their world, and Liverpool wasn't his anymore. As horrifying as it was, the trench was his home now. The fleeting friendships he made with his fellow soldiers, that was family. His old family couldn't, wouldn't, understand.

He was walking along the trench , nodding at the men he passed, and keeping his head down in the constant bent-back posture that all experienced soldiers of the trench occupied. It was second nature now, he didn't think about it. He was so experienced now, that the new soldiers all looked up to him as an older brother, as if he was anything but years younger than most of them. He might not have celebrated his last few birthdays, but in mental age he was much older than nineteen. He stroked the stripes on his arm. Age was no longer an indication of anything in this war.

A figure rushed in the opposite direction along the trench and George paid no attention, only to adjust his passage to allow the other man to pass, until he heard his name.

'George… George… there you are,' the other man said, panting for breath and now leaning with hands of his thighs. 'I've been running around trying to find you. I thought you would be at the muster point, but someone said you were still here.'

His accent was softer than George's, from somewhere in the south of England he guessed. The Corporal had found his way into their regiment through reinforcement after reinforcement, long cut off from his count-folk. He was around the same age as George, specks of blond bristles threatening to break out on his jaw, and he wore the grim expression that every soldier wore, never showing his teeth, lest they break up the grime of his face.

'Here I am indeed,' George said. He patted the other man on the arm. 'What do you want, Samuels?'

Samuels fought to catch his breath, doubled over and sucking in great draughts of air.

'The Captain, George… he… er.' He took another deep breath. 'He wants to see you… right away.'

'Where is he?' George suspected he knew the answer, but it was always good to check. Some officers had a habit of inspecting the troops and trenches and could be a bugger to find when you needed them.

385

'His dugout, sir,' Samuels said, managing to talk. 'He requested you there.'

It was a wonder this boy was so unfit. How did he expect to last in the army? Although it wasn't like he'd had any choice in the matter. Had George been that unfit when he had signed up? He couldn't remember, it had been so long ago now. Years, it seemed like.

'Get yourself some rum, and for pity's sake, sit down,' he said, patting Samuels on the shoulder in the way a father might. 'The Captain won't need you for a while. I'll go up and see him now. You just stay here and sort yourself out.'

Samuels started to protest, but George interrupted him.

'Don't worry, I'll tell the Captain I ordered you to stay until I got back.'

He didn't wait for a response, and left the private behind, walking along the trench towards the command dugout.

A few minutes later he pushed under the gas sheet, nodding to the adjutant as he did so. He hadn't seen this man before, the last one must have been killed. The officers were often quick to replace their aides, taking another man out of the immediate firing line. Some of the men welcomed the job with open arms. George wasn't sure that he would. They were often ridiculed for taking the easy way out, and for sometimes being too close to their officers. George much preferred the honest, working man's nature of the trench.

The Captain sat behind his desk, as usual poring over pieces of paper, moving one piece to the side of the desk and then picking up another and shaking his head. He didn't notice George come in, so George had to get his attention.

'You called for me, sir,' he said, whilst saluting.

'Ah, Sergeant. Come in. Come in.' He threw the papers to the side, no longer caring about them and looking up at George. He took off his spectacles and also placed them to one side. He rubbed his hand through his balding hair, then observed his hand for a moment as if he didn't recognise it. He sighed and, reaching for a handkerchief, he wiped the sweat and grime from his hand.

'Must I always tell you to sit down?' he asked.

'Regulation, sir.' George stayed standing. What would they be without rules? Their old Corporal had drummed that into them enough that he would never forget it.

'Yes, well, have a seat, Sergeant. I'm sick of craning my neck up at you.'

George took out the same old worn seat, the one that seemed to be reserved for visitors, and sat down, noticing a new creak in its frame. Where once he might have welcomed a seat, he found it very difficult to be at ease these days.

'Thank you, sir,' he said anyway.

The Captain took out his battered flask and filled himself a drink without saying a word to George or offering him any. It had become a kind of ritual in the few times that George had visited the Captain, and he suspected it was to allow the Captain time to gather his thoughts.

'Private Samuels told me that you wanted to see me, sir.'

'Yes, I did. He's a good lad, young Samuels. Always happy to please.'

'Only, I'm due to go on leave at any time, sir.'

The Captain stared at George for a long time, chewing his lip before speaking.

'I'm sorry for having to do this to you again, George.'

George's spirits dropped, and he looked down at the worn wooden table in front of him. He didn't know whether to be upset, or relieved. He wasn't surprised. As an NCO his time for leave often seemed to come at the most inappropriate times, right before another big assault.

'I'm guessing then, that I don't need to say what I'm about to say next, Sergeant. I truly am sorry you won't be going home to see your family. I will make sure that you are treated as a special

387

case, just as soon as this assault is over. I'll even drive you up to the coast myself if I have to.'

The Captain smiled a warm smile at George, with only a faint hint of sadness in the corner of his eyes. To see the Captain's compassion made him feel a little better. For the first time in a while he didn't feel alone out here.

The Captain stood up, took a glass from a nearby table and placed it in front of George. He unstoppered his flask and poured some of the golden amber liquid it contained out into the glass.

'I don't know if you drink, George, but now is as good a time as any to have a drink.'

'Thank you, sir,' he said. He smelt the liquid as it poured, and it burnt his nostrils, in a warm, pleasing way. It smelled of old wood.

'It's whisky, George. That one is one I keep for special occasions. It's an Auchentoshan. Quite delightful.' He sniffed the glass himself, took a sip and smacked his lips in appreciation. 'One of my absolute favourites, but an absolute bugger to get hold of at the moment.

'I must say. I don't often share, especially as it's so hard to come by. But you positively look as if you need a dram, or two for that matter. And no doubt you'll need more after I tell you about the next assault we're due on.'

'I'm guessing HQ think that we will be able to break through at last, sir?'

'Yes, well, don't they always?'

George was taken aback by the Captain's frankness. At first he had thought that the Captain felt sorry for him, but now he was beginning to feel that he was instead taking George into his confidence, that there was some grain of respect between Captain and Sergeant.

He put his hand around the glass of whisky and stopped. The grime that coated his skin and surrounded his fingernails was a stark difference to the immaculate crystal of the glass, and he felt a complete fraud to be touching it. He suspected that the Captain would be offended if he refused the drink. It was too good to waste.

He picked it up from the table bringing it closer to his lips and stopped again. The Captain had moved back to his chair and was fiddling with his papers. George was relieved that he wasn't watching. He wouldn't notice the fact that George's hand was shaking. He willed it to stop and that only made matters worse, as if the very act of concentration was causing the problem. He tried to forget about it but feared he would drop the expensive glass. All his pain, loss and lack of control was bundled up into his arm, and it threatened to overload. His nerves were on edge, and not because he was nervous of the Captain's presence, but because he couldn't take it anymore.

He almost threw the glass at his lips, wanting the shaking to stop. The liquid ran down his throat, warm and burning. He could feel it getting to work on his body and he started to feel warmer. The shaking in his hand subsided a little and he slammed the glass back on the table with more force than was necessary. The Captain took it as enjoyment of the drink and smiled at George, but in truth he couldn't offset the taste against the burning sensation. The drink wasn't for him.

'I'd better get back to my men, sir.'

George wasn't eager to be back in the trench, but the Captain's manner was becoming more distant, and George didn't want to be there anymore. The Captain's behaviour was making George uncomfortable. He was staring into the middle distance, with his glass hanging limp in one hand, whilst his lips moved as if in conversation, but no sound came out.

In a world of discomforts, emotional discomfort could still get to him, and he longed for his own company, or at least the trench where all the men kept to themselves. His new rank had made that even more pronounced.

'Hmmm, yes?' the Captain said after some moments.

'To prepare my men for the assault, sir. They'll have to be made ready.'

'Yes, you're right. Of course.'

The Captain appeared as if he had only just noticed that George was there and stood up abruptly, staring. He started pacing around the dugout, making use of the few metres of space that it afforded him.

'You're right, George. Of course. Get back to your men and get them ready for what may be.' He stopped dead in his tracks and stared at George again. 'You know, I'm not sure that I can go through with ordering men to their deaths again. It doesn't seem right somehow, making them give up their lives for us.'

'Every man out there, sir, knows what is at stake, and they know their duty.'

'Of course, of course.' The Captain threw an awkward, forced smile at George. 'Make sure you look after them, Sergeant. Oh, and look after yourself.

'You make sure you come and see me as soon as this is done and we'll get you back to Blighty.'

George nodded. 'I will, sir. Um, thank you.'

'Oh, and send Samuels back when you're done with him. I've got some more errands for him to run before we go.'

George saluted and pushed his way out of the dugout.

By the sounds of things, the Germans had increased their bombardment on the British lines. Other soldiers were rushing up and down the trench, keeping their heads down. One man ran past with his hand on the top of his steel helmet in case it should fall off. George always thought that had been weird. Why put your hand over something that was designed to protect you from harm? The trenches couldn't destroy human instinct. Old habits die hard.

He pushed his way down the trench, crouching low whilst maintaining a jogging pace. As always it was the best way to avoid being shot by a sniper, without running so fast that you would slip in the mud and gunk in the bottom of the trench. The duckboards, when they were present, could be slippery.

There was a blast of light up ahead, then shingle and clods of mud sprayed across him and the men around him. They cowered back from it, then stood up when it had gone. He didn't even bother wiping the mud off his uniform, it could just join the rest already there. Perhaps the lice would enjoy the added habitat.

The trench wall had subsided ahead of him, but there was still room to squeeze through. Within minutes he was back with his section. They were no longer sat around cooking, but perched on the firing step in wait. He checked his men. They were ready.

'Where is Samuels? I left him with you.'

One of his men, Walters, slowly shook his head. It was an unspoken sign between them all. There was only a hint of sadness in his eyes; instead they were filled with the distant, regretful look of the trench soldier.

George felt the guilt that he guessed all officers felt, even non-commissioned ones such as himself. He had ordered Samuels to stay, if he hadn't he may be somewhere else now, running errands for the Captain. That was no guarantee of his safety, but George had been responsible for his death this way. He added another name to the mental list of families he would have to visit when he got home. If he ever got home.

*

The sun hadn't risen above the horizon when George was standing in the trench alongside the men of his section, yet its rays were silently creeping across the land. It was time for the next assault. They had been given their objective of the village of Cambrai, and he had made sure that every man he was responsible for knew their duty. They stood in silence, waiting for the whistles that would signal the advance. The artillery had been softening up the Germans since reveille, but they would have to be quick – the sun was rising and would give away their positions.

George noticed movement to his right. The Captain was walking down the trench accompanied by his adjutants. He often inspected the troops before an assault, but this time he appeared different, more commanding. He held his Webley revolver in one hand and his whistle in the other. He nodded at each soldier he passed.

'Ready?' he asked George as he strode past, trying to give of the air of a noble commander.

'Er… yes, sir.'

'Good.'

With that, he checked his watch, and then with a large breath, blew his whistle. Similar bursts broke out along the line, as the other officers joined in. The man in front of George was first up the ladder, and George followed. The sounds of gunfire barked out as the Germans heard them coming.

The man in front of him was cut down by machine gun fire that sounded like slaps against his body. George ducked out of the way and used some of the wooden joists that used to hold barbed wire as cover for his advance. He noticed the Captain a few metres to his left, walking towards the enemy with his pistol raised in an outstretched arm in front of him, firing off rounds at an enemy he couldn't see.

There was the bang of a trench mortar going off, and George moved forward with the rest of his men, trying to move away from the Germans' target. More bullets whistled past, followed by other explosions.

A dull crump to his left blocked out his hearing, and he felt a sudden sharp pain in his right leg. He couldn't see what had happened, his senses were too blurred. He couldn't move his leg and he thought he could feel a wetness there. He tried to shake his head to clear the fog, but his head hurt more with the movement. He couldn't move and fell backwards unable to stop his fall.

Another explosion boomed nearby, covering him in mud and blood. He no longer cared to do anything about it. He couldn't move out of the way. He couldn't wipe his face clean.

The last thing he saw was a ray of sunshine as it broke through the thick black clouds, then everything turned black.

Chapter 39

The heavy bolt of the cell door clanged open, and light spilt into the chamber. Joe didn't bother to look up at his captors. He knew who they were and he didn't care to see their smug, self-satisfied faces. He continued staring at the ground. They didn't say a word to him as their feet drew nearer, making long shadows across the floor that wobbled as they drew nearer.

'Still refusing to eat?' one of them said, scoffing. Joe didn't see who it was. He didn't answer. Couldn't answer. Words were a foreign concept to him. He had been alone so long, and he had given up trying to articulate his feelings. It was as if these men spoke a different language to him. Even his letters had dropped off. He couldn't write anymore. Couldn't hold the pencil that he had hidden under the corner of his mattress, or even lift the mattress to get to it for that matter. He was alone with his thoughts.

They hauled him to his feet, each man grabbing him under the arm and dragging him up from his knees. He was so light now, so weak, that they didn't need to put much effort in. It only served to make them more rough in their purchase. Or perhaps it was just because he was so weak.

He had lost so much weight, but he couldn't bring himself to eat the swill they called food that was pushed through the small slit in the door a few times a day. It wasn't just that he refused to give in to their demands until they listened to his genuine objections, it was also because the food was almost inedible. But he had paid the price. His body had withered, beginning to consume itself.

There were often times where he slipped between consciousness and unconsciousness. It sometimes helped to pass the time, as there was very little to do in his cell. He had one book available to him that he had already read several times. He wasn't sure what was worse, the dreams he had when he lapsed, or the waking-nightmare he awoke into.

This was one such occasion that was worse. They dragged him out of the cell, only just raising him above the ground so that his knees scuffed along the floor, ripping the cheap cloth of the prison uniform he had been given. At least he had managed to refuse to wear khaki when they had left him with nothing but that to wear. It gave him hope that he could overcome anything, even this hunger strike.

He didn't know where they were taking him. At first his knees and legs rubbed along coarse concrete, but now they were clanging against metal, as each of the wardens' footsteps brought him nearer to the gantry they were walking on. He could see through the metal at the levels of the prison below, and men looked back in his direction, muttering amongst themselves. Joe didn't have much energy to wonder himself, but at least they were not forcing him to walk, as they might have done in his early days in prison.

After many painful strides they ascended the walkways and out of the main prison block. The staring eyes disappeared and Joe was once again left with only the warders for company. They strode into the large room that served as the medical wing of the prison, where gurneys dressed in off-white sheets lined either side of the room in pairs. No other medical equipment could be seen as it was all locked away lest some prisoner decided to use it for something they shouldn't.

They dropped him on one gurney, and one of them lifted him as his body drooped towards the ground. He didn't know whether he was struggling to control his muscles, or whether he no longer cared. One of the other prisoners was on an opposite gurney surrounded by wardens, the doctor, and some macabre equipment. Joe couldn't see him clearly from where he sat, and it was an effort to lift his head and to the side to peer around the warders.

A strange gurgle emitted from the other prisoner, and Joe noticed that the two warders were holding the man down. After a few seconds of gurgling the man screamed. It was a high shrill scream, which pierced the infirmary and hurt Joe's ears. Fear welled up inside him.

'Will you be silent?' the doctor said, and the warders doubled their grip on the man, who was no longer screaming, but wailing in pain, amid wracking sobs.

'No,' Joe said, only a whisper from between his parched lips. No one heard him, or at least no one turned around. The warder holding him upright didn't even react. He just stared, holding Joe with a passive expression on his face.

After he was done, the doctor extricated himself from the group and turned around. He saw Joe and smiled. He was a corpulent man, who lived a full life. His balding hair was plastered across his head where sweat kept it down. He must eat all that spare prison food, Joe thought. He was too tired to laugh.

'Ah, Mr Abbott,' he said, as if seeing an old friend. 'Ready, are we?'

He walked over to the gurney and inspected Joe, lifting his arms, much like the warders had done, without take any care about his wellbeing. He pulled Joe's prison shirt down and placed a cold stethoscope on his back. Joe winced at the coldness, but it didn't stop the doctor.

'You've been naughty, Mr Abbott. You need to take better care of yourself.'

He took the stethoscope away and begun checking his jaw and teeth, as if he were an animal. Not a prize race horse, an animal.

'Though you have been exceptionally strong willed. Much stronger than I would expect for a coward like you.'

'I'm not a co...' He had lost all strength to complain. The doctor was taunting him and he refused to cooperate. Even with the fear, he wished they would get whatever they were planning over and done with so he could return to his cell in peace. Peace was all he had ever wanted.

The doctor had finished his ministrations and dragged a tray across from the opposite gurney. The other prisoner had gone, but Joe didn't see where, or what his condition was. The doctor had taken up all of his small attention span.

'Now,' the doctor said, lifting Joe's head up by the chin. 'I will give you one last chance to eat of your own volition. Your lack of food has left you in this state. Look at how pathetic you are, you cannot even lift your own head.'

Joe wanted so much to lift his head and defy the doctor, but his body betrayed him.

'If you don't eat, you will die. It's that simple. As your own life is so precious to you, so precious that you won't even fight for your own country, to protect your own countrymen, why won't you eat and protect your own life?'

The doctor must have known that he couldn't answer, he was having fun with him, enjoying the sense of power it gave him.

The warders held a tray of crusty bread and slop in front of him.

'Eat,' the doctor urged. 'Eat and you will feel better.'

Joe held the stare for as long as he could. He would not, could not let this vile specimen of a doctor win. With all the strength he could muster, he reached towards the tray of food. The doctor smiled, it was a serpentine smile, full of evil and malice. Joe lifted his arm, and let it drop on the tray, which crashed out of the warder's arm and spilled all over the pristine white-tiled floor. The slop stained it a blood-brown mess.

The warder was furious and punched Joe across the face. His head snapped back. It could be that he had lost the ability to feel pain, or perhaps it was that his body was already broken, but he just felt numb.

'Now, now, Mr Abbott,' the doctor said, as one of the warders attempted to clean up the mess. 'That was rude. We are only trying to help, although you are not deserving of our help. If you will not eat, then you have left me with little choice. Remember that we tried to give you food. This is a result of your actions, or rather your lack of action.'

He laughed at his own joke with a deep, rich boom of a laugh.

Without a further word the warders lifted Joe's legs up and positioned him on the gurney. He sat back against the head of the bed, which had only one narrow pillow perpendicular to the surface. It was the most comfortable he had been in weeks. He let his arms and legs go limp, hanging off the gurney, and relaxed, if such a thing were possible, on the bed.

The doctor frowned at him.

'Lazy. Coward,' he said, almost spitting at Joe, and motioned for the warders to lift up his arms and place them back on the gurney. Each warder held an arm down on the side of the bed. They held him firm, but as Joe stopped resisting they loosened their grip.

'Hold him,' the doctor said, matter-of-factly, and one warder reached up and gripped Joe's chin in a meaty fist. He clamped down on Joe's mouth making him unable to open it. Even with all his strength remaining, Joe wouldn't have been able to move in that steel grip.

The doctor reached up to him, but the contents of his hand were obscured by the warder's fist. Joe didn't squirm, he didn't want to give the doctor the satisfaction. He just sat and let them do whatever they were planning to do. His life was easier this way. The doctor pushed one nostril closed and he felt something hard enter the other. There was a resistance at first, but then the doctor redoubled his efforts, frowning and pursing his lips.

There was a sharp jab in his nostril and then the resistance ended in pain. It sent a jolt into his head, and he wanted to cry out as the other patient had done before him. He couldn't move his head, and the doctor kept pushing the tube into his nostril. He had the intense feeling of needing to sneeze, but his body wouldn't comply. Instead he had the numb pain like the beginning of a headache, it itched inside his head, a horrible itch that couldn't be scratched.

The tube pushed through into his mouth and he felt it tickle the back of his tongue. He wanted to gag, but everything was pressed shut. It felt cold in his mouth, which was dry and burning up. He pressed against his restraints, feeling a renewed vigour in his desperation to escape. How could they be doing this to him? Was he just some animal to them? He pushed and he thrashed, and no matter how hard he tried he couldn't move an inch. The doctor was not even aware that he was trying to resist. After a few more seconds Joe could feel a warmness permeate his throat, like he had just had a hot drink. Except it wasn't a drink that was being forced down his throat, it was food. He had refused to eat for so long that they had resorted to force-feeding him. He wanted to gag, to force the liquid food away, not because of his protest, but because of the unnatural presence of the tube down his nose. He wanted to gag, but he couldn't. The doctor had worked his way into Joe's oesophagus. Joe had no choice but to eat. He felt like a slave, a worthless being that had no choice but to be kept alive. He felt worse than that, he felt like an animal being fattened up for the slaughter. No doubt they still intended that he should put on the khaki and go out to France to join all the other brave boys.

But to the slaughter he would not go. They would have to force something else down his throat to make him do that, and they had yet to liquidise nationalism. He didn't know what they had hoped to achieve, but they were forcing him to eat all the same. He wouldn't change his stance, he wanted out of the prison, but he wouldn't fight, not ever. He didn't even fight now as the liquid rolled down into his stomach.

It burned as it went, like eating food that was too hot. His chest made him aware of the force with a hot, burning pain across his ribs. He rocked against the restraints, trying with futility to dislodge the pain. It made his eyes water and his vision blur.

The tube pulled back and his nose felt free. He could breathe again and he sneezed violently. The warder let go to wipe his hand, with a scowl on his face. Joe lurched forward to throw up, but the warder, seeing him, clamped his hand back down over Joe's mouth. Snot, mixed with whatever they had been feeding him, flew out of his nostrils. It stung. The warder was even less pleased, but what was Joe supposed to do?

He swallowed, forcing the bile back into his throat. After a few moments of swallowing and gagging, the urge to vomit subsided. After some time, the warder let go and observed him warily. He almost dared him to try again.

Joe needed to drink. His throat was so dry and his lips were broken after months of punishment and neglect.

'Water', he said. It was an animalistic croak, the sound of dry bark being snapped. He wasn't sure that they could hear, or even understand him. He tried again, but the pain in his chest robbed him of breath.

The doctor turned back and held out a zinc mug before him.

'If you want to drink, you need merely take this cup and drink,' he said. He must enjoy toying with his patients. The warders undid his restraints and stepped back. The strength needed to lift his arm was almost beyond his wasted muscles, but the overriding thirst lent him some momentum. He took the cup from the doctor, whose smile faltered for a second, before he let go.

As soon as the doctor let go, the cup felt like a lead weight in Joe's hand. He shook violently and water spilled over the sides and onto the floor. He cursed, not just because he would be punished for the spill, but also at his own lack of strength. He had never thought of himself as a strong man, but he hated how feeble he had become. Even a child could hold a cup of water without spilling it everywhere. They were right, he *was* pathetic. He was doing it for the right reasons though, he had to keep telling himself that. Sooner or later, someone would take notice and stand up for not just him, but all those who opposed the war.

He brought the cup to his mouth gradually, still spilling water from side to side. There was only a small amount left when he touched the zinc to his lips, but he drank it greedily all the same. He had expected it to feel refreshing, a relief. Instead it felt wrong. He couldn't swallow and the paltry water made him feel as if he had a giant lump in his throat. He coughed, trying to dislodge it, and had the sudden feeling of drowning. He dropped the cup, and it clattered against the floor.

The coughs wracked his body and the rest of his pains flared and shocked him. He felt desperate, trying to cling for air and he grabbed hold of the gurney, but his fragile body wouldn't let him gain any grip.

'That's enough,' one of the warders said, taking Joe by the shoulders in an iron grip. He turned to his colleague. 'Help me with him.'

Together they picked him up off the gurney, and for some reason his body straightening up helped ease the coughs and the pressure on his chest. He gulped down some air, before they started moving. He saw a patina of concern cross the doctor's features, and he watched as they dragged Joe away in the same way they had brought him in. It struck Joe as at odds with the doctor's behaviour.

'*Help!*' he wanted to shout. He was screaming within himself at a world that wouldn't listen, banging in frustration at the edge of consciousness. Why wouldn't anyone help? The doctor alone had the power to help Joe, but perhaps the prisoners weren't the only ones trapped in the prison against their will.

They dragged him back out onto the gantry again, in the direction of his cell. The clanking of his boots against the metal flooring was comforting, like the clacking of a train against its rails.

He saw the small group of conscientious objectors going about their work, stitching together the sacking that would end up as sandbags. He was glad he had refused that work, but he didn't condemn the others for it. They looked up as he passed and one of the men dropped his bag and needle, clutching a hand to his mouth. The others were just as shocked at Joe's appearance, but then they were gone as they passed outside Joe's field of vision.

He was almost thrown back into his cell, as the warders dropped him onto his hard pallet and retreated, locking the door behind them with a clang. He didn't notice the pain of being dropped, over the other pains in his body screaming for attention.

He knew something was wrong. The feeding hadn't gone as they had planned. He was still in so much pain, and his weak body wasn't fighting anymore. His chest felt like it was encased in a vice, and he couldn't breathe. Each breath was a shallow wheeze that caused more stabs of pain in his chest. It was like the feeling of needing to burp, and not being able to, but much more extreme. His lungs burnt with each breath, as he imagined a heavy smoker might feel.

He couldn't shake the feeling that something was wrong. His vision had darkened, and even though he knew it was day it felt like night. His body wanted him to sleep and his eyelids became heavy with lethargy. He would never have dared sleep so much in his life before the prison. But it was all he had now. The prison and his objection had reduced him to this. He closed his eyes and allowed himself to be immersed in the pain.

He knew then that he was dying. He hoped it was just melancholy, but his body betrayed the lie. Something had gone horribly wrong.

All was darkness.

1923

They all stood in silence, with hats and caps doffed under arms, focusing their vision on their shoes. Meanwhile the bishop droned on in his fashion, extolling the virtues of sacrifice.

He stared with them, trying not to dredge up the memories of the past. *I have lived through hell, but in that I am not alone,* he thought. Bile stuck in his throat and he desperately tried to swallow it away. No one noticed, or if they did they attributed it to his grief.

Everyone had suffered and sacrificed, not just the soldiers. He wondered how his brother might be now. How much he would have been changed by the war. They had both endured their own private hells, and as the dead would keep their solace, so would the living. No one would ever truly understand their plight and those that had experienced it didn't need the others to remind them. That was what the nightmares were for.

So he stood there, in silence, with their neighbours and people from the nearby streets, waiting for the bishop to finish his sermon, for the memorial to be revealed.

Somewhere in the distance a baby cried. No one reacted, empathising with the child, who was probably too young to know what was going on, but was joining in nonetheless.

The bishop stopped and was replaced by a Major young enough to have been a junior Lieutenant at the outbreak of war. His voice broke as he began reading out the names of the lost, Morgan, Norris, Oliver, the endless torrent of the dead. They were just names now. Their legacy the brass plaque that was being unveiled.

He patted his coat pocket, remembering the bundle of letters that he kept there. That's where they would stay, sealed, but not forgotten.

The Major continued reading out the names of the fallen, some of whom he knew, others he had never met.

When he could bear to think of him, he had spent most of the war angry with his brother. Not angry, that wasn't strictly the right emotion. They had never really understood each other. They were very different people, with different stories. He had had high hopes for his brother, they all had, yet he threw it all away. He chose his path. When he should have turned to his family he turned away. It was hard now to remember him as they were when they were children. Too much had happened. His name had not been spoken aloud since. They all missed him, but it was too painful a memory.

The Major had finished now, and had disappeared. There was a cough from someone amongst the crowd. The only sound apart from that was the occasional sniffle of a nose, or the sound of stifled weeping. Heads were still bowed and would remain that way for some time, some years perhaps.

At first he hadn't understood his brother's decision; they stood on opposite sides. But as the war dragged on and on, past its first Christmas and into a new year, year after year, he had started to understand his brother a lot more. He began to understand the need to fight for something, to believe in something and to not give up. No matter what life would throw at you. That was a sentiment he could agree on, and he guessed it was something their father had managed to instil in them both, despite their differing opinions. It had been a clear dividing line at first, but things were less clear now. The world had changed for all of them. The horror of the war had left no family unaffected. They couldn't change their decisions, but they could make sure that they counted for something. That things hadn't just changed for the worst, but would be allowed to change for the better too.

He just wished his brother was still around to say this to, but he would never have the chance now. Their paths drifted apart, on what was to be a fateful day for millions of people.

There was a moment of silence.

Somewhere amongst the reverent crowd the baby continued

408

to cry, with thick sorrowful wails, the sound reverberating off the surrounding buildings, eerily loud in the gathering silence. He could well imagine the child was crying over some lost father. Many had lost their fathers, but the infant was probably too young to even know that fact yet.

He turned to walk away once the ceremony had finished. Most of the crowd had disappeared now, standing at the edges as they watched and making a quick getaway. He didn't want to make a quick getaway. Where would he go? It was so unusual, having the freedom of Liverpool again, that he was completely lost.

Really, he just wanted to stand for a while longer and think about what had come to be. He had always found time for inner reflection, and no matter how much the thoughts and memories hurt, his mind always wandered back to the pain. He could see the faces of those they had lost during the war. Lots of faces.

He thought it better that he left now, otherwise his family would begin to worry. They, like the others, had already gone. What did they have to stay for? There was nothing left here for them but haunted memories. But all he had were the memories. There was nothing left in Liverpool for him.

He limped away, feeling the old pain in his right leg. His bones clicked together with every stride, but at least it reminded him that he was still alive. Some of the crowd in front of him were walking very slowly, and he mentally willed them forward, wishing they would go faster so that his leg would hurt less. He had to walk at a certain speed, otherwise the pain would be overwhelming. A slow walk was excruciating, like a cold night when every old joint ached with frost. It was still too recent an injury. The doctors told him it would wear off, and would heal eventually, but he didn't believe them. In some sadistic way, he also liked the pain. It reminded him of those that had died, and that he had been the lucky one that was left. He felt that it was only fair. They had suffered the ultimate injury, what was this pain to them?

Finally, the crowd parted, and he eased into a faster pace, feeling more comfortable with each passing step. He almost bumped into someone as he passed, not noticing them as the crowd passed. He stopped and said sorry, looking up into the face of a young woman. She had clearly been crying, her blue eyes were bloodshot, and tears still ran down her pronounced cheeks. She looked at him for a long moment, shocked, then pushed a long strand of black hair back under her hood and nodded at him saying that it was okay, it was her fault anyway for standing in the way.

He had the odd feeling that he recognised her, but to his knowledge he had never met her before in his life. Then it hit him. It had been years since he had seen that face, but he remembered her clearly now. She had been at the station on that fateful day when he had shipped out to… where was it, Redhill, Canterbury? It was so long ago now that he barely remembered, even though it had actually only been a few years. It seemed like he had lived an entire lifetime in those short years. How odd that he should remember that face on that day amongst everything.

After she walked away he sat on a bench nearby, waiting for the crowd to dissipate. There was no point trying to force the issue and causing himself more pain. The pain of easing himself down on the seat would do for now, that would be enough pain. He looked up at the giant edifice of St George's Hall, and he smiled, remembering the time before they had set off to war fondly. Everything had been so different then, happier. They were young and full of vim and vigour. Setting off to a new world. It certainly was a new world, and the one he had come back to was even more different. Not far from here he had played as a child in the Gardens with his father and brother. But that was now lost to him.

At the end of the war he had woken up in severe pain, disorientated and not knowing where he was. He didn't remember falling asleep and for some reason that confused him. He didn't know it was the end of the war then, of course, he knew only pain. He body was entirely numb with it, and it had taken some time of waking nightmares for his mind to realise he had awoken in a hospital.

Once a nurse had noticed that he was awake, a doctor had come to him, dressed in his pristine white coat. It was the only thing he could remember about the doctor at the time.

'Sergeant Abbott,' he had said. 'Everything is going to be okay. You were blown up in the trench, but you're here now and in hospital. You've been asleep for some time, recovering.'

He had spoken as if George couldn't hear, but he could hear him well enough.

'You'll feel some pain, but I expect you to make a full recovery in time. And you'll have plenty of time. But for you the war is over.'

George's only response at the time had been to break down crying. Tears had fallen down his cheeks and dripped onto the bedspread. Nothing in his body could make him reach up and wipe away the tears. He couldn't control it. He had just wept. No one could console him. He had spent the rest of the war, with the medical staff, learning how to walk again.

Ever since getting back he had been distant from his family. He had found living in the same house to be completely unbearable, as it held so many memories for him from a lifetime ago. He had found himself a small house on the outskirts of the city and had tried to make it his home. Every now and then he would forgo his bed and curl up in the corner wrapped in his greatcoat, rocking silently while nodding off to sleep.

The rare occasions he spent with his family, either in their house or elsewhere, they wanted to know what it had been like for him 'out there'. Only his father had sensed that George couldn't and wouldn't talk about it. He couldn't allow his fragile psyche to relive what had happened to him out in France. His father would nod at him, and usher the girls out of the room, distracting them with something else, and for that he would always love his father.

George wasn't the same boy that had gone to war. It might have been a cliché, but he had become a man. He had also lost everything he held dear, and his family only served to remind him of that. He had had to distance himself from them for his own sanity.

As he sat on the bench now, he thought of all those that had not been as lucky as he, and nothing in him could stop the tears from coming again. He felt his brother's letters in his jacket pocket, including his final ones from prison, and thought about all the others that were gone.

Despite his objection, once again, he wept.

Acknowledgements

First I would like to thank my parents, without their love and support I would not have had the opportunity to write this novel, or be the person I am. I cannot thank them enough. Then I would like to thank my lovely editor Hannah Smith, Nia Beynon and everyone at HQ Digital/HarperCollins, who have been so welcoming and encouraging, and for having faith in this story; my tutors James Friel and Jeff Young on the MA in Writing at Liverpool John Moores University for everything they taught me, and giving me the confidence to write this novel; Rob Knipe, Laura Bennett, Reece Dinn, John Warner, Brett Janes and Adam Waller for reading early drafts and offering improvements; Carl Hellicar, for lending me piles of books about the First World War, and using his wealth of knowledge to make great suggestions; the staff at the Liverpool Central Library for showing me how to use the microfilm viewer and tolerating my presence during hours and hours of reading them; the staff at Caffè Nero Liverpool One for keeping me caffeinated; and everyone else who contributed in any small way, I'm eternally grateful. Thank you all so much.

Dear Reader,

Thank you so much for reading. I hope it meant as much to you as it did to me.

Ever since visiting the battlefields of Ypres and Northern France as an almost-teenager, I felt the need to write this story. Sitting in trenches that somehow still existed after almost a hundred years, and unexpectedly seeing several instances of my surname on the memorial at Thiepval, I couldn't help but think of all the men that had fought and died there. There was a special feeling about those places, and it was overflowing with potential stories. The journey also included the last total eclipse of the sun seen in this part of Europe. To say the trip was special is an understatement.

It wasn't until years later, while studying for my MA in Writing, that I gained the confidence to write the story. The more I researched, the more I realised how closely linked to the First World War the city of Liverpool was. Not only did many regiments leave from this very city to fight on the Western Front, and further afield, but many of the war's Conscientious Objectors were imprisoned locally in Walton Prison.

The story of the Great War will never not be poignant, but I hope that by telling these stories we can learn from the lessons of our past.

Reviews mean so much to writers, I would be grateful if you could spare time to leave a review on Amazon or Goodreads, and feel free to follow me on Twitter @MikeHollows

Thank you for reading.
Lest we forget.

Michael

Dear Reader,

Thank you so much for taking the time to read this book – we hope you enjoyed it! If you did, we'd be so appreciative if you left a review.

Here at HQ Digital we are dedicated to publishing fiction that will keep you turning the pages into the early hours. We publish a variety of genres, from heartwarming romance, to thrilling crime and sweeping historical fiction.

To find out more about our books, enter competitions and discover exclusive content, please join our community of readers by following us at:

🐦 *@HQDigitalUK*

f *facebook.com/HQDigitalUK*

Are you a budding writer? We're also looking for authors to join the HQ Digital family! Please submit your manuscript to:

HQDigital@harpercollins.co.uk.

Hope to hear from you soon!

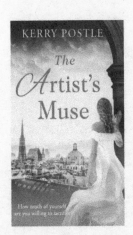
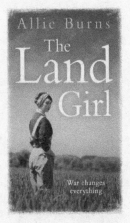